LOST
in the
LONG
MARCH

ALSO BY MICHAEL X. WANG

Further News of Defeat: Stories

LOST
in the
LONG
MARCH

MICHAEL X. WANG

The Overlook Press, New York

This edition first published in hardcover in 2022 by
The Overlook Press, an imprint of ABRAMS
195 Broadway, 9th floor
New York, NY 10007
www.overlookpress.com

Abrams books are available at special discounts when
purchased in quantity for premiums and promotions
as well as fundraising or educational use.
Special editions can also be created to specification. For details,
contact specialsales@abramsbooks.com or the address above.

Library of Congress Control Number: 2022933715

Printed and bound in the United States

1 3 5 7 9 10 8 6 4 2
ISBN: 978-1-4197-5975-8
eISBN: 978-1-64700-583-2

ABRAMS The Art of Books
195 Broadway, New York, NY 10007
abramsbooks.com

To my family, always.

LOST
in the
LONG
MARCH

Red Guards' Battle Song

We are Chairman Mao's Red Guards,
We steel our red hearts in great winds and waves.
We arm ourselves with Mao Zedong Thought
To sweep away all pests.

We are Chairman Mao's Red Guards,
Utterly firm in our proletarian stand,
Marching on the revolutionary road of our forebears,
We shoulder the weighty task of our age.

We are Chairman Mao's Red Guards,
Vanguards of the cultural revolution.
We unite with the masses and plunge into battle
To wipe out all monsters and demons.

Dare to criticize and repudiate, dare to struggle,
Never stop creating revolutionary rebellion.
We will smash the old world
And keep our revolutionary state red for ten thousand generations.

PART I

COURTSHIP

1

1934

WHEN NEWS OF THE MOST recent Kuomintang invasion arrived, Ping and the other platoon members were more interested in its carrier, a new comrade that would join their unit—a girl this time—named Yong. She had transferred to Iron Well Mountain from Ruijin, the administrative capital, by her own request, and because she had fought in the shorthanded eastern divisions during the second and third encirclement campaigns, the Politburo had decided to place her with a combat unit instead of the medical or propaganda detachments. She wanted to be here at Iron Well and defend the birthplace of the revolution. She was honored, she told the platoon, to fight with those who'd been with General Mao the longest.

At first, Ping couldn't tell if her words were merely meant to sound charming. Nearly all the soldiers had been bandits or prisoners, and they cared about the Communist ideals about as much as they did their body odor. Ping was a gunsmith. Back in Canton, he'd also been a gangster, someone who traded a week's work for a night with a perfumed courtesan. He'd shove his way into the brightest building on the street, throw a rifle to the cashier as payment, and ask the lady of the house, "Take me to your finest!"

Yong had a crooked nose—a gift from the landlord her parents had sold her to when she was eight. Her hips were narrow, her chest was flat, and her arms were as skinny as bamboo shoots. When Ping handed her one of the extra flintlocks he'd made—his elbow grazing her sharp shoulder as she turned away—the thought of lying with her, like lying with a quiver of arrows, made him shiver.

Yet there she was in the cave, snoring with the other members of their platoon. There she was carrying a bag of rice peels, the sack so heavy she looked like an ant lugging a pebble. There she was, drenched in rain, setting up a machine-gun emplacement. There she was squatting on the edge of a bluff, her feces splattering onto the mountainside like spilled ink. And there she was again behind a tree—perhaps this was when his desires emerged—waiting for the whistle so she could turn around and blow the Nationalists to smithereens.

He didn't think his attraction resulted only from proximity. Otherwise, he figured, he'd be enamored with the peasant girls at the marketplace or the older ladies who served him rations at the Great Hall of the Proletariat. No, Yong was attractive for a more elusive reason. He found out that she truly believed in the words of the leaders, something that he, at times, wished he could believe in himself. Back from combat, she attended every party meeting, roundtable discussion, and lecture on Pear Tree Hill. She shushed those around her when the familiar mumbo-jumbo came on over the loudspeakers, urging them to memorize the words of Engels and Marx. She'd stare, doe-eyed and drooling, at the educated men babbling under the hammer-and-sickle banner. Winning her affection, Ping began to realize, was like winning China. Her very being resonated with the goal to build a new nation. Winning her would take, as the leaders might say, an ideological battle.

The leaders proclaimed that having a girl around was good for the unit. The old, bourgeois ways of forcing women into arranged marriages would be abandoned for that of free will, for love. One or two women had been placed in every platoon, and darlings like Yong had many admirers. Not often openly, but Ping knew. He could tell by their sideways glances and fake smiles. "Let me help you carry that spade." "Here, take half of my sweet potato porridge." "You'll catch cold standing in the rain like that! Come, sit under this tree with me!" They were thugs, just like him, lordless mercenaries in a fractured country. He wouldn't pursue her in the same clumsy manner the rest of them did, though he didn't know what a graceful approach would be either—not yet. He would let them fight over her first—rush to her door, shoulder to shoulder, like a herd of donkeys.

She wasn't pretty enough, he was certain, to catch the eyes of the leadership, though would she settle for a member of her own platoon—a common foot soldier? Would she care that Ping was the only one among them with a trade? Surely being a gunsmith would give him a leg up on the competition. After all, where else was she going to get her bullets?

2

PING WORKED ON A CLIFF overlooking the valley, in a make-shift armory next to his unit's cave. The rock formation—wavy lines of blue, gray, and burgundy—stretched from ceiling to floor, the crystals lighting up during mornings and afternoons like fireworks during the Spring Festival. Moldy water ran down the crevices whenever it rained.

Ever since the Nationalists had started retreating, the fighting was light, and Ping and his assistant, Luo, were ordered to stay in the rear and manufacture supplies. At first Ping had objected, but then he thought staying back only emphasized his importance in Yong's eyes, and so he agreed.

The Nationalists were led by Kuomintang general Chiang Kai-shek. A decade earlier, he had reunited most of the wealthy coastal cities—Nanjing to Shanghai to Canton—but his troops couldn't penetrate the rural interior, which was still in the hands of the local warlords that had always controlled those provinces, ever since the end of the Qing dynasty. The Nationalists considered the Communist guerrillas the most powerful of these warlords—a threat, both martially and ideologically, to total military dictatorship of the country. And the Nationalists were losing.

Chiang Kai-shek had never reached the gates of the mountain, not in '32 or '33, and certainly not now. They fell for the same tricks again and again. A Communist unit would sneak to the other side of the valley, shoot at an encampment, and lure the Nationalists back to hillsides or river crossings, where an ambush always waited. "Like cocking your fist before throwing a punch," Mao had told them, squatting down at the base of Pear Tree Hill, where a semicircle of fruit trees shaded an amphitheater.

Since the beginning of spring, petals from the trees had drifted as far up as the mountain caves and as far below as the rice paddies. The local peasants gathered the flowers in flat baskets, laid them out to dry, and dropped them in water jugs to be used as tea and on their spicy turnip breakfasts. Still, the petals were everywhere, and the soldiers took extra awkward steps to avoid them when climbing the mountain pass.

Ping was standing over a limestone protrusion, smoothed out and made into an anvil, getting ready to cast another batch of shells, when Luo hurried in with two buckets of well water over his shoulders.

"You see them yet, Little Brother?" Luo asked.

Luo was taller than Ping by four centimeters and older by four years, and he was the only person Ping knew from before Iron Well. They weren't real brothers—only sworn ones. They had come to Chiang-hsi Province together after the 1931 purge that had killed most of the gang leaders in Canton, including their own.

"Not yet," Ping said. "All I see are farmers on the road."

He reached for the nearest ingot from a tall stack. He dropped it in an iron wok and put the wok over a fire. Waiting for the lead to melt, he dangled his legs over the cliff and stared out at the valley below. After a few minutes, he caught sight of his unit marching through the village, passing wattle-and-daub huts, peasants in straw hats, and water buffalo. Yong was among them, the third behind their platoon leader, who pulled on a horse that carried two injured men belly-down on its back.

"Anyone dead?" Luo asked.

"Can't say," said Ping. "I see bodies on Broadax, but can't tell if they're moving."

Luo squatted and fanned the flame, which needed constant attention. Too hot, the lead and wax would separate. Too cold, the ingot wouldn't pour.

"At least Yong's not injured," Ping added. "Ah Guang and Malin are as busy as ever trying to talk to her."

"Don't pretend you don't want to join them, Little Brother," Luo said.

A month earlier, in the village square celebrating a victory and drunk on rice wine, Ping had mentioned how he'd like to spend some more time alone with Yong—not to become a pair with her, but to talk to her and learn more about women—real women—so that when the time came, he could find a wife. As always, Luo saw through Ping's words and recommended that his friend get his head examined if he thought Yong would be interested in him. "You see the way she looks at the leaders?" Luo said. "Her neck lengthens like a crane's. She's straining so much she can't even look down at the dirt, and that's where you are." From then on, whenever Ping mentioned her, Luo would make fun of him. During midday snoozes for the last week, since the rest of the squad had left for assignment, Luo often elevated his pitch to mimic Yong's, whispering, *"Did you miss me, my prince? How many times have you thought about me? How many nights?"*

The ridicule, Ping decided, was better than keeping his desire to himself. It made it somewhat bearable, having someone laugh at him. If he laughed at himself more, maybe his yearnings would just go away, fade out like a dream after being awake long enough.

After the platoon circled the mountain and reached their cave, the soldiers with faulty weapons lined up in front of Ping's workshop. There were half a dozen of them, and when it was Yong's turn, she shoved her rifle to his chest.

"Rounds get stuck after twenty or thirty shots," she said. "Maybe something's wrong with the mechanism, or maybe a few of the bullets are too large. I don't know. The flint might also be too worn. Make sure it can survive our next outing."

She turned and started to walk away. Her rigid stride reminded him of the heroine Hua Mulan, and he was proud to be in love with someone so similar to a historical figure.

"Wait a second," Ping said. "Let me inspect it first."

He had been hoping for a moment like this all week. He wanted to make it last as long as possible. He picked up the rifle, looked through the barrel, lowered it, stuck a cotton cleaning rod through, then lifted the rifle up and looked through the barrel again.

"You need to scrub it more. Just as a sword needs to be sharpened or a horse needs to be fed, a rifle needs to be cleaned. It's not like a pair of chopsticks. You don't just pick it up and expect it to work every time." He used this tone with her often, attempting to imitate the leaders.

"Chopsticks need to be washed, too." Yong laughed, tilting her head back. A pear petal wafted up into her nose. She reached inside and scraped it out.

"Give it attention and respect," Ping said. "That's all I'm saying."

When Yong left, Luo took the rifle and set it on the rack with the others that needed repair. "Give it attention and respect." He laughed. "In Canton, I once saw a Western man carrying around a device that could capture the appearance of any moment in time. I wish I'd stolen it so I could show you how stupid you looked saying that."

"Your ancestors are a bunch of incestuous turtles."

Their platoon leader, Lieutenant Dao, tied Broadax to the mail post—a hollowed-out tree trunk—and came in with his head down. His family had once owned twenty *mu* of land in eastern Manchuria, before the Japanese occupation, and he was one of the few people in the unit with a European bolt-action rifle. Ping had examined the weapon and tried, without success, to produce a working replica.

Everyone stood up when Dao entered, waiting for news of their injured comrades.

"Well, it's both good and bad," he said. He took off his brown cap, the star on it tarnished and rusty. "Comrade Enling is fine—his ribs are healing—but Haiwu needs to have his left leg amputated. They're performing the operation now."

Haiwu was a Long Fist master, or so he had boasted, skilled in the Mantis and Sparrow Hawk stances, and had been, by Ping's estimation, the leading contender for Yong's heart. Haiwu carried around a saber he'd inherited from his uncle, who'd led a charge during the Boxer Rebellion. In the morning he would wake up before dawn and practice flying kicks and somersaults. Ping had hardly spoken a few sentences to Haiwu—"Here's your gun," "To your left!"—but he thought the man was a showoff and buffoon. What good could a sword do now that everyone had guns? Those Boxers were idiots, believers in empty mysticism that got them killed. He wouldn't be surprised if Haiwu had stabbed his own leg, the blade rattling around and accidentally poking his butt as he was running for cover.

"Sad news," Luo said, shaking his head. "He's been promising to teach me his techniques ever since I got here. A generous, selfless man."

Ping thought he caught a smirk on his friend's face. He had told Luo that he believed Haiwu had the best chance with Yong, and his friend had dismissed the kung fu champ as quickly as he dismissed Ping, citing Haiwu's short stature and often incomprehensible Manchu dialect.

Ping glanced toward the back of the cave at Yong, checking for any trace of grief. She combed her hair away from her mouth and bit into a half-peeled sweet potato, the juices running down her chin. Just as Ping was coming to the conclusion that Haiwu meant nothing to her, she started to talk.

"He was a fool, but a brave one." She examined the sweet potato. "He swore that he could turn his limbs as hard as iron if he breathed in and out enough times." The cave swelled with laughter, and Ping knew everyone was thinking about the same limb he was. "Anyway, he had his talents. He might've been better suited for combat if we were fighting a hundred years ago. I'm glad he only lost a leg and not his life."

Lieutenant Dao took a seat on a jut of rock crusted with fungus. "He'll be transferred out. The politburo will place him in the treasury department or with the candlemakers' union. He'll be taken care of. Tomorrow morning, you can visit him in the field hospital and say your farewells."

Ping felt energized. This was the opportunity he needed. Now that Haiwu was out of the picture, he could try for Yong relatively unimpeded. And he had the perfect means to get closer: her rifle. He would say that her old one was in worse shape than his initial inspection had suggested. He would build her a new one, a better one, but he needed her help. Designs for a fresh shoulder strap would be offered; hand sizes would be measured. She would begin to respect him through watching him work, and with respect came friendship, and with friendship came love.

That night, he was so excited he couldn't fall asleep. He planned on approaching her as soon as they woke up, before breakfast. He lifted his head slightly, peering past the rows of sleeping men to catch a glimpse of her silhouette. The moonlight reached into the cave like a finger, and there she was in the corner, away from the men, wrapped in rabbit's fur with a leg sticking out and a line of spittle running down her chin.

Suddenly Luo shot up, blocking Ping's view.

"Go to sleep, Little Brother," Luo whispered. "You can't see her that clearly anyway."

3

PING AWOKE TO A STRONG kick in the rear. When he opened his eyes, a man was standing over him like a giant, and for a second, before Ping realized who it was, he thought he was ten years old again, back in the slums of Canton, where the orphan matrons would tilt the bunks of the children who slept late so that they fell to the floor. Then they would march to the building's first level—a hall with long metal tables—and sew socks, shirts, or gloves for ten hours.

"Wake up, you lazy egg. I had to march thirty miles yesterday and I still woke up before dawn." Lieutenant Dao squatted, smiling. "It's not a problem when no one else is around, but for the sake of the others' respect, don't be the last bum out of the hay again."

The rest of the platoon had already left for the Great Hall of the Proletariat, which was the largest cavern among those settled in Iron Well. Platoons usually ate in their designated caves or huts, but on special occasions—after a victory, before shipping out, or during the lunar new year—the Great Hall would be open for a few days and offer communal feasts. Ping had slept with his blanket over his head and must've missed the roosters and the 5:00, 6:00, and 7:00 a.m. bugles. He buttoned his shirt, threw on his cotton-stuffed chinos, and sprinted out of the cave, holding down his cap to prevent the high-altitude wind from blowing it away. When he crossed the rickety bridge over Longtan Waterfall and arrived at the eastern side of the mountain, the Great Hall was packed.

He had to wait in line for twenty minutes before a seat was available. Once inside, he found that the benches reserved for his platoon were completely full. At first he was relieved to see Luo sitting next to Yong—he thought his friend was saving him a seat—but when he patted Luo's back and tried squeezing a foot between them, his friend swatted his leg away. Without bothering to look up, Luo said, "Come on, Little Brother. Can't you tell this jar's filled to the brim?" Ping had to sit six benches away, where another unit's mortarman waved for him to join them because a year ago Ping had made the man his sidearm out of a dented canteen.

Seething, Ping ate his cornmeal, sweet potato, and turnip breakfast while staring at Luo and Yong. From the looks of it, the two were having an engaging conversation. Luo stole a chunk of cornbread from Yong's plate, and she laughed several times, tilting her head back as if they had been friends for years. Only once did they glance in Ping's direction—or was it something behind him that made them chuckle? He turned around but only saw a soldier blowing his nose. *What could they possibly be laughing about?* Ping wondered. He had never seen them talk to each other before, not like this.

When the Great Hall was starting to empty out, he got up and made his way over. Halfway there, Luo and Yong got up and began walking in his direction.

"Luo—" Ping tried to find the right words.

"Ah, Little Brother. We've been meaning to speak with you." Luo put a hand on Ping's shoulder, his face growing serious. "Remember that dirty rifle of hers from yesterday?"

Ping nodded.

"Well, we have a plan to fix it, and without you having to do any work." Luo turned to Yong and smiled. "We're going to ask Lieutenant Dao for a Western rifle for our crack shot here. I'm sure the Lieutenant will agree that it's time."

"What?" Ping was taken aback. "That's absurd."

"Why? Yong's the best shot in the platoon, maybe the entire battalion. Why's it so absurd?"

"Yes, but—"

"But what? Shouldn't the best shot have a good rifle?"

"That's not to say the rifle you made for me is a bad one," Yong added. She put a hand on Ping's arm. Her fingers were sticky with sweet potato residue. "It has served me well. I'm sure any comrade who's lucky enough to inherit it will be a lucky guy."

"An extra gun for the unit." Luo winked. "This is a blessing."

Ping's innards felt as if they were being yanked apart by a team of oxen. When he didn't say anything, the two walked past him, Luo with his hands behind his back, looking at the ceiling. Ping lingered there, slowly breathing in and out. The room smelled like sulfur. The quartz and gypsum on the walls glittered like a thousand staring eyes. He heard a familiar laugh coming from the door. Turning around, he caught a glimpse of Yong walking out the cavern entrance and tilting her head back at something funny Luo had said.

4

FOR THE NEXT THREE DAYS he spent much of his time in his workshop. Even though his work had become less urgent now that the Nationalists had retreated, he found solace in the repetitive motions and the view of the countryside. Luo hadn't shown his face, thankfully, but Ping still had to endure the sight of the two together in the cave. They seemed almost inseparable, though they didn't hold hands or pet each other and he couldn't tell for sure how far their relationship had developed. Somehow Luo got the other two interested men to back off. Ping wasn't surprised, since Luo had been the leading browbeater in their gang and had often intimidated debtors to pay back what they owed without breaking their legs or kidnapping their children. Luo must've been planning this for a long time, taking mental notes of exploitable weaknesses. He probably didn't even bother thinking much about Ping, knowing his friend too well, how Ping would just cower away somewhere by himself until everything was forgotten, returning after a week wanting to be friends again.

Back in Canton, they'd been known as Smoke and Whispers. Ping was Smoke, because he made guns, and Luo was Whispers, for his skills in persuasion. Luo was the one who got him a membership with Twin Tea Gang. Before, Ping had been twelfth apprentice to a blacksmith who fed his workers the same slop he fed his pigs. Ping stole scraps of metal and made weapons at night, selling them to the gangs for pocket money. Luo was so impressed with the pistol that Ping had made for him, he introduced Ping to Lord Tea, who gave him a permanent position. At seventeen, Ping was glad to finally have a friend in the world, someone who took him to brothels and showed him how to be a man.

Then the Nationalist army cracked down on Canton's underworld. Once the city was no longer safe—not even for those who belonged in the gangs—Luo led them to the countryside. He'd heard a rumor about a sanctuary run by poor farmers and mountain bandits where the only senseless killings were those of the gentry—people who didn't deserve sympathy anyway. Luo went to Chiang-hsi Province wanting to see such a place firsthand, and Ping tagged along because he had nowhere else to go.

Comrade Mao greeted them personally: "If you want to know the taste of a pear, you must try it yourself. Join us and see how *real* folks work to create a perfect society." He told them that although the Red Road Army asked much of each soldier, they shouldn't think of it as an army in the traditional sense. They were a guerrilla force of like-minded individuals, without the rigors and constraints of full-time soldiers, free to live their current lives as they fought for a better one. He assigned Ping and Luo a unit and gave them uniforms. Ping didn't fully understand or believe in the principles the leaders taught, but he had to admit that he had never lived in a place where the people were as energized, where he felt as safe, and where he was treated almost like an equal.

In a way, he was indebted to Luo, but he often wondered what it would take for him to truly break with his friend, who seemed adept at teetering on that thin tightrope between trust and hatred.

What troubled Ping the most was not knowing whether Luo had been interested in Yong all along or if he had just decided to steal her from him out of sadistic fun—to prove that he could. Ping wasn't good enough, nor Haiwu, and somehow Luo *was*? Ping would gladly go down on his knees, perform a dozen kowtows, and proclaim Luo to be the emperor of the human race if it meant his friend would leave Yong alone.

One day, while Yong was off with the other army women distributing leaflets to the villages surrounding Iron Well, Ping found the opportunity to speak with Luo alone. Their unit was in the valley helping the peasants plant rice seeds. It was an hour past noon and the sun sizzled on their backs like a frying pan cooking eggs. Ping inserted a seed deep into the mud, lifted his foot out of the water, and inserted another seed ten centimeters next to it. After finishing a column, he moved to the one his friend was working in.

"You miss her," Ping said. "I can tell."

Luo reached for a seed in his basket. "You're imagining things, Little Brother."

"A week ago I could've never imagined this." Ping swatted flies around his ankles.

Luo inserted a seed into the mud. "There's your problem. You're always imagining the wrong things. You don't stop and look around. You live in your head, like an opium addict."

"Careful, now. I'm serious this time."

Luo laughed. "You don't know it yet, but I'm doing you a favor. It's a bad thing to have someone in your head like that. You'll thank me once you're older."

Ping stopped planting. He unslung the bag of seeds from his shoulder, walked to the other side of the column, and stood facing his friend. It bothered him that Luo's words made even the least bit of sense.

"Stand up," he said. "Look at me when you're talking. I can't tell if you're being serious."

Luo stood up and sighed. "Listen. When have I ever deceived you, Little Brother? *Truly* deceived you? Take it from someone with more knowledge of the heart: You can't be with a woman you like as much as you like Yong. Successful relationships—and marriages—are the ones where both sides just like each other a little bit. Passion will get you hurt or even killed. Take a look at what happened to Haiwu, that one-legged victim of passion."

"He lost his leg to a stray bullet."

"Wrong, Little Brother, all wrong." Luo shook his head. "It wasn't a stray bullet at all. It was a bullet deflected by passion. I had my suspicions even before Yong confessed that Haiwu had saved her life, but now I'm positive."

What Luo said about Haiwu didn't surprise Ping as much as the fact that it had come from Yong's mouth. He suddenly remembered a quote by Marx, one that was often repeated over the loudspeakers: "Our mutual value is for us the value of our mutual objects." But he knew Haiwu hadn't done it for that reason. He had done it for the selfish value of love.

"Don't believe me, Little Brother? Go ask Haiwu himself. See what passion can do to a person. If a visit with him doesn't scare you to reason, come back. I won't be too long with Yong. You can have what's left after I'm through."

Ping lifted his foot and found a seed sticking between his toes. No matter who planted the seed, a stalk would spring up and be ready to harvest in the fall, and it occurred to him that his feeling for Yong was such an ordinary thing and that even a monkey like Haiwu had felt it. Loving someone was as simple as planting a seed: All this time he had lifted Yong as high up as the swan goddess Chang'e, who lived in a pavilion on the moon. And the base way in which Luo talked about Yong comforted Ping by showing him that she was nothing special—just another seed in the ground. Perhaps visiting Haiwu would be a good idea. At the very least it would ease Ping's mind: seeing the fool who Yong almost gave in to—someone who contorted his body into animal shapes.

5

THE GREAT MOBILE HOSPITAL OF the Masses—a line of tents
on the far side of Iron Well—was drawn up on soil too rocky to cultivate.
The wind swept around the back of the mountain and onto the roofs
of the tents, making a sound that always stirred Ping to imagine that
some great dragon was trapped inside, trying to pound its way out. He
had spent a week here during the second Kuomintang invasion, after a
piece of shrapnel had lodged itself below his collarbone. He was given
acupuncture and chloroform and lived in a state of blissful drowsiness
for three days, playing cards with his neighbors and listening to operas
on the windup gramophone before being sent back to his platoon with
a cast.

Lieutenant Dao had said that Haiwu, after the surgery, was placed
in the last row of tents, with the patients who didn't require immediate
care. Ping walked past the first couple of rows, heard screams, and had
a strong feeling that it was stupid of him to be there, that there was no
lesson to be learned at all, and that somehow Luo had tricked him. But
he felt better when he reached the end, where it was quiet, and after
lowering his head and parting the canvas an almost unexplainable sense
of euphoria came over him. This was a place of healing, he thought, and,
yes, this just might be the place where he was going to start feeling like
himself again.

He found Haiwu in a bright corner of the room, surrounded by rib-
bons of drying bandages still pink after washing. Staring outside, the

man had a smirk on his face. Ping guessed he was on the same medication the doctors had given him.

"Hello, Ping, you wonderful maker of guns. I never thought I'd see you here."

The medication slurred Haiwu's speech, causing his accent to become even more difficult to decipher. If it weren't for the man's content expression, Ping wouldn't have been able to tell if Haiwu had just complimented him or told him to go shoot himself.

Ping grabbed a stool from the end of a bed. "How are you feeling?"

"Pretty good. It feels like it's still there." He scratched his chest and nodded to the flat spot under the sheets where his leg would've been. "You can't see them, but there are ten needles on the stump. Can you believe that? I've lost a leg and gained a stump."

During the procedure to remove the bullet from his shoulder, Ping had been afraid the doctor would have to take out his collarbone, leaving him an unbalanced, narrow-shouldered shrimp. Ping unfastened the top two buttons of his uniform. Then he stuck out his shoulder for Haiwu to see.

"It still hurts when I lift my arm," he said. "Sometimes, when I reach around to scratch my back, it feels like I've been shot again."

Haiwu shook his head. "I'll never be able to practice kung fu in this life, not with this stump, unless I can somehow invent Tree form."

Ping laughed but quickly regretted it. He cleared his throat. "Have the others come to visit you?"

Haiwu nodded. "A few. The lieutenant comes almost every day. The person I want to see most, though, has been absent."

"Who is that?" Ping asked. He didn't want to be the one to mention her name, but he wanted to hear it.

"Yong." Haiwu pressed both hands on the bed and pushed himself up so that his back was against the wall. "Maybe you can do me a favor? Can you ask her to come? You hold a certain prestige in the unit. She will listen to you."

Ping thought about this. What Haiwu proposed would give him an excuse to talk to her, but did he want to approach her in service of

Haiwu? She might confuse his intentions, think him as just a matchmaker. "I don't think it's my place. I don't hold as much sway as you think I do. At least, not anymore. She's been given a medal and now she has this new German-built gun. I don't think she held much respect for me before, and she certainly thinks less of me now."

"No, no, no, you have it all wrong. Sometimes she acts tough around the people she regards most highly. She respects you, she's told me. She said, 'We'd win the war a lot quicker if we were all more like Ping Pei-hsu: so talented, serious, and devoted to the cause.' Her exact words."

"I'm not that gullible." Ping tried to hide his smile.

"She thinks you're special—really. Now, tell her I just need to see her for a minute. Even half a minute will do." Haiwu coughed. "Tell her I know she's a woman without pity and that I don't expect her to be with me now because of this. Tell her I know it's over between us. Tell her—can you remember all of this?"

Ping got up, moved the stool to the side of the bed, and leaned into Haiwu's face. "Listen, I'm sorry to be the one telling you this, but Yong has already moved on. She's been spending a lot of time with Luo."

"She's what? With that weasel?"

Usually Ping would defend his friend—*Oh, he's conniving, for sure, but he wouldn't hurt anyone who didn't have it coming*—but this time he just nodded.

"I know you're close with that scoundrel, but Yong deserves better."

Ping nodded again. He ran his hand through his hair, pulled out a louse, and pinched it dead between his fingers. "I've been thinking about this, too, and you know what? I think they might be the perfect couple after all. They're both cold, callous, and amoral."

Haiwu blinked a few times. Then he leaned back and laughed. "Oh, I see now," he said. "You like her, too."

Ping stared at Haiwu, dumbstruck. Why, he wondered, did people see through him like a stagnant pond? Did he sweat out words that revealed his emotions? Were the characters for "hate" and "love" painted across his forehead in careful calligraphy?

"I should head back. I hope you'll feel better soon." He stood up and fumbled for his cap, which was folded and stuffed inside his pocket.

Haiwu had his hands locked behind his neck and was reclining his head back and forth. "I'll tell you this much, Ping, I'd much rather see you with her than that swine."

Ping paused. He turned around and sat back down. "What do you mean?"

"I mean I'll help you."

"What?" Ping didn't think he understood correctly. In the Szechuan dialect, the word for "help" sounded similar to the one for "shoot."

"As my master told me on top of Mount Hua, the keys to Long Fist are discipline, form, and technique—not so dissimilar to that of seduction."

Ping doubted how much talking to Haiwu would help his situation, but out of desperation and curiosity he stayed in the hospital late into the night, taking a break only when Haiwu was hungry and asked if Ping could buy him a bowl of glass noodles from the villagers. When Ping returned, they continued their discussion, talking and slurping. Haiwu told Ping what Yong liked—sparrow nests in roofs, marching along the river, wading barefoot through swampland—and what she didn't—chili paste, small talk, carrying bamboo stretchers. He revealed the extent of their relationship: a kiss on the cheek after he had climbed a date tree and shook the top branch; a stroke of her chest while they were camping behind enemy lines; and a kiss on the mouth after he had stepped between her and a 7.7mm bullet from a British machine gun. Slowly, it became apparent to Ping that Haiwu was telling him all of this not just because he'd rather see him with Yong than Luo but because he wanted someone to know about the times he had shared with her. Perhaps he wanted to validate his desires, just as Ping had done by telling Luo. Perhaps he was afraid he might forget—or hoping he *would* forget. Perhaps he was simply tired of being cooped up and wanted to talk to someone he knew.

When it was close to midnight, a nurse told them their voices were disturbing the other patients. Ping said farewell, promising that he'd visit again the next day. Parting the canvas and stepping outside, he breathed in the fresh air and felt rejuvenated. He realized he had never seen this side of Iron Well Mountain at night before. There was a reflective white sheen to the graveled soil, and the mountaintop—or the portion of it that wasn't concealed by gray, smoky clouds—loomed a festive red, burning like an imminent volcano.

6

MOST PEOPLE IN THE PLATOON, Haiwu had mentioned, had a problem or two with Luo. Of course, this didn't surprise Ping, but what did surprise him was the extent to which they would go out of their way to avoid his friend. Hearing Haiwu talk about how Luo had stolen Chuang's Buddhist prayer beads and sold them to an antique dealer or how Luo had fabricated a heartbreaking story of a dead uncle just to get an extra piece of squash cake from the mess hall, Ping thought: No wonder! No wonder they were never invited to mahjong on Sundays or badminton games on Pear Tree Hill. Luo had likely spread lies about Ping to prevent his friend from bonding with the others. Not even Lieutenant Dao liked Luo, and Haiwu told Ping that the Lieutenant only agreed that Luo should stay behind on this last outing because Luo would be out of his sight for an entire week.

There were two kinds of bandits in the army: the decent kind and the indiscriminate kind. The decent kind stole only from the rich and killed only when they had to. The indiscriminate kind said, *Fuck you, People!* and did anything to anyone so that their bellies were full and their members were satisfied. While Ping had always placed himself in the former group, the others had lumped him together with Luo in the latter. Haiwu suggested that Ping's first order of business in winning Yong should be to distance himself further from Luo.

"What about the fact that Yong is with Luo now?" Ping asked. He took the crutches from Haiwu and helped him into a wheelchair made from old rickshaw parts.

It had been a week since Ping had last talked to Luo. In order to avoid seeing him with Yong, he visited Haiwu almost every day. Since the army had just won a battle, duties were light, and Ping often wandered around the village with his new friend, coming up with the best approach to win over Yong.

Today they were heading out to the Black Croc River, a tributary of Poyang Lake where the locals fished. If Haiwu was lucky, the army doctor had told him, the fishermen might have recently caught a dolphin, the backbone of which could be sanded down and crafted into a fine prosthetic—much safer and more comfortable than wood or bamboo.

"What does it say about Yong's character to fall for someone like Luo?" Ping asked again.

"Absolutely nothing," Haiwu said. "She hasn't fallen for Luo, trust me. At most, she's with him because she finds him fresh. You have to understand that the others don't really tell her anything—nothing about us, anyway." This was true, Ping considered, since she had her own circle of friends outside of the platoon—the cooks in the Great Hall or the dancers in the army's morale detachments—whom she hung around with more than the people from her own unit. Haiwu continued, "It wouldn't take her long to find out who Luo really is, and when she does, you'll be at a good place for not being his friend anymore."

Ping wiped sweat from his forehead, pushing the wheelchair with one hand. "So I'm just supposed to wait until she discovers what a bad person he is?" he said. "That doesn't sound like a good plan. Luo is more persuasive than you think, and he can pretend for a long while. Anyway, don't women fall for bad men all the time? What makes you believe she's not with Luo *because* he's a terrible person?"

Haiwu took off his straw hat, looked up at Ping, and squinted a smile. "Because she liked me, and I'm not a terrible person."

When they reached the docks, several soldiers were raising a flagpole next to the tallest building, a two-story pavilion with a green *wa*-tiled roof that sold fishing supplies and river mud, which was used for making pigpens. The sign, which had read *Huang's Fishery Stock* the last time Ping had been here, now stated in bold red characters: *Great Proletarian Naval Reserves, Run by Huang Tingting.*

Ping pushed Haiwu into the store, his nostrils filling with the pungent odor of soft-shell crab and dried grass fish. The room was almost barren. Four dusty stools lined the entrance, and all he could see in terms of merchandise were a few recently returned fishing poles—still dripping—in a brown vase with a crack running down its side. Most of the product, he guessed, was either behind the counter or stored away upstairs. The old man who ran the store, Huang himself, wore round glasses and waved to them.

"We're looking for dolphin bone," Haiwu said. "The good kind, to be used to make a new this." He pointed to his missing leg.

The man craned his head around the counter to have a look. "You're in luck. I think I have enough dolphin vertebrae left for one more limb."

He went to the back of the store and came out with a long package. He unwrapped it and showed them its contents. The bones, rounded into cylinders, were strung together with copper wires and were already indented in four spots to fit the support railings. Haiwu nodded, and the man wrapped the package back up and put it in his lap.

"How much do I owe you?"

"For a soldier," the man said, "I'll take whatever you can afford."

Haiwu gave the man four silver coins—two months' wages—and bid him farewell.

On the way back, Ping wondered how Luo would have run a store like that. For sure, he would set a price, and he would sell pig bone when dolphin was in short supply. Rounded out like that, a bone from any animal would look the same, although the man with the prosthetic would know he'd been swindled once the product shattered after a week. In the end, Ping came to the conclusion that Luo wouldn't even have the decency to run a store in the first place. Why open a store when you could just take from those who have one? Since the revolution began, the man who sold Haiwu the bones ran a store the only way he could: by changing the name and giving discounts to those who could protect him.

"So I can't just sit around," Ping said when they were outside again. "I need to be more active."

"Maybe waiting for her is a bad idea," Haiwu agreed, "but you don't seem to be the type who's able to skillfully pester a woman until she gives in. You don't seem to have the patience or the ability to stomach such a loss of face."

"I don't want Yong to like me because I can pester her into submission," Ping said. "It didn't work for you, did it? All you got for being shot was a peck on the mouth. I don't want her to like me because she thinks I'm someone I'm not."

"So what? You want her to like you *for you*?" Haiwu laughed. "This is why mothers arrange marriages for their sons: because of idiots like you. Tell me, what qualities do you have that make you believe Yong should fall in love with you?"

Ping was hurt. Wasn't it just a couple of days ago that this man in the wheelchair told him that he was unique, that he had a special place in the unit? "Well, none of the others can make guns," he said, almost in a whisper.

"You don't say. You can make guns? Why don't you just tell her that? 'Yong, you should love me. If you haven't noticed, I can make guns. Any questions, or should we start our affair now?'" Haiwu glanced up, and when he saw that Ping wasn't laughing, he asked, "Have you ever read *Outlaws of the Marsh*?"

"Now you're telling me you can read?" Ping was getting tired. He rolled the wheelchair away from the dirt path and parked it under an elm tree. Then he sat down on the dirt and crossed his legs.

"A little," Haiwu said. "Well, my master could, and before the local lord shot him for not paying the land tax, he'd often read me passages from famous books while I stared at the words on the page. I learned a lot of stuff that way, including the qualities that women are attracted to. *Outlaws of the Marsh* gives famous examples of highly attractive men throughout history and breaks male attraction down to five categories named after five famous men: Teng, Lo, Pan, Hsiao, Hsian. Do you want to know what they are?"

Though skeptical, Ping nodded. Didn't women like men for the same reason that men liked women? He took off his cap, rearranged his hair, and put the cap back on so that it covered his eyes. Then he leaned back on the elm.

"I'll give you the shortened versions," Haiwu said. His face took on an expression of learned delight. He spoke in an almost rehearsed way, as though he'd been waiting to pass down his knowledge for a long time. "Teng was a wealthy silk trader in northern China and his method of seduction was buying women a lot of really expensive stuff—jade hair clips, pearl earrings, silk gowns—so his name is shorthand for 'wealth.' Lo was a male courtesan for Empress Tz'u-his during the Tang dynasty, rumored to have been able to pleasure the empress for hours upon hours, so his name is shorthand for, well, the ability to do *that*. Are you following me so far?"

"Go on," Ping said, chewing on a blade of grass.

"Pan was a great poet during the Song dynasty, smartly dressed with long straight hair and neat whiskers that surrounded his lips like wings—someone who could make women fall in love with him just by smiling at them, so his name is shorthand for 'handsomeness.' Hsiao was an ugly and lame mule driver, but he was the husband to a beautiful woman famous in the province for her wrath. A lot of suitors wanted to marry her, but they were all too afraid and not willing to part with their pride and act submissively in front of her. Well, none except Hsiao, and so his name is shorthand for 'humiliation.' Finally, Hsian was a famous beggar in Mongolia who followed the women he loved—women who had scorned him and told him to go away—for days on the Mongolian plains. He didn't take no for an answer, and acted with forbearance and kindness and determination for as long as it took to win a girl's heart, so his name is shorthand for 'patience.' Put them all together, and you have Teng, Lo, Pan, Hsiao, Hsian: wealth, pleasure, looks, humility, and patience."

Ping didn't want to believe what Haiwu was saying, but his words made so much sense that he found them difficult to reject. He repeated the names of the five men in his head, trying to memorize them.

"Shall we go over which of these traits you possess?" Haiwu asked. Ping nodded.

"Teng—wealth," Haiwu said. "Nope, you have no money, just like me, to buy a woman anything. Lo—pleasure. Doubt it."

"I've been to brothels," Ping was quick to add, lifting an index finger. "They told me I was good."

"Unfortunately, Lo is only good at keeping a woman once you have her, not at getting her in the first place. Moving on. Pan—looks. Nope, you're short, though not as short as me, and your face resembles a fox's. So we're left with Hsiao and Hsian, the two most important traits, and, lucky for you, the two that any man can have if he puts in enough will-power and practice."

"Hsiao and Hsian," Ping said.

"Humility and patience," Haiwu repeated.

7

IT WAS DUSK BY THE time they got back to Iron Well Mountain, the red sun setting between peaks like a ripe tomato. There was a great bustle in the valley, soldiers walking shoulder to shoulder in one direction. Ping asked someone what was going on, and a boy told him that the army was heading to Pear Tree Hill. The members of the politburo, including General Mao, had driven down from Ruijin and were conducting an emergency meeting. "A change in leadership," he said, "so the rumor goes."

Ping joined the traffic, pushing Haiwu in the direction of the outdoor lecture hall. He suspected that the meeting was an award ceremony, where Mao would give official promotions to those who had contributed the most in the last campaign.

Reaching the stairs that led to the top of the amphitheater, Haiwu said that it would be fine if Ping just left him there and that he could see better from their current spot. Ping shook his head and insisted on lifting Haiwu's wheelchair step-by-step to the northern corner, the designated area for their unit. When he got there, he was short of breath. He saw Lieutenant Dao at the edge of the row, his arms crossed. Several comrades waved, and Haiwu tipped his hat. Luo and Yong were at the other end, sitting on a green army jacket—Luo's probably—that covered the dusty red earth.

"Wheel me over to her," Haiwu said.

"You think that's a good idea?" Ping hadn't planned on a confrontation this early. He should have just left Haiwu at the spot where he'd said he'd be fine.

Ping backed up the wheelchair and went around the perimeter of the amphitheater, his elbow grazing the branches of pear trees, to the empty spot next to Luo and Yong. Luo eyed Ping and frowned as if asking, *What's going on?* and Yong pretended—or so Ping guessed—to not notice them.

When the loudspeaker started blaring the "Internationale"—"Rise up, you who are damned; rise up, you suffering people of the world"—the crowds quieted and a ring of torches was lit onstage. Even after two years Ping hadn't memorized all the words, but out of the corner of his eye he noticed Yong singing along. From his position—a hundred and fifty meters or so from the base—the leaders' faces were small, but he could still make out Mao in the middle, the pink ribbon of the politburo above his left breast pocket. He was flanked by Zhou Enlai and Bo Gu, who were both sitting in wicker chairs. They had just returned from Moscow, bringing with them a German advisor, also sitting, who could barely speak Chinese and who everybody called Li De. Mao waved his arms for the crowd to settle down. Then he stepped onto the red bamboo podium with the hammer-and-sickle emblem circled by a gold wreath.

"First, I'd like to thank you all for your hard work in this last battle. Our Communist Party and the Peasants' Red Army are true battalions of the revolution! Many comrades have died, my friends included, but as we all know, death varies in its significance. The ancient historian Sima Qian wrote, 'Though death befalls all men, it can be lighter than goose hair or weightier than Mount Tai.' And it is times like this when we realize how true the words of the ancients are, for dying for the people has the weight of Mount Tai, while dying for landlords and exploiters has the false weight of hair!"

Everybody cheered. The leaders onstage clapped, and Bo Gu got up and stepped onto the podium next to Mao.

"That said, I'd like to take this opportunity to announce my formal resignation from the position of frontline general," Mao continued. "I will still serve the Party in other ways, but just as the seasons need to change, the standing committee has decided that Comrade Bo Gu, recently returned from Russia and more knowledgeable on how the true form of communism operates, will take over as the supreme field commander."

The crowd began to murmur; someone even shouted, "We will not accept this!" and Ping echoed their disbelief. He couldn't have guessed that Mao was replacing himself. Maybe this was a promotion in disguise. He wouldn't be surprised if the chubby-faced man was going to make everyone called him "Grand Leader" Mao now. He glanced over at Yong, who had her hand over her mouth, and at Luo, who saw Ping looking, and shrugged.

When Mao left the podium, Bo Gu gestured for the crowd to quiet down. He was tall and skinny, with wide spectacles and hair almost as immense as his head, giving him the impression of a giant paintbrush. His shirt was crisper and tighter-fitting than Mao's, and when he raised his hands his sleeves retreated to his elbows.

"My name is Bo Gu, as many of you already know, and I thank Comrade Mao for his belief in my abilities. He has led us through half a decade of hard times and we are all here in no small part because of his guidance. But I believe we need a different battle plan now. We have defeated the Nationalists time and time again and I believe we no longer need to retreat and fight. We can take out Chiang Kai-shek tit for tat! Guided by Li De"—he pointed to the German man behind him—"we will build fortifications along our border and defend until we stop the Nationalists for good! No retreat, I say!"

In the middle of the speech, Haiwu tugged on Ping's pants, told him to step back a second, and with his remaining leg nudged himself over to Yong.

"Why haven't you visited me?" he whispered.

Yong looked forward. "Do you have to do this now, while the leaders are talking?"

"I think I deserve an answer."

Yong glanced over at Luo, who stepped around and took her spot. "How are you feeling, kung fu champ?" he asked.

Haiwu ignored him. "I took a bullet for you and now you have this idiot step forward to take another? You're shameless, Yong Yaozhong, shameless!"

Ping put a hand on Haiwu's shoulder. "Hey, why don't we wait until tomorrow, when we're all a little more clearheaded?"

"Listen to your *friend*," Luo said. "Show the generals some respect."

Haiwu angled the wheelchair to the side and then, with his remaining foot, kicked Luo between the legs, sending him flying into the soldiers behind them. "Hey, what's up, fellow?" someone shouted. "We're trying to listen to the speech." Luo pushed himself up, grabbed Haiwu by the collar, and cocked his hand. Yong stepped forward and bounced him away with her sharp hip.

"All right," she said, her eyes as fierce as a falcon's. "You want an answer? I didn't want to tell you this, but I would've much preferred it if I'd taken that bullet myself. It was, after all, intended for *me*. What you did, though brave, was unfair and selfish. You left me with the option to feel indebted or heartless. Well, I choose the latter, because I think giving my life to the cause is more important than giving it to you. I'd rather make one person unhappy and do my best for the rest than shun the people for the sake of guilt. Do you understand *now*?"

Haiwu started to cry, making a squeaky, mouselike noise between his fingers. Yong steadied her breathing, sat back down, and pretended to focus on the speech again. Luo gave his shirt a stiff tug, stared at Ping as if this was *his* fault, and plopped down between Yong and Haiwu, shoving the wheelchair away.

Lieutenant Dao rushed over and asked, "What's going on?" When nobody replied, he looked at Haiwu and then at Yong and said, "Even during an hour like this, you're consumed by nonsense. Ping, take Haiwu back to the hospital."

Pushing Haiwu down the stairs, Ping wondered whose words had more merit. On the one hand, the leaders always told the soldiers to be brave and selfless, and Yong had even admitted that Haiwu's act had been courageous. Yet he also agreed with Yong that Haiwu's valor wasn't the selfless kind but was performed out of selfish motives. It seemed strange to Ping that bravery and selfishness were not mutually exclusive.

This was the reason he couldn't fully accept the Communist teachings: There were too many contradictions. Mao had told them to "learn from the masses, and then teach them," but Ping didn't know what should be learned and what should be taught. How can you learn from someone and then teach him?

Arriving at the bottom of the hill, he decided that Yong was more in the right, and despite her display of callousness he found that he loved her more for it. Perhaps her attitude was what it took to change the country. He envied her for her dedication to the cause and understood that the only way to impress her was to be as certain as she was about the Communist ideals. He was selfish to question the teaching of the leaders. It wasn't his job to think. Comrades like Yong already knew this—even Luo understood his role in the larger scheme of things—and they plunged into their work with bravery and conviction. Suddenly Ping felt very foolish for taking so much pride in his gun-making abilities. He was a common soldier, just like them, except they knew who they were. There wasn't anything for her to desire in someone as confused as he was. He didn't deserve her, as he had once believed. She was too good for him.

8

NEXT MORNING, WHEN PING RETURNED to his platoon, he noticed that everyone's expressions had changed. There was barely a whisper in the cave, and most people sat in their corners, doing something private. Shaohu, their standard-bearer, was sharpening the spearpoint at the top of his flag, while Pengpeng, the most literate person in the unit, was writing a letter to his parents.

"We're heading out soon," Lieutenant Dao explained, catching Ping up on the parts of the meeting that he'd missed. Apparently Generalissimo Chiang Kai-shek was building a perimeter of thick, concrete pillboxes a hundred kilometers outside the Communist base. "Operation Iron Bucket, our spies are calling it," Dao continued. "Next week we're joining the rest of Third Legion at the front to make our own defenses and engage the Nationalists head-on. Can't spare a man, so you and Luo are coming, too."

Ping was glad they were moving out. The action would keep his hands busy and keep his mind from thinking about his inadequacies.

Over the next few days, their unit prepared for war. In addition to the supplies that the other soldiers had to carry, Ping packed into his bags four lead ingots, several hand clamps with different-sized bullet molds, and a pair of tongs. He slung an enormous twenty-kilogram wok—to melt the lead in—over his backpack. Luo carried the remaining bullet-making supplies, including another eight ingots, twenty spare flint mechanisms, and three dozen triggers. In her corner, Yong wiped her new gun and counted out the number of shells the official supply officer had allocated her, polishing each of their brass tips like pearls on a necklace.

The day before departure, she was off saying farewell to her friends from the other units. Luo walked over to Ping's spot and handed him a canteen of hot pear cider.

"How have you been, Little Brother?" he asked.

Surprised, Ping counted the number of backpacks he had to carry, making sure none were missing. "A little nervous, I guess," he said. "This campaign feels different from the ones before it."

Luo smiled. He grabbed one of the larger packs that Ping had to carry and threw it into his own pile. "I wouldn't worry. We're in good hands," he said. "Bo Gu learned a lot in Russia and we even have a Western guy in our ranks." He lifted his foot and smacked his shoes until a dust cloud surrounded them. "Still, just like before, we only have each other."

"You're probably right," Ping said.

"I always am." Luo put on his gear and headed down to join the others.

Ping thought he should say goodbye to Haiwu before leaving, so he walked in the direction of the Great Mobile Hospital of the Masses. He felt uncomfortable. Luo wanted to be friends again, but Ping didn't think Luo's idea of friendship was as simple as watching each other's back at the front. His instincts told him that Luo's friendliness was a harbinger of bad news, though he couldn't quite figure out exactly what that was yet. As if carrying around an extra bag was enough to amend for what he'd done! Ping thought, getting angrier.

When he arrived at the other side of the mountain, he saw that the Great Mobile Hospital had just a third of its tents up. The rest had been taken down and put on mules, a long line of which was marching with the army down the plateau and into the valley. Engineers were still dismantling the last roll of the ones that would be mobilized, and Ping ducked under a beam to reach Haiwu's tent.

"Third Legion heading out?" Haiwu asked, scratching his stump. The bandages had been removed and Ping could see the ten holes where the needles had been inserted. "I've never had such a bad itch before."

"Try putting it in mud," Ping said, "to cool it off."

"Good idea," Haiwu said. "So did they say when you'll be back?"

Ping shook his head. "I have a bad feeling about this. The enemy's not fighting like before. *We're* not fighting like before."

"And you don't have a kung fu champ in your ranks—like before." Haiwu smiled, showing a roll of uneven teeth.

"That's the only thing that makes me feel better. I don't need to watch out for your sword swinging in my face anymore."

Haiwu lowered his head, his smile fading.

"It was a bad joke," Ping said.

"Has she said anything about me? What's she like these days?"

Ping shrugged, fidgeting with a rip in his pants that he had sewn together with burlap. "I try not to think about her anymore. I avoid looking at her. Anyway, Luo's gotten a lot nicer these last few days, and we're going to war. It might be better just to become friends again."

Haiwu appeared startled, glancing around the tent as if a bat had snuck its way inside. "Luo's gotten nicer?" he repeated. "That's bad news. That means he's in love with her."

Of course, Ping thought. This was why he'd felt uncomfortable earlier. "I think you're right. Like I said before, maybe it's for the best. Why fight it? I'm tired."

Haiwu kicked Ping in the shin. "What kind of attitude is that? You're leaving for battle and you already reek of defeat. You're *tired*? I have one leg and I have more energy."

Ping rubbed his shin, letting out a *shh* sound.

"Have you forgotten what I taught you?" Haiwu continued. "Hsiao and Hsian? Well, it seems like you have the Hsiao down; you're so humble, you'll probably call a duck your sovereign. But what about Hsian, the most important of the five traits? A tasty soup takes hours to simmer, and you want to dump it in the trash before even lighting the fire?"

"All right, all right," Ping said. "What do you want me to do?"

"Small signals of love," said Haiwu, standing up and hopping from bed to bed, pacing and contemplating. "You'll have a lot of opportunities for those. During the march over, during nighttime, and during battle. Hand her a tarpaulin when it rains. Lend her a clean pair of chopsticks.

Clean her gun for her. Show that you care, but in small increments. This is what Hsian means. When pressed, never admit to your feelings, and no large gestures—that was my mistake. And never be defeated."

When Ping left the Great Mobile Hospital, he still wasn't sure if he should continue pursuing Yong. Haiwu's encouragement didn't hit him until three hours later, when Ping was out of the valley. In front of him, the line of soldiers extended beyond what his eyes could see, meandering like a bristled python down the dusty country road. Behind him, Iron Well Mountain had become only one of many sharp precipices and appeared as small as a rooster's comb. The air, no longer the pungent odor of mold on limestone, tasted as sweet and fresh as hawthorn juice. He jumped up a few times, peering over the shoulders of his comrades, and saw Yong in brief glimpses, the third behind Broadax, marching with Luo. One second, it seemed like they were holding hands; the next, their arms swung in wide arcs across their bodies.

"Never be defeated," Ping whispered to himself. "Small signals."

9

THIS TIME OF THE YEAR, southern Chiang-hsi Province's flowers—yellow, red, and orange—bloomed with the urgency of the Yangtze River, flooding the hillsides and fields and even poking out from the nooks of centuries-old Buddhist monasteries and stone bridges. It always amazed him, whenever he marched down, that there could exist anything but peace among the folding layers of rice paddies and the wafting strands of tall grass. He could see why so many songs were written about the province. If he could choose somewhere to have grown up, he'd pick the straw hut a kilometer to his west, one of many in a ravine, with an oval hole for a window and chickens running around its yard.

A few steps in front of him, he could hear Luo talking to Yong about how he'd like to live in a place like this when he got older, and Yong saying that people their age shouldn't be thinking about retirement and should be prepared to die without seeing their fortieth birthday. Ping enjoyed hearing them disagree. "Remember this view!" yelled Lieutenant Dao, on horseback. "This is why we're fighting!"

Their march to the front took three days, and although mosquito bites covered Ping's arms and legs every morning, he appreciated the chance to sleep out in the open again. The view of the stars cleared his mind and made him forget about his fear of battle. The designated cook boiled their meals in a crock the size of an open hammock—corn, sweet potatoes, tiny shreds of dried pork, and rice—and each soldier filled up his canteen with a ladleful of the stew and gathered around the fire.

As Haiwu had predicted, Ping found many opportunities on the journey for small signals. First, it was a knee-deep hole in the ground. Ping saw a soldier falling into it and gashing his thighs open, and when Yong was about to step into it, Ping ran back and lifted her by her armpits. A little winded, she thanked him, and he told her that she should pay more attention to where she was going. "Where would we be if our crack shot were unable to walk?" he asked, smiling. Then there was the evening at Panda Village, where the locals contributed half of their shacks for the Red Army to rest in. The one designated for Ping's unit had only enough space for two-thirds of the platoon, and he gave Yong the long straw that allowed her to go inside, saying that he'd been in the cave for too long and would rather sleep outside anyway. Yong shrugged, and forced him to use her rabbit-fur quilt for the night, citing the frosty spring winds. Under the stars, Ping wrapped the blanket tightly around him, breathing in the smell of her: an unfamiliar but pleasantly sour tang. Finally, there was the argument over the wine. Standard-bearer Shaohu was caught stashing a bottle of lychee liquor, and instead of pouring it out as Lieutenant Dao had instructed, he decided to go off into the fields and drink it all at once. When he came back it was close to midnight, and on his way to his bedroll he tripped over Yong. Yong got up, furious, and started yelling about how Shaohu was a slob who disobeyed orders. Shaohu, in return, told Yong that she should mind her own business and that a woman had no right telling a man what to do. Ping usually didn't want to get involved in arguments, but he forced himself to go against his instincts. He got out of his blanket and told Shaohu that he'd seen his shooting abilities and that even if Ping made him the most accurate gun in the world, Shaohu still wouldn't be half as valuable as Yong. After Shaohu waved them both away and stumbled off to his corner, Yong nodded to Ping in gratitude.

Surprisingly, Luo didn't seem to mind these incidents. *He probably thought I was trying to be friends again,* Ping guessed, *or he thought I posed no threat.* Whatever the case, the only acknowledgments Luo gave was a pat on the back when Ping prevented Yong from falling into the hole and a brief remark—"I'm glad we're getting along"—the day after their night at Panda Village, while they were casting bullets at lunchtime. He slept through the disagreement over the wine.

10

WHEN THEIR UNIT REACHED THE front—a half-mile line of machine-gun positions on hills and partially built brick houses shrouded by a thin bamboo forest—they were tasked with helping the engineers finish the fortifications and defending them at all costs. Past the forest was the eastern bank of the Fu River, and past that the town of Southern Abundance, where the Nationalists were hiding inside thick walls of concrete, waiting for their tanks and artillery to arrive before making their push across the river. It was Third Legion's job to take the town before the cowardly arrival of the Nationalists' technology, so that the enemy would not have a base of operations from which to advance on Iron Well Mountain. "Since our platoon has proven itself in ambush warfare," Lieutenant Dao explained, "we will not be the ones making the initial assault. We will be here in these bunkers—once they're finished—waiting, and we will open fire as soon as our comrades have lured the enemy out of their holes."

It was a strategy they had executed many times before, except instead of ambushing the enemy in a forest they would be firing from bunkers. On the surface, the plan should work just as it had in the past, but Ping couldn't help but think that there was some flaw in it. After all, the trees had concealed their unit from the enemy, but the enemy knew they were in the bunkers this time around. There were murmurs of reservation from some of the other members of the platoon as well, and Lieutenant Dao added, "We should trust the orders given to us. The generals have never given us bad orders before, and we shouldn't have misgivings now."

Still, Ping was concerned. He pictured Haiwu charging at the Nationalist emplacements with his sword drawn. It was good that he was injured. Otherwise, because of his kung fu abilities, he might have been transferred to join the initial wave of troops as bait. His bravery, Ping supposed, might have proven to be more selfish than even Haiwu had intended.

For the next couple of days, Ping and Luo were ordered to help the others finish perimeter defenses. Their area to guard, sandwiched between two hills, was more of a wall than a pillbox, the material made from clay and straw. The wall sloped in the rear, giving the defenders easy access to the top, and sacks of rice peels lined the crest with spaces in between for machine guns and riflemen. Their unit slept two hundred meters behind the perimeter, in a clearing next to the brickmaking facility, where it always smelled like burnt glue.

One morning, Ping grabbed a tile from an oxcart carrying recently dried bricks and lugged it to the wall. Then he dropped it in the empty slot on the slope and coated a spatula-full of wheat paste over the brick. Luo and Yong were next to him, doing the same.

"I'd rather be making bullets," Ping said to no one in particular.

"I'd rather be in Canton watching an opera," Luo said.

Yong put several bricks in a straw basket and dragged it over to the slope. "I'm from Canton, too, you know."

"I know," Ping said.

"But I never liked the operas there," Yong continued. "They always play the same stories about concubines and noblemen, romanticizing the lives of the wicked, and I don't like how all the female characters are played by men."

Ping wanted to say that not all aristocrats were evil; there'd been an old gentleman who lived a block down from his orphanage and brought by candied dates on Sundays. Instead, he just recited a line that he happened to remember from a lecture: "It's true. Women hold up half the sky."

"Oh, please, Little Brother," Luo said, lifting a stack of five bricks onto his shoulder. "Did you hear that silly quote from one of your prostitutes back home?"

"Comrade Mao said that." Yong rested her arms on her waist. "What's so silly about it?"

Luo dropped the bricks onto the slope and made his way over to Yong. He pecked her on the cheek.

"Don't do that again." She pushed him away and glanced over at Ping. "Treat me like a comrade or I'll report you to the lieutenant."

Luo turned to Ping and shrugged, which made Ping suspect that his friend was more embarrassed than he was letting on.

"To a girl like you," Luo said, "that quote might sound like some kind of fact. And if every girl *were* like you—strong, dedicated, and serious—then I'd even agree with it. But we all know that's not the case, so why argue?"

Yong stormed off to work on another section of the wall, and Luo laughed. He went over to the oxcart, tilted half of its contents onto the ground, and began pulling it in Yong's direction.

"You see what I have to deal with?" he shouted to Ping. "Now do you understand how I've done you a favor?"

Pleased with Luo's embarrassment, Ping finished laying the remaining bricks and headed to the brickmaking compound to produce more. He was certain now that, despite his friend's efforts in the last couple of weeks, Yong had not made any real commitment. The fish hadn't left the delta. They were still swimming upstream, searching for the best spot to lay their eggs.

11

HE HAD NEVER SEEN ONE in the air before: a machine with four wings made from wood and metal. He'd heard about them a few times, sure, from the commanders and educated men who knew about the other side of the world. There'd even been a model of something like them inside Lord Tea's mansion back in Canton, but that one had eight or ten wings and appeared to be made fully from wood. It didn't seem durable, as if a toss of a torch could bring it to the ground. But to witness one in person—to see it gliding, impossibly, in the air faster than a hawk, to smell the gasoline burning in its engine, and to hear its deafening noise as it descended over their camp and strafed their ranks—was something that Ping never thought he would encounter during his lifetime, certainly not while fighting the Nationalists, who were, after all, Chinese as well. They had better rifles and more trucks. Ping could even accept their armored vehicles and tanks, but what were they supposed to do about something that could attack one second and then disappear the next?

"We work at night," Lieutenant Dao told them. During their first encounter with the flying machines, thirty soldiers had been killed and ninety injured. There was a group funeral with a currency-burning ceremony, after which the army moved their camp away from the forest clearing and into the forest itself. The casualties, luckily, were in other units—in those stationed on the two hills surrounding their wall. Ping's platoon was fortunate to have been assigned the ravine, which provided a natural trench that the flying machines could not dive low enough to reach. The only person in their unit who was injured—Pengpeng, the literate letter writer—had been out fetching water for the platoon when the planes descended and blasted the buckets on both side of his bamboo pole, shattering the wood and shooting the splinters into his arms. He was on a mule now, trekking back to Iron Well Mountain.

At night they lit torches. When the bugles sounded, they ran over and extinguished the flames. Ping was in charge of snuffing out the two closest to their camp, so he stayed near where the platoon slept and worked in the brickmaking facility full-time. Until now, night fighting had been rare, and the use of it signaled a crushing desperation that lowered morale and instilled fear. He could hear the apprehensive units, whose job tomorrow night was to swim across the river and rush the strongholds. "How are we supposed to lure the Nationalists out in the dark when they're asleep?" they asked one another. "Would they even know which direction to follow us?"

It was close to dawn—the sky somewhere between black and purple and the sun as thin as a blade's edge—when Ping heard the flying machines again, descending on the perimeter two hundred meters away. From their height, he guessed they could make better use of the morning light and see greater distances. He ran to the torches, snuffed them out, and headed into the forest as instructed. Between trees he could see enemy bullets—bright and quick—hissing to the ground, and friendly ones—tiny and slow—arching through the air. He could tell which were the bullets fired by the rifles he'd made—they were the dimmest, because they didn't have tracer rounds—and he felt sorry for Luo and Shaohu and all the others who were not adequately equipped.

Suddenly a flying machine hovered so close to one of the hills that it crashed. It rolled on the ground a few times, spinning like a sheet of paper, and drifted out of view. The guns stopped. A few minutes later, troops came rushing into the forest with the soldiers injured by the planes, carrying them on their backs and dragging them on bamboo stretchers. Ping got up and, not seeing machines in the air anymore, walked out of the forest. When most of the soldiers from his platoon had arrived, he began to worry that something might have happened to Luo and Yong.

"Are there any others?" he asked Guan Ye, one of three soldiers in their unit who operated the Russian-manufactured heavy machine gun.

The fat man, out of breath, nodded behind him and collapsed onto the grass.

Ping walked forward and, halfway to the wall, saw Yong running in his direction.

"We got one!" Yong yelled, pointing to the crashed machine to his left, its tail crumpled and smoldering. "I hit it a few times, I'm sure, and then it started burning on one side, and then the man inside limped out, and now we have taken him prisoner."

This was an appropriate occasion, Ping thought, and he gave her a hug. "Where's Luo?"

"He's with Lieutenant Dao and some of the leaders. They're questioning the driver. They know Luo's a good talker."

Ping nodded. He looked her over and saw that one side of her pants was ripped and her ankle was cut and bleeding.

"You need to see a doctor," he said, kneeling and examining the wound. The dawn light made her calves reflect a pale blue. His mind went back to the time when he'd thought they resembled bamboo shoots, and he laughed at himself. He ripped a portion of his sleeve and wrapped it around the cut.

"Don't you know what this means?" Yong said. "They're not invincible! We probably don't even need to fight in the dark anymore!"

"Come," said Ping, holding her arm. "Let me take you to the field hospital."

"It's fine. I just scraped it on construction material when we were ordered to dive for cover. I can still walk."

But she let him clutch her arm all the way to the forest, and when her excitement died down and her pain began to set in, she started to hobble.

The field hospital—the same tents used for the Great Mobile Hospital but painted green to match the forest—was filled with the injured. Even the critically wounded were left in rows on the ground and made to wait. The place smelled like dried blood and herbal medicine. A medic glanced at Yong's injury, threw her a vial of alcohol and some bandage, and told her that she could wrap it herself.

Ping helped her back to camp. Along the way, he wondered if he should tend to her wound. No grand gestures, Haiwu had told him, but was this a grand gesture? He was just a comrade helping another comrade when the doctors were busy. It felt natural and uncomplicated, and he didn't even ask for her permission when he sat her down around the fire, knelt, and began untying the scrap of his sleeve. Most of the soldiers in their unit were exhausted and had already put leaves over their eyes to sleep.

"I didn't know you were this way," Yong said.

"What way?"

"So attentive." She smiled. "Luo told me you were a little boy, fussy and arrogant, but I don't see that at all."

Ping bit his tongue. He wanted to say something nasty about Luo in return, but any such remark would ruin the compliment.

"What else did he say about me?"

"Oh, I don't remember. He told me you've never *had* a real woman before—that you liked to go to brothels when you were in Canton."

Ping swabbed the wound with alcohol, hearing her stifle a hiss. "Did he say he was the one who introduced me to those places?"

She nodded. "Only as a joke, he told me, but he said you took it seriously."

He shook his head, untangling the roll of bandage. "He's a lying sack of turtle dung," he said, "and he doesn't know me at all."

"That's no way to talk about a fellow comrade—a friend, no less." Her tone changed. It no longer held the lightness of chitchat and took on a firmer tenor of reprimand.

Ping wasn't sure how to continue the conversation. He could drop the subject and ask for more details about the crashed flying machine, or he could grow serious and accuse Luo even more. He knew the former was correct, but he was angry enough not to care.

"He doesn't deserve someone like you," he said.

She pulled her leg away, and he knew immediately he'd made a mistake.

"What are you trying to say?" she asked.

"Nothing. Never mind."

She paused, stretching her leg out and then back in. "All right, I'll say it if you don't want to. I know how you feel. Maybe not exactly, but I'm not stupid and I know enough. I like you"—hearing this, Ping looked up—"and in any other circumstance I'd be glad to have someone like you feel that way about me. I appreciate you as a friend. But Luo is the one for me. I think I've known this for a while now."

Ping paused. He wanted to run into the woods and be by himself, but he remembered what Luo had said and forced himself to go against his instincts. "What's there to like about him?" he asked. "I've known him longer than you have. You won't be happy. He's conniving and selfish, and he lies a lot."

"True," Yong said. "But he's also clever, strong, and independent. When I'm with him, I don't need to worry about him, which is more than I can say for a lot of the other men. I can focus all my attention on the revolution."

Ping gave the bandage to Yong, moved next to a tree trunk, and leaned his head back. "I've embarrassed myself. I hope I didn't embarrass you."

Yong stood up and walked over to the tree. Her movement was swift, as if her wound didn't bother her anymore.

"You haven't embarrassed anyone," she said, then returned to her spot on the ground. After a few minutes, she started to snore.

He watched as the line of spittle began to run down her mouth, and he couldn't take being there anymore. He got up and walked over to Shaohu's sleeping bag, knowing the standard-bearer still had a bottle of wine left. He shook him with his foot.

Shaohu awoke with a start, pointing the flagpole at him. "What's wrong? Are we under attack?"

"No," Ping said. "I was just looking for some wine. I know you have some."

Shaohu yawned, reaching deep into his bedroll and pulling out a bottle. "Here," he said. "Just don't be a snitch next time."

12

THERE WAS HARDLY A DESERTED spot in the woods, so Ping decided to drink at the stables—a clearing in the forest fenced in with wire—where horses, mules, and cattle grazed and sipped from buckets of well water. "It's all so silly," he said to a donkey, pulling on its leash. "We're in the middle of a war, and instead of worrying about losing my head I'm depressed over an ugly girl." He laughed. "Do you have someone special, Mr. Donkey? What's she like? Does she have wide hips to make baby donkeys for you?" The animal turned and started grazing in another corner. "Don't walk away when I'm talking to you!" Ping jerked the leash, whipping the animal's head back. In response, the donkey pounded the ground and kicked dust into Ping's face. "All right, all right," Ping said, coughing. "I get it. You don't like me, either."

He was drunk enough to sleep, so he trudged back in the direction of the camp. All around him were four thousand men snoring in unison like a cluster of chubby crickets. The sun was halfway to its zenith, and he estimated that it was close to ten in the morning. When he got to his camp, the only person in the platoon still awake was Luo. He was excited, Ping could tell, gnawing on a sweet potato.

"I was wondering where you were," Luo said. "Did Yong tell you about the flying machine? We have the driver in custody. He gave us information about the Nationalists' position and he's even agreed to defect. Can you believe that? We have someone who can operate a flying machine!"

"Except we don't have a machine of our own." Ping laughed loud enough for a few soldiers to stir. He stood there swaying left and right.

"You're drunk," Luo said, but there was no accusation in his voice. "Have any of that stuff left?"

Ping shook his head. "All gone!"

"A pity."

Luo helped Ping regain his balance. Then he brought him over to his spot near the fire and sat him down. He took out the rifle Ping had made and began cleaning it.

"I've never said I'm sorry about that." He nodded toward Yong, his eyes on the lines of the rifle. "I'm a scoundrel, but you know that already."

"You are," Ping said. He was no longer laughing. He remembered his conversation with Yong and he resented the fact that Luo was bringing it up and souring his good mood.

"It's different this time," Luo said. "I don't know what it is about her."

"It's love." Ping grinned.

"Ha, you're imagining things again, Little Brother." Luo lay down and put a leaf over his eyes. "But this time you might not be so far off."

Ping stood up and stared at Luo, rocking back and forth on the balls of his feet. The rifle, now glittering as if the metal were fresh from the forge, leaned on a rock next to his friend's cheek. Ping remembered crafting it during their first weeks at Iron Well. He had used a lightweight steel trigger salvaged from a Kuomintang pistol and had taken great care in polishing the insides of the barrel so that a bullet could never get caught. In fact, he had spent more time constructing Luo's weapon than his own. And for what? For Luo to steal the woman he loved and to make fun of him afterward? It seemed to Ping that his *imagination* was the only thing that got the two of them anywhere. The Communists might not have even taken them in if they hadn't known about Ping's abilities. Where would Luo be *without* his imagination? Ping thought. Then he wondered: Where would *he* be without Luo? And he saw Yong having lunch with him instead of with Luo. He saw her marching next to him in those orange and yellow valleys, wearing the wildflowers he would've picked for her. He saw him tending to her wounds and her smiling back, not as a friend but as a wife, and this body on the ground right now wouldn't even be there, and in its place would be an oversized cot, wide enough for two, where Yong's skinny frame would be locked next to his own.

When Luo's breathing steadied, Ping reached over and grabbed the rifle. He stuck his hands into his pocket and took out a lump of lead left over from a session of bullet molding. It was still soft, like a chunk of smooth sparkly clay. He'd planned on melting it down later in case the campaign dragged on longer than expected. But now he turned it over in his palms, thinking about the deadly potential for this innocuous material. That was all it had, though: potential. How many bullets found their mark? One in ten? One in twenty? Maybe one in a hundred? So much of his time he had spent creating objects that ended up lost in a field or lodged in a tree, never to be noticed again. Very suddenly a kinship for the lead chunk welled up in the pit of his stomach, and he didn't want its fate to end up like the others, with its potential wasted.

He rolled the lead into a cylindrical shape and inserted it inside Luo's rifle, using a cleaning rod to lodge it as deep as he could. He blew the excess lead shredding away from the muzzle and replaced the rifle next to Luo. Then he waddled over to his spot on the ground.

Curled inside his sleeping bag, he gargled with a mouthful of wine. He swallowed it and closed his eyes. His belly churning, he fell asleep not sure if he should've thrown up first.

13

AT DUSK, ARTILLERY SLUGS STARTED landing in the Fu River: arcing whistles followed by splashing thuds. Then shells exploded near the hills, and staccato bursts of bugles signaled the advance of Kuomintang troops. When Ping opened his eyes, most of his unit was already awake and running to their stations on the wall. "Up, up, up!" Lieutenant Dao yelled. "For the sake of each other's respect!" He nodded toward Ping, then got on Broadax and dashed to the front.

Ping had a piercing headache. He grabbed his gun and reached for his jute pouch full of bullets. Running out of the forest and down into the ravine, he saw Luo taking large steps up the top of the wall, using his rifle as a walking stick. Suddenly Ping remembered what he'd done that morning. He tucked his head down and ran faster. His lungs burned and his legs were sore, and he reached the top of the wall just as Luo and Yong were lying down between sacks and pointing their rifles forward.

"Glad you've come, Little Brother." Luo squinted through the flint hole on top of his gun.

Yong, who was resting her body on one shoulder and loading bullets into her newly issued bolt-action rifle, breathed in through her nose and exhaled from her mouth, a routine that steadied her aim. "Looks like they've taken the bait again," she said. "They'll be like mice trapped in a sack without rice."

"Except we're not in the forest," Luo said. "And where's our bait?"

A shell landed just a few meters in front of the wall, kicking up mud and splattering it on their faces. Lieutenant Dao yelled for Yong to leave her position and come down to where the machine gun was. "We need your accuracy up front!" he said. Yong wiped her face and crawled away on all fours.

The artillery stopped, and out of the bamboo forest soldiers started appearing. There were only a few at first, dressed in brown and gray with metal helmets and stiff, wide caps. Then more soldiers ran out waving blue-and-white banners. Next, the main group followed, and abruptly, as if a rock where beetles and centipedes hid had been turned over, there were hundreds of them, more than Ping could count, and they were sprinting toward him with their bayonets pointing forward.

"Not until they reach the edge of the hills!" Lieutenant Dao shouted, silencing the few potshots coming from the wall.

Luo reached for a bullet from his pouch, his eyes not leaving the enemy, and inserted it into the muzzle of his rifle.

"Let's switch guns," Ping said. He tried coming up with an excuse—something to add so that his suggestion made sense.

"What are you talking about?" Luo stared at his friend.

"Give me your gun," Ping repeated. "I want to see something."

"You're crazy." Luo returned his gaze to the front.

The shouting grew closer, and their comrades opened fire. Ping grabbed Luo's rifle and tried to yank it from his friend's hand, but Luo pushed Ping away so hard that he rolled a few steps down the side of the wall. His head struck brick, and when he peered up, he saw Luo on his knees, pointing down the wall and pulling the trigger. There was a boom and smoke, and when it cleared, Luo was on his back, his torso bending from his legs at a sharp and unnatural manner.

Ping rushed over. He lifted Luo in his arms and saw the lead bullet he had cast earlier that week lodged just above the right brow. Luo's eyes were still open, and when Ping glanced around, trying to find help, he saw Yong staring up at him from her position. Her expression was blank, waiting for Ping to fill it with whatever news he had to report. Lieutenant Dao tapped her on the shoulder, and after blinking a couple of times she lifted her rifle again and continued firing.

Ping started dragging Luo's body down the side of the wall even before the bugles sounded the retreat, before the tanks charged from the direction of the crashed plane and blasted a hole in the Communist left flank, before the hills were overrun by the Nationalist banners, and before his platoon followed Broadax to the rallying point. He dragged Luo until he reached the forest, placed the punctured body onto a bamboo stretcher, and then pulled some more. He didn't look back. When his right arm got tired, he pulled with his left. He didn't notice his comrades sprinting in the same direction, especially not Yong, who was running with him and yelling for him to stop, please stop, that he didn't need to wear himself out like that, that he should tie the stretcher to a horse or mule like the other casualties, and that Luo was already dead.

14

"THEY GOT NEARLY HALF OF US," Lieutenant Dao said. The
Nationalists had killed twenty-nine out of sixty-five soldiers in their
platoon, but Ping knew the number was one less than that. All morning and afternoon they ran, the flying machines picking off their rear
guard like stray sheep. The Communist army had reached a narrow stretch of land thirty kilometers from the Fu River, in between
two high peaks, called Buddha's Cleavage. The area was too narrow
for further Kuomintang pursuit, so Third Legion set up camp and
tallied heads. They dug as many graves as they could. When they
finished, the educated men in the army wrote the names of the dead
on thin sheets of paper and pasted them on logs collected for firewood and stuck them atop the mounds. They didn't have any fake
currency to burn, so they pulled out bills printed at the Communist
minting facility and scattered them in the air. They weren't worth
much anyway, since most vendors in the provinces accepted only
silver dollars.

The Communist soldiers who had crossed the river to lure the
Nationalists had never made it back, and the clay-and-straw block-
houses had not withstood the artillery or tank fire. They had lost
60 percent of their beasts of burden, 25 percent of their vehicles,
and 100 percent of their morale. Fighting Chiang Kai-shek's army
tit-for-tat, it seemed, had only proven how inferior their material and
equipment were.

Ping sat next to Yong at the campfire. He balled his hands to fists to keep them from shaking. His fingers felt the cuts and blisters on his palms. It would be a stupid thing to admit to what he'd done, but at that moment he wanted nothing more than to tell Yong.

"You were brave today," she said. She'd finished crying hours before, though for a moment Ping thought she might start again. "Spending all that time on top of the wall, where the enemy was shooting, holding him. Then dragging him here yourself."

Had there been so many bullets? He couldn't remember. It wasn't bravery, he wanted to say, but his explanation would have come across as arrogant and false. It was guilt, of course, that had caused him to do what he had done, though perhaps guilt, like selfishness, sometimes took on the form of valor.

Yong moved closer to him and put her head on his shoulder. "Who knew Old Man in the Sky was such a prankster?" She stared into the fire. "The moment I told someone I didn't worry about Luo was the moment he died."

"He knew you cared for him."

"Maybe," she said, facing Ping. "But no one else did." She sniffled and then sat up straight, placing her hands over the fire. "Anyway, many comrades died. Chairman Mao said it is selfish to feel too much grief. And I would rather be heartless than selfish."

Ping nodded. Could she really? he wondered. Could he?

Later that morning, when most of the other soldiers were asleep, Yong walked over to his spot, held out her hand, and invited him to take a stroll with her.

"Bring your bedroll," she said.

Lieutenant Dao was still awake. Ping was sure he noticed them walking hand in hand deeper into the valley. Love was allowed—even encouraged—but not during campaigns, and Ping almost wanted the lieutenant to intervene—to stop them from violating army policy so blatantly—but the Lieutenant just looked away. They had suffered a major defeat. Much of the army was in disarray, and policy became lax. Dao continued brushing Broadax's coat as if saying, *I have my partner; you can have yours.*

They found an area under three finger-like boulders pointing to the sky. The ground was dense with gravel, and the cotton inside the bedroll was not thick enough to prevent their backs from feeling the sharp edges and scattered lumps. They took turns being on top. Ping preferred being on the bottom because he wanted the moment to be as painful as possible.

When they finished, he asked, "Are we being heartless for doing this?"

"I am," Yong said, kissing him on his shoulder. "But you're indebted to no one."

Ping shook his head. He closed his eyes and saw Luo again, kneeling on the wall and pulling the trigger. The puff of smoke, like some shadowy demon, taking his friend's life. And he was the creator of that demon. Over the years, the only productive thing he'd done was create instruments that took the lives of people, and he'd never felt guilty about it—had never even thought about it really until now. And he remembered how everyone had called him Smoke, and Luo, Whispers. How appropriate, he thought. From this moment forward, he knew his life would be tarnished and black, while Luo's would be nothing more than fleeting recollections.

15

AT DUSK, UPON RETURNING TO camp, clutching the bedroll and holding hands, they saw the other soldiers look up from what they were doing to stare at them. Naturally, there would be some gossip in the platoon. Most soldiers shook Ping's hand and congratulated him. "Even during catastrophe, there are things one can salvage," Lieutenant Dao said. But AGuang, the only other man interested in Yong, swore to them that he would report them to the politburo for neglecting their duties and fornicating during wartime. "You'll both be court-martialed!" he yelled. The lieutenant tugged at AGuang's rifle strap and asked, "Should I replace this with a spear now, or do you want Ping to make sure nothing is broken before you go tell the Central Committee? I'm sure the leaders, despite their preoccupation with war matters, will surely put some serious thought in determining the appropriate punishment for this heinous crime." The others laughed, and Ping felt so ashamed that he almost wanted to tell AGuang what he had done to Luo so that the man had something real to report.

The journey back to Iron Well took four days. Due to the possibility of ambushes, the army avoided the main roads and swerved through gorges, swamps, and other difficult terrain. They marched during the day now, since the Nationalists had caught on to their tactics and expected night movement. Local villagers couldn't be trusted—not with news of their defeat—so they had to ration whatever supplies they were carrying and make them last until they reached their base. Under the sun for ten hours a day, their skin darkened until bits flaked off and their faces resembled long-extinct reptiles. Nobody paid attention to the scenery, which, as if in mockery, was more breathtaking than what they had seen during their march forward. The mountain vistas, waterfalls, and lush green canyons appeared undisturbed and ancient, as if no one had noticed their beauty save for the hawks and river trout. They crossed the Black Croc River on wooden skiffs, a single pole used for propulsion, and when they entered the Great Plebeian Naval Reserves, nobody was inside and they scavenged the shop for dried fish and seaweed and materials that could be made into bandages.

By the time the army reached the outer perimeter of the villages surrounding Iron Well Mountain, everyone was starving. All Ping had eaten that afternoon were some sour berries he'd found on a bush and the peel of the sweet potato that he'd had that morning. The Great Hall would surely be open when they arrived, and he looked forward to the communal banquet.

Nearing the northern gate of Third Well Village, where a watch tower stood guard, he noticed that there was no one to greet them. At first, he thought the soldier must be taking a nap in one of the village huts, but when he entered the village, he saw that the huts were also deserted. In fact, the whole town was empty, the only sound coming from a creaky well pulley, a bucket swinging at the end of a rope. Was there a meeting taking place farther up on the mountain? Were the villagers gathered somewhere for instruction on how to handle the coming of the Kuomintang army? Lieutenant Dao told them to take out their weapons and be ready for anything.

Then, at the base of the plateau to Iron Well proper, they saw the fires. The scattered alcoves on the mountainside were lit up—the flames tiny from their position—as if the lights were nothing more than an infestation of fireflies. Tentatively, scouts started making their way up the familiar trek of the mountain, through the sparse forest that pointed them to the first level of caves. But before they reached the Great Hall of the Proletariat, there were flashes of machine-gun fire: The scouts were shot down by emplacements hidden somewhere farther up.

When Lieutenant Dao returned from his meeting with the generals, he told the platoon that pathfinders had spotted the remainder of the Communist First and Fourth Armies on the other side of the mountains. Assaulting Iron Well head-on was too risky: Nobody knew how many Nationalists were up there. The Third Legion was commanded to circle the mountain and link up with the other Communist forces.

Approaching the far side of Iron Well, Ping noticed the remaining tents of the Great Mobile Hospital. Above them, a wooden pavilion was smoldering on a mountain cliff. Its roof was already burnt black and the wind was blowing embers down the crag and onto the tops of the tents. *Haiwu!* he remembered. With all that had happened these last few days, he'd almost forgotten that he'd made a new friend.

He needed to take a detour and reach the hospital. He needed to somehow skulk away from his unit without being suspected of desertion. How could he forgive himself if he missed this chance at redemption?

"Can you do me a favor?" he asked Yong, who was moving alongside him, her shoulders scrunched low like the rest of the army. They were spread out a few meters away from each other so that, when spotted, the machine guns wouldn't be able to take out more than one soldier at a time.

"What?" she asked.

"I need to pee," he whispered. "I'm going to head over there." He nodded in the direction of the tents. "If the lieutenant asks, tell him I'll be back soon."

"Hold it," she said, "or go in your pants."

He shook his head. "No, I need to go over there."

She turned to him and her eyes narrowed. "What's going on? You don't need to pee."

Why even bother lying when everybody could see through him like a silk handkerchief? He took off his backpack and laid the iron wok on the ground. Then he shuffled away from her, ducked under a tree branch, and headed to the clearing.

"I'm going to save Haiwu," he said.

"Come back," she whispered as loudly as she could without letting the others hear. "What does he even mean to you?"

"He's my friend—the only one I have left."

"Don't be stupid. He might not even be there anymore."

This was true, Ping considered, but it didn't matter. "He's there. I'm sure of it."

"Don't make me worry about you."

"Then don't worry about me." He glanced back and smiled. "Treat me just as you would've treated Luo."

He stepped out of the forest and threw himself on the ground. It would take five or six hundred steps to reach the hospital. It was a clear day and he could see birds in the sky: hawks, crows, and vultures. He wasn't a fast runner, but his shoulder wouldn't be able to handle too much more crawling. There might be any number of snipers in the area above the tents, surrounding the pavilion, in the shadowy nooks at the top of the mountain, or even behind the hospital itself.

"Get back here," Yong whispered.

Her voice was softer, more distant now, and when he looked back again, he couldn't see her face anymore. "When you perform an action," Mao had told them, "you will not know the laws governing it, or how to do it, or be able to do it well. You will understand its nature and its relation to other things only once you do it."

Repeating the words, Ping sniffed the dirt: it smelled of mushroom and pine. Then he got to his feet and took off as fast as he could.

PART II

DEVOTION

16

IF IT WAS OLD MAN in the Sky's intention that she should lose two suitors in so many weeks, then so be it. She wasn't going to worry. There were others in the platoon who'd gladly take Ping's place. Finding someone was easy, although it was true that none of them had as much to contribute to the cause as Ping did, except for maybe the lieutenant, who was a fair and competent leader. But someone could easily take his place as well; Ping's successor, however, had to go through at least a few years of training to become a gunsmith. In any case, the lieutenant had a wife in Manchuria—he swore he'd go there to find her once they'd defeated the Japanese occupiers—and Yong had already decided on Ping.

They had slept together after all, and not in the way that Lord Zhu, the crooked old man her father had sold her to, had forced her to sleep with him every night, until she took a pair of scissors to his bladder and ran away. The horny pig hadn't bound her feet, even though he'd grown up during the old dynasty and enjoyed the tiny, mutilated toes of his other wives. He told his senior wife that Yong was too old to get hers bound and that he wanted a different delicacy this time around. His one act of mercy, Yong reflected, led to his demise. She would never have been able to work up the courage to kill him if she didn't have her agile, tree-climbing toes to escape on.

At the edge of the clearing, she waited for Ping to return until the sun had almost set, and then crawled back to her platoon. When the Third Legion made contact with the other Communist forces, despite her best efforts not to worry, she searched the neighboring camps anxiously, hoping somehow Ping had already made it back. The lieutenant did a head count, and when he noticed one person missing, Yong stepped forward and told him that Ping was gone.

"He's on a mission of bravery," she said, "to save an injured comrade."

"He's being selfish." Lieutenant Dao chewed on some tofu jerky the other army's supply officer had given the platoon. "Bringing a cripple back to camp doesn't help us win the war, while losing a gunsmith will likely cause a lot of deaths. He's putting the life of one over those of the many."

Yong couldn't object to this, and she cursed Ping for forcing her to stand up for him and lose face in front of the lieutenant.

"I'll go look for him," she said, grabbing her rifle.

"You stay!" Dao stomped his foot. "I looked the other way when the two of you got together. Don't make me regret it."

There was nothing that Yong could do but pace at the edge of the forest, stopping only to stare out at the mountain for any sign of Ping's return. The combined Communist forces had to move out before dawn, before the Nationalists could find their position and before the arrival of the bulk of Chiang Kai-shek's troops in pursuit. If Ping still didn't make it back by then, they would label him a deserter and leave without him. She grew tired of walking and leaned against a sycamore, staring at the hilltops burning in the distance.

She never thought she would have to abandon Iron Well Mountain. She had never prepared for it, mentally. She saw herself living in the cave as an old woman, the war having been won, her children grown up and working with the villagers in the rice paddies. There would be fish and milk on every table, even those of the peasants, and the Great Hall's storehouses would be overflowing with their collective bounty. Recently, she had even started including Ping in her reveries. He would grow to be a wise old man, sage-like, with a long gray beard. He would enjoy the veneration of being a teacher in the new China, instructing the next generation on how to craft weapons more advanced than the ones from Japan or Russia. Perhaps she would be a teacher as well, an army instructor who drilled recruits on handling their rifles and steadying their breathing.

She awoke to a strong wind howling through the branches and carrying the smell of smoke. She sat up and sneezed. She wiped her nose with her sleeve and returned to camp, hoping to find Ping snoozing in his bedroll somewhere. The chances were low, she figured, since, if he'd returned, the first thing he would have done was come looking for her.

She saluted the lieutenant. "I'd like permission to stay here a while longer, sir."

Lieutenant Dao was saddling Broadax with supplies—his own along with those of the injured who couldn't lift their bags.

"No way," he said, giving the strap a tight tug. "And let me remind you that desertion under Communist law is the same as treason. After the defeat at the Fu River, the leaders have put a premium on prosecuting the crime."

"Fine." She kicked a log at Broadax.

Behind the lieutenant, the Third Legion was gathering in two columns. Just as Yong was trying to think up another excuse to stay behind, she saw Ping's silhouette in the distance. It was a hot morning and Ping's image shimmered off the white gravel, as if appearing out of thin air. There was someone on his shoulders, and when he got close, she was sure that someone was Haiwu.

"I'm so sorry," Ping said, panting and dropping Haiwu to the ground.

The kung fu master looked up at her and grinned.

"A unit was patrolling the mountainside and I had to go all the way around," Ping continued. "I almost thought we wouldn't make it. In fact, it's a minor miracle we did. I think it has more to do with the Nationalists not wanting to waste bullets on a crazy man and a cripple than with them not seeing us."

Haiwu grabbed a branch on a tree and pulled himself up. Out of the left side of his pants jutted a smooth, pearly stub.

"I'm one-sixth dolphin now," he said. He hobbled around her in a showy sort of way, his shoulder rising and falling. "Maybe I should add that to my list of kung fu stances: Tiger, Mantis, Sparrow Hawk, *Dolphin*."

Haiwu. What an annoying little man. He may have lost a leg, but still retained his irritating ebullience. Her words on Pear Tree Hill during Mao's abdication had only been partially true. She did think his action had been brave, but his valor was offset by a meddlesome kind of pushiness that made her want to grab him by his arms and shake him. She didn't do so because she was afraid he might mistake her action for a passion for him. When he'd climbed the date tree for her, she hadn't known him that well and pecked him on the cheek. Then he wouldn't stop bothering her, walking next to her every chance he got to talk about martial arts or books or whatever nonsense was on his mind. She'd only let him touch her chest because he'd promised to leave her alone afterward—a pledge he failed to keep.

"So Ping risked his life for nothing, I see." She examined an orange lizard crawling on his prosthetic. "You could've just walked out of there yourself."

Ping kicked the lizard away and steadied Haiwu with his arm. "The dolphin bone takes some getting used to," he said. "But the doctors told him that even when he's proficient, he shouldn't expect to run again."

"I can still do other stuff." Haiwu winked. "The same stuff you did with Ping, if you know what I mean."

She rolled her eyes. "Come on. If we stay here one more minute, we'll all be labeled deserters."

17

THE COMBINED COMMUNIST FORCES TOTALED about twenty thousand soldiers. Lieutenant Dao told the platoon they were heading east to defend the administrative capital of Ruijin, a two-week trek. Surprisingly, Haiwu didn't require as much assistance as Yong had thought. He kept up with the platoon well, and except for the rainy days when the mud reached ankle level, he didn't need Ping to carry him. Whenever the army stopped, they took the time to fight local bandits. Sponsored by the rich, packs of marauding highwaymen waited for any chance to rob villagers and capture Communist sympathizers to sell to the Kuomintang. It was imperative that the People's Army chase them down at every opportunity so that the peasants knew the Reds had not been defeated.

Food was severely rationed. The only time they ate meat was at the edge of a lake, when strange walking fish crawled onto the muddy shore to mate. The locals called them *wawas*: Their calls sounded like crying babies. At night, soldiers rolled up their pant legs, lit torches, and stuck them into the sludge. Attracted by the brightness, the *wawa*s slunk toward the flames in huge schools, only to be snatched up with nets. Yong and Ping had forty or fifty of the tasty creatures in their bucket, and even Haiwu, his prosthetic getting stuck in the mud every other step, managed to catch half a dozen.

Still, by the time they arrived at South Ji Village—a densely populated rural area forty miles from Ruijin—the army had nearly exhausted its food and supplies. Stealing from the peasantry was a hanging offense, and, to keep up with wages, commanders collected duties from landowning villagers and the civic administrator, a shrewd and wizened farmer who informed them that just a week earlier Lord Kai had harbored Kuomintang troops in his mansion atop Cloud Hill. When Yong heard their platoon was among those ordered to storm the hill and put Kai in his place, she shivered with excitement.

As a part-time member of the army's propaganda attachment, she had participated in public denunciations three times before. She knew that Kai, like other members of the privileged class, had had his land partitioned by the Communists and couldn't wait until the Kuomintang reestablished authority in the area. Men like him believed their wealth and titles had come from divine providence and that it was their right to collect taxes from peasants ten years in advance and coerce women to give them favors in return for letting their families stay on their land. Yong didn't believe in the Confucian concept of the moral baron—some fantastical entity who used his status and learning for the betterment of those he ruled. To her, there were only two types of noblemen: the corrupt and the slightly less corrupt.

The Kai mansion was built atop a cliff overlooking lychee orchards. A gentle waterfall dropped from the lowest point of the hill and emptied into a man-made pond, the water clean enough for Yong to notice tiny clear fish. The manor floated above the stream, the gnarled trunks, and the windswept branches as if on a cloud, and the curled-roof pavilions and red mahogany walls might have been mistaken for the summer home of emperors or the earthly dwelling of the gods.

On her way up, she stuffed a handful of the succulent lychees into her pocket and gave some to Ping, who for some reason appeared glum. She suspected that he was feeling guilty for not wanting to carry Haiwu. The little man had begged Ping to carry him so he could see the mansion, too.

"Cheer up," she said, popping a lychee into her mouth. "You've done more for Haiwu than his own mother."

Ping shook his head. "Oh, it's not that. I've never been to one of these condemnations before." He gestured to the mansion with his stubbly chin. "I'm a little nervous."

"There's nothing to be nervous about. You'll get to spit on their proud faces and rummage through their expensive stuff. Then they'll be just like the rest of us: equal in the way nature intended."

"I know we're bringing justice," Ping said. "But what we're doing makes me feel like I'm not in an army anymore, like I'm a thug again. I don't know. I think wronging those who wronged you will just make people want to wrong you again."

Poor honest Ping, Yong thought. *If all men in China were like you, there would be no need for revolutions.*

"You've got it backward," she said. "You treat someone who wronged you well and they'll still want to wrong you. And what about the people who treated you well all along? They get no credit. So you're basically saying to the world: 'Hey, it doesn't matter if you're good or bad to me; I'll treat you the same! Take advantage of me all you want!'"

"You're right," Ping said, though she couldn't tell if he truly agreed.

To reach the mansion, the platoon steadied their feet on the side of the cliff and climbed a thick hemp rope. Normally an excellent climber, Yong was so tired by the time she was over the edge that she held on to the rope for a couple of seconds, panting. Ping helped her to her feet and apologized to the soldiers behind them. He asked her if she was all right, and although her fatigue did worry her a little, she told him she was fine and jogged to the mansion door to prove it.

Lieutenant Dao was the one who knocked, lifting the ornate brass handle and letting it drop. "Open up for the People's Red Army!"

When there was no response, Yong and three other soldiers lifted a marble bench in the courtyard's garden and rammed it against the door until it gave way. Two servants, who still had the front halves of their heads shaved in the old style of the Qing dynasty, dropped their staves and raised their arms. Behind them, a woman dressed in silk with butterfly designs let out a scream, covered her mouth with a handkerchief, and ran up the circular stairwell.

"Hold it!" Lieutenant Dao shouted.

He patted Yong on the back and nodded in the direction of the woman. The interior of the mansion glowed a soothing red, like being inside an orange. Yong hesitated for a moment before dropping the bench, stepping with her muddy shoes onto the carpet, and running up with the rest of the battering ram crew. At the top of the stairs, under an electric lantern, the woman was huddling with two girls in a corner. In one of the rooms nearby a phonograph played "The Wandering Songstress," a hit song by a Shanghai singer. Up close, Yong saw that the woman who had run was around forty or fifty—older than she had first seemed—and the girls, presumably her daughters, were about sixteen or seventeen. They were twins, except one had a swollen belly. Yong hadn't encountered too many pregnant women in her lifetime, but she could still tell that the girl was pretty far along.

"Where's your husband?" she yelled, lowering her rifle. "Where's Lord Kai?"

The mother nodded to a room across from her, and when Yong nudged the door open, she saw an old man, no less than sixty, passed out on a cushiony, Western-style bed with phoenix-embroidered curtains. Immediately, because she had grown up around the poison, she recognized the aroma of flavored opium.

By the time the platoon finished dragging the members of the Kai family out into the courtyard, a crowd of villagers had gathered in a semicircle around the mansion. As was customary, Kai's hands and ankles were tied, and he was made to sit on a short stool so that everyone else towered over him. His family—the three women—were stripped clean of their bracelets and rings and were made to stand beside him with their heads down, wearing signs that read, "Sluts of an Exploiter." The two girls, the civil administrator informed them, were not Kai's daughters but were in fact his second and third wives. His real children had left the area long ago: His son was a colonel in Chiang Kai-shek's army and his daughter was a singer in Shanghai.

"A despicable family!" the leader of the propaganda attachment declared, his armband the deep, flaring red of the Party.

A helper handed him a bucket of water and he splashed it on Kai's face. The old man, who still didn't seem fully sober, squinted around the yard. Water droplets dripped from his white beard and curled it up, making him resemble a goat.

The leader of the propaganda detachment read out the list of charges: harboring the enemy, mistreatment of the peasants, and usage of mind-decaying substances. "Do you have anything to say for yourself?"

The old man looked up, licked his lips, and cleared his throat. "I've never—" he began, but then closed his eyes again. He was given another splash of water. "I've never smoked any mind-decaying substances in my life!" he said, and the crowds roared with laughter.

When the denunciations were coming to an end, Yong, Ping and the rest of the platoon were tasked with going through the house and looking for valuables. Currency, jewelry, or anything made from gold or silver needed to be turned in, but they could keep whatever else they could fit inside their pockets or carry in their arms.

"You're right," Ping said, handing Yong a glossy wooden snuff box. "That guy deserved to be punished. Someone like him shouldn't be rewarded with land and privilege over simple folks who work with their hands."

"What changed your mind?" Yong asked.

"His uselessness." Ping shook his head. "No one as brainless as he is should live as well as he does. And what really troubles me is how he doesn't feel guilty about any of it. If I knew people around me were surviving on tree bark, I'd be too ashamed to eat date cake."

Yong put the snuff box back on the table and touched her throat. Maybe it was the mention of food or the smell of the place bringing back old memories, but she suddenly felt queasy.

"You all right?" Ping asked.

"Fine," she said. "Just need to go to the bathroom."

She rushed to the one across the hall, collapsed onto the ceramic Western-style toilet, and vomited her breakfast, tasting the sour return of sweet potato and the lingering zest of spicy turnip. Her abdomen hurt, as if a rat were gnawing on her intestines, and when she returned to the bedroom to grab the snuff box, Ping was gone. She needed to lie down, so she rested her head on Kai's comfortable pillow. It even crossed her mind to take a puff of the opium.

"Come downstairs!" Ping called. "I have a surprise for you!"

She eased herself out of the bed and leaned on her rifle to stand up. At the top of the stairs, she saw Ping and Lieutenant Dao covering a table with bright red fabric. The soldiers of their platoon were pouring one another sorghum liquor and drinking out of glossy green shot glasses. Somehow Haiwu had made it up to the mansion as well and was now showing a soldier how to sidekick with his prosthetic. Pasted on the door was a gigantic *hsi*—the character for happiness.

Halfway down the stairs, when the light from the first-floor windows shined on Yong's face, everybody cheered.

"What's going on?" she asked.

"Blame Ping, blame Ping!" Lieutenant Dao spun Ping around and patted him on the back, on which there was strapped a huge red flower.

"No, no, no," Ping laughed. "This was all the lieutenant's idea."

"All right, it *was* my idea. But I wouldn't have thought of it if Ping hadn't pointed out how lovely Kai's mansion was—how suitable it was for a wedding."

"A wedding?" Yong asked, scratching her scalp with her pinky. "Do you think this is the best time?"

Ping stared at her in surprise, his eyes round and frozen. "I thought you wanted this. Wasn't this what we've talked about?"

Vaguely she remembered exchanging a sentence or two about how she had hated the way in which Lord Zhu had paraded his betrothed around town, showing off the young girls he intended to marry, and how she wanted her own wedding, when the time came, to be simple and surrounded only by those she respected . . . but she'd only meant for her words to fill time.

"Ping's right," Lieutenant Dao said. "What better place to get married than in here? The house is beautiful, we have plenty of tasty food"—he pointed to the boiled chicken and carrot casserole on the table—"and everyone's around. Who knows where we'll be in the coming weeks? We might be marching for months. You don't want to have the ceremony in the woods, with crickets beneath your feet and everyone eating around a fire, do you? Also, as your superior officer, I should warn you about how it reflects on your character to spend your nights with a man and not being married. People might not be saying anything now, but give them a few weeks and see how their expressions change."

The Lieutenant's words reminded Yong of a story a nurse at the Great Mobile Hospital had told her. The nurse—Yong couldn't remember her name—was seventeen and married to one of Mao's personal assistants. Before she was married, the nurse told her, she had treated the assistant for a burn wound. Two weeks later, Mao came into the hospital and thanked her for saving his assistant's life. By then, she couldn't remember who his assistant had been. "Brave men need to be with brave women," Mao told her. Then he lifted her chin and said, "You understand?" She didn't understand, but she also didn't want to seem like an idiot, so she said, "Yes, of course I understand." "Great!" Mao said, and led her to his side of the mountain, where the assistant was waiting with a red flower on his chest. Without her knowing it, she had agreed to marry him!

When she told Yong the story, Yong had thought the girl lucky for being picked by one of the leaders, but now she felt that she finally understood what the girl's state of mind had been.

"I understand," Yong said. She smiled at Ping and stood by his side. "Let's just make this fast. My belly's been hurting all day."

"What did you eat this morning?" Ping said.

"The same thing you did." She kneaded her stomach. "It feels like something just wants to burst from my body."

Haiwu, who was sitting at the table, tipping back glass after glass of sorghum liquor, roared with laughter. "You're pregnant and you don't even know it!"

Yong straightened herself. She looked at Lieutenant Dao, who was staring at her belly, and then at Ping, who looked as if he'd just been struck by lightning.

"Can't be," she said. "Impossible."

18

THAT NIGHT, LYING NEXT TO Ping in Lord Kai's bed—the lieutenant allowed them to sleep in the mansion, since it was their wedding night—she examined her breasts. The areas around her nipples had started to swell. Before today, she had attributed the change to eating better since arriving at South Ji Village, but she couldn't deny that pregnancy made more sense. After Haiwu's rude accusation, she had tried to persuade her comrades that she wasn't pregnant. She pointed out that she'd had her period two weeks earlier, and Haiwu explained that pregnant women occasionally bled, too, especially in the beginning. She dismissed his explanation as unscientific: "Where did you learn about medicine?" she asked. Lieutenant Dao told her to calm down and emphasized that this was good news, worthy of additional celebration. Everybody toasted her and wished her luck in bringing into the world a fat baby boy. By the end of the festivities, she didn't bother denying it anymore, and when Ping asked if he was really going to be a father, she told him not to look so damn happy about it.

She sat up and rubbed her lower back. The bed was too soft, and it contorted her body in a way that made her spine ache. Snoring like a wild boar, Ping was curled tight, taking up as much space as he had in his corner of the cave. He'd been confused by her misery over the news of the pregnancy, and she didn't want to spoil his glee by asking the obvious questions: How were they going to take care of the child? How could they keep it and still stay with the army?

When she closed her eyes, she saw Lord Kai's pregnant young wife standing over the chair with the sign around her neck: "Slut of an Exploiter." For the first time, she wondered if such propaganda was too harsh. Lord Kai should be condemned, surely, but should his wives suffer with him? After all, they weren't the ones who decided to tax the peasants. They didn't harbor enemy soldiers. They probably hadn't even wanted to marry the old man to begin with. Why should they be made to pay? Their punishment reminded Yong of China's first emperor, Qin Shi Huang, and how he had buried his wives and servants alive with him after his death. How was propaganda like that sign on the pregnant girl any different? The women, she decided, only deserved to be disciplined if they had actively wanted to marry Lord Kai and live a lavish lifestyle. The pregnant girl should be given the most leniency, since the child in her belly had committed no crime at all.

The next morning she would go to the town hall where the propaganda detachment was stationed and talk to the pregnant girl herself.

19

THE GUARD OUTSIDE THE TOWN hall—a twitchy new transfer she hadn't seen before—wouldn't let her inside the building even though she told him she was a part-time member of the detachment. "Where's your identification card?" he asked, and when she said she'd lost it back at Iron Well Mountain, he shook his head. "Sorry. No card, no entry." She called him an idiot and was about to storm inside without his permission when the door opened, and Meishi, the vice secretary of the department and the one who had helped Yong transfer to the Third Legion, told the guard that Yong was telling the truth.

The windows of the propaganda unit had been blackened with tar and the main source of light came from candles. Once inside, Yong understood why the unit members were being so cautious. Around a long wooden table were stacks of silver and banknotes. Soldiers were examining the currency under a magnifying glass and separating coins into piles from most valuable to least. The majority of the silver was sterling, though it wasn't uncommon for banks or private minting presses to melt the precious metal down and blend it with iron or lead. In the back of the room, on a smaller round table, a man and woman inserted rings, bracelets, and necklaces around their belts and onto the spokes of an umbrella. They were dressed in silk, and they were going to smuggle the jewelry into cities controlled by the Nationalists to raise funds. Yong knew this because she had been part of such an operation herself, one that had stranded her in the Communist eastern divisions during the second and third encirclement campaigns.

"The army hasn't been paid in months," Meishi explained. "We're afraid of break-ins now more than ever."

She was a tall woman with a strong jawline and wide shoulders. Yong envied her for having attended the prestigious Whampoa Military Academy, where many of the top leaders had been educated, and being married to Huang Dashu, a communications officer who worked with the politburo directly.

"I came here to speak with Lord Kai's pregnant wife." Yong knew Meishi liked people who got to the point as soon as possible.

"Why's that?" Meishi asked, taking a seat at the end of the long table, where she counted the silver dollars in a stack and jotted the number down in a notebook.

"Can I be honest with you?" Yong said. She leaned her rifle against the wall and pulled up a stool.

"I hope so."

"Do you think it's right to be punishing her like this? She couldn't have been an accomplice to any of Lord Kai's crimes. She was just at the wrong place at the wrong time. And it saddens me to think of her child, still unborn."

Meishi put her pen down. "You're probably right. I don't believe the girl deserves what she's going through, either. But—and you know this more than most—there are so many other people in the world suffering for even more unjust reasons. We've laid out our agenda, and it isn't perfect, but we must adhere to it or else lose everything we have fought for. Surely the third wife of a rich landowner is worth sacrificing for the benefit of the masses?"

Yong nodded. "Can I see her at least? It would make me feel better."

Meishi tilted her head, staring at Yong as if she were someone she didn't recognize. "What's gotten into you?" she asked. "This person in front of me isn't the hero of Ji'an that I remember—the fierce girl who took on a squad of Kuomintang troops and saved the lives of five comrade intelligence officers."

Yong wiped her nose with her thumb and looked away. "Are you going to take me to her or not?"

Meishi smiled. "Of course, if you insist. First, tell me what's *really* going on."

"You'll laugh at me."

"Now I must know."

Yong told her she wanted to speak somewhere more private, and in Meishi's office, where the windows weren't darkened, Yong paced back and forth.

"What the hell," she said. "You'll find out sooner or later anyway. And it's nothing certain yet. I'm just—" She took a deep breath. "I might be pregnant."

Meishi stuck her pen into her hair and gave Yong a hug. "Congratulations! Why did you think I'd laugh at you?"

"I don't know," Yong said. Escaping from Iron Well Mountain, Ping had called her "Comrade Mulan" as a joke, but she liked the nickname, and now she wanted to tell Meishi that she hadn't planned on having a baby before saving China from the Nationalists. "It embarrasses me, not being in full possession of my body. I just want it gone."

"I know how you feel. At first, I felt the same way when I was pregnant with my son." Meishi took a sip of steaming tea from the cup on her table. "But trust me, you'll feel different once you have him in your hands. My father was forty when I was born, and he told me his one regret in life was not having me sooner so he could be with me longer."

"That's a good story," Yong said, though it didn't make her feel any better. She saw her own dad, huddling over dice at Lord Zhu's casino, losing his daughter, whom he'd had for five years, and then his rickshaw, which he'd worked ten years to own.

"So who's the father?" Meishi asked. "Is it that guy named Luo you told me about?"

Yong was silent, staring through the brick-lined tall window. There was a sparrow's nest on the other side of the glass, and the female was feeding an earthworm to her chick.

"I take it the father isn't Luo."

"I got married yesterday," Yong said.

Meishi's eyes widened. "Why wasn't I invited? Do I know him?"

Yong tried to come up with the best way to clarify what had happened. "It was a surprise wedding," she said, and then explained that Luo had died at the Battle of the Fu River and that Ping had been his best friend. Then she added that Ping was also a gunsmith and that he was the kindest, most generous person she knew.

Meishi smiled. "You need a nickname for the baby," she said. "Something that sounds terrible, like Little Pest, to prevent Old Man in the Sky from claiming it." She reached into her pocket and took out a silver dollar. "Take it. Think of it as a wedding gift."

"Thank you." Yong took it and got up to leave, but then she remembered why she was there in the first place. "Now can you take me to the pregnant girl?"

Meishi frowned. "I was hoping you forgot."

20

THE GIRL'S NAME WAS CHO, and she was thrown in the village granary with Lord Kai and the other wives. When Meishi opened the door, a rat scurried by. The three wives were in a corner of the room, lying on sacks of rice, and Lord Kai was shivering in another corner, saliva foaming around his mouth. His hands and feet were bound together by chains, preventing him from fully extending his body.

"Cho." Meishi pointed to the pregnant girl. "Stand up and come over here."

The girl got up and hobbled over. Yong suspected one of her legs was asleep. Her clothes, so bright and clean the day before, were grimy with dirt streaks and prickly with bits of hay. Her hair, though disheveled, had a white jade clip holding it together. Yong thought she was prettier like this—without the pretensions of the upper class.

"Well, now you've seen her." Meishi crossed her arms. "Do you feel better?"

Yong took a step closer to Cho and moved the girl's hands away from her belly. "How many months pregnant are you?"

"Seven," the girl said, glancing between Yong and Meishi with her head low. "What's going to happen to me?"

"That depends on your behavior," Meishi said. "Do you wish to repent for your past as the slut of an exploiter?"

"Leave her alone!" Lord Kai choked out, his eyes filled with momentary clarity.

"Shut up!" Meishi shouted. "Your fate's already sealed!"

The girl nodded. "I wish to repent," she whispered.

Meishi nodded toward the door, and Yong took the girl by the arm and helped her walk outside. A drizzle had developed. The dirt road was slowly becoming muddy, and brown water gathered around in uneven pools. Yong was surprised Meishi had allowed the girl out of her prison. She wondered where they were taking her.

"Now, this isn't a pardon," Meishi said, stretching her dull green army jacket over her head. "I'm simply giving you the opportunity to absolve yourself in other ways. Do you understand?"

Cho nodded, her arm shivering in Yong's hand. Meishi was walking too fast and it felt as if the girl might collapse at any moment.

"Under army supervision, you'll work with a common villager of my choosing. You'll do whatever they tell you. You'll plow the fields, feed the chickens, clean the pigsty—whatever. If I get one complaint, I'll throw you back in prison. If you try to escape, we'll shoot you." Meishi stopped, turning around and staring at the girl for emphasis. "Got it?"

"I understand." Cho wiped rainwater off her brow.

Yong smiled at Meishi in gratitude.

The hut they finally stopped at was one of the smallest in the village. Its roof was made of hay tied in bundles to bamboo planks, and pillars of sandstone sheets elevated the shack a meter or so off the ground, creating a space where its inhabitants kept firewood, rakes, and extra roofing daub. Behind it stretched two *mu* of rice paddies, where a family of ducks were weaving through the stalks. Meishi informed the residents—a forty-year-old couple and their two daughters—of the situation and told Cho to kowtow. The two daughters giggled, but the older couple quickly lifted Cho to her feet and said they wouldn't dare work her too hard.

"No!" Meishi shook her head. "Don't go soft on her! It wouldn't be called punishment if it was easy."

After the couple put a blanket around Cho's shoulders and took her inside, Meishi raked her fingers through her hair, shook it dry, and turned to Yong.

"Well?" she asked. "Are you happy now?"

"Smart," Yong said. "I wouldn't have done it any differently."

"Now she'll know what it feels like to live the life of those she's oppressed. She's at the mercy of the people responsible for her meals—as it should be." With one eye closed, Meishi surveyed the fields, measuring the property size in thumb lengths. "Just about the same as Lord Kai's orchards, except not nearly as wasteful." She leaned in and whispered to Yong, "By the way, have you seen that garden? So extravagant. It's the perfect place to raise a kid."

Yong nodded. She didn't like to be reminded that she was pregnant. She reached for her gun leaning against the chicken coop and started walking back up the hill.

"You're not getting off the hook easily, either," Meishi shouted. "Since you were so insistent on getting the girl justice, I'm making her your responsibility. Check up on her frequently. Keep me posted. If anything goes wrong, it's all on you."

21

AFTERWARD, YONG WENT TO THE field hospital at the edge of the village. Inside the tent, the pregnancy specialist, an old man with a hunched back and a long, curly beard, squeezed her abdomen. Then he pointed to a secluded spot by some bushes and told her to pee over there. When she finished, he knelt down, examined the warm fluid, and nodded. Yong felt as though the sky had suddenly been painted black: Little Pest was real; the doctor had seen him there, inside her urine.

On her way back to the mansion, she passed through the lychee orchards again, and the taste of the fresh fruits washed by rain lifted her mood a little. The day before, in her haste to reach the top of the hill, she hadn't noticed the way in which the trees were patterned, twisting to form the character *tian*—for sweetness. She started to see what Meishi had meant. Yes, she agreed, this *would* be a great place to raise a kid. She pictured Little Pest's fat hands reaching to grab the fruit, his clumsy legs trying to find his footing on one of the gnarled branches. An orchard like this would allow a rascal like him plenty of space to expend his energy. Kai might be an evil exploiter, but he certainly knew how to design a garden!

She climbed the rope and, with her feet over the edge, found Ping squatting over a fire casting bullets. Haiwu was sitting on the ground next to him, blowing on the flame.

"You've found a new assistant," she yelled.

"I'm not good for much else," Haiwu said, "though I'll never replace Luo." He turned to Ping with a concerned expression.

Ping gave the hand clamp a hard squeeze, and when he released the pressure, two pointy bullets fell into the pail, the hill reverberating with their clinking. "It's my fault, really," Ping said. "I should've trained someone else other than Luo."

Yong brought over a stool—the same one that Lord Kai had sat on the day before—and dried her hands over the fire. "I want to ask you something, husband." It was the first time she had used the word, and she was surprised that it came out of her mouth so easily. "I've come up with a name for our kid. What do you think of Little Pest?"

Ping looked up, putting on that same dumbfounded face that made him seem so trustworthy. "Little Pest," he said, drawing out the word. "I was thinking maybe naming him after a food might be better. Little Carrot, or Little Spinach."

Haiwu laughed. "Or Little Turnip. We eat so much of the stuff, we might as well salute it by naming a baby after it. Plus, it's a good name even if the baby turns out to be a girl."

"Little Turnip," Yong said. The sound smacked on her lips like crisp spring water. "All right. Little Turnip it is."

That night they snuck back into the mansion. Yong figured even if they were caught, the lieutenant wouldn't make a big deal of it. Ping hadn't liked the idea, saying the punishment outweighed the rewards—"What's so great about the place anyway?"—but gave in to her demands when she said they could do *it* again just like the previous night.

An hour later, panting in the bed, she was surprised by how much she had enjoyed doing it. The old nurse who had taken care of her at Lord Zhu's mansion had always warned her about doing it when she was pregnant. "You must push him off if he tries anything!" the old woman had said. "Your baby's life depends on it." Now Yong hoped the old woman was right. She pictured Little Turnip's tiny hairless head being rammed again and again. He would get fed up with the pain and decide to go back to whatever heaven he had come from, leaving her with a few more years to improve China enough for his return. Perhaps he might be so shaken up that he would warn the child inside Cho's belly as well. All babies, Yong imagined, resided in some place of limbo where they drank milk tea, looked through a watery window, and chatted about what was on the other side and whether they should cross into it. If they saw something they didn't like, they would simply pay their tab and ride their mule back to paradise. How else could one explain all the miscarriages? Her own mother had had three before Yong was born. They probably had seen what a terrible person her father was and made a break for it before they, too, were sold into slavery. This was why her and her comrades' mission was so important: Eventually, if the world got awful enough, no one would want to cross over, there would be no more children, and all that would be left of China and its four-thousand-year history would be a barren, deserted wasteland. Up until yesterday, Cho's baby, seeing nothing but fruit trees and embroidery, would have been impatient to be born. From now on it would know only hard work and straw beds. Had it set its foot too far across the threshold? Yong wondered. Could it still communicate with the other side?

"I went to see Kai's pregnant wife today," Yong said, "but going there might have been a mistake."

Ping was across the hall, the hiss of his pee the only response she got. He tiptoed back into the room and got in the bed.

"Did you say something?" he asked, rubbing his shoulders for warmth.

"I wish Lord Kai's young wife weren't pregnant."

Ping narrowed his eyes. "Why's that?"

Yong wanted to tell him about her ideas of pregnancy. She wanted to say the propaganda unit should've left the girl alone and let her stay in the mansion. They should have respected her pregnant state and used her condition as an opportunity to send a positive message to the celestial world. They were the propaganda unit, after all. Why should their duties not extend beyond the physical realm?

Yong chided herself. She was being superstitious—a defect passed on to her by her father, who had been sure their ancestors were moving the casino dice based on how much he had visited their shrines.

"It's so unlucky for her kid," she finally said. "It's one thing to be born knowing your family has always been poor, but his mother will be constantly telling him about the lifestyle he lost."

Ping turned toward her and took her hand in his. "Didn't you say Lord Kai and his family deserved whatever punishment they received?" Ping smiled. "I've never seen this side of you before, this hidden care you have for others."

Yong stiffened her expression. "Lord Kai deserves to be beheaded in his next seven lifetimes. And I'm not saying countless others aren't suffering for even more unjust reasons. The only reason I care is because Meishi, the vice secretary of the propaganda detachment, tasked me to oversee the pregnant girl's punishment. Meishi's a good friend of mine and she gave me this easy assignment when she found out about my condition."

Ping's eyes widened, lighting up in the moonlight like polished opals. "That's great news! I was just about to suggest that we should find something else for you to do. Supply officer, garrison duty, nursing. But this is even better. Tomorrow, I'll ask the lieutenant if you can get transferred to the propaganda detachment permanently—at least until you have Little Turnip—and maybe you can even stay in this village after the army starts moving again."

Yong was horrified by Ping's suggestion. She couldn't imagine leaving the platoon, raising chickens and harvesting crops in some remote village while he and the rest of the unit fought on the front lines.

"No, you don't understand," Yong said. "The assignment is a temporary one, a week or two at most. I'm the best shot in the unit. The lieutenant would never let me leave."

"Things have changed, Yong." Ping spoke slower now, taking on the annoying tenor he had used to remind her to clean her rifle. "Just imagine a few months from now when we're forced to engage the Nationalists again. You with your large belly. How will you be able to lie prone? How will you have enough energy to retreat or advance? Can you walk thirty kilometers a day on swollen feet?"

"Worry about yourself." Yong was annoyed. She had always been more athletic than Ping and now he was doubting her abilities just because she was pregnant. "I could run twice as fast as you even if I were carrying ten babies!"

"My darling wife, you have to be smarter than this. You have more than your pride to lose now. Let me talk with—"

"My answer is no!" Yong yelled. "Just because you've written your name in the dirt doesn't mean the entire plot belongs to you! *I'll* decide how I should best serve the Party."

Below their window, there came a series of knocks on the drainage basin. "Do we have a couple of thieves up there?" The voice, a rising whisper, belonged to Lieutenant Dao. "Can the thieves stay quiet while the soldiers sleep?"

Yong glared at Ping, who caressed her cheek with his index finger. She swatted it away, turned around, and closed her eyes.

22

THE NEXT MORNING SHE ARRIVED at the hut where Cho was staying and found the girl already awake and raking leaves away from the squash garden. She had her arms fully extended, making sure with her strokes that the handle of the rake missed her belly. Her hair was tied in a bun without any jade or pearl clips. She had shed her old clothes entirely and was wearing a brown blouse and a pair of loose-fitting peasant trousers—no doubt given to her by the family she was staying with.

"I'm glad to see you working," Yong said. "If you keep it up, this'll be an easy assignment for both of us."

The girl smiled. Up close, the sweat on her forehead shimmered like sand on a beach. She tried to hide her fatigue by holding her breath, but this only made her gasp more when she inhaled again. "My parents had a squash rack when my sister and I were growing up," she said. "They made it my responsibility. My sister raised rabbits, but it was my job to make sure we had sweet squash in our soup during winter. I used to be so jealous of her. I hated my parents for giving her the better chore. I volunteered to kill her bunnies once they got fat enough to make into—"

"Slow down," Yong said. "Take a breath. I'll be here all day to listen to your stories."

Cho seemed embarrassed. She stopped talking and began to rake faster, even over the spots where there were no more leaves.

"And you can take a break, too," Yong added. "I'm not the vice secretary. You don't have to perform in front of me." She paused. Maybe she was being too lenient. "Not *too* much, anyway."

"I'm sorry." Cho slowed her raking.

Yong sat on a stool and put her feet up on another. "Just don't try to escape and everything'll be fine."

After a few strokes, Cho leaned the rake against the side of a pole that supported the squash racks, headed into the hut, and came out with a tin pail. She walked over to the racks again and began ladling wooden spoonfuls of liquid onto the budding plants. From where Yong was sitting—twenty meters or so from the garden—she could tell Cho was pouring urine. Over the last year Yong had eaten raw venison, buried corpses, and defecated in holes that a hundred men had used. She had a strong stomach even some of the officers envied, but watching the ladle get so close to Cho's mouth as she reached up to water the plants on the upper racks made Yong look away and put her hand on her temple.

"Is everything all right?" Cho asked.

Yong tilted her head down and waved the girl away. Then she turned around, kneaded her belly, and vomited. Before she could get up and clean the mess, Cho was kneeling next to her and patting her back.

"Let it all out," the girl said, "until there's nothing left."

Yong nodded. She was surprised the third wife of a peasant exploiter could act so casual around disgusting things. When Yong was a girl, Lord Zhu's other wives had fainted at the sight of a paper cut and wouldn't even bandage her elbow when she had scrapped it on a stone bench, but Cho took a broom to the vomit as if she had cleaned up after people all her life. Either the girl had come from much humbler beginnings than Yong had given her credit for or she had attended some famous acting school in Hong Kong.

"The best way to cleanse your system of last night's liquor is to just throw it up with the food." Cho swept dirt over the remaining vomit. "Don't worry about wasting a meal."

"I don't drink," Yong said.

The girl stared at her and then clapped her hands and laughed. "Oh, I understand now why you saved me."

"Who said I saved you?"

"The officer from yesterday." Cho's smile widened as if she had just written a perfect line of poetry. "After you left, she told me you had taken a special interest in me, and for the entire night I tried to figure out why. I thought maybe we had met before. Maybe you knew my parents. Maybe we came from the same village. But then I wondered: Why save me and not my sister? Now I know how similar we are."

"You don't know anything," Yong said, trying to stand up. "I haven't taken a 'special interest' in you. I found the child inside your body pathetic and too innocent to suffer because of your crimes. Don't for a second think I saved you or want to be your friend."

For a moment the girl was speechless, but then her smile returned and she took Yong's arm and helped her up.

"Of course," the girl said. "I shouldn't have spoken so arrogantly. But you're a person who sees innocence when everyone else sees guilt, and you're a hero in my eyes. I can count the number of female heroes on one hand. You are like Qin Liangyu, the girl general who defended the Ming from the Manchus, or Yuenü, the greatest swordswoman of the Han dynasty, or—"

"Hua Mulan?" Yong added. Cho's words were as sweet as nectar. Yong tried not to let it go to her head.

"Exactly." Cho led Yong into the house and sat her down on one of the wicker chairs around the three-legged table. She squatted next to the wood-burning stove, lifted a pot of cooled boiled water, and poured it into a clay cup.

"I bet Mulan never had to fight carrying a baby," Yong said dully.

"She carried plenty of babies after winning the war," Cho said, handing Yong the cup. "When I found out I was pregnant with Pig Feet, I felt terrible, too. The first few months are the worst, but it gets better after a while. Just look how energetic I am. Trust me, you'll feel normal again in no time."

What the girl said made Yong feel a little better. At least she wouldn't be incapacitated for all nine months.

After drinking the cup of water, they walked out of the hut and back to the squash racks, but Cho said they shouldn't risk another episode and promised Yong she'd finish up work there the next morning, before her arrival. They spent the next few hours helping the family of the house weed out moth larvae, stink beetles, and chinch bugs from the rice paddies. They pulled a short iron-filament sifter through the stalks and dropped the insects into a vase with a tiny hole on top. Later, the critters would be used as feed for livestock. Yong asked if Cho had done anything like this before, and the girl told her that she was born in a town north of the Yellow River and that her family had only harvested wheat. "Wheat's easier than rice," she said. "You don't have to get your feet wet." She raised a muddy foot for emphasis.

Over lunch, Yong found out that Lord Kai's relatives had owned the land Cho's parents worked on and that her father had agreed to marry their daughters to Kai in exchange for the right to stay on the land for another twenty years. "It was a win-win," Cho said, crunching on roasted walnuts. "I would live well and my family wouldn't be homeless. With enough time, I might even have enough influence to purchase the land for my family outright." She added that even though she was sure Kai exploited the farmers on his property, he really wasn't such a bad husband. "When he wasn't smoking opium, he was attentive to his wives. He told us jokes and cooked for us once in a while. He even continued the education my parents had started for my sister and me, hiring a good tutor who taught us many fancy words."

At the end of the day, when Yong and Cho had cleaned the mud from their feet and Yong was getting ready to leave, Cho put a hand on Yong's arm and told her there was something else she wanted to say.

"You mean you haven't told me enough already?" Yong slung her rifle over her shoulder.

Cho seemed embarrassed. "I don't know if it's my place to ask, but I guess I have to anyway. It's about my sister, you see. I was hoping she could join me here. Just like me, she needs to be reminded of the importance of hard work, and the family needs all the help they can get. A win-win."

"I'll see what I can do," Yong said.

"That's all I ask."

The sun was low and burned red on the leaves of the rice paddies. Yong waved goodbye and headed over to the town hall to report to Meishi. If it was up to Yong, she would have the entire Kai family working the plot. Nothing sobers up the mind faster than getting your limbs dirty, and Kai and his first wife, both haughty from years of folk operas and date pudding, needed to be educated even more than Cho and her sister. Still, she doubted Meishi would agree to let Lord Kai off the hook so easily, but as Cho had suggested, there was a good chance she might put his other wives to work.

Standing at attention, Yong informed the vice secretary of Cho's good behavior and decided to just ask her bluntly about the girl's sister.

"That poor family could really use the extra help," Yong said. "No matter how hard the girl tries, it's difficult for her to do a lot with a belly that big. How about sending her sister there as another helping hand?"

Sitting on the other side of the desk, Meishi finished signing papers and put them on top of a stack. "You should have asked me yesterday when you pleaded for the girl's life." She looked up casually. "Just this morning Kai and his other wives were sentenced for their crimes. They will be hanged at the town square in three days."

"So soon?" Yong asked, though by army standards the sentencing was late. Three years earlier, at the end of the first denunciation she had attended, the landlord had shown no remorse and was shot at sunset. "Is there any chance you can have it postponed?" she asked again.

Meishi shook her head. "It's a waste of manpower as it is with the guard there. And the whole town is expecting a show."

23

THE ORCHARD, UNDER THE GLOW of the setting sun, appeared this time of the afternoon as if caramelized, the orange reflecting off the waterfall, the smooth crescent tiles of the walkway, and the branches of the lychee trees. Soon, Yong reflected, the army would order the villagers to tear down these luxuries and partition the land for more practical purposes. In a month's time, these hills would be littered with grazing sheep and peasant children flying kites. The memory of the orchard, like that of its owners, would fade away as completely as incense.

On her walk up the hill, she wondered how she was going to tell Cho of the news the next day. She just had to be stern about it. If the girl objected, she would say, "The only reason *you're* not with them is because of Pig Feet in your stomach." She would say she should be ashamed of herself for being Kai's wife and seeing the poor hungry around her while living in luxury herself. Complicity meant guilt, and seeing those who suffered and doing nothing about it was a worse crime in the eyes of Old Man in the Sky. After all, there were people in the world suffering for even more unjust reasons.

At the top of the hill, Yong found Ping leaning against Broadax. He was looking at the grass and talking to Lieutenant Dao. The lieutenant, half a head taller, nodded, smiled, and patted Ping on the shoulder. The rest of the platoon was out on the other side of the hill running laps. When the two of them noticed Yong approaching, they turned and waved.

"Your husband just had a great idea," the lieutenant said.

"He's been having a lot of those lately." Yong stared at Ping, who avoided her eyes by stroking Broadax's mane.

"We've been thinking. Because of your condition, maybe it would be best if you stayed here for the next few months. You know, take care of yourself so that you'll be ready to kill more Nationalists when you're normal again. Anyway, you've been working with the propaganda detachment a lot these days and the change wouldn't be so dramatic."

Yong continued to stare at Ping. Sooner or later he had to make eye contact. "With all respect, sir, the Kuomintang forces are chasing us. We need every soldier we can muster, and I'm the best shot in the unit."

The lieutenant laughed. "Of course. Everyone knows that. But you're going to be a mother soon, and, to be honest, no matter how tough you think you are, a pregnant woman is always going to be a liability on the march."

"I won't be. I don't want any special attention." Yong stood up straighter. "I will always put the needs of the unit above those of my own."

Lieutenant Dao removed his cap and scratched his scalp. His face took on a pained expression, and his eyes darted around as if searching for someone to take his place in this conversation. Finally, Ping shot her a glance. She gave him a gaze as cold as limestone, and he let out a forced yawn and bit his lower lip.

"Didn't General Mao's wife have his first son in the middle of the Siege of Nanchang?" Yong asked. "Surely not every female revolutionary whose belly is big is a burden."

"You're right," the lieutenant said. "But it'd do you good to remember that the esteemed general had to leave the child with a peasant family when the operation went south. It's against army policy to keep an infant at camp. Not even the General could keep his child. Do you want to sentence your baby to death before it is even born? Do you want Little—" He turned to Ping.

"Turnip," Ping said.

"Right, Little Turnip. Do you want Little Turnip to not know his own mother?"

Yong shook her head. "No, of course not, but I'm a soldier first, and I'm—"

"Good," the lieutenant interrupted. "It's settled, then. I'll speak to the secretary of the propaganda detachment tomorrow and make it official."

Yong sighed. The lieutenant wasn't going to change his mind—not now, anyway. She would make a tactical retreat and continue the fight later.

"I'll talk to her," she said. "I know the vice secretary personally. It's better coming from me."

"Very well. Do it as soon as possible. Our scouts near Hejiang County have been seeing increased Nationalist activity. Something big is coming." Dao turned to Ping. "You make sure she does what she's told."

24

OVER THE NEXT FEW DAYS, despite her husband's apologies, she wouldn't talk to him. He wasn't *really* sorry, and she had a bigger problem on her mind: Cho's sister. Yong told the girl she'd made the request to get her sister out of prison and that Meishi would give the idea some thought. In the meantime, Yong accepted the walnuts and berries the girl gave her every afternoon, took them to the granary, and watched as the guard delivered the snacks to the prisoners inside. Yong managed to avoid revealing how soon the executions would be. In fact, she almost avoided talking altogether, choosing instead to listen to the girl go on about her childhood farm and the boy she had wanted to marry.

On the eve of the executions, Yong felt she couldn't hide the truth from the girl any longer, and she needed to clear her mind of the burden even if it meant Cho would hate her forever. She sat on a wicker chair opposite the girl and took a deep breath. Again she told herself she had to be stern. The girl deserved this minor injustice. She had enjoyed a life of luxury. She had watched those around her suffer and did nothing about it.

"I'm afraid I have news of your sister," Yong said.

Cho, who a moment ago had been discussing with glee the intricacies of frying cicadas on her family's land, stared at her. "You're afraid of having the news?"

"No, I'm not afraid of having the news. I'm afraid of the news itself. Not even that. It's not so much I'm afraid of the news as I'm afraid of you hearing the news."

The girl waited for her to finish. Yong wanted Ping with her just now. He was good at this kind of stuff. There was always an incompetent sincerity in his eyes that made those around him accept both what was going to happen and also believe it wasn't his fault.

"I'm making it worse," Yong said. "What I want to say is that Lord Kai's sentencing is being carried out tomorrow. They're going to hang him."

"But his wives are spared?" There was a hint of hope in the question.

"One of them."

"My sister?"

Yong shook her head. How could the girl, being as smart as she was, not figure out what she was trying to say?

Very quietly, she said, "No. You."

For a second, Cho's expression seemed to be one of confusion. She twisted a strand of her hair, stuck it in her mouth, and started chewing on it. A bee had strayed into the hut, and Yong followed its buzzing as it landed on the straw-filled bed and then, feeling the despondency in the room—she imagined—headed back outside. She couldn't tell at what point the girl started to cry.

"How long have you known?" Cho asked.

"Since the second day you were here."

"And you just let me simmer in the sun without telling me?"

"I was protecting you," Yong said.

It was true, but for some reason her words sounded false. They reminded her of what Lieutenant Dao had said a couple days ago: how it was for her own good she was being transferred to the propaganda detachment.

"If I had said something sooner," Yong continued, "you would have tried to save your sister, and that would have only led to you being up there with her. I know what's good for you." She paused. "I'm your friend."

"You're not," Cho said, crying into her handkerchief. "Not now. Not in a thousand years."

25

THE NEXT MORNING, THE BUGLES around the town square blared the same way as always. There were five notes repeated four times—cheerful and brave—and they didn't give any indication three people were going to be put to death. Still, word had traveled fast in South Ji Village. The night before, the shrewd civic administrator had passed out a flyer with the mustached face of Kai drawn in black and a headline that read "Finally Dead!" in big crimson characters. According to a rumor, the civic administrator had once worked for the landlord but had been fired for embezzling money at one of Kai's silkworm farms.

In the middle of the town square, atop the scaffold, Meishi stood with a dozen soldiers next to the sickle-and-hammer banner, reading out the heroic goals of the People's Red Army. By the time Yong arrived, several hundred villagers had gathered around and were eagerly awaiting the entrance of the condemned landlord. A vendor pushed around a cart selling dried tofu, and children played hide-and-seek, their faces flush with excitement.

It was a chilly morning. A thin film of frost covered Yong's rifle. Toward the back of the crowd, Ping and Haiwu threw sticks into a wok and started a fire. Haiwu was getting better with the dolphin bone every day. He didn't even need Ping to carry him anymore. They squatted around the fire and brushed their fingers on the flame. They were laughing. Apparently, Haiwu had told a joke, and Ping found it so funny, he almost keeled over.

Yong's husband hadn't been curious as to why she had made him come to the execution. She had said, "It's important," and he had nodded and gone to the tent next to theirs to see if Haiwu wanted to come, too. Ping didn't bother asking about her days with the prisoner. In his simple unquestioning mind he must have thought the reason she was so distraught was because she was being transferred out of the platoon.

The previous afternoon, after leaving Cho's hut, Yong had asked Meishi to post a couple of soldiers in front of the family's farm to make sure the girl didn't do anything stupid. The vice secretary commended Yong for thinking so thoroughly. The girl wanted to come to the executions—had, in fact, begged Yong to let her—but Yong told her it would be best if she kept her distance from the proceedings. "Someone in the crowd might recognize you and shout for you to join your husband up there with his other wives," Yong said. "And to save face the Red Army just might put you up there with them."

There was another roar of laughter. A villager turned around and asked Ping what was so funny. Haiwu repeated the joke and the villager chuckled.

"Hey," Yong yelled to Ping and Haiwu. "Knock it off. This is a serious matter. Someone is going to die today."

"Sorry," Ping said, coughing out his last laugh.

"Someone dies every day." Haiwu spat into the flame. "Why should I have sympathy for an old exploiter and his harem?"

She ignored him. He was just a cripple who felt sorry for himself. It didn't matter if Buddha or Confucius were up there. In his eyes, no one deserved as much compassion as he did. She thought about him and Ping on the road together without her, the two of them talking and laughing. With Haiwu there, would her husband even miss her? Would he still laugh like that? She had once thought Ping—a man with a trade—would value others according to their usefulness to the cause. She had thought he loved her, at least a little, because of her prowess with a rifle. But now she saw he was just like other men. He didn't care whether she fought on the front line. He saw her just as any farmer saw his wife: as an instrument to carry his offspring.

"Come over here," she yelled to Ping. "I want to talk to you in private."

Ping brushed off his trousers and jogged over. "What is it?" he asked. "Are you feeling all right?"

"I'm fine." She pulled him from hearing distance of Haiwu. "Let me ask you something, husband: Why do you think I've made you come today?"

Ping scratched his chin, as if the answer was hidden somewhere in his stubbly goatee. "So we're not here to see an execution?"

"We are, but why have I asked you to come witness it with me?" When she didn't receive a reply, she added. "Think about where I've been this last week, what my job was. Lord Kai and his wives. The pregnant girl who I've been looking after."

Ping looked up, searching the sky. Then he snapped his fingers. "I got it! You want me here to see the Communist ideals in action. You want me to witness a victory of class struggle."

For a moment Yong didn't speak. She was surprised by Ping's answer, and then it occurred to her she shouldn't be surprised. After all, it was the right answer—or, in any other circumstance, it would have been the right answer. She was shocked by how different it was from the answer she wanted to hear. And what *did* she want to hear? That she had brought him to show him an *injustice*? That it would better serve the cause for Kai and his wives—especially for Cho's twin sister—to labor in the fields?

In the end, she was disappointed more in herself than his answer. Haiwu, that despicable little man, had a point: Why should she feel sympathy for an exploiter and his harem just because she was friends with Cho? A week earlier she had told Ping to enjoy his first denunciation, and now she was criticizing him for a lack of respect. She didn't feel like herself anymore. She didn't know which version of Yong Haobing to trust. Again she cursed the thing inside her. Not only was it taking control of her belly; it was also taking control of her mind, making her weak. She vowed she wouldn't feel sympathy for any member of the Kai household, not even for Cho's sister. Starting the next day, she would distance herself from Cho. She would act as her guard only and not her friend.

"Well?" Ping asked. "Was I right?"

She nodded, looked up, and gave him a half smile.

"I knew it," he said, and proudly rejoined Haiwu by the fire.

When Meishi finished reading out the list of heroic goals, she stepped down from the podium and rang a small bronze bell. Two soldiers made their way to the base of the scaffold, opened a pair of waist-high doors, and dragged out the members of the Kai family. They were all four tied together with a rusty chain with their backs to one another and gagged with their own blue-and-green silk handkerchiefs. The crowd gasped. A woman yelled for Kai to return her husband, who had been crushed by a falling boulder while working on the dam that powered Kai's waterfall. An elderly man threw an apple rind, hitting Kai's older wife on her neck. A boy, urged on by his father, ran up to the family and started peeing on their shoes.

Cho's sister was short and was the only one with her back toward the crowd. Yong couldn't make out her face. As she shoved her way farther to the front, trying to see if she could get a better view of the girl from a different angle, she felt her resolve to not feel sympathy waning. Everything the villagers did she had seen before. In fact, compared to the last two denunciations, they were tame. But today she couldn't help but feel their actions were excessive. They were not, as she had once believed, fueled by a revolutionary fervor to create a new nation; they were there out of vengeance and possibly wronging those who might not have wronged them at all. She was glad she couldn't get a good view of Cho's sister; at least Kai and his first wife shielded the girl from further humiliation.

The family was brought to the top of the scaffold, below three ropes. Their stooped stature made it apparent they were barely conscious. A soldier hit their knees with a spear, and they stood up straighter. They were made to turn around once in unison, allowing the crowd to see each of their faces. When Cho's sister finally came into view, Yong put a hand over her mouth.

From the moment she had first seen the girl huddling on the stairs of Kai's mansion, she had separated her from her pregnant sister. When Yong found out she herself was pregnant, she separated the two further.

One deserved more punishment, the other less. But now all she saw was Cho on the scaffold, a noose around her neck, straw bits in her matted hair, her eyes searching for a familiar face in the crowd—for a friend, perhaps. She was Cho, all right, a slightly different version, and what made it worse was that after all this time Yong didn't know her name—had never bothered asking her sister. So the girl couldn't be anyone else. She was Cho. Only she had raised rabbits instead of watering squash racks. She was the one, for whatever reason, favored by her parents, and the one, for whatever other reason, less favored by her husband. She was Cho, and after the lever was pulled and the plank gave way, the body that slowly stiffened was also Cho's, and as the three bodies were brought down and thrown into a mule cart, the wheels squeaking from the extra weight, Yong had to remind herself that her friend was still alive, that Pig Feet was not inside the girl at the end of the rope, whose feet had pointed downward. She had to repeat, again and again, in her head, *You're not. You're not. Not now. Not in a thousand years.*

26

THE WEEKS FOLLOWING THE EXECUTIONS were busy ones for the People's Red Army. A distressed runner informed the Eighth Legion's central command that the rumors were true: The Nationalists were preparing another offensive, this time from the north, south, and east. Capitalizing on their victory at the Fu River, they would cut through the lakes at Nanchang and swoop up from Foochow City, all while their main forces lay siege to Ruijin, the Communist capital. Other Red Army divisions were already on an interception course to meet and delay Chiang Kai-shek's forces in the north and south, and Lieutenant Dao informed his platoon that the Eighth Legion, being a veteran unit, was tasked to march east as planned and join General Mao in defending the capital.

Since it became known that the Nationalists were aware of the Eighth Legion's position at South Ji Village, the army would not have the opportunity to leave a garrison behind. Not a soldier would remain, especially not one from the propaganda detachment, every member of whom were high-priority targets for assassination. The new plan was to leave as little trace of a Communist occupation as possible, giving the enemy little indication of how many troops were there or where the legion was headed.

Meishi said she'd think about Yong's application to join the detachment permanently. "With everything as hectic as it is, it might be better to not confuse personnel." Then she leaned in and whispered, "Maybe

I can get you a secretarial position once we reach Ruijin, for the sake of your baby, but I can't guarantee anything." Hearing the good news, Yong smiled, thanked the vice secretary, and told her she just had to stay with her own unit, then.

Kai's mansion was now in the process of being converted into a hospital, and Ping, wheeling inside an IV stand, suggested that Yong could just stay there without the army's support and pretend she was a peasant. "A bad idea," Lieutenant Dao said. He carried a freshly made bamboo stretcher on his shoulder. "It's too dangerous. The Nationalists will come, and they'll ask every villager if there are any remaining Communists, and who knows where people's loyalties lie with a gun pointed at their head? It'll be all right," he reassured Ping. "Yong's not due for months. She can transfer out once we reach Ruijin." Dropping an armful of bandages on Lord Kai's old bed, Yong thought about asking the lieutenant for an additional request—bringing Cho, another pregnant woman, to march with the unit—but decided to hold off until she asked the girl first.

Later, a day before the army's departure, she went to look for Cho at the hut. The girl wasn't there, so Yong walked to the other side of the village, by the river in which Kai and his wives' bodies had been thrown. She found the girl staring out into the flowing water. Ever since the army was ordered to depart, security had become lax, and Cho took to spending most of her time by the riverbank, eulogizing her sister, praying to Old Man in the Sky, or scattering mulberry leaves in lieu of ghost money. Today she had stolen a few of the remaining lychee fruits from the orchard and laid them out with date cakes and corn bread—procured, Yong guessed, from the family she was staying with—on a lily pad next to the shore.

"My platoon's leaving tomorrow," Yong said, taking out more lychees from her pocket and putting them with the rest.

Cho reorganized the fruits so that they were in a perfect oval again. "Why are you telling me?"

"You won't be safe here once we leave."

The girl laughed as if she had just heard a bad joke. "If you didn't come, I wouldn't have had to worry about my safety at all. The

Nationalists are your enemy, right? When they hear of what you did to us, they'll make me into a hero."

"Keep dreaming." Yong skipped a pebble into the river. "What we did to your sister was unjust, and probably unnecessary, but it was done out of the desire to create a better China, a place where the children inside our bodies could be proud of. The Nationalists don't care. You wouldn't even have been married to Kai if it hadn't been for their corrupt policies. And in the meantime, before they arrive, there must be a hundred villagers who would love to pull you away from our protection and throw you in there with that exploiter."

"I don't care," Cho said. "I'm staying here with my sister."

Yong wasn't expecting this much resistance from the girl. Just a few days before, Cho had been showing signs of recovery. A snake had slithered across her feet in the rice paddies, and she was able to laugh at herself after running away and tripping in a hole. Yong thought the girl might even be excited by the prospect of leaving the village and going on an adventure.

She squatted down. "Come on," she said. "Does it really help to mope around like this?"

Yong herself had cried the night after the executions. What had made it worse was when Ping asked her what was wrong, she had to pretend that she was crying out of joy from witnessing a victory of the proletariat. She wanted to tell the girl that she hadn't been there when her own parents died from pneumonia and that she didn't even hear about their deaths until a year after their funeral, when Lord Zhu allowed her to visit them for the Spring Festival and she found her old house deserted and ransacked. But comparing tragedies was like counting nicks on a potato. Everyone had them, and she would come off as callous.

"How about you do something to forget about what happened?" Yong suggested. "How about you set a goal for yourself?"

Cho closed her eyes, said a prayer, and kowtowed to the river.

"You said your family was north of the Yellow River? Well, why not come with us to Ruijin? The city's close to Shanghai. Once you're there, you can find safe passage to a harbor and take a steamer up north. You could rejoin your family."

Hearing this, the girl turned and looked up at Yong. "The Communists will let me do that? Won't I continue to be your prisoner?"

Yong laughed. "Of course not. Now that the executions are over, nobody cares where you go. You can tag along with us, do whatever chores the army requires of you."

The girl lowered her head again. "I can't face my parents. I can't tell them my sister's dead. They would say it should have been me."

"Don't be such a coward," Yong said, lifting her up. "They wouldn't think that at all. They'd be praising the heavens for bringing back their long-lost daughter, who would soon make them grandparents."

Cho smiled weakly, and Yong took it as enough of a response to take her by the hand and bring her back to the platoon.

27

AT KAI'S MANSION, YONG PULLED Cho up and over the cliff and led her to the courtyard. Upon seeing another young woman, the other soldiers came over and circled them.

"Let me help you with your belongings," Malin, the herbal medic, said. "A pregnant woman shouldn't have to carry anything."

"Don't listen to him," another soldier added. "He's barely stronger than you are. Give it to me."

Yong shoved them aside. "Slow down, guys. You'll have plenty of time to get noticed. Cho is here to join the unit."

"Everything is so different now," the girl whispered, looking around. "Even with all the servants, there was never this many people by our house."

"A place as big as this shouldn't be used by just one family," Yong said. "Now, hush: I'm not sure how the lieutenant will respond yet."

Lieutenant Dao, who was resting his head on Broadax's belly, squinted at them, rose to his feet, and walked over.

"Weren't you Kai's young wife?" he asked. "What do you want from us?"

Cho kept her head down, cradling a wooden chicken crate that contained all her belongings.

"She's here to join the unit, sir," Yong said.

The lieutenant scanned Cho from head to foot. "I don't think so. Take

Kai's pregnant wife, someone who's lived a lavish lifestyle all her youth? How can having her possibly benefit us?"

"She hasn't lived a lavish lifestyle. Her parents are farmers." Yong nudged Cho with her elbow. "Tell him what you told me. The rabbits, the squash racks—everything."

The girl glanced from Lieutenant Dao to Ping and to Yong, then looked down again.

"Please," Yong said. "The girl just lost her sister and husband."

"All for good reason," the lieutenant said. "What would the other platoons think if we harbored the wife of a deceased exploiter?"

"I was once with an exploiter, too," Yong was quick to add. "What do they say about me?"

Lieutenant Dao waved her away. "That's different. You had no choice. You were sold into it. And eventually you even killed him."

"That's her story, too! Her parents married her off so they could stay on their land. She loved a boy in her village. And eventually her husband got killed."

Dao shook his head. "None of that matters. You have months until Little Turnip's ready to sprout. By the looks of it, this girl's due any day now. What if she goes into labor while our unit's being ambushed? A crying infant will give away our position faster than a clucking hen."

Yong exhaled, searching her brain for anything else to say. She took the crate from Cho and set it on a long stone bench, one armrest featuring a bust of a dragon and the other a bust of a lion. Two soldiers from her platoon were already sitting there. One of them offered Cho a cigarette. The girl eased herself down and took it.

"Leave," Dao said. "I don't want her here another minute."

"We're just taking a break," Yong said. "She's exhausted from the trip up."

"No, take her back now."

"What's wrong with you?" Yong asked. "Do you even have a heart anymore? Maybe you lost it back in Manchuria when your wife—"

Before she could say anything more, Ping touched her arm.

"I'm sorry," he said to Dao. "Yong doesn't mean to be disrespectful. She's not herself. Blame it on the child inside her."

"Just get them both out of my sight."

Yong had never seen the lieutenant, usually a patient commander, so unhinged before. Maybe it was the pressure of another possible defeat. After the Fu River, an uneasiness had saturated the army like a fog. There were murmurs that their good fortune might have finally run out. Their years up on Iron Well were beginning to feel distant, dreamlike, as if a rosy veil had been lifted and the devils of the old world had surrounded them when they weren't looking, dancing a bobbing dance of impending victory.

"I'm sorry, Lieutenant." Yong stood at attention, her arms behind her back. "I shouldn't have said what I did. Ping is right: I'm not myself. You've been an exemplary officer, and I'm proud to be serving under you. I know you're looking out for the unit."

The lieutenant leaned against the lion bust, his arms crossed.

"But didn't Marx say that to be radical is to grasp things by the roots? How can we see ourselves as any different from the exploiters of the old world if we don't help those who are most in need? How can you deny a fellow comrade, one who, very soon, will bring forth a new life into the world? Anyway, she won't be with us for long. All we need to do is take her to Ruijin and then she'll leave on a boat and find her family in Shanghai. It isn't a big sacrifice on our part at all."

"I can help her," Malin said. "I scavenged a delivery kit from Old Kai's mansion. I'll be ready when the baby comes."

"And I can help take care of it after it's born," Haiwu added. "I need to stay behind when you're all fighting anyway. I'll make sure the little creature doesn't make a sound."

The lieutenant looked to Ping for support.

"To be honest, sir," Ping said, "like the rest of us, I don't fully understand why we can't take her, either."

"Ruijin, then." The lieutenant pointed at Yong and then looked at Malin and Haiwu. "But to all of you: If things go wrong, don't say I didn't give fair warning."

28

THE NEXT MORNING THE ARMY left South Ji Village from the northern gate, marching under a tall arch painted red and green. Atop it was a sign with three characters. Yong only recognized the last one, *cūn*, or village. The paint looked fresh. The fancy golden calligraphy sparkled in the rays of the rising sun.

"They hire a crew to repaint it every year," Cho said. "Kai's grandfather was an advisor to the emperor. That's how the family made its riches. During the Spring Festival, Grandfather Kai came down from Beijing and this was the only gate he ever used. The town made a big deal about it, drums and firecrackers and such. Everybody wanted to be on the good side of our family, get a piece of our wealth. Of course, my husband never traveled to Beijing, but he made sure the arch always looked as new as the day his grandfather finished building it. It's the envy of the town."

"All history now," Yong replied.

She was surprised Cho referred to Lord Kai as her husband and his family as her own. During her rehabilitation, the girl had barely mentioned her husband, and she certainly wouldn't have spoken about his family with the fondness she seemed to feel for them now. *People*, Yong thought. How soon they showed their true colors once danger was gone! She had praised Meishi's idea to have Cho work in the fields as "smart," but perhaps that praise had been premature. She wondered if the girl had learned anything at all.

Still, Yong was glad Cho felt comfortable enough to be honest with her, to see her as a friend again. Honesty meant trust, and trust meant forgiveness.

Cho used the three-day trek to Ruijin to get to know the other members of their platoon, although it wasn't as if she had a choice. Ever since Yong had married Ping, many of her comrades had acted as though she didn't exist anymore, and she had been glad to be free of their fake smiles and hassling, like a dog shaking itself free of fleas. But it wouldn't be entirely accurate to say she didn't feel a tinge of envy seeing Shaohu, the standard-bearer, help Cho carry her crate on top of his head when they were trudging up a steep hill, the boy punching the ground with his other hand for balance. Or when Malin offered her roots from his personal stash of mint ginseng to help her with her queasiness. (The girl wasn't used to being around army men and their defecation habits.) Finally, she was surprised—although she really shouldn't have been—by Haiwu's immediate and unrelenting pestering of the girl, hobbling around her every chance he got, whispering his stories into her ears, even going so far as emptying her chamber pot in the morning to compete with Malin's herbal remedy. Moreover, Cho, for her part, seemed to be responding best to the kung fu champ's advances. She laughed at his Dolphin stance joke. She made fun of the fact that he still had his saber on his belt. Descending a dusty hill, she even lifted his arm to support him.

On the second night of their march, when the army was camping in a valley known by the locals as the Path of Snowing Leaves, Cho asked about Haiwu's past.

"Has he been married before?" The girl's eyes flickered red in the hue of the setting sun.

"Him?" Yong replied. "Who would marry a fool like that?"

Cho tucked a corner of her tent under a boulder. Yong rolled the stone back on top. The girl remained silent, and when she stood up, Yong saw that her lips were curled down as if she was disappointed.

"You would have preferred him to have been married?"

"I don't know. I guess it's not important. Pretend I never asked." Cho put her hands behind her lower back, extending her belly, and wobbled to the edge of their camp. She looked out over the valley below, at the other members of their platoon gathering firewood.

Yong grabbed an ax from her backpack and followed Cho. She was about to go down and join the others, but then the girl said, "It's just that it would have been something we'd have in common, you know?" She stared at her protruding stomach. "I wouldn't feel like such a used-up tablecloth when I was with him."

Yong slashed the ax into a tree. "Feeling like you're not good enough for Haiwu is like bowing to a monkey: Everyone will think you're a fool, and the monkey would be confused."

Cho shook her head. "The old folks say a pregnant girl without a husband steps in quicksand wherever she walks. Nobody is allowed to help her if she starts sinking."

"Well, that's not how it works here," Yong said, although she was reminded of what Lieutenant Dao had warned her of on the day of her own marriage: *See how their expressions change.*

"Haiwu's a good person," the girl responded. "I know he doesn't care about my past. I guess I'm just looking for an excuse to keep him at a distance."

"If that's the case, find more excuses." Yong lowered her voice to a whisper. "What about Malin or Shaohu? Either of them would make for a better match. To start, both have two legs." Yong laughed.

"That's not a nice thing to say about a friend."

"I never considered Haiwu a friend."

"He considers *you* a friend." The girl's voice was loud now, and she started talking quickly. "He couldn't say enough about how loyal you are, how you're one of the best soldiers in the army, and how lucky Ping is to have you."

Yong was taken aback. In the valley below, the little man limped next to Ping, carrying a basket of firewood. "He said all that?"

"Almost too much, like he was in love with you or something."

Yong searched Cho's expression to see what she meant, but the girl only smiled.

"Anyway, I don't like the others," Cho continued. "Remember the boy in my village I told you about? Haiwu reminds me of him." Her eyes never left Haiwu as she said this.

Yong shrugged, knowing the girl was too far gone to be convinced otherwise. "Do what you want. I'm not your mother."

But later that night, under the sheepskin blanket with Ping and staring out of an oval tear on the ceiling of the tent, she worried like a mother. Would Haiwu remain faithful to Cho? The kung fu champ was more boy than man, his head hopping from one thing to the next like an aimless cricket. And Cho—she was a child herself, sheltered from the real world first by her parents and then by Kai. Two kids walking through a field made for a pretty watercolor, but a stiff wind blowing past would rip it in half faster than a scythe through wheat.

"Has Haiwu said anything about Cho? Husband—" She gave Ping a shove.

"The gun needed more cleaning, Luo," Ping mumbled. "I swear, I didn't mean to—"

She shoved him again, and this time he awoke with a snore.

"What a nightmare." He slowed his breathing. In the moonlight, the beads of sweat on his cheek flickered. "What did you say?"

"Haiwu and the girl," Yong said. "Do you know what's going on between them?"

It took a few seconds for the question to register. "You know Haiwu. Always keeps himself busy. Thinks he's smarter than everyone else because he's read a few lines from some books. Doubt anything would come out of it."

"What if it did? Would he treat Cho right?"

Ping turned to his side and stared at her. "What do you mean?"

"What else can I mean? If they got married, do you think Haiwu would make a good husband?"

"It's gotten that serious? It's only been two days."

Yong sighed. "The girl's stepping on clouds. Listening to her talk, you'd think Haiwu was as charming as the Monkey King."

"He'll be happy to hear this. He's taught me everything I know about women, even though I suspect he's never been with one for more than a week."

"A boy, then, one who'd make a bad husband."

"I wouldn't be so quick to judge. I'm not much different, and we're happy together." When Yong rolled her eyes, Ping added, "More or less."

"I don't like it," Yong said. "I just don't see how this will end up as anything but a burden for both of them. A cripple barely able to take care of himself now needs to take care of a frantic girl and her newborn? A new mother who never had to fend for herself now needs to fend for a baby and a cripple?"

"Love doesn't make sense. It *isn't* convenient. It *is* a burden." Ping gazed up into the same hole in the tent. Staring at the Dragon Boat constellation, he seemed to be lost in thought. "And what else are we fighting for? Sure, arranging a girl's marriage might provide for her future and lead her to happiness, but it could also be used to form an alliance or pay a debt—all the corruptions of the old world. In the end," Ping continued, "at least it's keeping her mind off the past. You said it yourself: The girl's been through a lot. Why take away this thing that makes her happy, if only temporarily?"

Hearing her husband, Yong didn't know whether she was glad or upset to have brought up the subject. Ping, every so often, would display a strange and startling wisdom, blowing away weeks' worth of clumsy answers like an opening of clear blue sky between gray storm clouds.

29

THE EIGHTH LEGION ARRIVED AT Ruijin at dusk, right before the city was ordered to snuff out its lights. Although flying machines hadn't been sighted yet, there was always the risk of bombing runs or strafing attacks. General Mao told his divisions that he wouldn't take any more chances with their lives. The politburo had voted the general back in charge of a few divisions after the defeats of the last campaign, and Mao was now responsible for all forces tasked to defend Ruijin. The Communist capital, located on the western piedmont of the Wuyi Mountains, was a young city, and its downtown area consisted of three courtyards housing the different state departments and the minting press. They were sky well buildings: The apartments were interconnected with a center yard exposed to the clouds. Three years before, the first meeting of the National People's Congress had taken place in a barn, which was converted soon after into a three-story structure that featured whitewashed walls, a golden hammer-and-sickle emblem on two metal doors, and a gigantic red star that framed a black-and-white photo of Lenin.

Nowadays, however, General Mao and the politburo held most of their meetings ten kilometers away from the figurehead buildings, inside a four-hundred-year-old Buddhist temple atop a small, secluded hill. Besides the troops securing the towers, walls, and mountaintops surrounding the city, most of the remaining eighty-thousand-strong army group was garrisoned around the hill, where sprawling beeches and laurels made troop movement difficult to spot from the air.

After bringing the soldiers who were injured from the march to the hospital, the Eighth Legion was instructed to assemble by the temple and wait for deployment orders.

Yong shrugged her backpack off her shoulders, breathed in the deep, cherry-scented smell of the woods, and collapsed onto the ground. Other members of her platoon were doing the same. The Eighth Legion had marched the most on their last day, a trek made more difficult by sporadic rainfall and slippery mud. Cho lay down on the slope of a small incline and put her feet up on her crate. Haiwu massaged her calves, which were red and puffy. Ping dropped his heavy bullet-making equipment, the wok hitting the ground with a thwack, and didn't even bother to go after the lead ingots that rolled out of his pack and down the hill.

For Yong, it felt good to be a part of a larger crowd, to see new faces, and to be so near the heart of the cause once more. Soldiers were uniting with their loved ones. A lieutenant from another platoon lifted his daughter into the air, thanking Old Man in the Sky for not letting her be captured. The girl, no more than twelve or thirteen, wore a blue nurse's smock and glanced back at her unit in helpless embarrassment. In every direction people wept with joy. One of the Buddhist monks even hugged a soldier in front of the temple doors. Apparently the two were brothers: One had a bald head, while the other wore the gray cap of an artillery-man. Yong felt rejuvenated by the revolutionary spirit she sensed from those around her. It was as though she had awoken from a monthlong nightmare and returned to Iron Well.

At dusk, torches were lit, marking a path along the side of the hills. Then officers from the politburo came out of the temple and, through long voice funnels, told the army groups to gather in their respective units and stand at attention. Soldiers piled their belongings in messy pyramids, slung their rifles back on, and formed neat rows. When most of the army groups had finished assembling and the hillside began to resemble strings of firecrackers, General Mao and his aides exited the temple and stood under the Communist flag: a yellow star in the middle of a dark red background. He took the voice funnel from the officer and brought it up to his lips.

"At ease, everyone, at ease." His voice carried the warm tenor of someone born in rural Hunan. "You all are hungry, thirsty, and tired. Soon we'll have warm soup and straw beds for everyone, but we just need to do a quick head count first. In the meantime, continue your conversations. Rest your feet. Enjoy the stars!"

The soldiers in the back sat and relaxed, but the front rows remained standing at attention. The General walked through the lines with a clipboard tucked under his arm and a bowl of rice in his hands. He smiled at soldiers and chatted with everyone—regardless of rank—without a care in the world, as if the armies hadn't suffered any defeats, Ruijin wasn't in danger of being captured, and everything was happening according to some grand plan of his. Yong's platoon was near the front, and when the General walked over, he shoveled a chopstick-full of rice into his mouth and asked the unit, "Why not sit? None of you are tired?"

Lieutenant Dao turned and saluted Mao. "Never, sir! What are your orders?"

The General looked at his assistant, who was now carrying his clipboard and vacuum flask, and laughed.

"Even from inside the temple, I could tell this one was brave," Mao said, pointing to Dao.

He went down the line and surveyed each soldier in the Third Legion, giving them a thorough looking over from head to toe. He gave Ping a prolonged nod. "I remember this one," he said. "You grew up in an orphanage in Canton, didn't you?" Ping nodded. Mao moved on and touched Haiwu's shoulder, thanked him for his sacrifice, and kicked at his prosthetic leg playfully. When he got to Yong and Cho, he stopped and pointed at them. Yong swallowed. This close, Mao was handsome: His skin was pale and spotless, and his hair was as full and curly as a Russian actor's. She was so nervous, she could feel her arms shaking.

"What do we have here?" Mao asked. "A couple of female revolutionaries." He stared at Cho's belly. "And I see that one of them is festive."

"Both of them are festive, sir!" Lieutenant Dao said.

The General's eyes grew as wide as a panda's. "Two festive soldiers in one unit! I've never seen *this* before."

"I'm sorry, sir. I know it's against regulation. The slimmer one has been with us for over a year; she's the best shot in the unit. We picked up the more pregnant one during our stay at South Ji Village. If you need to discipline anyone, please blame me. I couldn't give the order to leave a pregnant woman behind."

Although Yong resented Dao for lying about accepting Cho, she was proud that he had mentioned her own combat abilities.

Mao dismissed the lieutenant's apology with a flick of his chopsticks. "It's perfectly all right. Sima Qian, the wise historian, once wrote that although numbers alone cannot win a war, one is foolish to underestimate their importance. You are blessed to have two festive women in your unit to bear the cause two more revolutionary rascals!"

Yong turned and smiled at Cho and felt herself blushing. General Mao scooped a portion of rice with a large chunk of sautéed turnip and pointed his chopsticks at Cho's mouth. The girl hesitated, glancing over at Yong helplessly. Yong shrugged and motioned with her hands for the girl to hurry up and eat it. What else could Cho do? The entire legion was staring at her.

"Quickly now," the General said, "before it falls."

Slowly, Cho extended her neck. When her lips touched the chopsticks, she tilted her head, sticking out her tongue to make sure none of the rice dropped.

The General moved on, and the entire platoon became excited. Soldiers congratulated Cho for having been so lucky to be singled out like that. The lieutenant thanked her for remaining so composed. Ping wiped sweat from his forehead with his sleeves. Haiwu gave Cho a deep kiss on the mouth, as if trying to taste what was left of the food on her tongue. Yong spread her arms out wide, and the two women hugged.

That night, much to Ping's dismay, Yong decided to share her tent with Cho. They were as giddy as circus monkeys and wanted to discuss what had happened with someone of the same gender. At first, Cho couldn't figure out why everyone had been congratulating her. She didn't know why her experience had been such a big deal.

"I've heard of him, of course," she told Yong, "but all the stories were about how vulgar, destitute, and thuggish the Communist leaders were. I wasn't expecting someone so enlightened and approachable. He's obviously wise but acts as playful and humble as a child."

Yong nodded. "I've seen him give a couple of speeches, but that was the first time our eyes met. Is it wrong that I regret being married?"

Cho shook her head. "I was probably more embarrassed. He couldn't possibly have any intentions, I kept telling myself, with my body as round as a lantern. Haiwu doesn't believe me, though. He gets jealous easily."

Yong smiled. Despite what Ping had said, she still couldn't fully swallow the idea of Cho and Haiwu as a couple.

"Has Lieutenant Dao agreed to the marriage yet?" Yong probed.

"Not yet." Cho beamed. "We wanted your approval first."

"*My* approval?" A trap, Yong realized. The girl was waiting for a chance to ask the question. Haiwu wasn't jealous of the General at all.

"You're the wisest person we know," Cho said, "and Haiwu and I have only met each other a few days ago. We don't want to rush into anything if you don't think we should."

Another trap: If Yong expressed her true reservations, she knew the girl wouldn't be happy. Cho wasn't really seeking approval but rather validation. In the end, Yong reassured herself that it wasn't important in the grand scheme of things whom the girl chose to marry. In a perfect Communist society, everyone would live with one another in a place of peace, prosperity, and harmony.

"You two can do whatever you want," Yong said. Then, noticing Cho's face growing serious, she added, "He's a good man."

"As good as the General?" the girl asked, and they both roared with laughter.

30

TWO DAYS LATER, THEY GOT married inside the Buddhist temple, which was decorated with red hammer-and-sickle wallpaper. Neither of them was religious, though the monks waved their incense sticks and shook their *damarus*. Lieutenant Dao told them that, under communist law, religion was forbidden in weddings, and the monks explained that a nuptial wasn't a religious occasion. Rather, it was a celebration of two souls joining together in lifelong search for wisdom.

"Doesn't even need to be lifelong," the eldest monk added. "If, after a few years, the pair, in their newly enlightened state, decides to part, no big deal."

Haiwu frowned. "Let's not talk about that now."

After Lieutenant Dao handed Haiwu and Cho fresh copies of *The Handheld Communist Manifesto*, the old monk reached into his sleeve for a ribbon and wrapped it around their wrists, tying it into the shape of a four-winged butterfly. The other monks clapped, prompting the soldiers to clap as well. Ping nudged Yong on the elbow to join him in the clapping.

The onlookers moved to the back of the temple, under the statuette of a bodhisattva, for the wine. They poured two wooden bowlfuls. Then Ping and Yong brought them up to the newlyweds and made sure they finished every drop. Because of the rationing, the Third Legion couldn't procure a chicken or goat, but they did manage to serve a thick porridge with tiny chunks of pickled duck egg and salted pork. The elder monk also volunteered his room—the largest in the temple—for the newlyweds to use on their first night. It featured a cushioned stone bed and a view of the countryside through a paper window with holes in it. After the feast, most people in the platoon were tipsy. Holding tin plates with nuggets of lit candlewax, they escorted the couple to their room. Haiwu lifted his prosthetic up to form the Crane stance and then kicked the door closed with a *hey-ya!* Everybody laughed.

Swaying in the damp corridor, Yong stared at the stone carving next to the door. The Buddha inside the wall was Vairocana, the embodiment of wisdom, or so she remembered from her years with Lord Zhu, who had kept a similar figurine under the paintings of his ancestors, all of whom he had prayed to nightly. This Vairocana had cobwebs on the folds of her robe and the straps of her sandals. She sat cross-legged, her hand pressed against her chest in prayer, and was missing an index finger. Yong despised the smug expression on her face, her eyes closed in prayer, shutting out the universe.

"You're a smart one, aren't you?" Yong said. "You knew the world was turning rotten and you left before it all spoiled. Yet you still have these fools praying for your return, praying for signs, praying for wisdom that you either don't possess or are too greedy to share."

"No blasphemy in the temple," a monk said.

"Come on." Ping took her arm. "Let's get out of here."

"All of you are fools!" Yong pulled her arm away and pointed to the monks one by one. "'Religion is the opiate of the masses!' You are no better than the landowners who exploit the people's labor. They sit around all day in their mansions collecting the food others have harvested. You sit around all day in this temple waiting for donations others have earned. You exploit their minds."

Lieutenant Dao, a little drunk himself, walked over and laughed. "Everything you say is true, Comrade Yong. But this isn't the time to say it."

Yong pressed on: "Pigs! Scoundrels! Filth!"

"*E mi tuo fo.*" The elder monk closed his eyes and lifted his fingers to his chin. "'Better than a thousand hollow words is one that brings peace.'"

"You old liar. You preach peace, but did what you just said really bring about it? No, you said those words to make yourself look good and make *me* look like a fool. What word can stop famine, war, or death? What word can feed a hungry child?"

One of the younger monks—no more than seventeen years old—sniggered. "You don't need our help to look like a fool," he said.

Yong pushed the boy down. "You're a coward. Kids half your age are dying to make this world a better place, and you sit here talking peace. You're nothing but a weakling."

"You had too much wine," Ping said. "Time to sleep."

"Listen to your husband," the lieutenant added, helping the boy to his feet.

Yong was about to saying something else but then suddenly she felt a tickle in her belly. At first she thought Ping had put his hand there, but then she felt it again and the tingle was coming from inside her. She looked around the hallway. Everyone was staring at her. The elder monk was patting dust away from the boy's robe and Dao was whispering apologies. The Third Legion had formed a blurry circle around them, and there were drunken smirks on their faces.

"I'm sorry," Yong said. "Don't know what came over me."

"It's all right, comrade," the lieutenant said. "We all know you're not yourself."

31

TWO WEEKS AFTER CHO'S MARRIAGE, her water broke. The girl cursed the timing. Days before, despite Yong's insistence that she stay until the baby was born, she and Haiwu had arranged passage on a fishing vessel docked at Ruijin's harbor, where they would steam north to Shanghai. It wasn't hard to get permission from Lieutenant Dao or Meishi. Both had wanted the girl and the kung fu champ to be out of the army's hair since South Ji Village. They were scheduled to leave the afternoon when Pig Feet was beginning to sprout, and while the girl hated the delay, Yong convinced her that she was fortunate to be delivering her child on land instead of on a rickety boat with fish stink everywhere.

Cho was put on a stretcher and taken to a well-known midwife in one of the surrounding villages. The trek took forty minutes, and Yong insisted on running alongside the stretcher and following them. Haiwu trudged behind for half a kilometer before collapsing on the ground and calling out, "I'm sorry, darling! I'm sorry!"

Ping, Lieutenant Dao, and the other men waited outside the hut, but Yong wanted to watch the entire procedure, partly out of concern for Cho and partly as a learning experience for Little Turnip's safety.

The midwife, an elderly woman with no teeth and a back that craned forward, poured rice peels on the ground until they formed mounds and then covered them with sheets of bull leather. She instructed Cho to stand up and come over to the mounds. Cho shook her head, and the woman stomped her foot and cursed at her in a native dialect.

"If you want to feel a lot of pain," the old woman said, "go ahead and lie there. Wait for it to crawl out. If you want this to be quick, squat on these mounds and let the ground do the work for you."

Reluctantly, Cho lifted herself from the stretcher. Yong and the old woman's daughter walked her to the mounds, a hand on each arm, and continued holding her as she slowly squatted down.

"Don't," Cho said, between breaths, "let go."

"I won't," Yong replied. Sweat dripped from her forehead down to her arms.

"You think"—Cho quickened her breathing—"she knows what she's doing?"

"She comes highly recommended from Meishi. Out of the hundreds of births the woman oversaw, only five mothers died. Meishi said the old woman could tell as soon as she saw you what position you should give birth in, what was the safest. She's had women give birth standing up, sitting down, lying on their sides. You name it, she's done it."

"Old Man in the Sky, help me!" the girl screamed. "Meishi recommended her? The woman who bullied me into working all those days in the fields while I was pregnant?"

Yong nodded. "Does the body good to work, even when it's pregnant. Don't worry. The old lady even helped Meishi give birth to her little boy. If I'm so lucky, Little Turnip will come out in the same spot you're standing on."

"Less talk," the old woman said, slapping Cho's arm with a soft braid. "More push!" Then she added, "*Ji! Ji! Ji!* Push! Push! Push!"

A few minutes later, Pig Feet slid out of Cho like an egg from a hen, landing headfirst on a cushiony mound. The old woman cut the umbilical cord and dipped the infant in a lukewarm tub of boiled river water. With practiced efficiency, she wiped the blood from its arms, legs, stomach, back, and face. Then she put it on one end of a scale and measured its weight, thumbing the center of the ruler until it balanced.

"Wow," she said. "Heavy boy. Almost four kilograms."

"It's a boy?" Cho asked. She was still squatting, her arms hanging exhaustedly between her legs.

"You can lie down now," the woman said.

Yong lifted Cho up and helped her back to the stretcher.

"Is he healthy?" Cho asked.

"For now." The old woman cradled the infant in her arms and brought her to Cho. "The real test is still to come. What did you name him?"

"Pig Feet."

"Good name. Should ward off most evils." She turned to Yong and extended her hand. "The agreed-to amount, please," she said.

Yong reached into her khakis, took out two silver dollars—four months' wages which she had saved for emergencies—and placed them on the woman's palm.

"I'll pay you back," Cho whispered, barely conscious. Her hair was matted and wet, and her lips were as parched as the Gobi Desert. "I have some savings in my crate."

"Hush," Yong said. "Those coins I gave her—they will mean nothing once the war is won. Don't you know? No one will need to buy food and no one will go hungry."

"I wish I could believe you. If what you say is true, I don't think I'd ever . . ." But the girl fell asleep before she could finish her sentence.

The old woman placed Pig Feet in one of a dozen premade baskets stacked in a corner of the room. Then she covered him with the bull leather he had fallen on: the first thing in the world he had touched. Yong was relieved he hadn't been stillborn. After all that rocking back and forth on the march from South Ji Village to Ruijin, all the emotional turmoil Cho had gone through, Yong had worried that Pig Feet had long ago decided to forsake this world and would come out stiff and black like a lump of coal. Perhaps, while in heaven, he saw China's future, saw it bright and pure and full of prosperity. Perhaps he saw a life after the war—a good life with his caring mother and adopted father—one where he drank orange peel tea after practicing martial arts, where he attended an industrial school or military college, and where nobody would look down on him for being born poor or landless. He would be best friends with Little Turnip, who, just a few days ago, seemed to have been equally excited to enter the world. They'd be two strapping boys wearing their military stars, marching at the fronts of their platoons: the future leaders of the Party.

32

OVER THE NEXT FEW HOURS, the members of the Third Legion took turns coming in and looking at Pig Feet. Ping remarked on how plump his fingers were, like fig leaves wrapped around sweet sticky rice—treats he had eaten at the orphanage. Shaohu, the standard-bearer, said he had his mother's eyes, while Lieutenant Dao added that he had the thick lips of his exploiter father. But everyone, including Yong, was most curious about how Haiwu would respond when he saw the baby. After he and Cho had become a couple, many soldiers in the unit teased him about raising another man's child, calling him an eater of leftovers and a wearer of oversized shoes. Still, they were silent now as Haiwu walked into the room, took off his army cap, and stared into the basket.

The kung fu champ, so chatty and droll most of the time, kept quiet. He tilted his head to one side and then the other. He inserted a finger into one of Pig Feet's hands and rocked it up and down. The entire time, his lightly mustached face remained as difficult to read as oracle bones from the Shang dynasty.

Finally, he giggled. "He's so ugly," he said, "like a skinned and uncooked rabbit."

The old lady turned the basket around. "If I was a gambler, I'd wager you were twice as ugly when you were his age."

Lieutenant Dao patted Haiwu on the back. "I warned you, didn't I? If that thing had been yours, even if he were a chunk of dirt, you'd be calling it the incarnation of Pan An."

"At last," Yong said, smiling, "Haiwu and I agree on something."

The kung fu champ had said what had been on her mind the moment that fleshy ball dropped on the mound. *How could a thing like that be in my body?* she wondered, and if it hadn't been for how relaxed the old woman's face looked while cleaning and handling the thing, Yong might have even thought something was wrong with it.

"Haiwu seems happy," Ping said, offering her his hand.

"He does." She accepted it. "I'm still worried about the two of them, though," she said. "A spoiled girl and a cripple."

"Haiwu's hardier than you think. Back on Iron Well, he hid in the hospital for two days without food or water. The Nationalists captured all the other patients in the tents. Only he survived. He'll take care of them both."

"Let's just hope we don't end up becoming parents to all three." She touched her belly. "We've got enough to worry about on our own."

Cho slept through the morning and into the afternoon, waking for a few minutes to hold the baby before falling back to sleep. The old woman agreed to let the girl rest in her hut for two more days, although she complained that such a request was unusual and that most village women were back out in the fields the day after they had given birth. Yong handed the woman another silver dollar for her trouble.

The truth was Yong would've paid any price to leave Cho there so that she could worry about other things, like her duties to the army. Ever since arriving at Ruijin, she had been so caught up with the girl that she hadn't been able to practice at the firing range or speak to Meishi about her obligations as a propaganda officer. She had even missed General Mao's speech earlier that morning, assigning duties to the different army groups.

By noon, when everything was settled with Cho, she sprinted back to Ruijin and finally reached the wooded hill where the army was gathered. Creeping up the Third Legion's knoll, she found Lieutenant Dao in the middle of a lecture, pointing to a hand-drawn map nailed to a tree. She joined her unit, who were sitting cross-legged in a semicircle in front of the lieutenant.

"Good of you to join us," Dao said. "Shall I get you a cup of tea?"

"Sorry, Lieutenant. This won't happen again."

Dao scoffed and then resumed his lecture. From what Yong gathered, General Mao was planning a surprise offensive. The Nationalists expected the Red Army to stay quiet and hide in the mountains surrounding Ruijin. They were building a wall of pillboxes in a ten-kilometer arc outside of the city, preventing supplies and equipment from coming in or going out.

"They mean to suffocate us," the lieutenant said, "but General Mao, like his zodiac sign, the serpent, has a plan for us to slither free. The tighter the enemy's grip, the easier it will be to sting his eyes."

Only a small contingent of the Red Army would remain at Ruijin to defend the city. Along the watchtowers and inside the buildings in the central square, straw mannequins dressed up in army attire would give off the appearance that the city was heavily defended. Double the amount of torches would be lit at dusk, and gramophones would play at full blast. Meanwhile, in a month or so—the General hadn't given an exact date—the bulk of the army groups would travel quietly through the treacherous swamps and steep cliffs of Ruijin's western mountains, swinging around the city and cutting off the supply lines of the Nationalist bunkers before dismantling them one by one.

"A great plan," Yong whispered to Ping, who nodded. "I'm excited."

33

SHE WAS STILL EXCITED THE next morning, so she grabbed some bullets from Ping's stash and headed for the firing range to practice her marksmanship. The range consisted of around thirty human-shaped targets on the other side of Mianshui River, just a short distance from the docks. Trainees would fire on the side closer to the mountains, either prone, crouched, or standing, and if a target collapsed, the soldier responsible would cross the river on a rattan skiff and prop it back up.

All the lanes were occupied by the time she got there. Apparently, the General's plan excited the entire army as well. Soldiers waited in long lines, smoking and chatting and yelling at the person at the front to hurry up. The staff sergeant keeping order had to restrict each man to twenty-shot turns. By the looks of it, it could be an hour before Yong got a chance to practice. "Just what I needed," she said, and left the firing range.

She walked along the edge of the river, hoping to find another area suitable for training. The Mianshui River, or the Stream of Flour, became milky after rainfall, the result of disturbing the chalky mud at the river's bottom. Such an opaque surface was what she saw now, and when she reached the fishermen sitting in their rowboats not far from the merchant docks, she wondered if they could catch anything.

"Snag any fish in this mud?" she yelled to the closest one. Maybe she could buy a carp for a cheap price and brew a soup for Cho.

"Not many today." The man took off his straw hat and fanned himself. "I can thank your friends down there for scaring all the fish away. No disrespect, but can't your army find somewhere else to shoot your guns?"

"The riverbank's the safest place," Yong said, shielding her eyes from the sun with her palm. "With the water in between, soldiers can't accidentally walk through and get hit."

"But on busy days like today, we fishermen lose half the river."

"You'll gain the whole country when we win the war." She didn't want to waste any more daylight and started marching away from the riverbank.

"And there are other times when you folks take up the docks, too," the man continued, "loading and unloading your treasure chests. Some days I can't sell my fish to the merchants until well past sundown."

Yong stopped and turned around. The man was referring to the brave smugglers who transported goods confiscated from landowners and sold them in Nationalist-controlled cities.

"They've been doing that again lately?" she asked.

The man nodded. "I saw some today before I unlatched my boat. They're probably still there. And let me tell you about your engineers on the other end of the river. They're no better than the soldiers. They dig up all that chalk from the shore to build Lord knows what, making the river so cloudy I can't even see my catch."

Yong headed north toward the merchant docks. Maybe she'd meet someone she had known from her smuggling days. Even if she didn't, maybe they'd still recognize her. She was something of a legend, after all, saving those five intelligence officers at Ji'an.

At the entrance to the docks, hand-drawn wagons weaved along piers so narrow that when one cart passed another, a wheel often had to leave the pier and hover above the water. Garbage floated on the milky river, and the premises stank of spoiled fish and pickled cabbage. It was just how Yong had remembered it.

There were no traces of any smugglers—the dock master told her they usually left before dawn—but she was surprised to see another familiar face: Haiwu's. He was standing with one foot on a pier and his prosthetic on a boat, throwing supplies onto the deck: fishing nets, two hay pillows, Cho's crate, and his saber. She was surprised how natural Haiwu looked, as if he'd worked as a sailor all his life.

"This is the thing you'll be traveling to Shanghai on?" Yong asked.

"The most luxurious boat on the river," Haiwu said.

The boat before them had a cylindrical roof, over which rested two sets of triangular sails, and its hull was painted the same white as the water, probably using the chalk found at its bottom. In the back, an old man with a silver tooth sat sleeping on a stool, resting his back against the long pole that controlled the rudder.

"You two are leaving so soon?" Yong asked. "It hasn't even been forty-eight hours since Pig Feet's birth."

"Not our decision." Haiwu nodded to the man in the back. "Old Meng needs to reach Shanghai before tea season ends. He's got twenty jars of aromatic leaves belowdecks, and we've delayed him enough. If we don't leave within the next few days, we'll have to wait months."

Yong stared at the two characters on the ship's stern. She recognized them: *Cha Ye*, or *Tea Leaf*.

"And I heard there's an offensive starting soon. Ruijin won't have many defenders in the coming weeks, and it's not going to help the Third Legion if Cho and Pig Feet and I have to tag along. We'll cause you and Ping a lot of trouble."

Yong couldn't argue with his reasoning. She was glad to hear the kung fu champ was thinking about others for a change. Perhaps having a family had made him more mature.

"The captain has been to Shanghai many times?"

"Tons," Haiwu said. "I've asked around. Old Meng is well respected by everyone. He's been sailing these waters for thirty years."

Perhaps she had been wrong to expect Haiwu to be a bad husband. Maybe he really was as resourceful as Ping had claimed him to be. She should trust her husband's judgment, she decided, and feel secure in handing Cho over to his closest friend. She wished Haiwu the best of luck on his journey and told him that, with his charm, Cho's family was sure to accept him.

Afterward she trudged back up the hills and found a secluded cliff to practice her aim.

34

OVER THE NEXT FEW DAYS, the army was busier than ever, preparing for the upcoming operations. On top of her rifle training and the now mandatory daily exercise regiments, which included formation drills, camouflage preparation, and three kilometers of mountain climbing, Yong had to help Ping cast bullets at night. Despite her objections, her husband asked the lieutenant if she could be excused from combat duties—as they'd discussed before—and Dao said that the army needed every able soldier they could get now. When Ping pressed him further, the lieutenant told him, with restrained hostility, to stop being so selfish and start thinking about the sacrifices that everybody had to make for the greater good. Yong was glad to have the lieutenant on her side.

It was difficult for her to find time to visit Cho, who had moved onto the ship with Haiwu and Pig Feet. Still, the night before they were scheduled to sail north, she managed to sneak away from camp and drop by the docks to say goodbye.

Captain Meng let the couple stay in a walled corner under the cylindrical roof. They placed Pig Feet's cradle on a tea barrel protected from splashing currents by fishing nets, under which their bedding lay folded. When Yong came in, they were eating dinner in the communal dining area: four tree stumps glued down with wheat putty and a piece of driftwood punched through the base of the mast. She watched as Haiwu fed Cho cod-and-lentil stew and then as the girl took Pig Feet to her chest to suckle from her breasts. Afterward she scratched her nipples, complaining that they itched.

"I made fun of my mother for doing this when she had our little brother." Cho cringed. "But I can't help it. It's like someone lit them on fire."

"Maybe you're allergic to something," Yong said. "I'll ask Malin to make you an herb bundle before you leave."

"Allergic to Pig Feet." Haiwu laughed. He rocked the cradle on the barrel. "Did you hear that, little one? Your mother's allergic to you."

Cho threw a fishbone at him.

"You should come to the hills tonight and say goodbye," Yong said, "both of you."

"Nobody will miss me. I was barely in the unit."

"The only person who'll miss me is Ping," Haiwu added, "and he isn't even here. Shows what kind of friend he is."

"Ping has to cast enough bullets for twenty soldiers," Yong replied, "and he's short one assistant who'd rather waste his last night being lazy on a boat than helping his comrades on the hills. I should report that person for insubordination."

"Always the stickler," Haiwu said. "The good Communist soldier."

"Maybe I should work in the communes one last time, too." Cho nodded to her husband. "Serve out the reminder of my punishment."

"You two make a good pair," Yong said. "I don't know if you've always been this annoying or if you're learning from your husband."

When she got up to leave, Cho and Haiwu laughed and got up as well.

"Come on, husband. It's a nice night out, cool and fragrant. A walk will do us good."

Haiwu reached into the cradle for Pig Feet.

"You're bringing him with you?" Yong asked.

"Doesn't the Third Legion want to say goodbye to its youngest member?"

Yong wasn't joking when she said Ping needed help. Because Haiwu was familiar with her husband's process, even a few hours of assistance would be of benefit. They wouldn't get anything done with a baby around.

"Up to you," she said.

"You want me to bring him?" he asked Cho.

The girl looked at Haiwu and then at Yong. Then she looked past them at the captain dozing near the stern with his back against the rudder pole.

"You awake, Old Meng?" the girl called. "Can you take care of Pig Feet for a few hours?"

The old man, his eyes still closed, gave them a thumb's-up.

They walked up the hills in silence, slowing every few steps for Haiwu to catch up. There was a full moon out, and it was so bright, the stars around it dissolved like grains of salt. Arriving at Ruijin, the first thing the army groups had done was plant fruit trees by the Buddhist temple, hoping to re-create the amphitheater on Pear Tree Hill. Now Yong imagined neat rows of blooming trees like those in Kai's gardens, except they would be harbingers of the Communist ideals rather than those preserving a corrupt past.

"I've never thanked you for bringing me out here," Cho said. I know I could be difficult, and you've been kind and patient. You've been more of a friend to me these last few weeks than my own mother has her entire life."

Yong wanted to say something about how her strength and passion came from the teachings of Engels and Marx, but she knew that any passage she'd cite would ruin the moment.

"You shouldn't thank me," she said. The girl shook her head and was about to say something else, but Yong stopped her. "I haven't been acting like myself lately, or so everybody keeps telling me. If you want to thank anyone, thank Little Turnip in my belly."

"And he wouldn't have existed without his mother," Cho said.

"Nor would he without his father!" Haiwu shouted from the back. "And I haven't thanked you yet, either. Thank you and Ping both! You for finding me a wife, and Ping for saving my life!"

"Stop." Yong was getting tired of all this praise. "At least wait until we reach camp. You can tell Ping in person."

They continued on in good spirits, passing trees blown sideways. The summer breeze felt cool on Yong's face, and she could smell the aroma of boiling onions and sesame from the soldiers' cookpots farther up the hill. Haiwu began to whistle an unfamiliar tune. Cho sang along:

> *My parents grow old with each Spring Festival.*
> *Their hair turns gray, their backs start to ache.*
> *What have they worked for all their life?*
> *Where do their hopes lie?*
> *Tell them I'm coming home this winter!*
> *Tell them I'm coming home to see them!*
> *Tell them I'm coming home!*

She was still singing halfway to the camp, even when the sirens started drowning out her voice. They were coming from the central plaza, near downtown Ruijin. The noise crawled over the hilltop like a swarm of locusts: at first a quiet buzz, slowly increasing in volume until the rasping filled their ears. The sky flashed orange in a quick succession of threes and fours, and when they realized the color was coming from behind them, they turned and saw a half dozen flying machines descending toward them and then swooping past their heads.

Yong pulled Cho and Haiwu to the ground, clutching them under her arms. The earth started to quake, and dirt and grass flew up in ripples. For three minutes she counted in sixes, the number of shots per cartridge for her rifle, to calm her nerves. It felt as though there were a hundred thunderstorms above her head, as if Old Man in the Sky were fighting some primordial demon bent on turning this mountainside into its domain and that they didn't know anyone else was there. Just as during her first encounter with flying machines, Yong felt trivial, insect-like, a splinter on a decaying log, a smudge on a gun scope—not the end goal that the world was created for but the pests struggling to prevent it from becoming whatever it was destined to become.

When the ringing in her ears had settled, she lifted her head. The sky was empty. Plumes of curly smoke rose over the hill. The machines had hit Ruijin's central square. The sirens had stopped not because someone turned them off but because they were blown apart.

Cho shook free of Yong's arm, stood up, and stared in the direction of the docks. The woods blocked their view and prevented moonlight from piercing the treetops, but the three of them were high above sea level, and they caught sight of the same kind of smoke, its tendrils weaving between the branches and then rising above the canopy.

Immediately Cho began running down. Haiwu followed.

"Stop," he said, and when he couldn't run any faster, he yelled to Yong, "Follow her! Follow her!"

But Yong was already in front of him. She had been a soldier for a long time and had gone through many weeks of rigorous training, but she was surprised how difficult it was to keep up with the girl. The hill wasn't steep, but she found herself taking halting steps every few seconds to avoid tripping over branches or slipping on pebbles. The girl must have been running as fast as she could, without glancing down at all. By the time Yong caught up to her, the docks were in full view.

"Don't get any closer!" Yong yelled.

Below them, the docks burned.

None of the piers were standing; only their posts protruded from the surface. Debris from wagons and boats floated on the water, which was itself in flames. The cries on the river were indistinguishable from those on land. A man on fire, stuck between a burning ship and a section of wharf, had submerged to put himself out, only to float back up seconds later, lifeless. A boy—some fisherman's apprentice—swam to shore, discovered he was missing a leg, and dove in again to search for it.

Yong followed Cho, who was trying to retrace the path to their spot on the docks, staring at the location *Tea Leaf* should have been. Only a torn slice of sail attached to a blasted-off section of mast remained bobbing on the river. There was a winding path of debris that led to the boat, and the girl stepped ankle-deep into the water to swim toward it. Yong pulled her back and pushed her to the ground.

"I'm a better swimmer," she said, "but if I go in, you have to promise you won't follow. Do you promise?"

The girl brushed her eyes dry, tried to remain composed, and nodded.

Yong took off her shoes and then slogged into the water.

The water was cold. Her slack pants felt heavy in the current. Dipping her eyes below the surface, she tasted gasoline and saw a murky view of driftwood, seaweed, and anchor chain. Tiny fish glimmered and vanished into nooks at the bottom of the river. Yong resurfaced, took a great gulp of air, and followed the winding path to the bobbing mast. Pulling away the debris of *Tea Leaf*, she saw what was on the other side: barrels, fishing poles, half a bedroll with the cotton spilling out, Cho's chicken crate, and Old Meng, facedown on the surface, holding Pig Feet between his chest and elbow, the infant's cheeks and ears the only parts above the milky waters of Mianshui River.

35

A SUCCESS IN DECEPTION, MEISHI called the attack. "Too much success, in fact. Our spies inside the Kuomintang high command informed the Nationalist generals that we were preparing a defense of the city, but we hadn't yet propped up the mannequins or lit the torches. We weren't expecting an air raid until at least a month."

Yong laid her rifle on the vice secretary's desk. They were in a reinforced room below the Buddhist temple. The bunker was cramped, small slits below the ceiling its only source of sunlight. The structure had one entrance, which was the size of a well opening, but it would keep the politburo safe even if the temple above collapsed.

"The attack was good for us, overall," Meishi continued. "Casualties in the army were light and we don't have to waste resources or manpower rebuilding decoys. Let the Nationalists waste their shells on empty buildings."

"What about the docks?"

"Ah, the docks." Meishi tapped her pen against her canteen. "The attack on the docks was a surprise. We didn't think the Kuomintang would go so far as to bomb the local population. They're only fueling people's hatred for them, which, in the end, also supports the cause. We did lose some good people there, though—people who made countless trips for us to Nanjing and Su-Chou and Shanghai. They were heroes, but you know that already."

Yong couldn't control herself anymore: She was crying, and in front of someone she knew would respect her less for crying.

"Let it out now," Meishi said. "Let it all out. And then let it turn into hatred. Use it in the battles to come."

"Pig Feet died." Yong knew she shouldn't be saying this. "His fat little fingers were clutching the old man's arm, and I pried it open and saw his little face. It was white, like the river, and his expression was stuck like he was still crying. I can't stop thinking about it. I see him when I close my eyes, when I wake, when I pee, when I'm eating lunch. I see my own Little Turnip in his cheeks, his nose, his strands of new hair, his toothless mouth that once suckled on his mother's breasts, his tiny legs and the rolls of fat on them. I've tried everything, and I can't stop seeing him. And it's my fault, all my fault—I was the one who stopped Haiwu from taking him out of his cradle. I took his life then and I didn't even know it!"

Meishi's eye twitched. "Pig Feet was Kai's newborn?"

Yong nodded, wiping her nose with her sleeve.

"What did I tell you about getting involved? Why waste sympathy on the son of an exploiter? I just told you your comrades—some of who you even knew—were killed in the attack, and you cry for someone who's contributed nothing to the cause. In fact, he's part of the reason we're fighting."

Yong sat up straight, took her rifle from the desk, and put it back on her lap. "I know, I know. You're right. It's just been a difficult couple of months. I've never been pregnant before. I shouldn't have embarrassed myself like this."

Meishi softened her expression. "It's all right. I'm glad you came to me. We've known each other a long time, and what are good friends for but to share our embarrassments?" She sighed. "I don't know how you do it, spending your days in the Third Legion with those dirty, smelly criminals, no women around to talk to, letting your thoughts get cooped up inside you until they get twisted and unbearable. You're stronger than I am, that's for sure."

"I should go," Yong said. She had fully regained control of herself. "I've taken up enough of your time."

The vice secretary escorted Yong through the tunnels to the entrance of the bunker. Yong climbed to the top and twisted the hatch open. The afternoon sun poured inside and revealed the ants and centipedes crawling around the dirt walls.

"You're a stronger woman than I am," Meishi's voice echoed up. "You're the hero of Ji'an!"

36

ON LORD ZHU'S DOORSTEP, RIGHT before giving her to the old man, her father had told her that life was a roll of the dice. By giving her to someone wealthy, he ensured that she rolled at least a four: She didn't need to worry about food or shelter, and in a few years, when the old man died, she could do anything she wanted. "Everyone needs to live a few shitty years. Better when you're young than when you're old." Those were the last words her father had said to her, but, like much of his wisdom, Yong came to believe in the opposite. Life couldn't be decided by chance; that would mean there was no right or wrong, and the *Manifesto* spoke of uprising, of karma, of the good being rewarded and the wicked punished. And then there were those who lived a lifetime of bad years and also those who lived a lifetime of good ones, and the only way to explain why that happened was the existence of another world, one where things became balanced. The way she saw it—and she knew this wasn't the way Marx meant for his words to be understood—what the *Manifesto* was really urging was bringing the decency of that world to this one. Why wait until death when equality could be achieved here in life?

Ping was the only one around when she returned to their knoll. Taking a seat next to his workshop, she reached into a pail of cold water, grabbed a handful of submerged bullets, and started drying them with a piece of burlap.

"Where are they?" she asked.

"They're out practicing drills."

"No, I mean, where are Cho and Haiwu?"

"Oh, they're by the docks, scavenging more of the wreckage." Using tongs, Ping poured another batch of hot ammunition into the pail.

Yong separated the dried bullets into piles of twenty and placed them in coin purses next to waterproof pouches with enough powder in them to ignite twenty shots.

"You don't need to do that," Ping said. "Rest a little. Take a nap."

"I can't sleep. I'll just see him again."

Ping dropped the tongs and squatted in front of her. "Forget this guilt. It's not good for you. It's not good for the baby."

"You don't need to console me," Yong said, looking away. "Go back to your work."

"I know something about what you're going through. I have the same guilt."

Yong laughed. "How many combat missions have you been on? You spend most of your time behind the front lines. You've never killed anyone."

"My bullets kill people." Ping paused. "But that's not what I mean, either." He opened his mouth but no words came out. Then he said, "Back in Canton, when I didn't have much experience, I made a gun that wasn't any good. I was an apprentice, but I pretended that I was just as good as my master, and I sold a gun that backfired on its user. During a fight, the bullet ricocheted and hit the shooter straight in the head. I didn't know that would happen. I mean, I knew the gun wasn't accurate, but I didn't know it could kill the person shooting it. I've lived with that guilt for a long time now without telling anyone. Well"—he paused again—"Luo knew, but he's dead."

"That was different," Yong said. "That was a gang member. He wasn't a good person, not someone innocent like Pig Feet."

"But you didn't ask Haiwu to leave Pig Feet behind out of greed. You asked out of the desire to help the Third Legion." When Yong shook her head, Ping added, "My point is, you need to separate intention from outcome. If your intention was good, you shouldn't feel guilty. Not even Cho blames you."

It was true. It had been three days since the attack, and the girl, though inconsolable, never once mentioned Yong's question to Haiwu before they'd left the boat: *You're bringing him with you, too?* Perhaps the girl didn't remember. Perhaps she only remembered the way Pig Feet looked when Yong carried him out of the water and placed him on the ground. The closest the girl had come to blame was to ask why she herself hadn't been on *Tea Leaf*, why Old Man in the Sky spared her life but took her child's. These last few nights, Yong and Haiwu took turns staying awake, watching over the girl so she wouldn't do anything stupid.

"Did you hear me?" Ping asked.

"You're right." Yong tried to smile.

Ping kissed her on the cheek and picked up his tongs again. She went back to sorting bullets.

A moment later Haiwu came hobbling up the hill. Out of breath, he shouted something she couldn't understand. When he reached their knoll, he fell to his knee.

"It's all my fault." His shirt and pants were wet, and he was sobbing. "I shouldn't have fallen asleep. I shouldn't have even agreed to go down there. But she told me she wanted to go to the river again, to see if his cradle would wash up, to see if we could find the bull leather that first touched his face. She told me she wanted to say goodbye to him one last time. She was crying so much. What could I do?"

Yong grabbed Haiwu by the arm and shook him. "What happened?"

He reached into his pocket and took out an inkpot the size of a plum and a folded-up sheet of paper. He lay them before Yong and then lowered his head.

"I don't understand," she said. "What is this?"

"Cho's gone! Cho's gone! They found her body in the river!"

Ping walked over, picked up the inkpot, and put it in his palms. "I've seen this before," he said. "Where did you get this?"

Staring at Ping holding the pot, Yong remembered seeing such objects in Lord Zhu's manor. Usually they contained ink for calligraphy, but the vessel was also ideal for a single dose of arsenic or cyanide.

"Beauty supplies, she told me." Haiwu slapped himself twice, once on each cheek. "It was in her crate, and I could've just thrown it into the river days ago and she couldn't have swallowed the poison."

Yong unfolded the sheet of paper. Staring at the characters, she recognized only a few. They were distant, remote, a reminder of the girl's educated upbringing. They could've been written by anyone and she wouldn't have known the difference.

"These are her final words?"

Haiwu nodded.

"Read them to me."

"I can't bear to look at it again. Take them to Dao."

Yong pulled up Haiwu by the collar and stuffed the letter into his hand. "Read them to me, you useless oaf."

Ping stepped in between them and separated Haiwu from Yong. "Control yourself," he said, smoothing Haiwu's uniform. "This isn't helping."

"Read them to me," Yong repeated. "I want it to come from your voice."

The kung fu champ slowly lifted the letter to his face.

"You don't have to read it," Ping said.

But Haiwu had already begun:

Dear Family,

I call you all my family because you are the only people Pig Feet knew. I don't take back what I said that night, about thanking Yong and Ping and the rest of Third Legion. I should have stayed here with all of you, I realize that now. I should've had Pig Feet brought up by the Red Road Army and raised as a soldier. I should have listened to you, Yong, my closest friend.

He stopped.

"I know that wasn't all there was," Yong said. "Read me the rest."

Haiwu, sniffling, continued:

To my husband, my dear Haiwu, I know you will miss me. I will miss you, too. But even from my brief time with you, I know you are

the kind of person who will recover quickly. I don't say this as a form
of admonishment. You give your heart readily. You are passionate. It is
why I love you. You will suffer greatly for a while, more than anyone
can mourn for someone else, but then you will recover.

I must go now. I was of no use to Pig Feet, and I am sure I'll be of
no use to anyone else now that he's dead. Do not try and find my body.
I don't want you to see me that way. I am in the river with my sister.
Knowing that should suffice.

With love,
Cho.

The words felt distant, foreign, written by someone else in another
language, not by the Cho in Yong's memories. The Cho she remembered
would never have used words like "admonishment" or "suffice" like
some midlevel bureaucrat. The letter was meant to bring Yong closer to
the girl, but it had the opposite effect. It felt like something Lord Zhu or
Kai would have written.

"Take me to her body," Yong ordered him.

Haiwu looked up from the letter.

"Didn't you hear what she said?"

"Please," Ping pleaded. "Can't you see he's suffering?"

"Never mind. She won't be difficult to find. I don't need you
anymore."

Yong stormed off in the direction of the docks. Ping followed, calling for her to come back. She started walking faster. At some point, she
couldn't hear his steps behind her anymore and thought, *Good.*

When the docks came into view, she headed toward a spot by the
shore where a crowd had gathered. She tapped a man on the shoulder,
and the mob—fishermen who themselves had almost lost their lives a
few days earlier—saw that she was from the army and parted for her.
Weaving among them, she heard whispers: "Pretty girl," "So young,"
"A shame."

At the front of the line, a skinny sailor stood over the body, his shirt
soaked and dripping. "You know her?" he asked.

Yong stared at the girl. She was lying on her side, one arm over the other, as though she had just found a comfortable position to sleep in. She wore the dull gray blouse the army had issued her, and the jade clip Lord Kai had given her. Her matted hair clung to her forehead. There were green weeds in it, some type of seagrass. Her profile resembled her twin's, and three words crossed Yong's mind: *You've joined her.*

But this time Yong didn't put her hand over her mouth. She didn't look away. She stared at the girl, and in her eyes the body changed from one belonging to her friend to just another casualty in a long list of combat losses.

"I know her," Yong said. "You two, help me bring her to camp. Quickly now."

There would be a funeral, of course, and then a burial, and then it would be over. She hoped it would all get done swiftly, efficiently. Who knew how soon the Kuomintang would begin their attack on Ruijin? There was no time to waste. The army groups had to be ready to move out at a moment's notice.

Watching the two men place the body on a bamboo stretcher, Yong breathed in and breathed out, steadying herself for the war to come.

PART III

BIRTH

37

WHEN I WAS A BOY, my grandfather often recited the fable of the footless man. There are many versions, but the one he told me went something like this:

Thousands of years ago, before the time of emperors, China was divided into many nations and city-states. The wealthy curried favor from local kings by offering gifts. Nobles gave a portion of their harvest. Intellectuals supplied the bounty of military advice or worldly philosophy. Those with neither land nor education had one remaining way to gain favor: possessing something the king personally desired. There were stories of how a blacksmith became a general after he had forged the king's sharpest blade; of how a cowherd became a magistrate after the king had wed his daughter; of how a weaver became a landowner after he had sewed the king's finest gown.

Such was the ambition of a lucky jade miner from Hubei. He had spent decades in the quarries without finding anything substantial, and then on his forty-fourth birthday he struck a prize so large and so fine that only a king could afford it. He shaped it into a lustrous cabbage, smoothing it until the leaves bloomed symmetrically on all sides. Holding it up to the sun, he felt pride when his work lit up like a lantern. It was rumored that, because of its purity, the jade cabbage could capture the light and glow even at night.

Confident in its worth, the miner took his prize to the king of Zhou, the most powerful king in the land. He lay the piece at the foot of the throne, his head bowed until the king's advisor finished examining it. The advisor, a sycophant easily moved to jealousy, held the jade cabbage between his long flowing sleeves and worried that such an awe-inspiring object might elevate the miner to a position above even his own.

"Nothing but a chunk of limestone," he yelled up to the king, who was sitting half-asleep behind a silken veil, "dressed up to look like treasure. The thing is worthless."

"Fine, fine," the king called down. "Get the man out of my sight."

"Your Majesty," the miner pleaded. "Ask any reputable jeweler. They will confirm the authenticity. I come bearing this gift as your honest servant. Why would I—"

"Might I suggest a punishment?" The advisor grinned at the miner. "One fit for a liar."

"Fine, fine," the king called down. "Chop off his right foot so he will be slower and lie to fewer people."

And thus the miner lost one of his feet.

On crutches, though still confident of the worth of his work, he took his prize to the king of Zheng, the second most powerful king. Again he lay the piece at the foot of the throne, his head bowed until the jade was examined. This time the king himself picked up the object and though he liked its shape—its craftsmanship—he was worried about its origins.

"I have heard another jade cabbage had come before the king of Zhou. Is this the same one?" he asked the miner.

The miner nodded. "The king of Zhou does not have as keen an eye as you do, my lord. He is not worthy of my prize."

"I heard a different story. I heard that he rejected the piece because it was nothing more than limestone." The king threw the jade cabbage into the miner's lap. "You bring me a gift that my rival has rejected. Are you suggesting that I should accept it because I am lesser than him, that the kingdom of Zheng is second to Zhou? If the object is as magnificent as you say it is, why not bring it to me first?"

"Sire," the miner pleaded, "I meant no disrespect. I was—"

"Guards!" the king called. "Get this man out of my sight. Chop off his other foot so that he knows the meaning of loyalty!"

And thus the miner lost his other foot.

With both feet gone, the miner became a beggar.

Years later, on the streets of his hometown, a wandering laborer approached the miner who had become a beggar. The laborer glanced at the coins in the shape of knives on the ground and then at the jade cabbage in the beggar's arm. By this point the beggar had become an old man. His hair was white, he had grown a gray beard, and his legs were covered with a brown cloth.

"What makes your life so pathetic that I should give you my hard-earned money?" the laborer asked the beggar.

The beggar uncovered his right leg and showed his missing foot. "I tried giving this jade cabbage to the king of Zhou. He refused it and chopped off my right foot."

"So?" The laborer wasn't impressed. "Many people have lost their right foot. What makes you so special?"

The beggar uncovered his other leg and showed that both his feet were missing. "Then I tried giving this jade cabbage to the king of Zheng. He refused it as well and chopped off my other foot."

"So?" Again the laborer wasn't impressed. "Many people have lost both their feet. I ask a second time: Why should I mourn for someone with missing feet?"

The beggar shook his head. "You misunderstand me. I mourn not for my missing feet. I mourn because no one will accept this jade cabbage, my life's work."

No one knows how the laborer reacted to this last revelation. Was he finally impressed, or did he remain unconvinced? Did he give the beggar knife money, or did he walk away?

I tell you this story because you're like me—a scholar of sorts—though your generation seems to have forgotten the fables of our ancestors or, worse, even distrusts them. And that's a shame, for in them hide morals that have persisted over the ages, morals that are relevant even today. On this the twenty-eighth anniversary of our republic, when the nation is still grieving the death of our great Chairman, it is particularly important to think about the wisdom of the ancients, who are all too eager to guide us if we are willing to hear them.

I see that look on your face. You want to shake your head. You want to ask: What was the moral of the footless man's fable? I have thought about this question a lot myself, and my answer has transformed a great deal over the years. At first, like you, I didn't believe there was any moral at all. I was just a boy and thought my grandfather had made the little tale up, but that changed once I grew older. It's peculiar the way some stories stay with you and others don't. My grandfather must have told hundreds of them, but I can only remember a few, and only this one from start to finish.

During my teens and early twenties, the country was a dangerous place, with hundreds of warlords and gangs vying for control of their tiny corner. China wasn't really a country at all. After seeing innocent people mutilated on the streets and thugs take what they wanted from every marketplace I visited, I was reminded of the brutal way the two kings treated the miner, who, despite his artisanship, was not a physically strong man. The story was a warning of the treacheries of the world, reminding us to always be prepared for the worst. I decided to practice martial arts. It was an easy decision, since my great-uncle took part in the Boxer Rebellion, whose members had believed they could turn their bodies as hard and impenetrable as iron. Of course, I don't need to remind you of how the rebellion ended. The Boxers are laughingstocks now, and while it's true they were overconfident, their martial arts weren't fake. In my prime, I could take on ten people hand-to-hand. If I had my saber, no one stood a chance. At least, not without a gun.

And ultimately it was a gun—a British automatic that fired 7.7mm rounds—that made me realize my original interpretation of the story was inadequate. Shortly after joining the People's Red Army at Iron Well Mountain, I lost one of my legs, and for a while the story was all I could think about. Lying in the hospital, wiggling the toes my mind felt but my eyes couldn't see, I wallowed in self-pity. I had never thought I would be the miner who became a beggar. I was prepared for the world. I read books, practiced martial arts, made myself strong—both in body and mind. I was supposed to be the laborer standing in front of the beggar, deciding whether to give him knife money. But as I continued retelling the story in my head, it dawned on me that my original interpretation didn't take into account that part of the story, the conversation between the beggar and the laborer, who harbored no ill will toward him at all. The true wisdom of the story, I came to believe, was not "Always be prepared" but rather "One can never truly be prepared." I felt better for many years after this realization. It snapped me out of my misery, made me appreciate the world again. In life, the story seemed to be saying, everyone experiences misfortunes they cannot anticipate. Do not lament for too long on yours. Cherish them as a fragment of your being.

But, once again, I misunderstood the story. I was taking the parts of it that suited me and not grasping the whole. In fact, it is only recently that I believe—I am not so proud anymore to say I am sure—that I have come to terms with the full meaning of the tale. Surprisingly, it was this event that has so consumed our great republic—this Cultural Revolution of the last decade—that made me see the light. I know it is somewhat irresponsible of me to say this, and if our illustrious Chairman were still alive, I wouldn't be so bold, but being an early member of the republic comes with certain privileges, and being an old cripple certain protections, and I am sure my mild criticisms won't be taken as anything more than a concerned grandpa looking out for his favorite grandson's best interest.

We all know, with the arrest of the Gang of Four, that the Great Leader hadn't been surrounded by the most reliable people during his final years. We also know the Chairman's final wife, Jiang Qing, was a disgraced actress with delusions of grandeur, and that it was her poisonous influence that caused millions of intellectuals, teachers, doctors, and scientists to suffer. Seen in the light of this recent knowledge, the fable of the footless man becomes a warning again: Those who are able to give truly valuable things to the king are punished, while sycophants whose only gift is flattery are rewarded. I know this interpretation isn't perfect, either. *What about the king of Zheng?* you want to ask. He decided to chop off the miner's other foot all on his own. I don't know how to answer your question—not yet anyway. I'm still trying to work that out.

In the meantime, let me tell you another story, a true one this time, about my experiences on the Long March. Of course, it will also include Yong and Ping. They are, after all, the reasons you searched for me in the first place. This story will be very different from the footless man's fable, and since it is true, there are no morals. In fact, you shouldn't compare the two at all.

38

THE LONG MARCH BEGAN, FOR me at least, with the death of my first wife, Cho, and our newborn son, Pig Feet. After his birth, we had gotten permission from the army to sail north and drop him off with my in-laws, but no one expected the Kuomintang to bomb Ruijin's harbor. Both Cho and Pig Feet were on the boat when the shells started to land, and the only thing that comforts me when thinking about this memory now is perhaps believing that they had been asleep and felt no pain.

I was still in a state of deep mourning when the Communist position at Ruijin became impossible. The enemy had surrounded us with concrete bunkers and advanced toward the city at a rapid rate. All our attempts to outflank them only managed to slow their progress for a few days. We had to evacuate, and we had to do so quickly. The wounded piled up along our hills and many died of curable wounds before a nurse could even get to them. In response, the army formed special "heroic" detachments. These detachments selected the elderly, injured, and diseased and had them man towers and trenches as a final delaying tactic while the main body of the army escaped through the steep cliffs of the western mountainside.

I passed many soldiers in these heroic detachments on my way up, and although some put on a brave face and waved to me, others crossed their arms and stared over my shoulder. If I had lost my leg at Ruijin instead of Iron Well, I surely would have been among them.

"The people of the new China will remember their sacrifice," Yong remarked.

"Will they remember Cho?" I asked. "Will they remember Pig Feet?"

I was naïve back then, and didn't believe much in the Communist ideals or their goal to build a new China. I had joined because I wanted to survive. In any case, I understood that a few wounded men weren't going to stop the Nationalists from pursuing us and that it was premature to think about who would remember who when there would still be many more casualties in the days to come.

As soon as the army left Ruijin, winter arrived. Snow fell in soft, warm chunks, and by the time we reached the Xiang River, it reached our ankles. The river was where the Kuomintang caught up to us. They gathered in full force on the other side. Because of the bad tactics of our German advisor, who suggested a direct attack, it took half our remaining fighting men to break through. Loaded down with baggage—sewing machines, minting presses, desks and chairs, chests full of silver coins, radio equipment, and all the other nonsense deemed necessary to run a government—they were easy pickings for the enemy artillery and sharpshooters.

I was lucky the battle took place on water, even if the surface was ice-cold, since I was a good swimmer; otherwise, I don't think I could have outrun the machine guns. Reaching the other side, I hid among tall stalks of brown river grass, covered my face and uniform with mud, which clung frozen to my chin, and watched as soldiers fell from the narrow bridge into the water dotted with pink.

Even after the rest of the army had crossed over, the enemy air force continued to chase us and strafe our ranks. Finally, we reached the relative safety of the walled city of Zunyi, which was just out of range of their planes. By that point, many battalions were completely wiped out, and others had neither the time nor the energy to properly mourn their losses. Morale was low, desertion became unmanageable, and the Red Road Army was like a spider that had lost all its legs: only a fragment of what it had been before. The Nationalists believed they had achieved a total and complete victory. They even played news reports on the radio claiming that Mao was already dead.

At Zunyi, the Third Legion camped below the city walls and huddled around a fire fueled by donkey dung. I remember Yong telling
Ping, "Little Turnip will come out a clay lump. I know it." She was
superstitious and believed that her unborn child would want to avoid
life if it saw how horrible the world was. Ping clung to her stomach,
too exhausted to say a word. The rest of the platoon slept on the dirt,
covering themselves with wood planks, hay, or, if they were lucky, the
bloody coats of the deceased.

No one paid any mind to me. Not even the lieutenant had enough
energy to see how I was doing. If I had drowned in the river and failed
to respond to his roll call, the other soldiers would only nod. "Not a big
loss," they would say. "He didn't do much for us anymore, anyway." I
had alienated myself weeks before when I had gotten special permission
to leave for Shanghai. After Cho and Pig Feet died, I had worn white
for a few days, and although I had every right to mourn my loss—it
was, in fact, my obligation as a father and a husband to do so—other
soldiers claimed that wearing such a bright color made the army more
susceptible to air raids. I was endangering their lives, they said, and so
I stopped my mourning after only three days, much shorter than the
traditional period of a month. But this did not make them hate me any
less. Many of them probably felt I should have been part of the special
detachment, even though I had little trouble keeping up with the army.

After leaving Zunyi, the German advisor and his cronies were pulled
from power, and Chairman Mao was put in full control of the army.
As you know, he made the famous—and ultimately correct—decision
to abandon the planned linkup with the other Communist forces and
instead march around the main roads and travel through the remote
province of Sichuan. The detour meant thousands of extra kilometers
for the already exhausted soldiers, but, almost immediately following
the change, the spirits of the vast majority of the survivors improved.
The enemy didn't know in which direction to pursue us, the landscape
changed from steep cliffs to rolling hills, and a warm wind blew up from
the south and made it feel like summer.

Soldiers started singing again. The Red Dramatic Society worked
overtime, composing tunes and short ten-minute "walking break" plays.

Many famous songs were composed during these months: "The Red Guards Are Not Afraid of Hardships," "Day by Day Victorious with Committee Member Mao," "Open Fire at the Black Line," and "Shaking the Four Seas, Shocking the Five Continents."

Our optimistic songs brought out scared villagers, who opened their shops and traded with us. We taught them our morality, showed them that we fought and suffered for the poor and not the imperialist-supported Kuomintang or the capitalist landlords. We encouraged local boys to run side by side with the army and attend recruitment rallies. In a few months' time, our numbers had reached half of what we had before Zunyi, and the army had enough spirit to fight once again.

My own spirit, on the other hand, had not improved. Before Xiang River, when there was the threat of attack at any moment, I didn't have time to let Cho and Pig Feet linger in my mind for too long, but, with the threat of immediate death gone, memories of Cho and Pig Feet rushed back into my mind like a deluge freed from a dam.

I couldn't join in the newfound joy of the other soldiers. I saw my family everywhere: in clouds over my head, in the shapes of trees, in patterns along the dirt road. The stars at night seemed to rearrange themselves into Cho's jade hair clip or Pig Feet's bamboo basket, and the wildflowers bloomed only with the scent of her perfume. The winds howled at my back like their collective last breaths, and the snowy motes of dust in the air scattered like ash from an urn. Sometimes my thoughts became so unbearable, I wished I *had* joined the special detachment, manning some machine-gun turret and giving the Kuomintang a few good slashes of my saber. At least I would have passed from this world with a clear head.

I trudged a fair ways behind my unit. Except for Ping, who'd run back once in a while to see if I was tired, no one bothered to glance at me. In one instance, I was told to move my sleeping roll away from our unit's main camp and make room for new recruits. Many of the soldiers who shunned me were the same ones whom, less than a year ago, I had taught martial arts to and played cards with.

How easily can friends turn to strangers! How soon can they cast you aside!

By the time spring came, we were averaging twenty to thirty kilometers a day. The journey took a toll on us physically. In several instances we had to leave behind hundreds of the sick and wounded, and those new recruits I spoke of—many couldn't keep up. Teenagers who had joined because their villages had suffered from a famine found themselves stranded hundreds of kilometers away from their homes, too exhausted to continue. An elderly soldier—a teacher back at Iron Well—was abandoned by his unit and left to fend for himself after a festering wound on his leg made it too painful for him to walk.

My own calf had swollen to the size of a drum. I had ripped open the heel of my shoe, and the bottom of my feet had blistered beyond feeling. The iron links connecting the different sections of dolphin bone on my prosthetic squeaked, and I had to get the hinges oiled. On the whole, though, I was one of the lucky ones: I suffered no serious injuries, and my training as a martial artist gave me the stamina to endure pain others couldn't.

In early April, we entered into the snowy highlands bordering Sichuan, where the color of the earth changed from the familiar brown to a bloody red. It was here that what happened next became significant, at least to me. A series of strange events—strange even for those days—altered the course of my life and changed me into the man I am today.

I remember those events vividly, as though I had lived them yesterday.

39

THE ARMY HAD STOPPED ABRUPTLY within a half day's dis-
tance to the foothills of Mount Liang. Thin strips of cloud hid the highest
peaks. The land before us was a series of rolling hills with muddy swaths
of burnt grass and patches of melting snow. Just coming into view were
the pines and cypresses and banyans dotting the mountainside.

Everyone was eager to proceed into the lush new terrain and
wondered what was holding us up. Lieutenant Dao sent a runner, an
eleven-year-old recruit—one of the "Little Red Devils" who never seem
to lack energy—to check with the vanguard. When the boy came back,
he told the lieutenant that the politburo thought the area had a high
possibility of being booby-trapped. We were about fifty kilometers from
Sichuan, and there was no other way of entering the secluded province
within a week's march. Although the Nationalists didn't have enough
manpower to cover all the rocky passageways, they were likely to have
hired local warlords to bury mines.

"General Mao's asking for volunteers," the runner told Lieutenant
Dao. The boy's cheeks were red and sweaty and snot dribbled from
his nose. "Brave men who will help the army plot a path through the
scrubland."

The lieutenant turned and stared at us. Most of the platoon were
squatting around a patch of prairie, washing their faces with snow.

"Come, come, come," the lieutenant said, almost in a whisper. "None
of you have to volunteer, but I still have to ask. There's a chance the area

in front of us contains explosives. It could be nothing. How about it? Who wants this opportunity for free honor?"

There were murmurs. "No such thing as free honor," one soldier said. Another agreed, adding, "You should just assign the task to someone and be done with it." Yong stood up and was about to walk over, but Ping pulled her down.

"You're risking two lives," he said. "It's one thing to do something dangerous yourself, but don't go volunteering for heroics until Little Turnip has come into the world and has a say in his life."

"He won't be a coward like his father," Yong shot back.

She was eight or nine months into her pregnancy and prone to anger. The two argued throughout the journey, always reconciling a few hours later. Ping rested his head against a tree, but she wasn't done scolding him yet.

"And now that we've scavenged so many enemy rifles, none of us need to use your pathetic little bird guns anymore. You're almost as worthless as that one there"—she nodded toward me—"who should've been the one to drown in the milky waters of Ruijin."

"I'll let you calm down," Ping said, and walked over to me.

I was sitting a few meters from our platoon, on another patch of grass.

"Don't listen to her," Ping said, squatting down. "She gets that way when she knows I'm right. She doesn't mean anything she says." He picked at dirt beneath his fingernails. "And I don't blame her for her outbursts, either. I can't imagine walking this far with a sack of flour between my arms."

"What about some squeaking hinges as your foot?" I smiled.

"Hey, at least you never have to do any of the really dangerous stuff. If somebody said I'd lose a leg but go through this journey otherwise unscathed, I might just take that deal." He looked up at the sky as if asking heaven to make him the offer.

Many of the Third Legion's veterans had taken their turn as the first to cross a bridge or walk through a tunnel, including Ping and Yong. Much of the soldiers' conversations revolved around who had been in more danger. It was a competition of bravery, one in which I should have been included. Did they forget that I had lost a leg to a Nationalist bullet? Did Yong really believe I was worthless—I who had risked my life to save hers? Cho and Pig Feet would turn in their graves knowing that others looked upon their man in such a way.

"I will go!" I suddenly shouted, using my cane to stand up.

Passing Ping's surprised stare, I joined the rest of the unit by the other patch.

When I reached the front of the lines, Chairman Mao was peering at the foothills through a pair of rusty binoculars. His hair, combed down the middle, matched the curvature of the lenses. Other members of the politburo and their staff were standing next to him, and when I saluted the colonel in charge of our battalion, he shushed me and directed my attention to an object in the distance.

"You might not be needed at all," he whispered. "Look."

I squinted at the spot the colonel was pointing to. Although there was snow, the ground shimmered with heat. The object in question was far away, and from this distance it was nothing more than a black splotch. At first, I thought it was a rock. After a few seconds the object started to bob, and then thin threads appeared under its body, which took on the shape of legs. Finally, there was another string that swung back and forth, sculpting the form into a half-moon: the swishing of its tail.

"If nothing happens to it, you're clear."

"Why not use more pack animals?" I asked. "Why risk lives at all?"

The colonel frowned. "You think the army is a polo stable? You think we have mules and donkeys to throw at every small obstacle? Who will carry the heavy equipment up the mountains? Who will lug the artillery?"

I was a little upset at how the colonel was speaking to me. I realized he didn't know I was volunteering for the task. He probably thought I'd been assigned to it. I couldn't correct him, though. That would only make me look more foolish. I ignored him and focused my attention back on the ambling animal.

It was about halfway to an area dotted with more trees—still a few hours from the safe point, which, I guessed, was where the hills turned into mountain. The animal stopped and lay down, its legs disappearing into its torso, and sat for a long time. One by one, the members of the politburo sat on the ground, too, but the Chairman's eyes never left the binoculars. He put his weight on one foot and then the other, his knees as jittery as bells.

I took his tenacity for nervousness, for I couldn't sit, either. My stomach curdled like tofu. My mind swayed from wanting the creature to survive and then to it finding a mine. The latter outcome had the upshot of giving me a real chance to prove my worth, while the former allowed me to save my neck. In the end—and I'm not going to lie and impress upon you a false sense of bravery—I wanted the animal to succeed. Even if it reached the foothills, I reasoned, I would garner some small amount of respect from my fellow Third Legion members purely for volunteering for the mission.

It was at the moment that I reached this conclusion that the animal stood back up and, taking no more than five or six steps, found a mine. The sound it made, though muffled, startled everyone. Its tremor reached us a second later and then hissed away. The brown-pink mist lasted much longer, hovering fog-like above the earth.

Chairman Mao lowered his binoculars, consulted his assistants, and then looked over behind them at the colonel. Even though our eyes never met, I knew he was asking for me.

"Well." The colonel nodded to the Chairman. "You won't feel anything if you step on one. That's more relief than any soldier could ask for before a mission like this."

There were no detachments trained to find mines, not even among the engineers. The army did have a metal detector scavenged after a skirmish with the Kuomintang, who had gotten it from the United States. The detector itself was light, but it had to be connected to the battery of a radio pack, and that was heavy. The politburo was worried that, because of my condition, I wouldn't be able to both carry it and walk. So I strapped it over my shoulders and limped around a bit, and it seemed like the leaders were satisfied enough with my abilities, for a moment later the young comrade in charge of the device walked over, unhooked the long wand from the backpack, and put around my head a pair of sand-colored earmuffs.

"If you hear a rapid beeping like this"—he swept the flat head over the barrel of a rifle—"you place a red flag beside the spot on the ground where the noise came from. Make sure the flag's *beside* the beeping spot and not *on* it. Very important. And don't turn it on until you've reached the spot where the donkey had been. We need to conserve the battery. Go slow, but not too slow. As it is, there might not be enough power left to reach the other side. If the machine stops beeping, that means the battery has died. If this happens, you are probably close to the mountains, and you have probably arrived in a safe area. If you are still a distance from the mountainside, place a line of flags where the machine stopped working and then just move as fast as you can toward your destination. You take fewer steps the faster you move. The less steps you take, the less chance you hit a mine. Got it?"

I nodded, more to assure myself than the young comrade. It was the first time I heard the word "battery."

I was in a foreign province with a strange device strapped on my back, and I had just witnessed a donkey turn into a cloud of dust. I was very certain I was minutes away from death.

40

FOR MUCH OF THE JOURNEY I had been ready to die. I had told myself if a sniper found my forehead or a landslide swallowed me whole, I would welcome the chance to end my lonesome wanderings—as long as the agent of death was swift and painless—and return again to my wife and son. However, once such an opportunity presented itself—and presented itself in such a prolonged manner—I found it difficult to return to that mindset.

I set out in the direction of the foothills with the heavy equipment strapped to my back, the beeping earmuffs pressed tightly against my scalp, and the flat-headed wand in my hands. Using it as a cane, I followed the hoofprints, and I wanted nothing more than to regain that sense of desolation I had felt leaving Ruijin. When thoughts of Cho and Pig Feet were not enough to adequately depress me, I tried thinking about all the other misfortunes I had suffered through: the death of my parents at the hands of the Japanese, my grandfather's passing, the loss of my leg, the many days of my youth I had spent hungry and homeless . . . But reflecting on these things had the opposite effect of preparing me for death; it made me want to live. Retracing the steps of the poor donkey, whose destiny I would most likely share, I felt the unshakable certainty that the world owed me. Why should I die at the young age of twenty-eight when I didn't have a penny in my pocket or a wife who'd mourn my death or a son to carry on my name? Why were there people in the world sitting on leather chairs, gold rings on their fingers, drinking wine and smoking Indian-grown opium, while I had never owned a *mu* of land nor known the comfort of silk against my skin?

When I saw a chunk of splintered bone next to a hoofprint, I glanced back to see how far I'd walked. The army was out of sight. They were over the ridge that the politburo were standing on, and the only thing I discerned were specks of light reflecting off the General's binoculars. A few more steps, and I noticed the smell: The carcass was more intact than I had expected. The donkey must have stepped on the mine with its hind leg, for the front half of its body, severed at the torso, lay a few meters from a black crater.

I stopped, not daring to take another step. I dropped the equipment to the ground, flicked the switch to turn on the battery, and slung it over my shoulders again. And I did all this as slowly as possible. Then I held the wand above the earth in front of me. Taking small, painstaking steps, I continued forward in the direction of the foothills. The beeping remained steady, and I suddenly remembered what the young engineer had advised me—that I should go quickly—and then I started walking faster.

For a hundred or so steps I listened closely to the rhythm of the beeps, noticing no change, and I feared that maybe my ears were deceiving me. I stopped, held the wand close to the iron links on my prosthetic, and sighed with relief when the sound turned frantic and nervous. I knew again what I should be listening for.

For a hundred or so more steps there was still no change, and I began to think that perhaps the warlords allied to the Nationalists didn't have too many mines and buried only a handful before the mountain entrance—and did so more out of necessity to maintain the alliance than a desire to do serious damage to the Red Army. (This, as it turned out, was a correct assumption.)

The more the machine continued its steady beeping, the more these comforting thoughts entered my mind. After two or three hours I was almost convinced that I would come out of this mission alive. If you can believe it, I even started to daydream. I pictured the faces of those in my platoon, young and old, reaching the foothills hours after I had arrived, regarding me as one of their own again. Maybe they'd even lift me on their shoulders and give me a dried plum or two. That was usually the prize for one who'd been in danger.

I was in the middle of such reveries when I suddenly noticed that there was no longer any noise coming from the earmuffs. As the battery lost power, the sound had become fainter and fainter, and I must have walked many steps without hearing anything at all. Panic gripped me. I dropped the equipment and inserted the small red flags into the earth, as I'd been instructed, and then I looked around to see how far I'd walked.

I had gone over many imperceptibly small hills and couldn't see a human figure in any direction. Behind me, even the donkey carcass had long been out of sight. In front of me, I could make out individual pines on both sides of the mountain pass, which meant the foothills were about a half hour away. But there were no huts or roads or any indication of human activity, and the area between the scrublands and foothills, as different as the two terrains were, blended into each other seamlessly, so that I didn't have a clue at which point I was safe from the mines and in which direction I should continue walking. My view was already starting to become limited due to the increasing amount of trees, and if I continued in my current direction, I would reach a thick section of forest that did not lead directly to the mountain pass, which was ultimately where the army wanted to go. In the end, I adjusted my direction slightly to the right, aligning myself with the place where the two mountains met. I told myself I would stop walking when the forest became too impenetrable and when I had come upon some distinguishing landmark, like a boulder or rock formation, where the army would naturally pass.

As I ventured farther into the woods, the sun began to set and the terrain became bumpy with branches and roots and pebbles. I tripped a dozen times. It was obvious the earth beneath me hadn't been touched in ages, and my concern changed from being blown up by a mine to getting lost in the forest. There was no distinguishing landmark to stop at, no sign or trail or any marker pointing to a village, and if I walked any farther, I would just become more lost. I decided to head back in the direction I had come, but the stars were out and it was difficult retracing my steps. All the trees looked alike, and when I left the denser woods, every patch of grass or snow appeared familiar and foreign at the same time, and I couldn't be sure I had walked past any of them. And there was still the issue of the mines, which made me think twice about going farther back.

At last, I was too tired and hungry to continue. I found a knoll in a relatively open clearing between forest and scrub, and I took the remaining flags and stuck them on the trees around me. Then I sat down and leaned my head against the most prominent one. After munching on a chunk of stale bun and a few strings of pickled turnips, I fell asleep.

41

MY GRANDFATHER ONCE TOLD ME that being lost with no one to see your face or hear your voice was a thousand times worse than being ridiculed even by your worst enemies. I was alone in the foothills of Mount Liang for five days, and I will say this: By the end of it, I likened myself more to a beast than a man. In my days practicing martial arts, I had learned many animal forms—Tiger, Snake, Mantis, Sparrow Hawk—but none had brought me closer to nature than those few days.

The food in my backpack was gone by the next noon, and I found out quickly that eating snow only made me thirstier. By nightfall, my mouth was chapped and my stomach ached as if insects were biting my intestines. I spent the entire night balled up under the stars, sweating profusely, and if a wolf had wandered down the hills searching for a free meal, I wouldn't have had the strength to prevent it from dragging me to its den. After that, I had to start a fire if I wanted a drink, boiling icy slush in a tin cup and then using a ripped-off piece of cloth to filter out any dirt or disease.

Over the next few days I continued wandering the foothills and stepping carefully around the sections of scrubland, looking for any indication of the army or the path I had previously taken. All to no avail. From afar, I could see my destination: the point where the two mountains converged. I knew that over the precipice there was a small lake from which a stream ran down the other side, and from there Sichuan, the province fabled in *Romance of the Three Kingdoms*, a province surrounded by mountains, making it the ideal location for any retreating army.

But I couldn't reach the spot where the two mountains met. No matter how many detours I took, I always came upon an obstacle: a cliff too steep, a hill too jagged, a forest too dense. Perhaps if I had two working legs and a set of climbing gear, I might have tried reaching the top, but with the way I was, I would've never made it. A wise man once said, "If you can't scale the mountain, you can't view the plains," but in my case, it was the opposite: I had full view of the mountains but I couldn't get through the plains.

By the fourth day I was ravenous. I shifted my priority from finding the army to finding food. I knew well enough to avoid plants with milky leaves, fine hairs, or an almond scent, and I went from tree to tree, bush to bush, licking leaves until I found one that tasted neither bitter nor soapy and had tiny black spots from insects. I reasoned: If these leaves were safe enough for an ant, surely my own belly could digest them. Digest them it did, but I didn't feel any fuller. On the contrary, I felt hungrier, and it wasn't until I came across a wild peppercorn tree and ate handfuls of the young budding berries that I was able to gain a small amount of satisfaction.

(A few years ago, I went back to Sichuan on an excursion for veterans and came across the berries once more in the wild. I popped a few in my mouth, bit into them, and tried to relive that sense of satisfaction. But they weren't at all what I had remembered. Chewing them was like chewing lightning bolts: The juices were sweet and sour, and spicy enough to numb your lips.)

I had found a temporary source of nutrition, but how could a man expect to survive for long purely on berries? When night fell again, my mind wandered back to thoughts of my past and what my life would mean if I died alone on the foothills of Mount Liang. But this time I managed to transcend my early self-pity to feel a kind of egalitarian regret at not having done more for the Red Army. I had been selfish for lamenting so long on what I'd lost; there were others in the army who'd suffered even more. Loneliness, as it turned out, could turn anyone into a true believer of the Communist ideals. The Party should sponsor exercises in which young cadre members are thrown into the wild for a few days and left to fend for themselves. It would teach them more about the importance of community than any textbook on Lenin or Marx.

Five nights in the mountains and I was scolding myself for squandering much of the journey from Ruijin to Sichuan on suicidal defeatism, wasting many opportunities to talk to the new recruits and learn their histories. I vowed that if I ever made it out of the mountains I would become a new man, thinking not about myself but embracing the Communist ideals and their emphasis on living for those around you. I got down on my knees and prayed to the night sky, which shone with the yellow stripes of the Silver River and the bright egg yolk near the horizon. I offered myself completely.

To my surprise, my prayers were answered, for the next morning a band of locals on their way to dismantle the mines found me, and through a hidden cave system on the far northern edge of the mountains took me to their village, where the Red Army had been resting for days.

42

SCHOOLCHILDREN OF YOUR GENERATION KNOW the
familiar story of the Yihai Alliance: The Red Army established communications with the Yi people of Sichuan; General Liu Bocheng became
sworn blood brothers with a Yi chieftain; and the Communist army was
able to safely cross Big Dam River and establish a second base in Shaanxi,
marking the end of the Long March.

But this simple narrative, propagated by the picturesque paintings
in textbooks of soldiers waving red flags and shaking hands with the
locals—always drawn to look like you or me—hide the fact that the Yi, or
the Lolos, as they called themselves, were very different back then, and
very different from the Han majority. Their culture was influenced by
their neighbors: Tibet to the northwest, Myanmar to the southwest, and
China all around them, but the remoteness of their mountains offered
them the opportunity to develop independently as well. Their beliefs
centered around nature. They worshipped animal gods and thought
everyone had lived as some sort of creature in their previous lives.
Their attire was colorful—sparkly green shirts with gold buttons and
baggy red pants and blue shoes—and they wore elaborate headdresses
that featured bells and feathers. Their young men painted their faces
to resemble panthers or falcons, and their women had jewelry on their
eyebrows, inside their nostrils, and across their lower lips.

They resembled, for all practical purposes, people who didn't want
to be people anymore—savages—and the Nationalists had looked

down on them for this very reason. Even though they were allies, the Kuomintang refused to provide them with enough mines to secure all the mountain passes and refrained from giving them modern weaponry to fight our army. The Communist forces, on the other hand, didn't have the luxury of discrimination, and General Bocheng and the Yi chieftain became brothers through a blood ritual: killing a rooster, mixing its raw innards with vinegar, and then drinking it together. Bocheng was close to Chairman Mao, who had chosen the general to spearhead the alliance because he had been born in the province and spoke a similar dialect.

I didn't have a chance to witness this ritual personally, but on the morning when I arrived in the Lolo village, their shamans were throwing dried pig blood into the air. It was a holiday, apparently—celebrating what, I didn't know. I stuck my tongue out and lapped up the nutritious powder. I even got down on my knee and, before Ping and Yong and the rest of the platoon, started licking it off the ground.

They all laughed, having been well fed for days, but I didn't mind. I welcomed their laughter, took it as their way of saying I was one of them again. I smiled back, my mouth covered in pink dust.

"You are unsinkable, my old friend!" Lieutenant Dao said. "You have as many lives as Tin Hau, the Goddess of the Sea."

Ping walked over and lifted me up. "I'm sorry," he whispered. "I would've looked for you if I could, but I've been preoccupied."

Behind him, between a shaman and a soldier, I saw Yong. Her stomach was small and she was cradling a baby wrapped in one of his father's gray uniforms. I looked back at Ping and he turned his head away guiltily, and I asked, "When did that happen?"

"The same day we lost you," he said. "Shortly after you started walking to the mountains, we caught a Lolo spying on us." General Bocheng, he continued, managed to convince the young man that the Red Army was not his enemy. Afterward, the scout led the army to another part of the mountain, away from the mines, and up a path that wound its way to the Lolo village. Ping and the lieutenant ran through a maze of caves holding the ends of a stretcher with Yong on it. She was in labor. Ping said, "Toward the front of the lines, we passed the Chairman looking through his binoculars. I guess he was still searching for you. I wanted to help him, I really did, but we were in too much of a hurry."

"All forgotten now. Give me a few dried prunes and all will be forgiven, too."

Ping nodded. He ran over to Yong, and a moment later they came over holding a handkerchief full of goodies: walnuts, dried fruits, and peppered jerky. I must have seemed like a wolf, the way I bolted it down.

"Well, look at that," Yong said. "There's your Uncle Haiwu, Little Turnip. He's not so useless after all."

She pulled back the shirt and for the first time I saw the baby's face. He was a handsome little thing, thin, with pudgy cheeks, and looked neither like his mother nor his father. His forehead was large and oily and shone like a lit lantern. I felt honored Yong had called me his uncle, although later on I would discover that she referred to all the soldiers in the Third Legion this way. But that didn't discourage me. I came to think of him as somehow connected to my return from the wild, as my savior, and although I wasn't his only uncle, I vowed to become his best. He was, I believed, the answer to my prayers: my penance for having been so selfish and defeated, for having let my wife and son die.

Over the next few days I looked after Little Turnip more than his parents did. Ping and Yong were busy teaching the Lolos about modern weaponry and communism, and they welcomed me as their new nanny. Each morning, after Yong had fed the infant, they handed him to me, and I grew happy, seeing his shiny head in my arms. He was a quiet baby for the most part, content whenever anyone held him, an unobtrusive jewel satisfied with its place around your neck.

I changed his rags morning and night, drying them on a boulder hot from the sun. I washed him with boiled water, made sure to clean the areas between his fingers and toes, and told him all the stories I remembered from the books I had read. The other soldiers teased that I had finally found a good listener.

As a whole, they started treating me with a great deal more respect after my return. They handed me whole portions of rations, as much as any other man would receive, and saved a spot for my bedroll on level ground free from pebbles and twigs. They even gave me a new title:

Haiwu the Groundskeeper—a pun that celebrated both my minesweeping adventure and my ability to make Little Turnip smile on the rare occasions when he cried, keeping the grounds quiet.

Strapped safely inside my cushioned pack with his head resting on the back of my neck, I took him everywhere: down to the base of the mountain, where a stream flowed into a pond as clear as sky and fishermen directed skiffs using long poles; and then through the village marketplace, where local goods such as fur, herbal medicine, and chili pepper were bartered for tea, weaponry, and salt. I took him to see the Lolo puppet show, a loud affair where children ranging from three to twenty-three gathered in front of men singing operas and waving sticks with the embroidered portraits colorful animals. Although Little Turnip was asleep for most of it, whenever he opened his eyes I leaned his head forward and made him giggle by pointing to the turtles and foxes bobbing up on the stage.

During the show, an old woman, wearing a black hat the shape of a hammer, sat down next to me. She parted her arm and showed me a baby girl, her granddaughter. Smiling, she pointed to the sky and held up eight fingers. By the looks of it, her child appeared to have been eight weeks old. Then she nodded to Little Turnip and I held up one finger. She made the shape of a rabbit with her free hand, which—as I had learned the day before at the market while buying a fur cap for Little Turnip—meant well-wishes. I tried doing the same. The woman pointed to my face and then to Little Turnip's and then she made a circle around her own face. I could be wrong, but what I interpreted that as: *You two look alike.*

I was thrilled. Imagine that: Little Turnip and me, looking alike!

43

BACK AT OUR UNIT'S SPOT on the mountain, I was so moved by the whole experience, by the fact that the old Lolo woman thought Little Turnip was my son, that I stared at him until the sky got dark. He was sleeping in the cradle Ping and I had made for him from a hollowed-out tree trunk that we covered with a layer of cotton and another layer of wool. Rocking him, I tried seeing what the woman had seen, tried finding the features that made us look alike. Was it the flat, persimmon-shaped nose, or the thin eyebrows? Were our pupils the same shade of brown? Or maybe it was the way he sat on my lap, like he was going to fall over. Maybe the woman was making fun of me because we both couldn't walk like normal people.

I was concentrating so hard, I didn't even notice when Ping had returned. He squatted next to me without a sound.

"Anything wrong?" he asked.

"No," I said. "Why do you ask?"

"You're staring at him like something's wrong."

I pulled the cradle closer to me. "Today a woman in the village said we look alike. Do you see it?"

Before he could answer, a pair of arms came between us, reached inside for Little Turnip, and lifted him up.

"We've just had dinner, kung fu champ. Don't make us throw it up."

I winked, glad that Yong and I were back on familiar terms. "Behind all these wrinkles lies a handsome face," I joked. "You should know. You kissed it once."

In her arms, Little Turnip awoke and started to cry. Yong opened the top buttons of her uniform and thrust him to her breast.

"See?" she said. "You've upset him."

Ping stood up, tilting his head to get a better peek at Little Turnip's profile. "I can see it," he said. "He has a flat, square head similar to Haiwu's."

"Idiot," said Yong. "When someone spits in your face, you lick your lips and say you want some more." She turned away from both of us. "Don't you know? To the locals, we all look alike. We dress the same, we don't have stuff painted on our cheeks, and we wear normal-colored shoes. And how could you understand what the woman said, anyway? Do you speak Lolo?"

Yong seemed more annoyed than usual. I sensed that something else might be wrong.

"What's gotten into her?" I asked Ping.

He shook his head. "Bad day at the village."

Yong turned Little Turnip around and held him to her other breast.

"I can't teach them anything," she said. "I tell them we are against the landlords. They ask me, 'What is a landlord?' I tell them, 'Those who eat the best but don't work.' They say, 'You mean the old and the young?' 'No,' I say, 'landlords are those with more wealth than others who use their wealth to become more powerful.' They say, 'Such people exist?'" She scoffed. "I'm not sure if the interpreter is bad or if they really don't understand. Teaching them communism is like teaching a rooster math."

"They learn how to use a gun easy enough." Ping shrugged. "Today I even managed to show a young man how to mold iron into a long barrel."

He lay down, rested his head on a brick, and closed his eyes.

For a while, nobody said anything. I stared out at the valley below, watching the locals bring up water to each level of rice paddy. They used what we would now call an elevator method, where each villager was responsible for bringing a pail of water up only a few meters and then handing it to the next person. This was not how most peasants tended their crops back on Iron Well or Ruijin. The land in those places was bought and sold by the highest bidder, and the poorest villagers usually farmed the topmost paddies, their shoulders crumbling over time to resemble those of a gorilla.

"Maybe they don't need to be taught communism," I suggested. "Look at the scene below. It looks like they're farming as a collective, doesn't it?"

Yong shook her head vigorously. "Don't be fooled. They still have landlords, but they call them chieftains. These chieftains control how the harvests are divided. And they keep slaves, you know, like the ones from the days of the ancient emperors. These slaves are worse off than concubines or girls sold as maids. They can't buy their own freedom or marry their way out of a family, and some are treated like dogs. One chieftain had his slave's tongue cut off because he talked back too much. Just the other day, the army had to teach him a lesson on humility. After he whipped his mute slave, we stripped his headdress—his 'crown'—and pushed him into the dirt. We would've given him the full landlord treatment, but General Bocheng came to his defense and reminded us that we were all guests here and that the army's survival depended on the strength of the alliance." Yong set Little Turnip, asleep again, back inside his cradle. Then she continued in a lower voice, " 'Alliance,' they call it. The way I see it, we don't need to ally ourselves with anyone who compromises our morals."

To this day, I'm not sure if what Yong had said about the Lolos was true, although I've never known her to be a liar. I will say that everything I had personally witnessed contradicted her accounts. But then again, I didn't spend much time with the chieftains, and I wasn't capable of asking anyone whether they owned slaves. The villagers I encountered were all hardworking, neighborly, and charitable, possessing the very virtues of ideal Communist citizens. Ping's opinion was somewhere between his wife's and mine. He spent his time on Mount Liang training fighters, a whole other caste of society made up, from what I gathered, of the children of chieftains and commoners alike.

In any case, our discussion of whether the Lolos were cultured proletarians or uncouth serfs turned to the question of Little Turnip and whether he would have a pleasant childhood here. For days we had avoided discussing the topic of leaving him behind, the image of setting his crib outside a hut or handing him to a villager festering in our minds like a neglected wound. Still, we knew the subject would eventually be brought up, if not by one of us than by others in our unit.

Keeping him was out of the question; not even Chairman Mao brought his children along. Perhaps as an example for the army, he had abandoned his newborn daughter years ago to a peasant woman; then, right before the March began, he left his two-year-old son with his brother, who was, soon afterward, chased down and killed by the Kuomintang. If we tried even talking about the possibility of keeping Little Turnip, Lieutenant Dao would surely use such stories to shame us into thinking otherwise. Moreover, we could tell by his increasingly irritated glances whenever Little Turnip made a noise that he was itching to be rid of the infant and was just calculating how long after his birth could he suggest to his mother that she should abandon her newborn.

Yong was the first to hint at the subject: "How unlucky I was giving birth here: so many kilometers from Iron Well, such a distance from the heart of the revolution."

"The women here seem like good parents," I said, trying to remain positive. "Their children are fat and happy, running around the mountainside like fluffy little sheep. The men are not abusive, either. They produce puppet shows during the day. They take their youths out fishing and hunting. You see how strong they look? Perhaps Little Turnip will grow to be tall and muscular, powerful enough to wrestle a battalion all by himself."

Brushing her son's hair with her fingertips, Yong seemed to consider what I'd said. "I still don't trust them. They might be nice at first, but who knows what they'll do to him when he gets older? Sell him to a chieftain? Make him a mute? He'll be among foreign people practicing strange customs, far away from kith and kin, and he's such a quiet, smiling boy that he'll probably do anything they tell him to without complaint."

"Ping"—I kicked at his thigh with my prosthetic—"what do you say?"

Ping kept his eyes closed, but his breathing was irregular and he didn't snore. I could tell he was only pretending to sleep.

Yong gave him a kick as well. "Wake up, husband. We both want to know what you think."

He turned his body away from us.

"We're talking about your son's future," I said, a little louder. "It would be nice if you contributed a few words, acted like you cared."

At this, he shot up, the brick that had been beneath his head trembling like a turtle that had retreated into its shell.

"You think I don't care?" he said. This was one of the few times I saw him genuinely angry. "Don't forget: I grew up in an orphanage. However wicked your father was, Yong, at least you knew him. You had your grandpa, too, Haiwu, even for those brief years. I didn't know any of my family, and now I'm condemning my son to suffer the same fate. You don't know how much this has been hurting me."

Yong and I were silent. A cold wind blew up the mountain and through our camp—the last breath of winter.

"We understand *now*," I said. "But understanding doesn't provide us with any new insight on what to do."

"What *can* we do?" Ping sighed. "We don't know for sure how they'll treat him, but at least he'll be safe here, hidden from the wars in the lowlands. At least there won't be gangs fighting in the streets, like in Canton. At least we don't need to worry about a stray bullet cracking his skull or thugs robbing him at the market. This place, I think, is better than most. High up in the mountains, it's between heaven and earth, and neither Old Man in the Sky nor the devils below can take him for an early servant."

Maybe it was the appearance of the moon next to the sun, covering the red horizon like an utterly inadequate bandage, or the other soldiers in the platoon returning with the lieutenant, but there was something poetically final about Ping's words. We dropped the subject and joined our comrades around the fire.

Later that night, I had a hard time falling asleep. I got up often, glancing over at the tree trunk cradle tucked between Ping and Yong's bedrolls.

I knew I wasn't the boy's father. I wasn't even his real uncle. At some level it was foolish of me to grow so attached. But my grandfather used to say that a swan rears its young by sneaking its egg into a duck's nest, and it is the mother duck who reaps the reward when the grown-up fowl flies at the front, leading them all south for the winter.

By my own choosing, I was the mother duck, and it broke my heart to know that my swan wasn't going to fly down the mountain with me.

44

THE NEXT MORNING, WHEN PING and Yong had left for their duties, I decided to take Little Turnip up to the top of the mountain, where there was a wooden temple sculpted into the soft sandstone bedrock for the worship of the animal gods. It was rumored that an old mystic wiser than Confucius had made his home next to the temple. The locals believed he could predict the destiny of anyone worthy enough to have a destiny, and after the discussion of Little Turnip's future the previous night, I couldn't resist bringing him to the mystic's abode to get a reading.

I passed the temple opening, which was framed with the chipped carvings of different animals interlocking paws and hooves, and turned the corner to another, much smaller opening. It was partially covered by a triangular slab of decaying wood. I knocked several times but no one answered. Next to the door, a large window, roughly in the shape of an oval, opened to the outside. I smelled burning incense and heard the sound of snoring.

"Esteemed master," I called forth. "May we disturb you for a small fraction of your day?"

"Go away," a feeble voice said. "The boy is not worthy, and neither are you."

I was taken aback. How did he know I was carrying a baby? How did he know Little Turnip was a boy? In a place as remote as this, how could he speak such a fluent Han dialect? Now I *had* to talk with him.

"You are right. We are not worthy, especially me. I have discovered this recently, while alone on the foothills of your mythic mountain. This is the very reason I must speak with you, wise one: to teach me and the boy how to become worthy of a destiny. Your reputation is without equal. They say you have attained a wisdom beyond those found in the *Dialects of Confucius* or the *Histories of Sima Qian*. Can you not provide us with the charity of an hour of dialogue?"

I heard the rustling of straw and then the approach of light steps. The door cracked open and a bald head protruded forth from one side of the triangle. The wrinkled wise master looked me up and down. I smiled, put my hands together, and bowed.

"Here's some advice: Mentioning a few over-read books won't impress anyone. Neither will flattery. Go away. I don't have many days left in this world. I won't spend even a portion of one with the likes of you."

He slammed the door shut, sending Little Turnip into a fit of crying.

From my extensive reading of the classics, I knew the master's actions were a test. The wisest sages often feigned disinterest as a means of determining merit.

I wasn't going to fail. After getting Little Turnip to settle down, I leaned my backpack with him inside it against the wall of the abode and carefully extended my prosthetic and leg through the window. Then I reached for the backpack and lifted Little Turnip up and over.

The inside was sparsely furnished. There was a stone stove, a long piece of varnished wood piled from end to end with scrolls, and a miniature shrine with the watercolors of two other bald men, presumably the mystic's ancestors. The incense had the strong spicy odor of ground black pepper, and it curled up around their faces like a pair of growing mustaches.

The mystic slept on a pile of hay in the corner farthest from the window. When I stepped closer, he turned over so that he faced me, not appearing the least bit surprised.

"The fool sees wine when there is only water." He sat up. "You are a bigger fool than I first predicted."

I placed my backpack underneath me and put Little Turnip on my lap. "When one looks down upon the world from a tower as high as clouds, men and ants are the same size."

He laughed. "You've got a clever tongue. Almost makes up for your missing leg." He squinted, trying, I imagined, to see if I was angry. "Tell me, did you also lose your parents when you lost that leg?" He paused. "Or was it your wife?"

I tried to remain stoic, but a twitch or a blink must have given me away.

"Ah, so it was your wife," he said, laughing again. "And that boy between your legs, he isn't yours, is he? But you treat him as your own, because like all weak men you need a purpose to keep on living. And you come to me believing that purpose is the same thing as destiny, even though in your heart you know that is not true. Your purpose, that thing between your legs, is a temporary one, and you are afraid that very soon you will have to part with it, and that when that day comes you will be left as you once were, when your wife died, purposeless." He rubbed his belly, satisfied with his deductions. "Well, here is your reading: It is true you will have to part with the boy. After all, you cannot carry him to war. Your army will not allow it. And you will feel very much the way you did before. But there is some relief to all this." He leaned in, his nostrils flaring and his head shining with sunlight. "The relief is: None of it will matter. People will kill each other, society will crumble, and you will lose this boy. You will lose him, but he will not be lost. He will live a life without destiny just as you have lived a life without destiny, and those without destiny cannot attain destiny; they need to settle for purpose. When one has purpose but not destiny, he cannot be truly lost, for he was never found."

The mystic's words, of course, were not the ones I wanted to hear. I had hoped he would have foreseen a great future for Little Turnip, one full of triumph and fortune. What did he mean when he said one can have purpose but not destiny? How could he tell?

"Destiny?" I asked. "Is it similar to fate? Or is it more like a calling, like a prince who knows he will be king?"

The mystic ground his teeth impatiently. "Destiny is destiny. You either know it or you don't. I can't define something that doesn't exist in your heart. Can you explain pants to a fish? What about paper to the sky?" Suddenly his eyes grew kind. "Do not be troubled that you are without a destiny. Most people are. I am as well. That is why I cannot define it for you. It is nothing. It is better this way. Once you've realized it is better this way—and it is beyond my powers to predict if you'll ever attain such insight—you will lose that burning feeling in the pit of your belly, which is ultimately what you should truly fear in this life, and not the false loss of a child who is not your own."

The way the mystic's words and expression turned kindly angered me. Who was he to tell me what I should fear? Who was he to say that Little Turnip and I would be without a destiny when he couldn't even define what that meant? I suddenly remembered the vow I had taken on the foothills—to live for others—and then this old man before me, who suggested that I should lose all hope and be happy with it, became very small in my eyes.

He seemed to read my mind, for what he said next was more surprising than anything he had uttered before.

"Yes," he said. "That is the way you should feel. You regard me with contempt because you *should* regard me with contempt. You should regard the world with contempt! You are not at fault for being without a destiny. The world is at fault for being mean and meager and not providing one for you." He touched his throat. Talking so much and so fast, it seemed, was causing him pain. But he continued: "Now, some might say that it is petty for one to place blame on the world and not on oneself, and I say to them, 'You are petty for thinking others petty!' It is the fortunate who cannot stand or understand the laments of the unfortunate. It is a lie they perpetuate to make the unfortunate blame themselves and not the world. But here is what the world really is: A place of beauty, sure, but also one of cruelty, and you should regard it with equal parts awe and contempt."

A bird flew into the room and landed near a nook in the ceiling. From the nest came forth eager chirping.

The mystic glanced in the direction of the nook, raised his eyebrows, and said, "The animals know this truth. They fear being eaten and they fear hunger. As soon as they are born, they are suspicious of this world."

I remained quiet for a while longer, waiting to see if he was finished. By this point my anger had subsided and I had come to the conclusion that what the old mystic said about the fortunate and unfortunate was, in some ways, not so dissimilar from what the army tried teaching us, though I didn't understand how it had to do with destiny and purpose. The reading also, to my disappointment, gave no advice on Little Turnip's future or his safety here with the Lolos. Still, however convoluted the mystic's words were, they had the effect of calming me, at least for a little while, and I told myself that an easy mind was the only thing a sage could truly offer.

I stared at Little Turnip sleeping in my lap. His serene eyebrows and fleshy cheeks seemed to say that he was going to be fine wherever he was. I was being selfish. Wanting him with the army was more for my benefit than his own; he would feel no sadness when we parted, and children are more adaptable than we give them credit for.

When I looked up, the mystic was lying on his side again, his face toward the wall. I reached into my pocket and dropped a few pieces of copper. Then I hurried down the mountain, trying to return to the village before nightfall. The leaders were making an announcement that afternoon, one that might impact the direction of the army in the days to come.

45

THE ANNOUNCEMENT TOOK PLACE ON the same platform
the Lolos put on their animal shows. The scaffold was dressed up in
crinkly red paper, illuminated by festive red lanterns, and flanked by
a pair of long spears supporting red windswept banners. Given by
Chairman Mao and General Bocheng and other members of the politburo,
the announcement spoke of courage, determination, and righteousness;
it read out the names of soldiers, both present and deceased, who had
taken part in heroic deeds since the last announcement. (My name was
mentioned.) To bolster courage, it listed the number of machine guns,
grenades, sabers, and pack animals we still had and it presented a map
of the route we had taken, indicating the number of kilometers we had
traveled. Finally, it revealed the news we were all afraid of: our eventual
departure from Mount Liang. Our location wasn't going to remain a
secret forever, and we had to be one step ahead of the Nationalists. We
could be moving out in as little as two days.

Hearing the nearness of the date, Ping dabbed his eyes with the ends
of his sleeves. Yong searched the crowd, looking for me. I had arrived
late and for an instant I hoped she wouldn't be able to find me. For the
briefest, faintest of moments, I considered disappearing into the crowds
and going down to the foothills so that I could take care of Little Turnip
all by myself. But she was a talented sniper and her eyes were as sharp
as a hawk's, and she stormed over faster than it took me to swing my
backpack around.

"Where were you all afternoon?" she asked.

"Nowhere," I said, embarrassed by my own superstition. "It doesn't matter."

"You really shouldn't be carrying him around like this so much. What if you tripped and fell? What if you dropped him?" She pulled Little Turnip out of my pack, scanning him for injuries.

"You could say thank you. Thank you for changing his rags. Thank you for washing him. Thank you for being the kindest uncle the world has known. Try it. Practice it." I debated whether I should say what I was going to say next. "You'll be needing to say it to a stranger soon."

It took her a second to catch my meaning. Then, without a word, without so much as a glare, she walked back over to Ping.

Squatting in a corner away from the others, I ate dinner alone, much as I had done for most of the Long March. I offered only a cold nod to the comrades who came over and congratulated me for having been mentioned by the leaders. My belly full, I didn't know what to do with myself. I was still ashamed for what I'd said to Yong, but I couldn't stand being away from Little Turnip for too long, especially since we had only a few days left together. In the end, I swallowed my pride, hobbled over to Yong's and Ping's bedrolls, and tried putting on a smile.

"I'm sorry about what I said—" I began.

"Haiwu," Yong interrupted me, and waved me closer. "You're just the person I wanted to see. I'm having trouble pinning his rags together. I think the pins are bent. Can you help?"

She held up the pins between her fingers, her expression kind and generous, not at all what I'd been used to.

I knelt down, scooted next to Little Turnip, and inserted the pins through the different layers of rags.

"They're bent on purpose," I said, "to poke through as many sheets of cloth as possible."

Ping squatted next to me. "You've done this more times than the two of us combined. Where would we be without you?"

"Pride" would be the wrong word to describe how I felt. "Pride" would imply that I had something to be proud of, and I knew they were only feigning ignorance.

I covered Little Turnip's legs with his quilt and shook my head. "Where would *I* be without *him*?"

There were many preparations to make before the army's departure, but from now on Ping and Yong tried to accomplish as much as possible without having to leave behind Little Turnip. Yong carried him to the communal cave beside the waterfall, where she bid farewell to the Lolos she'd tried teaching. Later, she nursed him in front of a whole company of muscular tattooed fighters as Ping distributed the final batch of used rifles. After reporting to General Bocheng that they had completed their duties with the locals, Yong held Little Turnip next to the general and he puked on the general's shirt. They cleaned the vomit off, embarrassed by the leftover streaks of white, which—I'm sure this was in all our minds—had come from Yong's breasts. I liked to think that the little rascal threw up because he wasn't used to his mother's efficient strides and preferred his uncle's bobbing steps, a motion that mimicked being rocked in his cradle. His parents let me tag along for all these events, saying that I had a calming effect on the boy, even though I could tell they would've preferred being alone with him, and that they were merely tolerating my presence like cattle tolerating egrets pecking insects off their backs.

I remember those last days on Mount Liang with fondness, but as the old mystic had predicted, such days wouldn't last, and soon there'd come a time when we couldn't put off the inevitable. That time came in the form of another announcement: Lieutenant Dao telling the platoon the army was leaving the village the next evening, as soon as the sun had set, and that we'd be crossing into Sichuan under cover of darkness.

He called Ping and Yong over, and although I wasn't officially part of the conversation, I was pacing close enough to hear it all.

"Now, I don't know if the two of you have been looking or have already found somebody," he said, "but if you haven't, I know a woman who would take in your child. She lives around the middle terrace of the mountain, next to good fields, and has an infant of her own, just a few months older than your boy. She says she doesn't mind the trouble, says that taking care of two babies is not much different from taking care of one. I could introduce you."

There was a long pause. Biting her lip, Yong looked away.

Ping asked, "How did you find her?"

"Last year she lost her husband in a landslide. She was one of the 'upright unfortunates' the other villagers singled out for special treatment. Depending on their level of misfortune, the Party gave them tools or seeds or silver."

"What level of misfortune is this woman?" Ping asked.

"We gave her all three."

"Being so poor, how can she feed another child?"

"She'll feed him from her own breasts." The lieutenant glanced at Yong, but she still wouldn't look at him. "As I said before, to her, raising two is no different from raising one."

"Until they grow up," Yong whispered. "When they only have one bowl of rice, who do you think the woman will give it to?"

"She'll care for yours enough if she suckles him. And he will earn his keep when he gets older. He will help out in the fields, along with his older brother, and they'll live as one family."

"I don't know any woman who loves another child equal to her own," Yong said.

"You can't expect the impossible." The lieutenant turned to me, his expression annoyed, his arms crossed. I couldn't tell if he wanted me to come over to support him or if he was simply wondering why I was walking back and forth like a madman. "Anyway, describing her like this is useless," he said. "Meet her. Talk with her." He put a hand on Yong's shoulder. "It will just be for a few years. When the war is won—or perhaps even earlier, when the army has settled down again—you can come back and get him."

Yong sucked in her lower lip, which was bleeding now, and played with the buttons on her uniform. Then she gave the lieutenant a weak nod.

"Tomorrow morning, then?" Ping asked.

Next to him, a soldier tripped on a bandolier. The lieutenant became momentarily distracted. The entire camp, in fact, was messy, with half-packed provisions, canteens, uniforms, and firewood thrown about.

"Who left that there?" the lieutenant yelled. "Clean it up!" Then, impatiently, he turned back to Ping. "Tomorrow morning. At dawn. Bring everything. All his belongings."

I couldn't bear hearing about Little Turnip's departure any longer—couldn't bear seeing him and knowing that we'd part in the morning—so I decided to try and keep my distance for the night. I had dinner by myself again and afterward got ready to take a walk along the mountainside. But before I could, Yong ran over and asked if I could help her with something.

"We want you to write a letter," she said, "for when he gets older. You're the best writer we know."

A part of me was thrilled to get the chance to spend more time with the boy, but I continued fighting the urge to become more attached.

"It's better coming from you and Ping," I said, a poor excuse.

"It will be from us, though. You can add whatever you want. We will just—what is the word?—dictate our thoughts to you."

"What good will it do? The Lolos can't read our language. They can't teach him, either. In all likelihood you will have him back before his fifth birthday, so it probably won't be read. It will be a piece of paper with symbols no one around will understand, written for one who might not even need to read it."

"Just in case," Yong said, trying to smile.

I shook my head.

"It will make me feel better, knowing he has a few words from his mother." She leaned in and kissed me on the cheek.

And so I found myself composing a letter by candlelight with Ping and Yong looking over my shoulder, surrounded by the soft snores of our comrades. Paper was scarce at the time. We had to use the clean side of a dispatch memo the colonel had given the lieutenant, crossing out revised instructions on preventing the loss of equipment.

"Remember," Yong said. "You can add anything you want, but no big words. I don't want my son thinking his parents are arrogant aristocrats."

"You don't need to worry," I said, and then began taking their dictation:

Dear Little Turnip,

> *If you are reading this, then either we have failed to create a better world for you or we have been killed trying to do so. You will live here with these people if it's safe, or you can try going down the mountain to be among your own.*
>
> *This is your mother. She wants you to know that you are the son of heroes, which means that you are also a hero. There isn't enough space here to talk about the details of the better world, but know that it is a paradise for the poor and a place worth sacrificing yourself for. If you are able to continue the fight, do so.*
>
> *This is your father now. He wants to tell you that he grew up just like you, without his parents. He didn't want to part with you, but at least with this letter you know who your parents are and have a few words from them. Try to be a good person. If you do things you're not proud of, they sit in your mind and stay with you forever. Try to avoid that.*

They were finished with their parts, and I hesitated for a moment, glancing over at Little Turnip sleeping in his crib, before beginning my section. I read it out loud for them to hear:

> *And this is your uncle Haiwu, the least important person of the three. He took care of you during your first week in this world, and even though he's not your relative, he cares about you very much. He has no advice to give you, because it's not his place. All he can say is that life*

is an adventure, and you will pass through it and become lost in it no matter what choices you make.

Signed,
Mother, Father, and Uncle

When the letter was finished, we folded it in half twice and inserted it into the pocket of Ping's shirt, on which Little Turnip had been born. There were things in the letter all of us wanted to change, but we didn't have the space to make corrections, and blackening out too many words caused the thin paper to tear.

In my bedroll, I found myself more attached to the boy than ever, unable, as the mystic suggested, to let it not matter.

46

OF COURSE, THE LOSS OF my first wife and son had been more devastating than the loss of Little Turnip. Of course, compared to what I had suffered at Ruijin, my distress on Mount Liang was minor, a scrape on the knee. I'm surprised you'd even compare the two. I'm telling you this story because I thought it was the one you wanted to hear. Are you or are you not interviewing me because of our mutual friends? Are you or are you not writing an article about them and not me? I'm not offended. They're big shots in the Party, so naturally readers will be more interested to learn about them than some minor soldier who was on the Long March. That is the reason I am obsessing over the details of Little Turnip's departure, because they are important to your work. I am trying to tell you that his loss, at the time, affected me deeply, almost equally, I suspect, to what his parents felt. You already know how this would all end, but you would be surprised by how differently things could've turned out if I had made a couple of different choices.

Anyway, the last morning on the mountain proved a busy one for both the army and the villagers. The marketplace clamored with soldiers making last-minute purchases. A line of fully saddled donkeys and mules rattled down the narrow road, stretching from valley to peak. And the Lolos' theater troupe played their horns and drums and cymbals inside a cave that acted as a loudspeaker. Half the mountainside heard their tunes, which sent off their new allies with what they considered to be the appropriate amount of pomp and spirit.

Accompanied by their mock-courageous songs, the three of us followed Lieutenant Dao and an interpreter some distance down the mountain. The latter was a gray-haired Lolo leader who often traveled to other parts of the country to barter. He was dressed in army attire—probably gotten from a trade—although the striped turban on his head gave him away. We turned into the terrace where the woman's hut would be, and Ping remarked that these homes looked cozy and rustic with their thick red beams for walls and their strings of chili peppers sunning outside their doors.

"The woman's home won't look like these," Yong said, wiping dirt from Little Turnip's cheek. "Or did you forget she's part of the highest level of misfortune?"

Indeed, the woman's hut was the smallest one in view: The walls were five logs high. Most of her neighbors had ten or twelve. Flat stones lay on her roof, preventing the shingles from sliding down or being blown away. Her neighbors didn't require these stones; between their shingles was some kind of hardened putty. Smoke the scent of rabbit meat rose out of a hole in her ceiling.

The lieutenant gave the door three hard pats.

The woman who came out wore a black vest with red sleeves and a pair of brown pants with enough dust on them to make a mouse sneeze. On her head was the same type of hammer-shaped hat that the woman at the puppet show had worn. At first I almost thought she was the same person, but underneath the dark attire was a young, smooth face. She was in her early twenties, by my estimate, and she held a baby dressed in fur, its forehead covered by a hood with whiskers for brows and fake catlike ears.

The interpreter was the first to approach. He introduced the lieutenant but did not gesture toward the rest of us. The woman shook her head and replied.

"She says she doesn't have anything to trade," the interpreter said.

"No, we're not here for that. Doesn't she remember me from the rally? I was the one who handed her those two silver coins, the seeds, and the newly polished spade." Lieutenant Dao made a plowing motion.

The interpreter translated the lieutenant's message. The woman narrowed her eyes and then, as if a veil had been lifted, smiled broadly. She said something else to the interpreter, who now gestured toward the three of us standing behind the lieutenant. The woman peered at Little Turnip in Yong's arms and then waved for her to come closer. Yong drew back, wrapping the sheets around her son tighter.

"Now that I've seen her, I don't like her," she said.

Trying to hold on to her smile, the woman turned to the interpreter, who looked to the lieutenant. Dao shook his head, and we all stood there awkwardly for as long as it takes an earthworm to cross a road.

"I have ten thousand other things to do, Private," the lieutenant said to Yong. "Burning Leopard is a chieftain, and he has ten thousand other things to do as well. Unless you know another option, you need to hand over your son now."

"What if I stayed?" Yong said. "That's an option."

"Stop this nonsense. Ping"—the lieutenant pointed to Yong's husband—"tell your wife she's wasting all of our time."

The gunmaker remained frozen as if he were one of his own bullets that had stopped midair, refusing to find its target. I looked from one friend to another, hopeful that something might come out of their determination.

"That's right," Yong said, her head tilted. "Little Turnip and I, we're a package. Either we both stay here or we both go with the army."

The lieutenant laughed. "I don't believe you," he said. "Another female, maybe. But the cause is too important. You believe in what we're fighting for more than anyone else I know. You're the most decorated soldier in our unit. I mean, the hero of Ji'an, suddenly a Lolo rice farmer? Who are you trying to fool?"

"I may be all those things, but if I can stay with him, I'll settle for just being a mother."

The lieutenant paced back and forth, so angry he was at a loss for words. The woman seemed to have figured out what was going on. She scooted next to Yong, their arms close enough for their baby's heads to touch. With her free hand she pointed to Little Turnip and then to her own child, and when Yong ignored her, she extended her arms, offering

Yong her baby. It was as if she was saying: *Let's switch for moment. I trust you. Do you trust me?*

"You see now the kind of woman she is?" the lieutenant pleaded. "She's doing you the biggest favor anyone can expect of a stranger, and *she's* the one who's trying to make *you* feel better."

Ping whispered something into his wife's ear. Afterward he reached into Yong's arms and held up Little Turnip. He then transferred his son to the woman and transferred the woman's baby to his wife's arms. Crying, Yong held on to the strange baby, a bundle of fur that resembled a bear cub more than it did a human infant. I was holding Little Turnip's cradle and, without asking, the lieutenant took it from me and laid it next to the woman's feet. The woman put Little Turnip inside, covered him with his blankets, and took her own son from Yong. When the ball of fur was with his mother again, Ping handed the woman the letter.

"For when he gets older," he said to the interpreter.

The woman bowed and we turned to leave.

After a few steps, Yong glanced back at the woman, staring at Little Turnip by her feet. The woman smiled and raised her hand. Her pinky and index finger pointed to the sky, her thumb and middle finger pressed together in the shape of a snout.

47

ALTHOUGH YONG'S BRIEF STANDOFF ENDED in defeat, it did give me an idea. The lieutenant was right: She couldn't stay. She was too important a soldier, she was too invested in the revolution, and she hated the Lolos. But what was preventing *me* from staying? I hardly mattered as a soldier anymore; I wasn't as well versed in Marxism; and I thought of the locals as a community of good parents, more or less. *I could be happy here,* I thought. My time alone in the foothills, and with it, my fondness for Little Turnip, had given me a sense of purpose. I could live with the old mystic at the top of the mountain, grow as wise as he had, all while checking up on the boy and making sure he didn't get sold into slavery. Perhaps I could even help out the woman in her fields; she was a poor widow, after all. Perhaps, with time, we could share more than our mutual love for Little Turnip and raise a family together.

While the rest of my unit was making their final preparations that afternoon—Ping trying to console Yong and Yong telling him she didn't require any consoling—I trudged up to the top of the mountain to see if I could persuade the mystic to let me stay with him. It would be difficult, I knew, but I had convinced him to give me a reading when he had wished to be alone, and I was confident he would relent if I pestered him enough. It was even possible he wanted a disciple. I remembered him talking vaguely about not knowing whether I would attain the peace that came with being without a destiny, and that sounded like a challenge he was preparing himself for. Maybe he had already predicted my return and had gathered another pile of hay inside his cave next to his own.

Reaching the triangular door, I didn't bother knocking. I came in as confident as a rooster, proclaiming, "Master! I am back!"

The old mystic was kneeling in front of the two portraits. He had a stick of incense in his hands and he was naked from head to foot.

"What are you doing in here? Get out!"

"Why are you praying naked?" I asked.

"It is best to lay yourself bare when addressing your ancestors. Now, get out!"

I thought about what I should say. I was amused, and I wanted very much to laugh, but sniggering at your master wasn't the most appropriate thing for an aspiring disciple to do, so I started taking off my clothes as well.

"It is something you must teach me," I said. "I have come here to be your humble servant. How can I be clothed while my master is naked? How can I stand while my master kneels?" Fully undressed, I knelt down next to him.

The mystic's mouth was agape, his eyes wide with bewilderment. "No, no, no. You have to leave right now."

"I won't." I kowtowed to his ancestors, keeping my head on the ground.

He tried pulling me up by my shoulders, but I was stronger than he was, and I needed to show him my resilience and dedication.

"Young man," he said, panting, "what can I do for you? I'll do anything, but you can't stay here."

From the corner of my eye I saw him reach for his rags, and when I righted myself again, he was dressed and sitting cross-legged on his bed. Fanning himself with a large dried leaf, he had regained his composure and was staring at me with eyes as sharp as a king's blade.

I remained kneeling and shifted my ankle to face him. "I apologize, Master, but the only reason I am here is to become your disciple. Your words the other day have affected me deeply, and I must stay until I fully understand them."

The mystic quickened the pace of his fanning, his eyes never leaving mine. They were a fierce snowstorm blowing away the outer shells of my cocoon. They were needles untangling the garment of my existence. After a few minutes, they had done their job, and suddenly he closed them. When he opened them again, he had a smile on his face.

"You will die here if you stay," he said. "Not in the painless, serene way in which your wife died. You will suffer like the ways of old executions, through ten thousand cuts."

"I am ready to suffer," I said.

"Were you ready to suffer when your wife died?" He crossed his arms. "You should have died with her, you know. That would have been what a brave man without a destiny would have done: given his life for his purpose. But you're not a brave one, are you? Far from it! Your entire life, you've acted with a cowardice that would shame even a toad."

"I've taken a bullet for a comrade," I said, keeping my body stiff, trying not to let his words anger me. "I've walked through a valley infested with mines."

"Your cowardly nature suits you, since you're surrounded by cowards." He started fanning himself again, slowly this time, letting his words linger, blowing them into my face. "Your army is one of cowards and criminals. The comrade you saved was a coward, too."

My eyes twitched. A surge ran down my neck and through my spine. I felt a chill on my missing leg. It started hurting again, as if it were still there, and I felt myself reliving the moment when the bullet had pierced the bone.

"Yes," he said. "You've been surrounded by cowards your entire life. You were raised by cowards, your children will be cowards, and the society you'll find yourself in will be run by cowards." He ran his tongue around his lips, cleaning the foam from them. "Even that wife of yours, some whore your army picked up on the road—she was a coward, too. Am I right?"

Upon hearing this last insult, I couldn't control myself anymore. I leapt at him with a speed that would have surprised even the version of me with both my feet. I started punching him. I pulled his ears to get a clear shot at the other side of his face, and I cuffed him across his temple. In the back of my mind, I knew he had said those things to get this response out of me, but I kept punching him all the same. When I got tired of hitting him, I unlatched my prosthetic and clubbed it across his cheek. And the little man made no sound the entire time, and for a moment, after gaining control of myself again, I became alert to the fact that I might have killed him, and then I started to shake. I got off him. I hopped around in front of his body, glanced at it, looked around to see if there was an herbal kit. Feeling sweat dripping down my back, I slapped myself, called myself a fool, and collapsed on the other side of the room, sliding down the cold, jagged wall.

Finally, there came a groan.

"So you've practiced martial arts." He tried to laugh. "I should've foreseen that."

I went over and helped him up.

"Bring me a cup of water." He nodded to the window.

Below it was a wok resting on a stack of bricks above a pile of ash. I ladled a cupful of water and returned to him. Wiping the blood from his nose, I brought the cup to his lips.

"This is what happens when you can't put away purpose," he said. "I wasn't lying when I said you'll die here if you stayed. Do you believe me now?"

I nodded and then exhaled.

"Young man." He brought my head very close to his, and I saw the bruises and scars I had made, his eyes swollen and small and purple. "The boy doesn't need you. Neither does the family caring for him. I, certainly, do not need you. You will not find happiness here. I see it now: You will never attain the wisdom of the joy of one without a destiny. You have to go with your army and seek out another purpose. And you will. For someone like you, it's impossible that you won't."

48

AND SO I HURRIED DOWN the mountain and rejoined my unit just as they were walking under the garrisoned gate of the Lolos. I marched behind Ping and Yong and Lieutenant Dao and, along with the rest of the Communist First Army, traveled another thousand miles until we reached Yan'an. There were no other major battles, nothing that compared to the crossing of Xiang River, and although we lost many good soldiers in the marshy flatlands of Tibet and the army made a big deal out of the victory at the Luding Bridge—which was, in truth, a trivial and easy skirmish—the interesting parts of the March, at least for me, had already passed.

But you know the rest of the story. You're not here for that. You're a chronicler of the children lost on the Long March. Chairman Mao never found his son nor his daughter, and my friends and I have never found our Little Turnip, though not from a lack of trying.

After the end of the revolution, the veterans' retreat to Sichuan yielded few clues. The population of the area had been greatly reduced. The woman, Little Turnip's caretaker, was gone; her house was replaced by another, more modern one, and much of the hillsides were partitioned and bulldozed. The lake between the mountains had been drained, the water diverted to a nearby dam. There were much fewer trees—most had been cut down during the Great Leap Forward to produce paper or firewood—and stumps littered the foothills of Mount Liang like so many scalped heads. I was lucky to have found a young peppercorn that day. I don't think anyone could get lost there anymore.

The only people who knew anything about what had happened to the missing locals were the chiefs and their sons. They spoke of a massive famine during the years following the Japanese invasion. At the Yihai Alliance, the Red Army had introduced opium, and many chieftains went back to their mountains and set aside as much as two-thirds of their terraces to the production of the cash crop. Then the cruelest winter of the last century ravaged the area in '43. Little Turnip must have been fourteen or fifteen. That year the Lolos left the mountainside by the hundreds. Some had relatives in nearby mountains. Others traveled to Chongqing or Chengdu to find work. The poorest joined the beggars' guild, which preyed on destitute areas for new recruits. Children were the most desirable: They had the most energy, garnered the most sympathy, and could endure the most suffering. A child missing an arm sitting on a city avenue could expect to make as much as a man with a factory job. Someone like Little Turnip, a boy far from his parents, hungry and cold, could easily be lured by a cunning recruiter with the promise of a soft bed and candied hawthorn. Afterward he belonged to the man, who would beat him and torture him and mutilate him, all for the purpose of making him look pathetic enough for the streets.

At least, this is what Ping and Yong have told me. They've done much more research than I have. They've gone back to Sichuan many times since the liberation of the Mainland in 1949. Each time they returned, they told me about their new leads: One year they found the headquarters of the Sichuan beggars' guild; the next, they tracked down an old crook who had been responsible for selling boys to the Japanese as servants. They've used all their leverage, which is considerable, given their prominence in the Party, to detain and question suspects, but their labors so far have produced only rumor after rumor. I'm sure they'll tell you all about it during your interview with them. For the last twenty years it has become their obsession. No, it is their purpose.

I've tried to persuade them to let go. "It doesn't matter if you find him," I said. "He might not have joined the beggars' guild at all. He might have found work in a nearby city. He might have married a girl below the mountains and joined their village. Whatever the case, he will live his life and be on his adventure regardless of whether you find him. Seeing him is more for *your* benefit than it is for *his*."

But then they told me something else: Little Turnip was the only child they'd ever have. During the last days of the March, Yong had suffered an injury on a reconnaissance mission: a cut along her abdomen after crawling through barbed wire. At the time, the wound appeared to have been minor. Years later, the doctors reexamined the scar and told her she couldn't become pregnant again.

Since learning this last detail, I've stopped telling them to give up. In fact, I've done all I could to support their search, including agreeing to do this interview. I've grown compassionate to their plight, sensitive to their situation. During the holidays, I don't bring my family around. I bring them to the gatherings of other Third Legion comrades, but not theirs. They don't say anything, of course, but I can tell they don't like seeing my children. Their house is a somber one. It used to belong to a Kuomintang general, and Chairman Mao saw to it personally that the mansion was given to them. All that space and nobody to fill it. They have couches from Poland, lamps from Germany, and jeweled eggs from Moscow. Yet, every time I walk by, it is as quiet as a mausoleum. Even the willows flanking their front door remain barren longer than those of their neighbors, the leaves not coming in until late spring.

Strange, isn't it, the way the world divides its bounty? I looked up to Ping and Yong, adored them, admired them—coveted them—for the first half of our friendship, and while they are still ahead of me in terms of position and power, I have prospered in other ways. My oldest has been married for two years now. A big wedding, attended by a number of former politburo members. My daughter-in-law is a beautiful girl, very fair, and from a good working-class family. She's due any day now. The doctors say it will be a boy—a little rascal for his grandfather to pass down his martial arts to! I hope I'll still be strong and healthy when he grows up. My body isn't what it used to be, and I forget things more often now.

Please give Ping and Yong my warmest regards. Tell them I think about them often. Almost every day my mind wanders back to our years together. I want to ask them to become god-grandparents to my grandson. I feel it will give them peace.

But I am afraid to bring up the subject. Perhaps you can ask for me?

PART IV

ESCAPE

49

1943

THE RABBIT CRAWLED INTO A hole. Little Mushroom placed a stone over it. He knew where the other openings were. The warren ran through rows of red and yellow poppy flowers and separated in two directions, coming out of mounds on opposite ends of the field. He leapt to the closer one, his legs poking between leafy shoots like needles on a quilt. He kept his eyes on the farther mound as he held another stone over the closer opening. He couldn't place the rock over the mound just yet. If the rabbit saw the light disappear, it would dash to the other opening immediately. He had to wait until the creature was close, until it had expended its energy, until the dirt near the mound started to shift and a screeching could be heard.

Sure enough, moments later a nose peeked into the sunlight. He didn't reach inside to grab it as he had done when he was little. He was eleven now, and he had learned enough from his failures to understand that this was what the rabbit wanted: Its twitching nose was bait, made just alluring enough for the thin arms of its predator to reach inside and struggle for it, giving it enough time to escape out the other end.

No, he waited until its ears sprang up around the corners of the tunnel. When its beady red eyes glanced up at him, the rabbit tried pushing itself back inside, but its retreat was slow, hindered by the need to rearrange its ears. Now he dropped the stone on top and sprinted for the final mound. The rabbit wouldn't be stuck for long. At the last opening, he squatted down and wiped sweat off his forehead with the back of his hand. Then he reached into a bush, took out a net with a bamboo handle, and waited.

Half an hour later, walking out of the poppy field with the net sagging under his arm, he tried to decide whether to bring the rabbit home or sell it whole at the marketplace. He would get more out of the creature if he skinned it, roasted the meat, and simmered the bones in a stew. The tannery paid almost as much for skins as the butcher did a whole rabbit, but bringing it home meant sharing it with his brother, Lucky Sheep, and his fake mother, A-ma, who would no doubt place a meaty hind leg in front of the monkey mural as an offering to her dead husband.

And why should *he* have any part of something that Little Mushroom caught? Monkey Father didn't want him for an heir. A-ma and the rest of the village made sure to remind him. Anytime anyone uttered his name he was reminded: Little Mushroom. He was taller and leaner than the other villagers, and his skin was as pale as candle wax, but none of these things stopped them from calling him names. To those who belonged there, he was a brown umbrella in a field of green sprouts. He was a rough mole on a smooth face. He was something unwanted, something dirty. A foreign leech.

He walked through the tall grass at the edge of the field. The market was up the hill. He weaved in and out of the mountain mist, passing women who carried clay grocery pots on their heads. The setting sun shimmered a dizzying red on the bamboo roofs of the storefront. Seeing the butcher throw a slab of fatty pork to his dog, Little Mushroom suddenly didn't want to sell him the rabbit anymore. A-ma, despite her intermittent cruelty, was still the woman who took care of him, and Lucky Sheep was still his best and perhaps only friend. None of them had eaten meat in over a month.

"Got anything for me today, boy?" the butcher yelled.

Little Mushroom shook his head.

"What about that in your net?"

"Turnips."

He turned and walked down the road. In any case, he figured, A-ma knew people at the market. She would find out if he'd sold a rabbit. Sooner or later he'd have to share. And it would be better to get some goodwill out of his bounty than a beating.

50

HE PARTED THE DOORWAY OF dried pepper strings and threw the net toward the center of the room. He was aiming for the stove, but the rabbit spun on the ground and toppled a jar of wood chips. A-ma was squatting next to the stove and grinding chili into powder, and when the jar shattered at her feet, she slammed the grain roller onto the grinding stone.

"Why would you do that?" she yelled. "Can't you ever act normally?"

Little Mushroom scratched his neck. "Sorry. I wanted to show off the rabbit I caught. Share it with the family."

"Family," she repeated. There was a subtle rise in tenor at the end of the word, as if she wanted it to become a question but then pulled back: *What do you know about family?*

"Where's Lucky Sheep?" he asked. "Don't want him to miss a meal this delicious."

"He's at the bottom of Home Mountain with the elders." She walked over to him and reached for the crow-tail broom leaning against the door. Her body was frail. Her neck hung low from years of cradling him and his brother and from carrying them for hours out in the fields.

"What's he doing there?" he asked. Lucky Sheep wasn't part of the traders' guild and none of the expedition teams wanted him because he had difficulty breathing. What business did he have at the bottom of the mountain?

"You haven't heard?" A-ma said. "You're usually the first to know everything."

"I was in the poppy bushes looking for the rabbit."

"Soldiers are at our gates. Twenty or thirty. The elders were busy all afternoon preparing the welcoming ceremony."

Hearing the news, he became so excited, his legs wobbled. There hadn't been contact with many people below the mountain, and the last soldiers who had appeared were so beaten and exhausted that half of them died on the way up to Ancestors' Quarry. He was only eight at the time, but he remembered that, before they left, the leaders of the soldiers had told the villagers that China was lost—that, worse still, it was irrecoverable. The soldiers were Nationalist troops retreating from invaders across the sea.

"Do they wear red stars?" Little Mushroom asked. "Are they led by the big man you told me about, the one named Mao?"

"I don't know. But from the way it sounds, I don't think so. Folks tell me they have curtains on their hats and carry a white flag with a bloody dot in the center."

He sighed. He knew he shouldn't have gotten his hopes up. He pulled out a stool, sat down, and rested his head on his arms.

"I could be wrong," A-ma said. "Go. Fetch your brother. I'll prepare the rabbit. By the time you two return, the entire street will be fragrant with peppered meat."

When he didn't rise any further, A-ma began sweeping the areas around his stool. She brushed his shoes again and again. Clay shards from the jar came off the broom and stabbed him in the foot.

"Stop it," he yelled, standing up. "That hurts."

"Get out of here," she said. "Don't sit around feeling sorry for yourself. Find your brother. Bring him back for supper."

51

AT THE BOTTOM OF THE mountain, he squeezed his arms through the mob of villagers. They all wore their shiniest gold-and-black robes, usually reserved for holidays and funerals. It was difficult to see over the wall of tall spotted hats or through the curtain of silver earrings and dangling head ornaments. To get a clearer view outside the gate, he climbed the bamboo ladder to the top of a rampart, where two sentries chewed on goat jerky.

"Hey! Get out of here, Little Fungus!" one of them shouted. He poked at Little Mushroom's chest with the dull end of his spear.

Little Mushroom raised his arms. "I'm just trying to find my brother. He's down there somewhere and I don't want to yell out his name like some worried grandma."

The other sentry lowered his friend's weapon. He was Burning Leopard the Younger. His father was one of the young men who, eleven years earlier, had gone with Mao to join the revolution. Burning Leopard was four years older than Little Mushroom. They had been friends when they were younger and had stolen eagle eggs from a cliffside nest. Burning Leopard had held Little Mushroom by his legs over the edge of the mountain while he reached down and scooped up the fist-sized eggs.

"He's all right," Burning Leopard said. "He won't cause trouble."

"I'll just be here for a few minutes."

The first sentry withdrew the spear and thumped it against the floor. "You'd better. The towers are a sacred place. Reserved for the Guardians of Home Mountain."

Burning Leopard smacked his friend on the back of his head. "Sacred? Did you tell that to Pink Lily when you brought her up here to fondle her chest?"

The first sentry shoved Burning Leopard away and walked over to the lookout.

"Thanks," Little Mushroom said.

Burning Leopard shook his head. "No big deal." He leaned in and whispered, "I've wanted to do that for a while now. Can't stand that kid." He brought Little Mushroom to the other side of the lookout. "Still, it's not a good idea to sneak up on us like that, especially during an important time like this. You were lucky we didn't open your gut." He winked. "Now, let's find that brother of yours."

Burning Leopard extended his neck over the straw edge, searching through the colorful hats of the villagers below the rampart. Secretly, Little Mushroom was more interested in the soldiers on the other side of the gate. Standing neatly in perfect squares, the strangers were accepting bouquets of purple wildflowers from the daughters of the village elders. Every once in a while, when Burning Leopard pointed to someone in the crowd, Little Mushroom glanced below him and shook his head. There was a pink mist in the air—dried pig's blood scented with horseradish—and it made it difficult for him to see the soldiers' faces clearly. Still, he could tell they were foreign, and not in the same way that he himself was foreign.

He counted twenty-nine of them: three squares with two leaders at the front. They had small, gleaming knives at the ends of their rifles and metal jugs on their belts. The one in the broad-brimmed cap—one of the leaders—carried a thin curved sword with golden bands on the handle. What impressed him more were the vehicles behind them: two open-roofed wagons with four seats and four wheels and an even larger closed-roof wagon with eight wheels. On Home Mountain, a few villagers owned bicycles—boys and girls rode them up and down the main road that ran down the mountain—but these vehicles before him now rumbled like sleeping water buffalo and farted plumes of gray smoke. From everything A-ma had told him about how desperate his parents and their generals had looked, Little Mushroom became aware that this was not the same army that his family belonged to. Nor were they the defeated Nationalist troops from when he was eight.

They were, he was now sure, the invaders from across the sea. The difference was important to him, although to the other villagers they were all the same—foreigners—neither friend nor foe.

"There!" Burning Leopard pointed to a hatless head coughing behind the elder's daughters. "That must be him!"

He was right. As soon as Little Mushroom saw the arched back, he knew it was Lucky Sheep hunched over in one of his coughing fits. Ushered by the elders, the foreign soldiers were walking past his brother through the gates. Little Mushroom said goodbye to Burning Leopard, walked over to the ladder, and swung his legs around.

"I'll see you at the feast tomorrow." Burning Leopard waved.

"What feast?"

"The one with them." He nodded to the soldiers. "When the elders have us meet them formally."

Shoving through the crowd, Little Mushroom thought about this feast—this formal meeting with the outsiders. He wondered who they were and why they had come to their village. They didn't look hungry. It didn't seem like they had come for medical attention, as his parents had. These soldiers weren't going up the hills to use the facilities of Ancestors' Quarry. Obviously they didn't require the broadswords, spears, or bows of the town militia, and their vehicles were, without a doubt, faster than the horses and yaks that the village's expedition teams and traders used. In the end, he couldn't come up with anything the foreigners needed other than passage through the mountains or labor hands to staff their armies. The Lolos had a habit of sending their sons to journey with those below the mountain—of scattering forth like seeds spinning in the wind.

He hoped the foreigners did need workers, because by the time he was walking back up the hill with Lucky Sheep, he was already planning what to stuff inside his knapsack after he had convinced the army to take him with them. He imagined that they would travel north to join up with his parents' army. He had learned from Burning Leopard that they had defeated the Nationalists, who were also Mao's enemies. Why wouldn't the two generals meet and fight alongside each other? They would help him find his parents, and before long he'd be coming back to Home Mountain triumphant in a shiny vehicle of his own, no longer poor or a bastard. The girls who had scorned him before would beg him to give them a ride, and he would choose the prettiest among them to be his wife. Imagine that: Little Mushroom, the fungus of the mountain, with an elder's daughter.

By the time he detected the smoky aroma of meat near his house, he had almost forgotten that he'd caught a rabbit that day.

52

NEXT MORNING, AN HOUR BEFORE the sun was up, he got up off his cot. Like a guard dog, he slept next to the door. He reached for his shirt, which he had stretched over the window to serve as a mosquito net, and put on his cotton trousers. Passed down by his brother, they were wide at the hips and short at the legs, extending just below his knees. He tied them with hemp.

It was his job in the morning to gather the day's water, so he grabbed a pole and hung a bucket on either end. When he returned from the well, he poured a bucketful into the iron crock, splashed some of it on his neck and face, threw a handful of wood chips under the stove, and started the fire. He heard blankets shuffling in the other room and then hurried steps on the stone bed. A-ma and Lucky Sheep were getting up. They had slept together for as long as Little Mushroom could remember. When he was little, the other village boys thought he slept with them, too, and made fun of him for it. It wasn't until A-ma beat him at the marketplace in front of a large crowd for stealing a handful of dates, kicking his ribs as he rolled on the ground, that the other kids became aware of his place in the family.

"Wear something nice today," A-ma said inside the bedroom. "The entire village will see you at the feast."

Lucky Sheep parted the bead curtain and walked into the den as slow as a tortoise. He smiled at Little Mushroom, who handed him a cup of boiled water.

"Got any of that leftover rabbit?" Lucky Sheep asked.

"Sure." Little Mushroom pointed to the strips of meat laid out to dry on the windowsill. "But you'll want to save your belly for the feast. I heard the elders are roasting goat."

His brother yawned. "Guess I'll go hungry for a few hours."

A-ma came out holding a blue robe with gold trim. She wore the headdress that she had worn at her wedding.

"I found it!" she said. "Your father's marriage cape! You'll look just as handsome in it as he did. Perhaps you'll catch the eye of a rich girl. Perhaps you'll find yourself a wife."

Lucky Sheep turned to Little Mushroom pleadingly. Little Mushroom grinned. There were times when he didn't mind not being A-ma's son. He dropped a dried pepper into his bowl of boiled water, blew away the steam, and tilted his head back. Instantly his eyes widened and his nose cleared. He swished the liquid around his mouth, gurgled, and spit it out onto the ground.

"Sometimes I think you're more Lolo than me," his brother said. "I can't stand the burn."

"The first few times are the worst." Little Mushroom bent his neck to the side until he heard a crack. "But you do it enough and you can't wake up without it. Tranquil Crane once said that a drop of pepper a day will keep the moon away."

"*He* should've been the one who raised you," A-ma said, fastening her son's last button on his neck. "I tell that to the old hermit every time I go up there. Nobody listens to a woman, though, especially not to a widow."

Lucky Sheep rolled his eyes and smiled at his brother. Little Mushroom nodded, although secretly he, too, had always wished he'd been left with the hermit on the mountaintop, who barely left his dusty, smelly bird's nest of a cave. Neither of them were Lolo, and they were both outcasts. There was even a rumor that the old recluse had considered taking him on as a pupil, and Little Mushroom had often gone up there to inquire about his parents and Mao's army. The hermit never provided anything specific, however, and always told him to stop gazing afar and instead focus on the present—useless drivel he'd say to any villager who sought his advice. Little Mushroom didn't think he meant much to the old man and was surprised when the hermit asked to see him right before he died. On his deathbed, Tranquil Crane looked like a shriveled apple. Waving for Little Mushroom to come close, he whispered three words into his ears: "There's no need." For the longest time Little Mushroom tried to figure out what he meant. A-ma told him not to dwell on it too much: "The last words of a confused old man are worth about as much as the grasps of a dying squirrel." She cooked him a hearty dinner that night and promised that he'd feel better in the morning.

"Nobody listens to a fungus, either," Little Mushroom said, even though he knew A-ma couldn't hear him.

She was already outside. She waved to their neighbors, to those who lived far below at the rim of the mountain, to villagers who owned more land than she did and to those who owned less—to anyone with a daughter.

53

AT THE CENTER OF THE marketplace, the foreigners sat in a semicircle with elbows forward, fists punching legs. They didn't speak or smile. Their dull yellow capes matched the curtains on their hats. Laid out between them and the elders were colorful maps the size of tearoom rugs. Stones were placed at their corners. The leader wearing the broad-brimmed cap whispered something to his interpreter, a younger man with glasses who didn't carry a rifle. The interpreter nodded and ran over to the map. He pointed to a section of green ridges and then spread his arms out wide and surveyed the marketplace. The elders nodded. The interpreter held up a hand with the palm forward, facing the elders, and shook it slightly. The leader in the broad-brimmed cap walked over and gave the interpreter a rolled-up sheet of paper. Uncoiled on top of the map, the black-and-white picture showed an army of soldiers gathered in neat squares with vehicles between their ranks. The interpreter rolled the picture back up and pointed to the map again. His fingers walked up the ridges and arrived at a black dot that had been circled in red. The elders looked at each other, nodding gravely a final time.

When negotiations ended, the villagers waited until their guests took their portion of the feast first before lining up and getting some for themselves. Little Mushroom piled onto his plate hunks of juicy mutton, boiled sweet potato, and scallion-spiced rice. He returned to the seat next to his brother, who was busy talking to a young girl his mother was pushing him into. Little Mushroom patted his brother on the back. Then he turned his attention to the soldiers.

The foreigners were drinking bamboo liquor and laughing at each other's jokes. The leader and an elder clinked bowls and drank them down as if their children had just gotten married. Wine flowed off their chins. Little Mushroom was waiting until the officer was alone. His plan was this: He would grab two bowls from the feast table, fill them up with wine, and offer to drink with the officer as the elders were doing. Then he would point to himself and make the walking motion with his fingers on their map, and hopefully they would understand that he wanted to join them.

As the festivities dragged on, he grew nervous. The elders stayed in their seats, and he was worried that he might not get a chance to speak with the soldiers. Even if he did, would the motion with his fingers be enough to let them know what he wanted? More importantly, why would they *let* him join them? In their eyes, he was probably just a skinny kid without even a proper pair of pants. Would they allow him to sit next to them when he offered the bowls of wine? Would they laugh at him? How could he prove his worth?

When the sun reached its highest point in the sky, lute players gathered in a circle in front of the foreigners. They began strumming cords. Moments later, the tallest girls in the village weaved into the circle, formed a butterfly, and danced. The musicians took a step forward and then a step back, their instruments bouncing like swooping nets. They were playing out the story of the butterfly catcher, whose betrothed had been transformed into a swallowtail. He had to seduce her with music and then catch her before the sun set, or else she would remain a butterfly forever. The foreigners clapped and hooted.

The scene gave Little Mushroom an idea. He would go home, grab his net and rabbit pelt, and show them to the soldiers. He might not be able to shoot a gun or drive a vehicle—not yet—but he was as good a hunter as anyone else in the village. He glanced at the soldiers and saw that some of them were dozing off. The elders had turned away and were talking to their families. The feast wasn't going to last much longer. He had to act fast.

He weaved through the crowd and ran down to his house. After grabbing the net and bringing the pelt down from the window, he sprinted back up the hill, lowering his head to gather speed. A hot gust of midday wind blew on top of his head, shaved bald just a few days ago. Staring at the dirt passing swiftly beneath his feet, he wondered if the ants on this mountain had always been there or if they, like him, had come from a faraway land.

He didn't notice the two young men carrying another goat to roast until his waist hit their bamboo pole. He slid forward a few meters, skinning his knees, and when he looked up to see what had happened, he saw one of the young men picking up the goat and brushing the dirt away while the other was storming over in his direction. His net and pelt had landed far away, down the hill.

"Little Mushroom?" the young man said. It was Burning Leopard. "What are you doing running on the street like that?"

"I had to get something from the house. Had to do it before the feast was over." He started limping toward the fields.

"Hey!" Burning Leopard yelled. "Come back here! You've dirtied our goat and you think you can just walk away?"

Little Mushroom stopped. He turned around and saw that the underbelly of the goat was covered with twigs.

"What did you need from your house?" Burning Leopard asked, his hands on his hips. "The feast has everything."

Little Mushroom wondered if he should tell Burning Leopard about his plans. He took a deep breath. "I want to leave with the soldiers," he said, "but I have to show them what I'm made of. I'm the best hunter in town, and my net will prove it."

Burning Leopard laughed. He yelled to his friend and told him why Little Mushroom had run into them. The other boy started laughing, too. Finally, Burning Leopard asked, "You really believe the soldiers care about your skills catching field mice? You're so skinny. Why would they want another kid to look after?"

Little Mushroom hadn't expected this from Burning Leopard, who, just the day before, had treated him as if they were best friends. Little Mushroom kicked at the dirt and spit out a few streams of saliva, trying to imitate some of the older boys. "I had my capping ceremony when I was ten," he said, "and I'm eleven now, which means I've been a man for over a year. I can take care of myself."

"True." Burning Leopard crossed his arms. "But tell me why. Why do you want to leave?"

Now Little Mushroom started to laugh, although he couldn't reproduce the same hearty, belly-stirring chortle that Burning Leopard had let out.

"Who am I here on Home Mountain?" he asked. "I'm not one of you. My parents are in the real China, fighting like the soldiers we met today. My place is with them."

Burning Leopard nodded, growing serious. His eyebrows slanted down like an owl's. "Good answer." He twisted the ends of his sprouting mustache, looking Little Mushroom up and down. "All right," he said. "You can come with me."

"I'm not helping you carry the goat up." Little Mushroom took a step back. "Like I said, I need to talk to the soldiers."

"No, you little fool. I mean you can come with me. I'm leaving with them, too." Burning Leopard pointed in the direction of the base of the mountain. From their position, it was hidden beneath the hill like the tucked-away entrance to animal heaven, where the dead had reverted back to their spirit creatures. "I'm going to find my father," Burning Leopard continued. "My grandpa has arranged it with the soldiers. It wasn't too hard. I'm a warrior and my father is a warrior. Just like yours." He told Little Mushroom that the foreigners needed helping hands. They wouldn't mind another tagging along, especially one whose parents were also soldiers. His grandfather had told him that although it wasn't likely that these foreigners would join up with Mao's troops, a small detachment led by the interpreter would separate from the main army and head north to Shaanxi Province. His grandpa had made a deal with the foreigners: In exchange for allowing their soldiers through Home Mountain, they would give the village weapons, spices, fabrics, and silver, and would agree to take his grandson with them. Burning Leopard would work as an errand boy until the interpreter's detachment reached Shaanxi, where he would be allowed to leave and travel on his own to the Communist base. "Our parents are in a city in the middle of the province, if you didn't know already. I wouldn't mind some company."

Little Mushroom couldn't believe what he was hearing. Could it be as easy as Burning Leopard was saying? He had been scheming this entire time and all he had to do was ask? He followed the two young men up the hill back to the feast, trying not to get his hopes up too much. This could all be a trick, an elaborate joke for the fungus of Home Mountain.

Burning Leopard set the goat down next to the tables, walked up to his grandfather—the elder sitting next to the lead soldier—and whispered something into his grandfather's ear. The elder glanced at Little Mushroom, his forehead creasing with annoyance, turned back to the interpreter, and tugged at the end of his sleeve. He was all smiles now, pointing to Little Mushroom and speaking in a strange language.

"My grandpa knows the common tongue," Burning Leopard said proudly. "He's even taught me a little."

The interpreter examined Little Mushroom and asked the lead soldier a question, to which the leader flicked his hands a few times, not even giving Little Mushroom a look.

"Are you going to be a good boy?" the elder asked Little Mushroom. "Are you going to work hard and follow orders?"

"I will."

"Good. Get your things together. Be ready to leave by tomorrow morning."

Hearing these words, Little Mushroom dropped the net with the pelt inside. No one had paid attention to what he was carrying. Although grateful for what Burning Leopard was doing, he couldn't help but feel that he was letting himself down a little. He wasn't joining the soldiers out of merit, but from the connection of a friend. Wait, he thought. Could he call Burning Leopard a friend?

"Thank you," he said. "So we're friends now?"

"We are." Burning Leopard winked. "Try not to be annoying."

54

A-MA PULLED OUT A WOODEN BIN underneath the stove and sifted through her belongings, searching for her largest knapsack. She unfolded a leather pouch, held it underneath the candlelight, and checked for holes.

"Well, it's risky," she said, "going to a new place with people you don't know. Then again, it was risky for your parents to leave you with people *they* didn't know in a land they never grew up in."

"They were lucky to have met you," Little Mushroom said.

A-ma sighed. "All the same, it *is* time for you to go look for them. Over a decade and still they haven't showed up." She gave the bag a few hard slaps, sending a cloud of dust into the air. "On your journey, leave enough room in your hope to expect worse. The afterlife is filled with animals. It is not so bad. It is a much better place than our own. If your parents are there, they will be happy."

Little Mushroom didn't say anything, annoyed at A-ma for giving a bad portent before his journey even began. He stuffed the few shirts he had into the sack and checked under his cot for anything he'd forgotten. A-ma reached deeper into the floor and took out a yellow envelope. She unfolded a brown piece of paper from inside. Then she laid it out in front of him.

"Show this to anyone literate when you're at your parents' camp."

"What does it say?"

"It has their names on it." A-ma brushed wood splinters off the sheet. "It also has your *real* name on it."

"I'm not Little Mushroom?"

She shook her head. "No, your parents called you Turnip. Little Turnip. It's the purple vegetable that grows in the ground. It's all in the letter."

Little Mushroom held up the paper and stared at the smeared ink. He didn't understand any of the words, but some of them told him who he was, while others told him who his parents were. "What are their names?" he asked.

"I don't remember. You should be grateful I remembered yours after all these years."

Lucky Sheep, who was in the other room, came out and kicked the compartment door shut. "Your name is Mushroom. Not Turnip. It'll always be Mushroom!" he yelled.

Little Mushroom smiled. "I won't forget you, older brother. But you'll have a wife soon, and there'll be a day when you won't even remember me."

Lucky Sheep grabbed the knapsack and stormed back into the bedroom. Little Mushroom got up to chase after him, but A-ma pulled him down.

"Get some rest," she said. "Clear your head. He'll be all right."

When A-ma went into the other room, Little Mushroom lay inside his cot and, under the moonlight, scanned the letter over and over again. From this day forward, he was Little Turnip. *Turnip, turnip, turnip,* he repeated. He would tell Burning Leopard to call him Turnip. He would introduce himself as Turnip to everyone he'd meet. This was the wish of his parents.

The next morning, A-ma made Little Turnip fetch one last bucket of water before handing him his knapsack. The moon was still out. It was so large that its divots and bumps were all visible, gleaming in the sky like great sapphires.

"You'll come back to visit, won't you?" Lucky Sheep asked, wiping snot away from his nose.

Little Turnip told his brother that he'd try.

Half an hour later, he reached the bottom of the hill, where the soldiers were staying inside emptied-out houses next to the towers. Just as he was about to approach one, he heard rapid footfalls behind him. Turning around, he saw A-ma running to him with what looked like a piece of white cloth dangling from her hand. He stopped, and when she got close enough, he saw that the cloth was actually the dried rabbit pelt.

"A mitten. In case your hand gets cold." She gave it to him. She reached into her cotton-stuffed trousers and took out several pieces of rabbit jerky. A hind leg was among them. "For the road," she said. "You'll get hungry."

He felt guilty. She had followed him all the way down to hand him something that he'd considered keeping for himself. He was suddenly ashamed he was leaving, and he had to tell himself that A-ma was stronger than she looked and that she didn't need help in the fields. He was a burden, he repeated, as she had made clear to him again and again.

He gave her a hug, and perhaps it was the morning moisture—or it could've just been sweat around her eyes—but as he was turning around, he thought she might have been crying.

55

AN HOUR LATER, IN THE back of the larger closed-roof vehicle—a truck, Burning Leopard had told him—the foreign soldiers asked Little Turnip to sing them a song. The interpreter was not among them. He had gotten on one of the smaller vehicles, which his friend had told him was called a Kurogane, and sat next to the officer. It was then that Little Turnip realized the man was someone important. Still, even without the interpreter, he could now tell that the other soldiers wanted a song. First they howled a discordant melody from their land across the sea, sharing metal containers of drink. Then they pointed to him, repeating in unison: *Utatte!*

Little Turnip and Burning Leopard looked at each other, and when his friend stepped forward and cleared his throat, a soldier shoved him back down.

"*Utatte!*" one of the soldiers shouted again, pointing fiercely at Little Turnip. He pulled him up and brought him to the center of the truck. The vehicle drove over a bump and Little Turnip fell into a soldier's lap. Instantly he was pushed back up.

He looked over to Burning Leopard, but his friend couldn't do anything but shrug. *They want a song?* his friend seemed to be saying. *Give them a song.* Little Turnip stared at the eager faces, trying to remember something A-ma had hummed in the fields. He felt his arms shaking. He lowered them to his side, licking his lips. "*We welcome you to the cloudy paradise,*" he sang.

No matter in rain or snow, our hearts are as sunny as a clear day.
The dragons carved the mountains with their tails.
We don't remember them.
Who says we were born from something evil?

He couldn't recall all the lyrics, but he figured none of the foreigners could tell the difference anyway. When he finished, there was a round of applause. A soldier put his hat over Little Turnip, pulling the curtains down so that they covered his ears.

Little Turnip returned to his seat at the back of the truck and exhaled.

"Good song," Burning Leopard said. "Dragons carving the mountains?"

"They liked it."

"Yeah, because they couldn't understand you."

Little Turnip opened a slit of the rubber flap to let in fresh air. Huffing, he stared out at the road hurrying away under his feet. It was the first time he'd ever been this far from the valleys of Home Mountain. The sky loomed wide and blue, like the skin of some magnificent fish, its scales stretching endlessly in all directions. Tapping Burning Leopard's shoulder, he pointed to the view above their heads.

"I never knew the heavens were so broad," he said. "Never thought there'd be this many clouds."

Burning Leopard poked his head outside the rubber flaps of the truck. "Yeah, it covers everything."

"Probably stretches to our parents."

His friend nodded.

One by one the soldiers, drunk on wine, fell asleep. Slowly, over the next few hours, the roads became smoother. Little Turnip's ears popped when the truck left dirt and continued over blackened cobblestone. City folk started appearing on either side of the road carrying sacks of hay, farming tools, babies, and pots and pans that rattled like wind chimes. Carriages flew by swift as diving hawks.

He had never seen so many horses before. Horses with bareback riders. Horses hauling carts of vegetables. Horses with their heads down, drinking from long troughs. And then there were people in areas where horses should've been. Men wearing straw hats pulled a carriage while the men inside of it were shaded by flowery umbrellas. A woman dragged a wagon of bamboo shoots all by herself. Children drank from the same troughs as the animals. Little Turnip pinched his nose: The street stank worse than Fishermen's End—the basin on the other side of Home Mountain, where the latrines emptied into.

"Disgusting," Burning Leopard said.

"Is this where they keep the garbage?" Little Turnip asked.

"Don't think so. Grandpa told me the people below are all dirty. I think this is normal for them."

When buildings started to appear, Little Turnip saw words everywhere. They were on peeling pieces of paper taped to walls. They were on signs hanging atop shops. They flew at him in leaflets in the air. He reached out and snatched one as easily as a tree branch. Could they all contain something important? The elders at Ancients' Quarry had written down only what was essential: who was born that year, who died, droughts, landslides, and floods—the history of their people. Could these floating sheets be the lives of those he was now seeing on the streets, recorded for all who passed? He had never expected to see so many words, had never known how important they were to the people below the mountain—to his own people.

"A new restaurant is opening." Burning Leopard nodded to the paper in Little Turnip's hands.

"You can read?"

"I know a few words." Burning Leopard pointed to a character. "*Fan,*" he said. "That's what the people below say when they want to eat."

"*Fan,*" Little Turnip repeated, grinning. "Let me guess. Grandpa taught you that, too."

Burning Leopard smacked Little Turnip on the back of his head. "What did I tell you about being annoying?"

The truck drove up a hill, turned left, and got on a dirt road again. The buildings vanished behind trees, bushes, and two huge gray stones with red words on them. Foreigners in clean suits and military uniforms started appearing on either side. The truck slowed and honked, and when it began to move again, a line of soldiers carrying rifles crossed the street, waving to them as they went. In the distance, more soldiers marched behind a colorfully dressed man who raised a baton over his head with every crisp step.

"You see that?" Burning Leopard said. "They all mean to cross our mountain."

"Our home's important," replied Little Turnip.

"Grandpa always said the people below only remember us when they fight each other."

When the truck made a complete stop, the soldiers inside motioned for Little Turnip and Burning Leopard to stand up. Little Turnip swung his legs around the edge of the truck and helped Burning Leopard down. He ran around to the other side of the truck and saw a building so massive that it seemed to have been built for giants. It had an arched entrance five times as tall as a man, with more glass windows than he could count on his fingers and toes, and three roofs whose corners curved up into lion heads. He had once believed that no building could be as grand as Ancestors' Quarry, but this one was twice as tall and wide as a delta—and it wasn't even beside a mountain.

"*Nimotsu!*" a soldier called. He walked over to Burning Leopard, leaned in, and yelled again, "*Nimotsu!*"

The interpreter got out of the jeep and pulled the soldier aside. This close, Little Turnip saw that the interpreter was not as young as he had believed. He had wrinkles around his nose, and his hair, which was slicked back with something that remained permanently wet, was beginning to thin above his temples. Still, there was a quality about the man's face that made Little Turnip trust him. Perhaps it was his down-cast eyes, small chin, or the roundness of his cheeks, but he believed that this man was there to help them—that somehow he was the key to finding their parents.

The interpreter said a few words to Burning Leopard, and Little Turnip was surprised that his friend was able to respond. Burning Leopard spoke slowly, pausing frequently and drawing out every syl-lable. When he finished, the interpreter nodded as if Burning Leopard's gibberish made perfect sense.

"It's our job to unload the bags every time we get off a vehicle," Burning Leopard said. "Next time they won't ask nicely."

Little Turnip followed his friend back onto the truck and stacked three duffel bags on his arms. His friend carried pouches and canteens and slung a basket of eggs around his neck. They wobbled to the interpreter, who was leaning against a wall and smoking a cigarette. When they passed under the archway, the soldiers from the truck threw more bags over their arms. Lifting a knee, Little Turnip strained to keep the items from falling.

They followed the interpreter up three flights of stairs hidden in a dark corner of the archway. Dropping the bags in a hallway, Little Turnip squatted, trying to catch his breath, and glanced into a large room that reminded him of the elder's discussion chamber. He was amazed that an area that big could be built so high. The room was carpeted, with circles of candles dangling from the ceiling and twenty or thirty tables. Soldiers sat around wearing silver earmuffs, tapping away at metal boxes. Again there were words. Thousands of them, written down on strips of paper that unrolled from a turning wheel.

"Come on," Burning Leopard said. "The interpreter will take us to where the servants live."

"Is that where we'll stay?"

"Yeah," Burning Leopard said, turning a corner. "We're servants, after all."

"But we'll move with the army when it leaves?" Little Turnip asked.

His friend nodded. "Grandpa made them give their promise."

They went down the stairs, passed the darkened archway, and headed into the central courtyard, where there were apple trees, cherry blossoms, and tall ginseng roots in reflective pots. A pond spouted out jets of water. Foreigners sat on benches reading pieces of paper while women tended flowers and poured tea. When Little Turnip walked by, several of them turned their heads, and he suddenly felt very conscious of the way he was dressed. On Home Mountain, he hadn't owned anything that rivaled the majestic hats and festive gowns of the other villagers, but he never felt out of place among them. Now, the men and women in front of him wore clothes so clean and consistent in their black-and-white coloring and their fit—more so than even the soldier's uniforms—that he felt as if he were from another time, as if Home Mountain existed not only hundreds of kilometers away but also hundreds of years in the past. What saddened him more was the casualness with which the people in the courtyard were behaving. They were leaning against the benches and letting their pants drag on the ground, their clothes getting dirty as though they had ten more to spare.

"What are you thinking?" he asked Burning Leopard.

"Not everyone below is dirty."

The interpreter led them across the courtyard into another archway. After going down another set of stairs, they entered into a kitchen, where the interpreter dropped them off with a fat cook wearing an oily apron. Five or six boys, none older than eight, stood on stacked limestone blocks and chopped vegetables. There was an aroma of sweet buns and leek.

"*Ts'ung na li lai te,*" the cook asked Little Turnip.

Little Turnip turned to Burning Leopard, who answered the man's question. Little Turnip heard the word "Lolo" in his friend's response and guessed that the cook had asked them where were they from. The cook pointed to a wooden bucket at the corner filled to the brim with plates. Burning Leopard took one side of the handle and Little Turnip the other. Together they climbed up the stairs, and put the clanking bucket under a spigot next to the garden.

"They sure don't waste our time," Burning Leopard said, spitting on a plate and rubbing a stain off with his thumb. "It's humiliating. Grandpa signed me up to help soldiers, not wash dishes."

Little Turnip examined the plate, running his fingers over the golden rim. He had never seen anything so smooth before. "The soldiers probably use these plates."

"Washing is for women," Burning Leopard said.

Little Turnip nodded, although A-ma had often made him wash their wooden bowls and scrub the side of the stove. If this was the price for being with his parents again, he'd gladly pay it tenfold. All in all, he thought, things weren't as bad as he had expected. Sure, the soldiers didn't treat them with much respect, but why should they? Unlike Burning Leopard, Little Turnip didn't think of himself as their equal.

Not yet, anyway. He had always been an outsider and understood that it took time for others to warm up to him. In any case, it wasn't *these* soldiers whom he sought respect from. They had nice things, sure, but they were only a bridge between mountains: It didn't matter if the overpass was a little rickety as long as it got him to the other side, where his parents were.

56

OVER THE NEXT FEW WEEKS, he started getting used to the schedule of his new life. It wasn't much different, in fact, from his old one. He offered to fetch water every morning, and the cook gladly agreed—the job having been his before. The cook had worked for the Nationalist government before the foreigners' arrival—the mansion had been an army training facility—and he'd managed to convince the invaders to let him stay on. From their mess officer he learned the proper way to set tables, polish silver, and roll sushi. He took in boys from the local orphanage as helpers, and the foreigners didn't mind, since the kids ate little and required no pay. "Just don't make trouble," he told Little Turnip and Burning Leopard. "The boys who cause trouble I throw away." When he was out of earshot, Burning Leopard spat on his stool. "Who does he think we are, five-year-olds?"

At dawn, Little Turnip made his way through the soldier's halls, collecting the empty vacuum flasks outside their door and filling them with boiling water. Like all the help, he ate the foreigner's leftovers in his quarters, which was a food storage closet he shared with Burning Leopard. They slept on a bunk bed between cans of fermented tofu, sweet potatoes, and peaches. If he stretched a foot too far from the bed, a can would roll down and the cook would pound on the wall. Burning Leopard, the taller of the two, had to fold his legs and sleep on his side.

On Sundays there was entertainment in the courtyard. The foreigners hired opera troupes or projected giant pictures on the walls. When he first saw the image of a black-and-white tiger moving about, he was terrified that it might leap out and attack him. Its teeth were as long as his arms and its fur shimmered like grass under sunlight. He covered his eyes, but Burning Leopard laughed and told him that none of it was real.

Little Turnip didn't think about A-ma or Lucky Sheep. Not that he expected to. He easily forgot the haggling at the marketplace and the rude looks the vendors had given him. The only things he missed about Home Mountain were the fields. He missed hunting—missed being out in nature. At night, on the top bunk, he stared at the dents in the ceiling, counting them as if they were stars, and petted the rabbit pelt until he fell asleep. It would make a great gift, he decided, when he met his parents. It would show them how skillful their son was.

Between midday and afternoon there wasn't much work, so Little Turnip took the time to read a picture book the interpreter had given him. It was a story about a wolf that lived among dogs. The dogs helped their farmer herd sheep, and when they trusted the wolf enough to leave it with the flock, the wolf killed a lamb and dragged it back into the forest to feed its pups. After reading it out loud and translating it, Burning Leopard asked, "What's it supposed to mean?" Little Turnip shrugged. "Foreigners are weird."

The interpreter came by the kitchen once a week. He told them how far along the army was in its preparations, gave them a list of jobs they needed to do—clean the officers' sheets, buy a special type of fish at the marketplace, wait on tables at a party in the grand ballroom—or just lingered on the steps smoking.

"He likes us," Little Turnip said to Burning Leopard one afternoon. They were out in the courtyard, hanging laundry up on wires.

His friend shook his head. "Don't be dumb. He likes *her*."

He nodded to a woman in a *cheongsam* dress sitting on a bench. She wore turquois bracelets and had bobbed black hair bound together with a white tortoiseshell clip. Her job was taking care of the boys who worked in the kitchen, giving them math and calligraphy lessons between their lunch and dinner shifts. Little Turnip had wanted to sit in during one of her lessons, but he was older than the others and figured that she'd probably kick him out.

"He likes Miss Choi?" Little Turnip asked. "But he never talks to her."

"He's shy. Doesn't know how to. They're from different worlds." Burning Leopard squeezed an officer's cap dry and hung it up on the wire. "I don't blame him, either. Look at her. She could tongue-tie the emperor."

"And she's smart, too," Little Turnip added. "She teaches the kids how to read."

Burning Leopard kicked up a wet shirt with his foot. He hung it up to dry, staring at Miss Choi from behind a brown uniform. Over the last few weeks, Little Turnip could tell that his friend had more difficulties adjusting to their new life. On Home Mountain, Burning Leopard was the envy of many boys. His grandfather had arranged a couple of girls for him to choose from, but he said he didn't want to get married until he had gone on some adventures.

When Little Turnip gave him the last piece of laundry, Burning Leopard said, "I can't stand this anymore, this doing nothing for days on end."

In front of them, the line of laundry they'd put up moved with the wind, hiding a pair of legs that was walking toward them.

"What dialect are you speaking?" Miss Choi tilted her head out from behind a bedsheet. "Which mountain?" Her intonations were all wrong—more nasal than his own—but they were familiar enough that Little Turnip could understand her.

"Home Mountain," he said.

"It's the tallest and most remote of all the peaks on Mount Liang," Burning Leopard added. "Also the most beautiful."

Miss Choi smirked, her eyes expanding into a pair of mischievous marbles. "I doubt it's the tallest, and everyone knows my hometown is the most beautiful."

"You're Lolo?" Little Turnip asked.

Miss Choi held up her palm, turned it on its side so that it resembled a triangle, and pointed at the fat of her thumb. "If this were Mount Liang, my home would be here. By donkey, it would take you two hours to get to the hillside where my house is. How far up is yours?"

Burning Leopard shoved Little Turnip aside. "Don't pay attention to him. He's not even Lolo. He doesn't have a home. My grandfather is an elder in the village. We live right next to Ancestors' Quarry, the highest point on Home Mountain. I'm the leader of the ceremonial guards that man our great towers."

"And now you're hanging laundry," Miss Choi said, taking a frilly white shirt off a wire. "*My* laundry, in fact. I've been looking for this all afternoon."

"Impossible," Burning Leopard said. "We only wash clothes for the foreigners. Any day now, they will take us to our fathers and make us soldiers."

She spread the shirt out and let it drop from her fingertips. The sides were thin at the waist and wide at the hips. "Which one of the foreigners do you think this belongs to?" she asked.

Back in the kitchen, Burning Leopard was so embarrassed, he threw a plate into the dish bucket, shattering several saucers underneath. Luckily the cook and the boys were bringing food up to the dining hall. Little Turnip gathered the pieces into a pail, replaced the broken plates in the bucket with new ones from the cabinet, and stuffed the broken fragments into the bottom of the trash basket.

"How long?" Burning Leopard yelled, pacing back and forth. "It's been over a month. When are the soldiers going to start moving?"

Little Turnip had been around when A-ma was mad, although her anger was never this destructive. As Burning Leopard continued shouting, Little Turnip reflected that everyone's anger subsided in different ways. Some people, like A-ma, relaxed if you were patient and kind; others, like Lucky Sheep, could only be calmed if you yelled back at them. Little Turnip still wasn't sure what type of angry person Burning Leopard was, so he decided to tread with caution.

"Did they tell your grandfather when they'll be going up the mountain?" he asked.

"I've never been so humiliated," Burning Leopard said. "If she was any girl in our village, I wouldn't have given her a second glance. *I* would've been the one to embarrass *her*."

Little Turnip tried asking the question again, and when his friend didn't respond, he tried changing the subject. "A month isn't that long, really," he said. "Do you remember the woman who worked for Strong Fox the lumberjack? Her parents owed him a lot of money and she was indentured for three years before he returned her to them."

"Washing dishes. Waiting tables. Doing laundry—women's laundry. I can't take it anymore!"

Ah, Little Turnip thought. His friend was the third type of angry: the deaf kind. He was oblivious to everything around him. Not bothering to say another word, he went to the closet to take a nap. He had two hours before dinner duties. Closing his eyes, he could still hear his friend shouting in the kitchen. Burning Leopard's bare feet clopped on the cement floor like a donkey's hooves.

57

NEXT MONDAY, THE INTERPRETER WAS waiting in the kitchen before Little Turnip had even woken up. As soon as he saw him, he ran back to the closet to shake Burning Leopard awake. When they came out, the interpreter dangled a string of bronze coins in front of them and tossed it onto the countertop. Then he took out a stack of papers so thin, they were almost translucent, and set it next to the coins. On the paper, a bloody fingerprint smeared the black brushstrokes. There were many characters on each page, and the way they connected to one another made Little Turnip believe they had been written quickly.

"A special mission," Burning Leopard translated. "We're to follow Miss Choi and the boys down to the city and steal papers like the kind here. She'll be our excuse to leave the mansion without rousing suspicion."

He did a snatching motion with his hands for the interpreter to see. The interpreter shook his head, gently pulling the sheet of paper on the countertop toward him, and said something to clarify.

"Not steal," Burning Leopard said, keeping his eyes on the interpreter. "Quietly retake. They belong to the foreigners. They're just trying to get back what's theirs."

Little Turnip wasn't buying the explanation. He'd lied to A-ma enough times to know when someone wasn't telling the truth, and there was blood on the paper before them. If the documents really belonged to the foreigners, why didn't they just ask for them back?

"Why us?" he asked his friend.

"What do you mean?"

"Why are they making us do it?"

Burning Leopard didn't bother translating the question to the interpreter. He pulled Little Turnip aside and whispered, "Don't you see? This is our chance to do something important. Before we left, you wanted to show them your rabbit net. You wanted to make them see what you're worth. Well, this is it."

His friend was right, although Little Turnip still had a sinking feeling in his belly. The task was obviously dangerous, but the interpreter had always been nice to them, giving them treats from his home across the sea and making sure the other soldiers didn't yell at them too much. He had also let Little Turnip have the book. Why should he *not* trust him? As soon as he nodded, Burning Leopard turned back to the interpreter for more information. The interpreter gestured with his hands as he spoke, gave his friend another piece of paper, and left through the stairs.

Later, while washing dishes, Burning Leopard gave Little Turnip the details. The next afternoon, Miss Choi would take the boys to a bathhouse. There were three buildings next to it that might have the documents. Burning Leopard took out a napkin with a drawing of the bathhouse and the three buildings: a vinegar merchant, an apothecary, and a massage parlor. Their job was to sneak into these venues and take any stacks of paper they encountered. Before they left on this assignment, the interpreter would give them a bag large enough to carry all the sheets. They should also report any buildings that had guns, bullets, or rifles—anything that looked like it shouldn't be there. On the way out, they should not follow Miss Choi and the boys too closely. The city folk shouldn't see them talking. When they arrive back at the mansion, they should go straight to the interpreter's office without stopping by the kitchen.

The next afternoon, after lunch duties, they rode a mule cart with Miss Choi and the boys down to the edge of the city. "Where are you two going?" she asked Little Turnip, but before he could answer, Burning Leopard pulled him up onto the wheel bed next to him. "Keep your questions to yourself," he said to her.

At the entrance to the city—an arched gateway with red characters—they waited until Miss Choi and the boys had walked a block away before following behind. When the bathhouse was in full view, Little Turnip became anxious. Bathers came out with towels on their shoulders and bars of soap around their necks. On the other side of the street, there were police officers eating at a noodle stand and burly shirtless men hacking at pork with machetes. If they got caught, Little Turnip wouldn't be surprised if Burning Leopard took off by himself, leaving him there with a bunch of people who couldn't understand a word he was saying.

"Maybe we shouldn't do it," he said. "We could tell the foreigner we didn't find anything."

"Don't be annoying." Burning Leopard loosened the cords of the bag that the interpreter had given him to stuff in the rolls of paper. "Come on," he said, shaking Little Turnip's shoulders. "You want to wash dishes all day?"

Little Turnip wobbled his head, a gesture between a nod and a shake.

"Didn't think so." Burning Leopard turned his attention back to the bathhouse.

They waited until Miss Choi and the boys went inside before crossing the street. The vinegar merchant was to the left of the bathhouse and the apothecary to the right. The massage parlor was behind it, out of view. It was an attachment to the saunas that bathers could reach by walking through a connecting pavilion. There were a lot of people on the avenue coming and going—more than what Little Turnip would have guessed was usual—and he thought that today was perhaps some sort of holiday.

First, he and Burning Leopard made their way to the vinegar merchant, which was the most crowded building. Inside the store, the line twisted around like a serpent, the shoppers all holding empty clay jars—the serpent's scales. At the counter, customers shouted and pushed and lifted their jars next to each other's heads. It was easy for Little Turnip and Burning Leopard to escape the shopkeeper's notice as they snuck behind the counter and walked into the storeroom. There they saw a few boys unscrewing the tops of huge vinegar jugs and pouring the fragrant black liquid into more manageable pitchers. It took three boys to tilt a jug and keep it steady, and when Burning Leopard walked by, they didn't even bother looking up. Little Turnip didn't see any tables, desks, or doors that led to other rooms. No guns or rifles, either. He did notice a wooden pistol on top of a jug, but there was a rubber band in it, and he thought better of telling Burning Leopard about this useless detail. "Damn," his friend said as they headed out of the store.

Next, they walked to the apothecary's shop. Only a few people were inside. One of them was talking to a man with a long white beard and pointing to some dried roots on the countertop. Little Turnip and Burning Leopard waited outside, trying to decide how to proceed.

"I'll distract the old man," Burning Leopard said. "I'll tell him my mother's sick and ask him what I should buy. You sneak past and search for the documents."

"Why me? Why can't you sneak inside while *I* distract him?"

"You don't speak their language, stupid."

Little Turnip wanted to say that he could spill the bag of strange red grain next to the counter or kick the legs that supported the cabinet, causing the jars of preserved organs on top to crash down, but he had to admit that those were riskier distractions than what his friend was suggesting.

"Don't run if I get caught," Little Turnip said.

"Of course not. Now, wait for my signal." Burning Leopard wet his eyes with saliva, put on an expression that suggested he had a sick mother, and went inside.

Little Turnip peeked through the doorway to the backroom. He saw a desk with an inkwell on it. The desk was so low that the person who used it probably had to sit on the floor cross-legged. On the back wall hung the red-and-white flag of the foreign soldiers. He didn't notice anyone in the room, although it extended beyond what he could see.

When Burning Leopard became first in line, the man in front of him walked out of the door carrying a box wrapped in newspapers. He stared at Little Turnip so hard that Little Turnip was sure the man knew something was up. But the man walked right past him, and when Little Turnip turned his attention back to his friend, Burning Leopard was waving to him angrily. The old apothecary was at the other side of the store, reaching for a container high up on a ledge. Little Turnip nodded and snuck inside.

Luckily, no one was in the back room. Shelves lined the top of the walls, the jars lit by candles placed behind them. It was obvious to Little Turnip that this room had also been open to customers at one point and perhaps would open again if the store had more business. He rushed over to the table and got on his knees. There were several sheets of paper beneath the inkwell, although none of them resembled the bloody document the interpreter had shown them. Still, he crumpled them up all the same and stuffed them into his pocket. He scanned the room one last time for any objects of value or any hidden doors. Then he made his way out the entryway, bending his head down just in case the old man had returned to his post.

Outside, he showed Burning Leopard what he'd found.

"Well, it's a start," his friend said. "One more to go."

At the massage parlor, the attendant at the door asked impatiently what service they wanted. She was tall and skinny. Her thin wrists crossed over the two tiny, berry-sized bumps on her chest. From behind her wafted the creamy scent of yak milk soap. Burning Leopard smiled, shook his head, and pulled Little Turnip away. They waited at the side of the building, out of the attendant's view.

"Did you see where the entrance to the back room was?" Little Turnip asked.

"Couldn't see anything," Burning Leopard said. "Too dark."

"What do we do?"

Burning Leopard searched his pocket and took out a few of the coins the interpreter had given them. The other half—Little Turnip's share—was promised upon delivery of the documents.

"Guess we get a massage," Burning Leopard said.

At the door again, the attendant wanted to take the pouch off Burning Leopard's shoulders, but he snatched it back, muttering something that Little Turnip suspected was offensive. The lady sneered, lazily lifting her finger to a young boy who carried yellowed towels behind her. They followed the boy up a wooden staircase to where the cheaper massages were given. On the way up, Little Turnip took note of all the rooms where wealthy customers received individual rubdowns. Between those chambers, there was a hallway lined with calligraphy. On two of the doors he recognized the characters for men and women—he'd seen the same ones plastered on the outhouses at the mansion—and wondered if the dark corridor contained other hidden quarters or doorways.

"Is the second floor the right place?" he whispered. "Maybe it's better if we checked that hallway there."

"We will," Burning Leopard said. "We can go anywhere now that we've paid. But we have to at least make it look like we're here for a reason."

Little Turnip had never heard of a massage parlor before. That morning, when Burning Leopard had explained that it was a place where people paid pretty girls to clean them, Little Turnip became excited. Now, after seeing the place, he was disappointed. Besides the woman at the door, there weren't many girls. Most of the folks inside were being scrubbed down by old ladies or plump men, and the groans the customers gave out sounded as if they were in pain. Lying down on the cushiony mat with a toothless lady chopping at his back, Little Turnip wondered what the fuss was about and what other pointless activities those below the mountain spent their money on.

"I don't feel any dirt coming off of me," he said to his friend.

"What did you expect?" Burning Leopard shook out his words. "We've seen their idea of cleanliness when we first came here."

After the message was over, walking down the stairs, Little Turnip reached above his neck and tried touching the spots that were still hot and aching. *How silly*, he thought. Folks below the mountain were as senseless as male mantises, eager to reproduce, knocking on the door of death.

They reached the suspicious hallway. Burning Leopard told Little Turnip to wait for him by the doors at the far end while he peeked inside the bathrooms. Little Turnip opened one of the wooden doors and saw brooms, buckets, and aprons. He moved on to the next one, but before he could unlatch the small hook, he heard a scream coming from his friend's direction. Burning Leopard gave an embarrassed bow to the lady in the bathroom and walked over to Little Turnip. Together they opened the next door. Besides a stack of firewood and some spark flints, which Burning Leopard put into his pocket, there wasn't anything of interest.

One more door remained. It was around the corner from the bathrooms. When they tried opening it, they found that it was locked. Burning Leopard took a step back, positioning his shoulders to ram it, but Little Turnip quickly stood in front of him.

"Someone might be inside," he whispered.

There was a hole by the doorknob where light was shining out. Little Turnip got on his knees and peeked inside. The opening was barely larger than his pupil, although he could still tell the room was more than just another closet. It contained a table, three chairs, and bookshelves, and the windowless area was illuminated by a bulb hanging from the ceiling. There was a man, too, a young soldier, perhaps—Little Turnip couldn't be sure—sleeping with his foot resting on one of the chairs.

"We should get out of here," Little Turnip said.

Burning Leopard scooted down and took a second peek. "This is it," he whispered.

"We could tell the interpreter we know where it's at."

His friend considered this. "Don't you see? He *knows* where it's at. They can't get inside without the enemy knowing it, too. That's why they've asked us."

"It's not worth it," Little Turnip said.

"This isn't a choice, brother. Think! What do we say when he asks us why we didn't try to go inside?" When Burning Leopard saw that Little Turnip was still hesitant, he put a hand on his friend's shoulders and stared into his eyes. "Think about our fathers. They'd want us to be brave."

Little Turnip turned away, exhaled, and peered through the opening again. The soldier was still asleep and snoring. Maybe, just maybe, they could get away with it. He gave his friend a faint nod. From the pouch, Burning Leopard removed a single sheet of paper—one taken from the apothecary's—and inserted it between the door and wall. He ran the paper slowly up the side of the door.

When he couldn't go up any farther, the sheet crumpled at one side, and he said, "Here it is. Here's the lock. Hand me my knife in the bag."

Inside the pouch Little Turnip found a bone-handle knife, one he had seen his friend use to cut goat meat at feasts. Burning Leopard unhooked the latch on the other side of the door and cracked the entrance open. Winking at Little Turnip, he crawled through with the blade between his teeth.

Little Turnip rested his head against the wall, too scared to check on his friend's progress. He had a bad feeling. They were going to be caught, he was sure. The man inside would take them to wherever the people below the mountain put their criminals, someplace smellier and dirtier than their latrines. The interpreter would pretend he didn't know them. They wouldn't see Home Mountain again. He would never marry, never have children—never even touch a woman. He would die in a dark hole without ever finding his parents.

A-ma's advice came back to him: *Leave enough room in your hope to expect worse.* What was animal heaven like? The elders had described it as a majestic valley of peach trees, waterfalls, and grazing buffalo. "You shouldn't feel bad about killing an animal for its meat," an elder had once told him at the marketplace. Little Turnip was six or seven years old, selling a rabbit for A-ma, watching the butcher hack its limbs off. "The guilt you feel now is one of the unenlightened. What you did will be forgiven when we reach paradise, which is the same for all." The same for all, he repeated.

"All right," Burning Leopard whispered, crawling out with a stack of papers and a handgun. "Let's get out of here."

Little Turnip followed Burning Leopard to the front door. His friend flicked a coin to the lady at the entrance, and when it rolled on the ground and the lady bent down to grab it, he tilted his head at Little Turnip and made a kissing action. Little Turnip forced out a laugh.

By the time they passed through the pavilion again, he wasn't nervous. People walked by without paying any attention to them, and Little Turnip's thoughts drifted toward the object they had found: the gun. He had never seen one out of its holster before. He wondered if it was heavy, what the grip felt like, whether the wheel in the middle turned. "Let me take a look," he said. "Let me feel it."

Burning Leopard pointed to a bench at the doorway to the bathhouse. Sitting down, he glanced around before loosening the strings of the pouch. Little Turnip took a peek but couldn't see much. He reached inside, pushed the papers out of the way, and found the gun. His fingers brushed the cold barrel and felt the coarse texture of the grip. Running his fingertips along the barrel, he tried inserting his pinky in the opening. He laughed when he discovered that his finger had become slightly stuck. With his other hand he found the outline pistol and held it in place while he pulled his pinky out.

Suddenly, Miss Choi and the boys walked out of the bathhouse, talking and laughing. She cast a glance at Little Turnip and looked away. Then, as if just recognizing them, she turned back and gazed at them with curiosity.

"What are you two doing?" she asked.

Quickly Burning Leopard pulled the pouch to his chest. "Get lost," he spat out, and flicked a pebble at her.

58

ON THE MULE CART RIDE back to the compound, Miss Choi kept staring at Little Turnip. Her expression was more serious than angry. He felt she almost wanted to smile. She didn't pay any attention to Burning Leopard. She continued to stare, and Little Turnip sensed that they'd been caught—that somehow she knew more about what they had done than they did themselves.

As instructed, they went straight to the interpreter's office. The interpreter handed Little Turnip the second half of their payment, dismissed him, and asked Burning Leopard to stay for a while longer. "He's impressed," Burning Leopard said when he rejoined Little Turnip, patting him on the back. When Little Turnip walked down the winding staircase and reached the courtyard to pull in the day's laundry, Miss Choi was sitting on a bench, waiting for him.

"What are you two doing here?" she asked. Her arms were crossed over a book.

He didn't know what to say. The only woman he had ever really talked with was A-ma, and half the time she was mad at him. He stood by the clotheslines, scratching his neck. A part of him didn't want to move out of the shadows—didn't want to reveal his face to her.

Finally he managed to say, "We work for the foreigners. Just like you."

She got up off the bench and walked over to him. Shaking her head, she said, "No, you're not like me. I work for the boys. Not *them*." When he didn't say anything, she added, "You don't know what's going on, do you? What about your friend? Does he know what's going on?"

"What do you mean?" he asked.

"*Them.* Do you know who they are?"

What was she asking him? Little Turnip wondered. Was this some type of trick question? She was a teacher, after all, and he could tell that some of the boys were afraid of her. "They're soldiers from across the sea."

She nodded. "Japanese. They've killed thousands of us. They're part of a terrible empire. And you're doing their dirty work."

"If they're so evil, why are you here?"

She turned away, giving him her shoulder, the shape of which reminded him of the smooth sandstone found near the lake between the highest peaks of Home Mountain. For a moment he thought he might have stumped her. Then he saw what she was looking at: the boys across the courtyard, drawing water into a bucket to be used for dinner.

"My nephew's with them," she said. "I'm all he has." She told him that she had been at the orphanage when the cook had arrived, inspecting the conditions, and she was just about to leave with her nephew when the cook was walking out with a dozen boys. He told her he'd take her nephew but that he didn't need a teacher. She followed him to the mansion anyway and went to the Japanese leaders to ask for a job herself. After she had spoken a few words of Japanese to the interpreter, she was hired.

Little Turnip squinted at the boys, scanning their features one by one, trying to find a resemblance. He wanted to ask which one was her nephew but then thought better of it. Why would she tell him? Why would she trust anyone whom she believed was working for the evil invaders?

"We're here because of family, too," he said. "We're looking for our fathers." He wasn't sure if this was the right thing to say, and he waited for a reaction before revealing anything more. When she turned around, he added, "Well, Burning Leopard is looking for his father. I'm trying to find both of my parents. Burning Leopard's mother is still on Home Mountain. He's Lolo and I'm not."

"I could tell." Sitting back down, Miss Choi patted the bench for Little Turnip to join her.

He tiptoed over, took the coins out of his pocket—he'd lost money the last time he'd sat on a bench like this—and plopped down on the corner, as far away from Miss Choi as the seat allowed.

"So tell me more about your parents," she said. "Are they in the city?"

"No, they're fighting for a general named Mao. Do you know him?"

She laughed. "Of course. Everyone knows the leader of the revolution. But the Red Road Army is thousands of miles away. Why are you two *here*?"

"The foreigners—they've promised to take us north after they've crossed our mountains. We'll ride as far up as Shaanxi. That's where our parents are."

Miss Choi bit her lip and stared at him.

"Listen," she said. "I don't know what they've promised you or your friend or the villagers on your mountain, but the Japanese are wicked. They don't care about anyone in this country. They want our farmland, our water, our jewels. Now, that doesn't mean they won't take you north with them. It doesn't mean they're not going to do what they've said. But my advice to you and your friend is to find some other way. The longer you stay with them, the more likely it is they will do something bad to you."

"If you're so afraid of them, why did you bring your nephew here?"

"It's better than an orphanage, where the kids are sure to go hungry. Here, at least they feed you." She turned and scooted next to him, close enough for him to notice her shampoo—winter melon. "Anyway, we won't be staying for long. As soon as I find another job, we'll be out of here. I suggest you two do the same. Find other people to take you up north."

Little Turnip wanted to talk more with her, but Burning Leopard's silhouette hurried past one of the windows on the second floor. He knew his friend wouldn't be happy if he saw him talking to Miss Choi. He got up quickly, thanked her, and made his way to the kitchen. While he washed dishes, his head raced like a rushing river. What should he believe? Whom should he trust? He felt like the plates in his hands, submerged in soapy water, where everything became murky.

59

MORE THAN ONCE OVER THE next few weeks, he almost told his friend what Miss Choi had said. But Burning Leopard was spending more time in the interpreter's office—on a few occasions he didn't even come down for dinner duties—and Little Turnip couldn't find the right words, or the heart, to break his friend's freshly found enthusiasm for their new life. Burning Leopard was in a better mood, he no longer complained as much, and they were becoming closer friends, talking late into the night in the stockroom, laughing at people they remembered or things that had happened on Home Mountain.

Burning Leopard didn't even make a big fuss about Little Turnip attending one or two of Miss Choi's lessons, only giving a slight shake of his head. If everything was going well, Little Turnip thought, why should he sour the mood by telling his friend something he didn't want to hear? Soon, Miss Choi's advice receded to the back of his mind like a tiny splinter into the flesh of his foot, bothering him only if he thought about it.

He needed time, he told himself, time to get ready for the eventual trip up north—with or without the foreigners' help. During Miss Choi's classes, he was beginning to improve his language skills. He was able to pronounce some common words now: *mi*, rice; *fu mu*, father and mother; *lan t'se*, the color blue. It was all very strange, he decided, the way those below the mountain spoke—their stresses and intonations and the manner in which their syllables were strung together. It clogged up his tongue like mongoose fur. Still, for the sake of surviving independently, he continued to attend the classes, and although he wasn't as confident speaking with city folk as his friend was, he hoped that he would know enough, when the time came, to exchange a few words with his parents.

One Sunday night, while watching moving images on the wall with the boys, Miss Choi, and the foreigners, Little Turnip suddenly felt a pair of hands squeezing his shoulders. He tried to rise, but the person behind him pushed him back down.

"*Gan ma?*" he asked in his newly learned, broken Mandarin. "What's up?"

"Another special mission, brother," Burning Leopard said. "Don't be too eager to get up. Leave your seat slowly and quietly."

"I don't want to go at all," Little Turnip whispered.

Sunday nights were the ones he looked forward to the most, and today the wall was showing a film about foreigners even more unusual than the Japanese. Men with bright hair and floppy hats rode horses, robbed banks, and shot at other men with feathers on their heads and paint on their cheeks. Little Turnip wanted to know how the show would end, who would blast away whom, and which one the pretty lady would pick to marry.

"Forget about that nonsense," Burning Leopard said, flicking his friend's ear. "We have our own war to fight."

Hearing that, Little Turnip wanted to stay in his seat even more. But his friend would think him a coward if he remained for much longer, so he sighed, ducked below the projected image, and followed Burning Leopard to the stairwell. He glanced back at the wall to catch a few more images and saw Miss Choi giving him the same stare she had given him on the mule ride home from the city. He quickened his pace to avoid her glare.

When they reached the second floor, the interpreter was locking the door of his office. He waved to four soldiers behind him, who ran up, and then together they walked past Burning Leopard and Little Turnip without so much as acknowledging their presence.

"Come on," Burning Leopard said.

Trailing him, Little Turnip asked, "What's this about?"

"You'll see. Tonight we get to ride in the Kurogane."

60

THERE WERE, IN FACT, TWO Kuroganes. They rode in the second one. Descending down the hill, they held on to the slanted metal poles toward the rear of the vehicle, which was cold from the recent summer chill. At first, since they were driving over dirt, it was difficult for Little Turnip to keep his balance. When the vehicle turned onto a paved avenue, the ride got much smoother. There were orange lanterns hanging outside the stores and smoke rising from the kabob vendors. Little Turnip found it surprising that, after all these weeks, he had never seen the city past dusk before. Nighttime on Home Mountain was near complete darkness. The mountain ranges often hid the moon, and candles were a luxury reserved for ceremonies that bid farewell to those on their way to animal heaven or ones that welcomed newborns still unfamiliar with their human forms. Little Turnip wondered how these folks, so busy and alive right now, would be awake enough in the morning to do their work.

They arrived at the city square. There were islands of people talking, laughing, and bartering. A crowd huddled over two old men, who placed black and white pebbles onto a sheet of gridded paper. For a moment, Little Turnip didn't recognize the shape of the bathhouse, its roof illuminated by two torches at the corners.

Before the vehicles had even come to a complete stop, the people on the sidewalk started dispersing. Upon seeing the foreigners storm off with their rifles pointing forward, the city folk ran in the opposite direction or fled inside the buildings. Parents yelled for their kids. An old man tripped over a flowerpot. The only people who lingered were those who were too drunk to get up or too greedy to leave their stalls.

The soldiers formed two columns and made their way to the other side of the street. The interpreter followed behind with Little Turnip and Burning Leopard. When they passed the bathhouse and reached the narrow alleyway where the pavilion stood, the soldiers quickened their pace. Little Turnip breathed heavily to keep up, the wind running through his hair and raising goose bumps on his arms. The soldiers didn't knock down the door of the massage parlor, as he had thought they might. Instead, they made their way to a structure behind it—a building that, because of its short oval door and windows crisscrossed with bamboo poles, seemed like it had been constructed a long time ago. The roof was lined with tar and the windows were darkened with black paper. When he had walked past it the last time he was here, he had thought it was abandoned.

The lead soldier lifted his fist and crouched down. Then the others hid behind a half-crumbled wall where garbage was kept, scattering a pack of rats. One scurried under Little Turnip's feet, close enough for him to catch it if he had his net.

"Wait here," Burning Leopard said.

He scooted over to the interpreter, who was rubbing his hands together, trying to scrape off something sticky. They exchanged a few words, and then the interpreter pointed to a few spots around the building. Burning Leopard crept back over.

"Okay," he said to Little Turnip. "You scout out the left side and I'll scout out the right. We'll meet up behind the building."

"What am I looking for?"

"Count the number of men inside. See if they have guns. See if they know we're here, if they're getting ready for our attack. Oh—" Burning Leopard nodded to the foreigners behind them. "And don't do anything stupid to embarrass us."

This last piece of advice, Little Turnip understood, was not given because his friend thought he'd actually do something stupid but because

he didn't want Little Turnip to act like a coward in front of the soldiers, who were all staring at them like a hungry pack of wolves. What
else could Little Turnip do but follow his friend along the side of the
half-crumbled wall, fingers pausing on the jagged brickwork with every
step, knees cold and shaky, the moon lighting the greasy cobblestones
brown and blue and silver?

They first snuck up to the crisscrossed windows on either side of
the door, the ones darkened with black paper. Little Turnip hid under
the left one, as instructed, and, with his hands clutching the railing,
slowly pulled his head up to the window until his nose was over one
of the small diamond holes. He poked a finger through the thin sheet
of paper that served as the window, and with one eye saw two dozen
men—many more than what he'd thought could fit inside from looking
at the structure in the alleyway. They were chatting at their desks, smoking, slurping on noodles, or sleeping on one of the many cots hanging
from the ceiling. There were machines on every table, not unlike the
ones he'd seen at the mansion, although these were rustier. There were
weapons as well—rifles, handguns, and spears—and one of the men
even had a saber in his lap and was rocking back and forth on his chair
while wiping the blade with a cloth.

From this angle, there appeared to be just the one large room. Little
Turnip lowered his head and made his way around the left side of the
building. The wall was long, and he was surprised to find near the ceiling a small square window that he hadn't noticed before. The fact that
it was dim and tiny made him think there was only a closet on the other
side, but he rose on his tiptoes and looked through anyway and he saw
a pair of stone beds separated by a frilly curtain. On them two women
were sleeping—wives of the soldiers, perhaps—and one of them had
her arms wrapped around a baby.

He turned the corner. There weren't any windows on the back of the
building. He knelt and waited for Burning Leopard. When he noticed
his friend's shadow creeping over the corner, he crawled over.

"I saw something," he whispered.

Burning Leopard brought his finger up to his mouth. "Not here," he
said. "Let's go back first."

As soon as they had returned to the garbage area, the interpreter scooted next to them. Burning Leopard told him to wait, and Little Turnip felt a slight thrill at having recognized the word.

"I saw two women and a kid in the bedroom," he told his friend.

"You saw a bedroom?" Burning Leopard asked, lifting an eyebrow.

Little Turnip pointed to the left side of the building, in the direction of the high window. "There. A small room with two beds. There are two women and a baby sleeping."

"I didn't see anything," Burning Leopard said.

"I'm not lying. I saw them."

His friend squinted at the left side of the building, rubbed his eyes, and squinted again. Then he turned to the interpreter.

Little Turnip grabbed his friend's shirt. "You'll tell him, won't you? You'll mention the bedroom with the women and baby?"

"Yeah, yeah," Burning Leopard said, pulling his shirt back. "Stop being annoying."

With the soldiers huddling around him, Burning Leopard smoothed the dirt under his feet and started drawing the floor plan. He marked the tables and chairs that were occupied. Then he raised four fingers and rested his head against his hand to indicate the men who were sleeping. The interpreter nodded, signaling to the columns of soldiers to go left and right. Little Turnip wanted to go over and remind Burning Leopard about the room again, but then his friend pointed to the left side of the building and waved to Little Turnip, which made him crouch back down. The interpreter nodded and gestured to the column going left to pay special attention. Finally, he started moving behind the soldiers as well.

Burning Leopard curled his index finger at Little Turnip. Little Turnip joined him, and his friend said, "Our job's done. Now we watch."

Little Turnip expected to see arrests. He expected the interpreter to knock on the door and capture the men inside for interrogation. When the soldiers around the building slung their submachine guns from their shoulders, he told himself that it was just a precaution in case any of the men inside tried to escape or, worse, leave through the windows and shoot at them from behind. It was only until the foreigners had fired continuously for half a minute—the night becoming bright with blips of orange; the guns a consistent, deafening series of cracking sounds; screams coming from inside and from people blocks away—that he realized there wouldn't be any prisoners. He had almost forgotten, by that point, the bedroom he'd found.

Then, during a lull in the shooting, the interpreter strode to the left side of the building and directed the soldiers' attention to the small, high window. They didn't kick the wall open to save the women or child inside. Instead, they reloaded their rifles, pointed just below the window, and fired off another series of rounds.

Then it dawned on Little Turnip that the men inside had picked this old structure because it had a space where their loved ones could stay during emergencies, hidden away like stick bugs on a branch. And then he thought back to what Miss Choi had said, about the foreigners being wicked, about bad things happening, about how he should leave as soon as he could, and he wondered if the women inside would still be alive had he taken her advice, and he couldn't help but feel a self-hatred rising in the pit of his belly, a guilt—like the leaflets in the air and the words on the placards outside the shops and the massage parlor—that he hadn't known such evil could exist in the world.

He did all he could to prevent himself from crying. Looking over to Burning Leopard, he checked to see if his friend was feeling the same thing.

Burning Leopard shrugged. "Well," he said, "I didn't expect that."

In his friend's hand was the pistol they had found at the massage parlor, and Little Turnip realized that Burning Leopard had been holding it the entire time, waiting for a chance to use it. After the soldiers had lowered their rifles, Burning Leopard started walking up to join them, kicking at the shells on the ground. Upon his approach, the front door opened. A man—the one who'd been cleaning the saber—ran out with the blade above his head, his shirt torn and bloody. Burning Leopard took a few quick steps backward, turned as if about to run, then straightened himself. He lifted the pistol and shot the man in the leg, falling down himself due to the recoil.

The interpreter marched over to the man writhing on the ground. He kicked the saber out of the man's hand and shot him in the head. He placed his gun back into his holster, which was strapped across his chest, and extended an arm to help Burning Leopard up. The two exchanged some words, the conversation ending with Burning Leopard lowering his head and handing over his weapon. Finally, his friend jogged back over to where Little Turnip was. There was a sheen of sweat below his hairline and his pupils reflected the moon.

"Ready for our next mission, brother?" he asked.

"You just killed that man," Little Turnip said. It was as if, by stating it, he was convincing himself that his friend had done what he had seen him do.

"What, back there? It was just reflexes. You didn't see the crazed way he was coming at me? And I didn't kill him. I injured him. The interpreter killed him." His friend stiffened his shoulders. "I would have killed him, though. If I had to. Kill a man. Now I know."

"And the women inside? The child? You would have killed them, too?"

"That was unfortunate," Burning Leopard said. "But I'm not blaming myself for it and you shouldn't blame yourself, either. This is what warriors do. They take no chances. They make sure no danger remains."

"What dangers are there with two sleeping women?" Little Turnip found his throat constricting, and he couldn't stop himself from crying.

"Please. I thought you were tougher than this. I thought you were the son of warriors. Your father's done what the soldiers just did." Burning Leopard nodded fiercely. "Yes. I'd bet my inheritance on it. Now clean yourself up. You're embarrassing yourself. More importantly, you're embarrassing me. And we still have work to do."

"What work?" Little Turnip wiped snot away from his nose. "Everyone inside is dead."

"You're a prophet, Turnip," Burning Leopard said. "That's our mission exactly."

They ducked their heads under the circular doorway. The foreigners followed. Light from the overhead lamps leaked out of the bullet holes on the walls and smoke rose from the blasted machinery. There was a smell of cooked meat, and as Little Turnip's gaze shifted from the cots to the chairs and then down to the floor, he saw men with their legs blown off, others with flesh hanging from their bellies, and still another whose facial features were no longer recognizable. He hadn't expected to see such devastation: The bullets had been so small, so quick, and he'd imagined that the men inside would be filled with tiny, clean holes, their bodies posed in various states of heroic defeat.

"Stop staring and give me a hand." Burning Leopard was kneeling on the ground, trying to turn over a body.

Little Turnip crouched and grabbed the man's pants, and together with Burning Leopard pushing the shoulder they flipped the body over. They saw the face of an old bearded man, and Burning Leopard reached into the man's pocket, pulled out a watch, and handed it to Little Turnip. Little Turnip almost dropped it, his palms shaking. The gold-colored band was shot straight through. A few links came undone and fell to the floor.

"Give it to the interpreter or one of the soldiers," Burning Leopard said, now working to slip off a silver ring.

Little Turnip walked over and handed the watch to the interpreter, who stuffed it into his shirt pocket, under his golden cigarette case.

"You feeling all right?" the interpreter asked. Little Turnip gave a nod, and the interpreter sucked in smoke. Then, picking tobacco off his tongue, he said, "*Na li, na li. Wo shih li. K'uai tien.*"

It took Little Turnip a few seconds to translate these last words, which, after taking into account the direction the interpreter was pointing at, he understood as, *There, there, in the bedroom. Quickly.*

61

FOR MANY NIGHTS LITTLE TURNIP had nightmares. He would be standing out in A-ma's sweet potato field or walking along the edge of one of Home Mountain's many familiar hills. Eventually his parents would appear lying alongside the road. His father had the same face as the old bearded man and his mother was the woman holding the infant in the secret room. He would try to shake them awake, yelling for them to get up off the ground, where, for some reason, he knew it was unsafe. "A-ma's house is around the corner!" he would shout. "It's pretty cramped and I don't know if she'd take you on, but it's worth a shot." And then they would all suddenly be in A-ma's kitchen. But something was wrong. Lifting the lid of the pot on the stove, he saw that his parents had shrunk down to the length of carrots, their bubbling faces still in the same positions as they'd been in on the road.

In the compound, Miss Choi knew something was off about him, glaring at him while he did his chores. It was impossible for him to put on a happy face, and he receded mostly to himself. He stopped coming to class and didn't show up at the movie that following Friday.

Finally, during the Dragon Boat Festival, after the foreigners had finished their feast of roast quail and sweet rice wrapped in bamboo leaves, she confronted him.

"What do you know about the massacre?" she asked.

They were in the grand dining hall. The dinner was over, and after dessert most of the foreigners had dispersed into the courtyard to observe the gas-filled lanterns floating toward the crescent moon. Little Turnip and Miss Choi were the only ones who remained, collecting plates and silverware in a wicker basket. Sometimes Miss Choi's classes went over the allotted hour, and she assisted the cook by occasionally helping out the kids with their chores. Burning Leopard had been excused from dinner duties and was instead washing the interpreter's Kurogane in the garage.

"It's all true, whatever people are saying. Whatever you heard, I saw it with my own eyes," Little Turnip replied. The words poured out of him like blood from a wound; he hadn't known until now how much he needed to tell someone.

Miss Choi collected the quail bones and dirty napkins and wrapped them in a tablecloth.

"Things like that happen all the time now," she said. "It's a shame they make kids like you take part. "

Little Turnip felt sick. In the servant's partition of the grand hall, waiting to serve the next course, the cook had given him and the other children some of the leftover dinner. The food was rich and oily, and now Little Turnip wanted to throw up.

"Do you think my parents are like them?" he asked.

"Like who?"

"The foreigners." He was wearing a suit and bow tie, oversized hand-me-downs he was required to put on whenever he served food at the grand dining hall. He had envied the foreigners' clothing when he first got here, but now he was disgusted that he looked like one of them. "They're soldiers just like my parents," he said. "My parents must have killed people, probably many people."

"Your parents are fighting for Mao," she said, "which means they're fighting for a better country. These foreigners fight to take that away from us. That alone makes them different."

"Have you found another job yet?" he asked. He looked up from what he was doing to check her reaction. He hoped he hadn't offended her.

She just shook her head. "No," she said, pouring the wine left over from multiple glasses into one cup. "But even if I don't, I'm not staying here much longer."

From below the window he heard the kitchen door open and the cook yelling for them to hurry up with the dishes. Soon he might come barging in, and then Little Turnip wouldn't have the opportunity to ask Miss Choi what he so desperately wanted to ask her.

He lowered the basket to the table and stared at her.

"I only ask because I don't know what to do anymore. Burning Leopard is one of them now, and I'm afraid of him. I'm afraid of everyone here—everyone except you. I was just wondering"—he paused, glancing around to make sure nobody was watching them—"if you could take me with you."

Miss Choi brushed away a long strand of curly hair from her eyes. There was no emotion on her pretty face, no indication that she was considering his request.

"I won't be a burden," he pleaded. "I won't even sit next to you on the mule cart if you don't want me to. I'll just run along the side of the wagon and follow you up north, if that's where you're going. Even if it's not, I'd still want to come. Maybe I could meet some people who know the way."

Miss Choi moved closer to him. "Stick out your hands," she said sternly, "palms up."

He did what she asked, and she examined the three creases below his fingers, first the left palm and then the right. Her hands were smooth but cold. Her nails glided across the lines in his palm like needles. He couldn't control his eyes anymore and started to cry.

"You poor thing," she finally said. "You should never have left the mountains; your life lines are scattered." She let go of his hands and touched his cheek. "You're a good boy. I suspected you were a good boy before and now I know for sure."

"So I can come?" he asked again. "You'll let me?"

She smiled now, moving back a step. Then she held her arms wide open, waiting for a hug. "Absolutely. You can absolutely come with me."

62

AFTER AGREEING TO TAKE HIM with her, Miss Choi admitted that she wanted to go north to join Mao at Yan'an, a small city in Shaanxi Province that the Communists had captured for their new capital. She had lived the easy life long enough, and now she must devote herself to making a future for the next generation, for boys like her nephew. The journey north would be tough. There were few roads and many bandits. But a resistance loyal to the cause was forming. Word had spread of a society without land tax or hereditary gentry, one based on shared suffering and full bellies. Safe houses were starting to spring up in villages all across the country. There were signs she and Little Turnip had to look for—a red dot on a gate, a sickle standing tall in a field, a crossed-out money emblem on a post—that directed them to safety. They could hop from one village to the next and be at Yan'an within a year. Little Turnip told her he was ready to go at any moment—that he could pack all his belongings before a rooster finished crowing. "It will take time for me to plan everything," she said. "I have to account for every stop we make."

And so over the next few weeks he waited, the summer chills becoming ever more common. The leaves all turned yellow and autumn crept up like mold over grain. The days shortened; the air grew damp and cold; and the foreign soldiers changed into different uniforms, marching around in tan long-sleeve jackets and thick, rusty khakis.

He began to spend more time with Miss Choi, and this didn't escape the notice of Burning Leopard, who made fun of him every chance he got, calling him "lady's man." Little Turnip didn't care; his Mandarin was improving rapidly. And luckily he didn't see too much of his friend anymore, either. Neither he nor the interpreter invited him on any more excursions. Often, Burning Leopard would come into the closet close to daybreak, plop down on the bottom bunk, and begin snoring without having uttered a word. His friend even received a special commendation from the foreigners: a paper medallion bearing the image of a soldier throwing a grenade. Little Turnip shuddered, wondering what they'd made him do to earn it. Watching him step onto the makeshift podium in the middle of the courtyard, he believed he finally understood why his friend felt an affinity with the foreigners and why he had shot the man that night. Like the Japanese, Burning Leopard saw those below the mountain as people not of his own kind. The flat land was alien, and he could care less whether its dirty citizens lived or died. He was so unlike Miss Choi, who was also from the mountains, who seemed to care about everyone.

"Does your friend still scare you?" she asked Little Turnip one day.

They were in a remote corner of the courtyard, reading books under a sheltering willow, a spot where there were few passersby in the afternoons. It was near the kitchen, so unless someone was part of the staff, there was no reason for him to be there. In fact, over the last few days, the foreign officers had been more aloof than usual, holed up in their quarters, not eating or executing drills. They barely came out at all. While picking up their vacuum bottles in the morning, Little Turnip had peeked into their dorms and seen them kneeling with their eyes closed, wearing white robes and beaded necklaces. Even the interpreter performed these rituals, his thin frame in front of a fat stone statue of a mendicant Buddhist monk.

"I barely see him anymore," Little Turnip replied. "Like I said, he's one of *them* now."

"I'm sure you know this already, but you mustn't tell him anything about our plans."

Little Turnip nodded, turning the page. The book they were reading was the one the interpreter had given him; he had read it until the bindings tore. They now reached the part where the wolf tried to blow down the third little pig's house, the one made from bricks. Failing to do so, he lit a pile of hay and stuffed it down the chimney. When the pigs stormed out, he clutched them in his arms and between his jaws. On the next page, there was a drawing of him wearing a bib and picking his teeth.

"This is a good book," Miss Choi said, smiling. "Mind if I show it to the kids tomorrow?"

He shrugged. Secretly, he wanted her to have it. He pictured it sitting beside her pillow. Maybe she would hold it while she slept.

"Which foreigner gave you this book again?"

"The one wearing glasses . . . the one who speaks our language."

"Oh," she said. Her eyebrows drew inward worriedly, and although her expression lasted for only a second, it was enough for Little Turnip to realize she knew him.

"He was the one who made us come to the massacre," he explained. "And"—he stumbled over the words—"and I think he likes you."

Miss Choi's concerned look returned. "You mustn't say that," she said. "You mustn't tell anyone. It's dangerous."

"*What* mustn't he tell? *What's* dangerous?" The voice came from the other side of the tree. Only one other person on the compound could speak Lolo.

"Nothing." Miss Choi closed the book and stuffed it into her purse. "Come to class tomorrow, Little Turnip. Don't be tardy."

She walked away, not even glancing at Burning Leopard.

"Well, well, well," his friend said, putting a foot onto the bench. He was wearing new rubber boots, the same kind the foreigners wore. "What a pair of lovebirds you two are."

Little Turnip shook his head. "I just want to learn how to read."

"Sure, sure," Burning Leopard said. After giving his boots a slap, he sat down. "I've been meaning to ask: Have you gotten over what happened that night, or are you still acting silly over nothing?"

"I'm all right," Little Turnip replied. He didn't like his friend's tone, and he didn't want to seem scared. "What about you?" he asked. "How have you been having fun with your new friends?"

"Nah." Burning Leopard scrunched up his face, as if in disgust. "They've been weird lately. They're on some sort of Buddhist fast."

Little Turnip didn't say anything. Burning Leopard got up off the bench and lay down on the ground, leaning on his elbow in the grass. He took out a new toy, a squeaky green ball—another present from the foreigners—and bounced it against the mansion's wall.

"Folks are acting crazy around here," he said. "You and your silliness. Miss Choi and her secrets. The foreigners and their fasting. Sometimes I think I'm the only normal one left."

"This place suits you," Little Turnip said.

"Let me tell you, brother, I don't mean to brag, but sometimes I think I know more about how these foreigners should do things than they do themselves. They mean to go up our mountain and conquer this city called Chongqing. That's where the Nationalist leader is located, you see, the last bastion of hope for those below the mountain. And the foreigners would make that task so much easier if they didn't follow their stupid rituals. Drowning men by the lake—at noon, no less, when the whole town was walking by. Beheadings in broad daylight. Burying folks alive . . ."

"I don't want to hear this." It was hard for Little Turnip to believe that this Burning Leopard, the one saying all this in such a smug way, was the same person who had come down the mountain with him. They had both left their homes with the same goal—to find their parents—but now it seemed like Burning Leopard had forgotten about that completely.

"I'm not saying they shouldn't do what they have to," he continued, "but why not show the folks below the mountain some mercy and compassion *most* of the time? That way the locals will help them and not make their operations miserable."

"Do you still think about your father?" Little Turnip asked.

"Of course. What kind of question is that?"

"It just seems like you don't talk about him anymore—like you've forgotten why we're here in the first place."

Burning Leopard gave out a shrill laugh, one that a foreigner might make. "Seems to me, brother, like *you're* the one who's forgotten. I'm doing what my father is doing while you're washing dishes and talking to pretty ladies." The ball bounced over his head, and he sat up to see where it went. "It's fine, though," he said. "Some people aren't cut out for this kind of life. They're squeamish, scared"—he reclined again—"like a turnip."

Little Turnip got up to leave. It was pointless trying to talk to his friend.

"Go." Burning Leopard laughed again. "Go back to washing dishes. Go back to eating scraps. Go to your little classes full of eight-year-olds, because that's where you belong."

63

BEFORE LITTLE TURNIP REACHED THE kitchen, something strange happened. He was staring at his feet, cursing his friend, and the ground started to shake. Then he heard an explosion that knocked him down. For a moment he was in a cloud of dust. Glass fell on him like droplets of rain. When everything cleared, he looked up and saw the right side of the mansion on fire. On the roof, the lion's head on that side was smoldering, its eyes turning molten and melting down to its fangs.

Foreigners in white robes funneled out of the archway, yelling and carrying buckets. More ran past him from behind. They splashed water up along the walls, trying to reach the windows. Driving up from the barracks, a brown truck pulled up to the courtyard and, from the back, soldiers came pouring out still buttoning up their shirts. They unrolled a long, floppy tube, pointed the tip at the lion's head, and fired a jet of water on its crumbling mane. A rainbow formed amid the spray, which floated into the woods.

"What the hell was that?" Burning Leopard said. He stood next to Little Turnip, shielding his eyes with a hand above his brow.

"No idea," Little Turnip managed to say. His lips were covered with ash.

Burning Leopard helped Little Turnip to his feet. Droplets from the hose cooled their faces. Despite the foreigners endlessly pouring water on the flames, the mansion continued to burn. Little Turnip had never seen a fire this destructive before. On Home Mountain, the elders had told stories about great immolations in the jungle that came once a century, clearing away entire generations of trees and shrubs and leaving bears and foxes charred on the forest floor, where villagers would forage the next day and eat the meats of the exotic animals as a way to conciliate the gods and beg that a similar blaze would not visit their settlement. He wondered if the foreigners had somehow angered the gods—if inside the mansion he would find human beings scorched in the same way.

After about ten minutes the fire was finally extinguished. The right side of the mansion was a crumbling ruin. Little Turnip learned that he was lucky the explosion had hit the side opposite the kitchen. Otherwise, he would have ended up a charred corpse.

That night, Miss Choi came back worried about her nephew. Little Turnip had anticipated this. He sat with the boy in the courtyard beneath the laundry lines. He wanted to make sure that his aunt could see him immediately so she wouldn't run around screaming his name. The boy was an eight-year-old named Rainy Cloud. He was responsible mainly for peeling potatoes and skinning cucumbers, and Little Turnip realized that night why the boy had never uttered a word in class and why her aunt talked about him only in passing and never introduced him. The boy was mute; he had suffered from throat disease from infancy. When Little Turnip had offered to bring him to a bench and wait for his aunt, the boy only nodded. When Little Turnip tried making conversation, the boy pointed to his mouth and showed him his tongue. Rushing to Rainy Cloud, Miss Choi thanked Little Turnip for looking out for him. "I made the right choice in taking you along with me," she said to Little Turnip. "If anything should happen to me, I trust you to care for Rainy Cloud." Wrapping her overcoat around her nephew's shoulders, she told Little Turnip that she had almost finished preparing for their journey and that they should be ready to leave within one or two weeks.

64

THE ATTACK ITSELF—AND IT WAS an attack, the interpreter told them—forced the foreigners to abandon the mansion's southwest wing and relocate the officers who had slept there to derelict log cabins in the hills. Although only two foreigners inside the mansion had been killed, a dozen or so had been burned, and one had lost an arm. Luckily, the blast hadn't struck the kitchen. All the boys were fine and their quarters unscathed.

Dynamite had caused the explosion—dynamite stolen by Nationalist operatives from the foreigners' tunnel-clearing detachment housed in another section of the city. It was in retaliation for the crackdown at the city square. The tunnel-clearer in charge of protecting the explosives was brought to the compound and whipped in the woods before the entire army. He wasn't tied down or handcuffed. He nodded when the general asked him to take off his uniform and pushed against a tree as the lashes licked his back. At least they were consistent, Little Turnip thought, watching with the cook and the boys in the back of the audience. The foreigners didn't show much mercy to their own, either. "Didn't I tell you?" Burning Leopard said, shaking his head. "None of this would have happened if they were only a little nicer."

Afterward the foreigners became more alert, more active. The red-and-white flag was raised every day. Soldiers started their drills again, gathering to run laps in the woods before Little Turnip had even collected their vacuum bottles. The sound of gunfire reverberated from the hills all morning and afternoon: target practice. Electrical equipment in the mansion was brought down, crated, and stashed onto trucks. Artillery pieces he hadn't even known existed were pulled from a camouflaged warehouse behind the barracks and wheeled out of the compound daily. He thought the foreigners were doing this only because they didn't want to lose more equipment to another attack, but Burning Leopard told him that it was for another reason entirely.

"Get ready for good news," his friend said. "We're moving out."

"When did the interpreter tell you?"

"He didn't. I got the news from him." Burning Leopard nodded to the cook, who was stir-frying glass noodles and scolding his helper for throwing in black pepper at the wrong moment.

"The cook told you?" Little Turnip wasn't buying the story. His friend had barely spoken to the cook, and the few times he had, he had done so with back talk and contempt.

"Not exactly. Yesterday, I saw the interpreter talking to the cook. The cook came out of the interpreter's office with his head as low as an anthill. Haven't you noticed the fits he's been throwing today? They're the kind that only someone who knows he'll lose his job could give."

It was true, Little Turnip considered. The cook had woken him up earlier than usual that morning, pounding on the closet door, yelling for him to refill the water in the vacuum bottles even though the foreigners wouldn't need them until they'd finished their run.

"He should treat the boys nicer," Little Turnip said. "He might find other work. They have nothing. They'll probably go back to the orphanage, where they'll starve."

"Oh, well. Nobody has it easy. Anyway, with him out of a job, we won't be needed here anymore, either." Burning Leopard brought the last load of diced mushrooms out of the wash bin and stood up to stretch his back. "I don't even know why I'm doing this. Like I should take orders from him anymore." Heading to the door, he nodded for Little Turnip to follow.

"Poor boys," Little Turnip said. "I bet a third of them will die by this time next year."

Burning Leopard put his arm around Little Turnip's shoulders. "Buck up, brother. We can't save everyone. It's time we think about our future. Didn't you hear what I said? We're moving out!"

It became clear, over the next two days, that his friend's information was correct. The foreigners began to withdraw from the compound, starting with the soldiers in the wooded barracks below the hill. There were usually two or three trucks leaving every day. Entire regiments sat inside the vehicles, hunched over from their heavy packs, their rifles between their legs. The loudspeakers, which had barely been used before, began playing brass-heavy martial music. The soldiers waiting to get on the next truck stared at the flag and sang with the music. When the song ended, they raised their arms and shouted, *"Tenno heika banzai!"* "Ten thousand years," Miss Choi whispered to Little Turnip. "They wish their emperor will live for ten thousand years." Little Turnip laughed. "But wouldn't he want to go to animal heaven after the first five hundred?"

Nowadays, he and Burning Leopard's duties consisted almost entirely of packing supplies and loading them onto the vehicles. There were no more afternoon naps, no more shows on Sunday. The foreigners made them take down and pack everything: the watercolors of mountains and fish hanging on the walls, the electric chandeliers, the celadon incense burners, the vases with the drawings of beautiful ancient women, the silk drapes, and the wool carpeting. On the general's order, even the busts of the three remaining lions sitting atop the mansion were carefully lowered using a crane and shipped out like eggs stolen from their nests.

He didn't know how long this was going to last. The courtyard looked emptier with each passing day. Every morning he hoped it would be the one Miss Choi told him that they were leaving, but he saw her less frequently now that all her classes were canceled. She didn't come to the compound regularly anymore; instead, she showed up every two or three days to check up on her nephew. When there was no work, Little Turnip paced around the courtyard trying to find her, checking their spot under the willow, inspecting the empty clotheslines, or just staring out the kitchen window. "Is your aunt coming today?" he'd ask Rainy Cloud impatiently, and the boy would only shrug.

Finally, on the morning when the cook moved out all his belongings—the other boys leaving for the orphanage each carried a bundle of rags and two cans of sardines (gifts from the cook)—Miss Choi came to the kitchen to pick up Rainy Cloud.

"Be ready to leave on the next full moon," she said. "That's tomorrow night." She took out a tiny green purse. She unfolded a few crumpled bills and gave them to her nephew, who smiled with delight, his ears wiggling. Then she handed some copper coins to Little Turnip. "Here's some money just in case you need it."

Taking the coins, he nodded fiercely. "Where do we meet?"

"Meet us at the courtyard, in our usual spot. When the view of the moon from the kitchen creeps past the tallest branches of the willow, that's the cue to come out. I've timed it myself. It should be around an hour past sundown." They would walk to the edge of the city, she continued. A peasant with a horse-drawn cart would be there to take them to his village, a town sympathetic to the cause. From there, they would wait until a band of Communist agents showed up. Then they would follow them north to Yan'an.

65

LITTLE TURNIP LOADED THE LAST crates of persimmons and bags of potatoes onto the supply truck. The vehicle shot a cough-inducing smoke at him as it rolled away. The courtyard was slippery from thousands of papers thrown out of the windows. Each page contained hundreds of characters written on them, and the ink made the entire compound smell of old, crackling paint. Office chairs were stacked underneath all four archways. Pillows and bedding material were placed on the topmost chairs. There would be one more truck, possibly two, and then nothing would be left. Overhead, a colony of bats flew by. The setting sun, an orange half dot on the horizon, promised night within the hour.

"Let's take a break," Burning Leopard said, washing his face in the courtyard's stagnant fountain, which also contained sheets of floating paper. "The interpreter said the other officers will handle all this easy stuff when they return with a new truck. Come tomorrow, we'll be out of here for good!"

The interpreter waved them over. He was standing in the shadows next to the chairs, his back against an archway buttress. He was drinking from a dimpled glass bottle with golden liquid inside. When they got close, Little Turnip smelled the bitter odor of liquor, so strong that it seemed to be spewing from every pore of the man's sweaty body. He gave the bottle to Burning Leopard, who took a hearty swig. His friend shoved the bottle to Little Turnip, but he pushed it back and shook his head.

"Come on, little brother," his friend said. "I know you've drunk before. There's plenty of wine at the feasts."

"I've never liked it," Little Turnip said, which was only partially true. He had enjoyed the way the bamboo liquor made him feel, but it also gave him rashes.

"*Drink!*" the interpreter commanded, eyeing him. His round spectacles drooped to the tip of his nose and his legs were swaying.

Little Turnip took a small sip and coughed. The stuff was stronger than anything they had back home.

The interpreter keeled over in a fit of laughter. Burning Leopard joined him. They brought three chairs down from the stack, slid two behind their backs, and pushed one to Little Turnip. Glancing in the direction of the willow, he reluctantly sat down. Burning Leopard and the interpreter returned to their drinking, laughing and telling each other stories as if they were best friends. Although Little Turnip's Mandarin had improved a lot since coming to the compound—to the point where he felt somewhat comfortable listening to those below the mountain—the two people in front of him were talking so fast and in such specific terms that it was difficult for him to make out what they were saying.

"I told him about my grandfather's accidental marriage to his cousin," Burning Leopard said in Lolo. "Surely you heard the story, too, Turnip. On an expedition to gather silkworm larvae when he was seventeen, my grandfather fell in love with a girl at the base of a neighboring mountain. She was ladling water from a stream, and my grandfather invited her up to our mountain. His father, the fabled elder Serene Stork, liked her immediately. They set a date. On their wedding night, after they'd completed the bonding dance and just as my grandfather was about to take her inside, my great-grandmother recognized the wrinkly birthmark on the forehead of her sister, who was sitting with the bride's family, cracking walnuts. And in front of the whole procession she yelled, 'Stop them now! The gods are watching!'" Burning Leopard laughed hysterically. Then he settled down enough to take another swig of the alcohol. "It's not really that great a story if you weren't there," he said, shaking his head. "I don't know why this guy found it so funny."

The interpreter waved for the bottle back. "*Wo hsiang ch`ü wo te piao mei,*" he said, and Burning Leopard translated: "He said he'd marry his cousin, too. She's a dancer in the navy, making sure the sailors are sent off from the port of"—the interpreter repeated the name of the city—"the port of O-sa-ka in high spirits. If he was in my grandfather's position that night, he'd tell his mother to shut up."

Little Turnip sat there listening, his hands locking together and then unlocking. The moon was out, although it hadn't crept past the willow yet, at least not from this angle. His mind raced trying to come up with a reason to excuse himself.

"*Ni,* Turnip." The interpreter pointed a wobbly finger at him. "What about you? Have you ever been with a girl?"

Little Turnip remained quiet. Trying to smile, he shook his head.

"Don't be shy," Burning Leopard said in Mandarin. He turned back to the interpreter. "You can't tell from the way he looks, but he's having quite the affair with his teacher, the pretty, pretty Miss Choi."

The interpreter stared at Little Turnip, his face turning hard. Then he took another long drink from his bottle. "Is that so?"

"It's true." Burning Leopard nodded. "They share books together. They shared that one about the wolves you gave us. I saw them myself. They were so adorable."

"I have to use the bathroom," Little Turnip said. All the supplies were packed and there was nothing left to do in the kitchen. It was the best excuse he could come up with.

"Pee in there." Burning Leopard kicked his feet in the direction of the fountain. "No one cares anymore."

"No, I have to do more than just pee."

"Me, too, come to think of it," Burning Leopard said. "I'll join you."

And just like that, Little Turnip found himself walking toward the willow with Burning Leopard. The kitchen was a short distance around the corner from the tree, and a plan formed in Little Turnip's head. He would stay in the bathroom for a long time, feigning diarrhea. When his friend left, he would sneak out and look for Miss Choi. Shaking off his friend wouldn't be a problem. What he was more worried about was whether Miss Choi could make it to their spot. Seeing the interpreter in the courtyard with Burning Leopard, she would have to explain why she was back at the compound. She might not risk coming to the willow at all. And what if she left without him? Where would he be then?

"Hurry up," Burning Leopard called from the kitchen.

"I have it bad," Little Turnip replied, squatting over the hole in the ground. Nothing was coming out, although he tried out of habit.

"Forget it," his friend said. "Find me in the courtyard when you're done."

There was the sound of footsteps and then the kitchen door slamming shut. Just to be safe, Little Turnip counted to one hundred before leaving the stall. Then he snuck out to the far side of the willow, ducking his head the entire time. The interpreter's laugher echoed up to him like the howling of a wild dog.

66

IT WAS GETTING DARK. The moon hid behind long sheets of passing clouds. Little Turnip didn't know for how long he'd been waiting, although it couldn't have been more than half an hour. Nobody had ever bothered giving him a watch—not that he knew, precisely, how to read one. The many arms, numbers, and circles were much more confusing than the simple sundial back home.

He leaned his head back against the trunk, feeling the knotted vines pushing against the base of his neck, and imagined the journey north with Miss Choi. Then he thought about his mother. He wondered whether she was nicer than Miss Choi. Probably not, he reasoned, since his mother was a soldier. But she was probably nicer than A-ma, who had beaten him every chance she got. His mother: not as nice as Miss Choi but nicer than A-ma. He could accept this. Now he wondered if she was pretty. . . .

In the distance, someone screamed. The sound came from the courtyard. He stood up and moved to the other side of the willow. He didn't see the source of the scream, although his vision was limited to just two of the archways and he couldn't even see the clotheslines. He had stopped hearing Burning Leopard's and the interpreter's laughter a while ago, which had made him more hopeful of Miss Choi's arrival. He had assumed they'd gone down the hill to the barrack's mess hall to scrounge up whatever food was still there.

Another scream, a longer one this time, followed by frantic breath-ing. The mansion and archways acted like an amphitheater, boxing the sound in and producing echoes. He took small steps down the hill, revealing more and more of the courtyard. Familiar benches came into view, then the fruit trees, and finally the gridiron gate of the mansion, flung open and swinging, as if water deer had just run through.

There were three more screams, short ones this time. When he reached the archway on the front side of the mansion, he turned the corner. He passed the stacks of chairs, which were now half as short as they'd been before. In between the two archways, near the front door, he saw the source of the screams. He hadn't wanted to believe it, but deep down he'd known ever since hearing the first shriek.

There, between the wicker backs of the chairs, on the yellow uphol-stered cushions—lined three to a side and pushed together to form a bed—Miss Choi lay facedown, her hair scattered and her white blouse ripped. The interpreter was clutching her arms together and pushing them against the small of her back, right above her bare buttocks. He was on top of her, a knee on one of her legs, spreading them apart. Burning Leopard stood behind the foreigner. He had taken off his pants, and was watching and waiting with anticipation. He glanced up briefly, and caught sight of Little Turnip.

"That was a long poop, little brother—ha-ha!—but I'm glad you made it. Look what we've found."

Stunned, Little Turnip covered his mouth with his hand. Of course he'd heard stories about what went on between a man and a woman, but the scene in front of him was so strange, so horrible, that he couldn't understand what he was seeing.

"Help me!" Miss Choi screamed. "Help!"

The interpreter stopped what he was doing for a moment, looking up. He lifted himself slightly off Miss Choi, grinned, and waved for Little Turnip to come closer. Miss Choi freed one of her hands, trying to crawl through the seat cushions. The interpreter grabbed her ankles. She turned and kicked him in the pelvis. Rolling, she dropped face-first onto the ground, then pushed herself up. Gathering her skirt in her hands, she limped toward Little Turnip.

"*Aiiii!*" the foreigner yelled in pain. He felt around the chairs for his glasses. He found them, put them back on, and laughed. "Ni, Turnip! He-he-he! Grab her!"

"Stop her, little brother!" Burning Leopard shouted, jogging toward him. "Don't let her get past you! We'll get her if she runs back to us, but you're the cap to this bottle! Ha-ha! You're the fence to this ranch!"

Miss Choi tripped on a torn piece of skirt. When Little Turnip lifted her up, he saw that she had a nosebleed.

"Go to Rainy Cloud," she said, crying. "He's just outside the compound, waiting on the street. He doesn't know anything. Go. Bring him to the farmer. Be brave and take care of my nephew."

She pushed him aside and ran past. The interpreter was buttoning up his pants, but Burning Leopard was still running straight at him.

"Why'd you let her go?" he yelled.

Little Turnip glanced behind at Miss Choi, who was rounding the corner. Should he follow her? Should he listen to Burning Leopard?

"Stay there!" Burning Leopard yelled. In the shadows of the archway, his friend resembled a demon.

Shaking, Little Turnip backed away a few steps. Then he turned and ran in the direction of the gates. He kept his head down to gain speed. The wind cut through his hair. Pebbles on the gravel road flew by, crunching under his feet.

He ran off the road and onto the grass. He stopped only when he was well inside the woods, where it was quiet, like a cemetery. His hands on his legs, catching his breath, he saw the outlines of the mansion, now as small as a beehive. Who would know such evil was taking place there? Over the gate he made out the archways, and between them Miss Choi—a tiny figure in a tiny dollhouse—running to the middle of the building. She stopped, hesitated, and starting sprinting to the gate, as he had done. The interpreter—a tiny man—leapt out from behind a bench. He snatched her up like a fish from a stream and carried her, feet kicking, back up the hill, emitting high-pitched laughs that drifted down into the woods like birdcalls.

Little Turnip couldn't bear to look anymore.

He climbed over the outer fence of the compound and found Rainy Cloud. The boy was squatting next to a bench and poking at ants with a stick. Little Turnip tapped him on the shoulder. The boy smiled, looking up at him out of the corner of his eye. Little Turnip opened his mouth but didn't know what to say. He had never learned words that could explain what had happened. The boy didn't have the ability to ask.

67

A FEW HOURS LATER, WHEN the cobblestone roads turned into unpaved dirt and the buildings started to border farmland, Little Turnip found the old farmer waiting atop a mule.

"Why so long?" the old farmer asked. "And where's the woman?" He was holding a horsewhip in one hand and smoking a pipe with the other.

"She's not coming," Little Turnip said. "It's just me and her nephew."

"What about the other half of the payment?"

Upon hearing the word "payment," Little Turnip reached into his cotton-stuffed pants and took out the coins Miss Choi had given him. Rainy Cloud also revealed the loose notes.

The farmer snatched them up. He counted them and shook his head. Puffing out a mouthful of smoke, he said, "This isn't enough."

"All we have," Little Turnip said.

The farmer frowned. Reluctantly, he stuffed the money into his sleeve. "Get on."

"We could wait for her," Little Turnip said. "She'll come, maybe."

The farmer shook his head. "Can't wait longer. Other things to do. If she wants to come, she'll find me when I return."

Exhausted, Little Turnip helped Rainy Cloud up to the wagon. Then he himself climbed on. The whip cracked. Clutching the boy in his arms, he closed his eyes. He smelled manure, felt the cart's gentle rocking, and quickly fell asleep.

In his dream he saw Tranquil Crane. The wise hermit became the old farmer atop the mule bringing them to their destination. Wearing his dirty rags, he was holding a blade of grass instead of the whip and playing a flute instead of smoking the pipe. "Why do I still need to do this?" he said between his playing. "Don't they know I'm old?" Little Turnip asked him where they were going, but the old hermit kept telling him the same thing: "Why do I still need to do this? Don't they know I'm old?" Little Turnip asked if they would see Miss Choi there, and still, the same reply. "We're here!" the hermit shouted. "Don't know why I'm doing this. . . ." They reached their destination. Before them was a shimmering pond of stars, the water just as dark and reflective as the sky. Deer lowered their heads to drink. Dragonflies zigzagged across the surface. "So beautiful," Little Turnip said. But nobody was there. As far as he could see, the landscape was flat, barren, devoid not of life but of people. "Don't they know I'm old?" The wise hermit walked straight across the water and into the horizon, and no matter how fast Little Turnip was running, he couldn't reach him.

He awoke with a start. Fragments of the dream still lingered, but Tranquil Crane was gone, and it was morning now. Rainy Cloud was asleep in his arms. Feeling the boy's breath on his skin, Little Turnip thought of Miss Choi and he wanted again to cry; he felt that he should. But so much had happened so fast, and all around him he heard the confusing sounds of children shouting and laughing, their cheerful, hurried steps like those of the kids on Home Mountain. He wanted to believe they were telling him that everything would be fine and that he was home now.

The farmer took the saddle off his mule and opened the back of the wagon.

"Get off," he said. "We're here."

"So soon?" Little Turnip asked. He remembered Miss Choi saying the journey to the sympathetic village would last at least two days and two nights.

"Get off," the farmer repeated.

When Little Turnip got off the wagon, he saw that they were indeed at a secluded village. In every direction there were low mountains that acted like clouds, preventing a view of the distance. The houses were small and misshapen, in parts flat stones stacked on top of another, in other parts crisscrossed wood. Straw covered the roofs. Villagers lowered their heads to exit their homes, shooing away the chickens that pecked near the entrances. In front of a hut, a dog with patches of missing fur was burying a bone.

Little Turnip took Rainy Cloud by the hand and followed the farmer to one of the larger structures, outside of which children both younger and older than them were kicking at a brown ball. They stopped playing when Little Turnip and Rainy Cloud walked by.

"What's your name?" one of the older boys asked Little Turnip.

"Where are you from?" a girl in pigtails said to Rainy Cloud.

"We're from the city," Little Turnip replied in his best Mandarin.

"And how old are you?" the girl asked Rainy Cloud, smiling. "You're cute. Do you like playing kick-the-ball? We're playing a game but the teams aren't fair. You want to join us?" When there was no reply, the girl asked Little Turnip, "Hey, is your friend stupid? Why won't he say anything?"

Little Turnip was about to say something, but the farmer grabbed their arms and pulled them into the building. He had seemed scrawny and old, and Little Turnip was surprised by his strength.

Inside, the dirt floor was uneven. Dead insects floated on muddy puddles. The roof was leaking, although it wasn't raining. Men sat on raised mounds, eating and drinking around a slab of wood. Teenagers were serving them food, throwing a grape or carrot into their mouths before squatting down and setting the plates on the table. A girl holding a fruit tray turned her face to the door, and Little Turnip noticed that she was missing an ear. The man at the end of the table stood up, walked over, and shook the farmer's hand.

"These two from the city?" he asked, nodding to Little Turnip and Rainy Cloud.

Up close, the man had the faint wrinkles of someone in his late thirties or early forties. His nose resembled a clove of garlic. He wore a green silk vest and smooth blue trousers, and his left arm sported the tattoo of a dragon with prominent crimson whiskers. He was short, almost as short as Little Turnip, and he had a hunched back. Nonetheless, there was no mistaking that he was the one in charge.

The farmer whispered something into the man's ear. The man nodded. Then he handed him three silver coins. The farmer let go of Little Turnip and Rainy Cloud and left without saying a word.

"I'm Red Whiskers, your new boss," the man said. "You two speak the common tongue?"

"A little," Little Turnip said. "I grew up in the mountains. My friend can't speak." He pointed to Rainy Cloud's mouth.

"No problem." Red Whiskers smiled, patting Little Turnip on the back.

He led them to the table. The others made room for them, and Little Turnip and Rainy Cloud sat down. The girl missing the ear poured water into wooden cups and handed one to Little Turnip. Afterward she giggled and whispered something to her friend.

"I'll tell you how everything works around here tomorrow, but today you rest." Red Whiskers took a chicken leg off his plate and handed it to Little Turnip. "Eat your fill. Sleep until whenever. You'll learn quickly that we don't have many rules, and there's plenty of time to play."

"You are part of the Communist army?" Little Turnip asked, unsure of the pronunciation. He had only recently learned the word from Miss Choi.

Red Whiskers laughed, and the others around the table joined him. Even the servers started to laugh.

"Communist?" he repeated. "Looks like we have a smart one here. Sure, we're the most Communist people we know. We only look out for each other. We share what we earn." He gestured to the kids behind him. "We're like a family."

Over the course of the day, Little Turnip got to know a few of the other children. Some had been in the house for years, while others had been there only a few months. "It's not so bad here," a boy playing soccer told him. He was about the same age. "Every other week we go to the city and beg, and then we come back and play." Little Turnip asked if they ever headed north, and the boy said, "Sure, we go everywhere. I heard about the Communist army you mentioned. We might just go there, too." But some of the older kids wouldn't talk to Little Turnip. When he asked the girl with one ear if she liked it here, she turned away as if he didn't exist. He guessed that maybe she didn't want to bother with those younger than her.

By the end of the day, he determined that conditions in this village were much worse than those at the foreigners' compound. But Red Whiskers seemed nice, and the children here seemed happy, more or less. In any case, he was glad to be away from the foreigners. Perhaps the Communist agents would arrive soon, as Miss Choi had said, and he would be with his parents by year's end.

At night, Red Whiskers brought him to one of the children's bedrooms, which was just a small nook behind the dining area. Little Turnip lay atop a large stone bed next to Rainy Cloud and ten other boys. They slept crisscrossed, their feet touching each other's heads, and Little Turnip could smell the fungus between their toes. Something scurried across his legs. When he bent forward slightly to look down, a cockroach darted through a section of the straw bedding lit by moonlight. For many hours he couldn't sleep. He felt hopeful, wondering what his life was going to be like from now on.

PART V

REUNION

68

1978

IT IS DARK NOW. NOT yet five and the sky has turned muddy, swamp-like, as polluted as the bogs around the Gobi Desert. Ping and Yong have lived in Beijing for twenty years and still they are not used to the winters. They prefer the south, where they could walk barefoot all year round. Here, the short days surprise them. Even in February, the streetlamps are not turned on until nine, then shut off a few minutes before midnight. They know the schedule better than most: Yong is a member of the committee on energy consumption, and it was a matter of debate—of embarrassment—when it was decided that the capital should be illuminated for only three hours in winter.

Ping gathers the glittering candy wrappers and throws them into the trash tin. Yong sweeps the peanut shells. The interview was brief, though not due to the fault of the interviewer. Their answers were too short. Even after being pressed, they could not find the words to elaborate on the matter of their missing son. They preferred discussing the weather and told the young man to hurry home before the storm. The roads would be icy, they said, and the lights wouldn't come on for hours. They hoped their offer of foreign delicacies and roasted nuts, which the young man helped himself to, filled his belly when their words could not fill his notebook.

The cleaning done, they sit quietly on either side of their Russian-made tea table, adorned with trimmings of horse-drawn carriages and flute-playing angels. Their armchairs are cushiony, stuffed with goose feathers inside green silk coverings. The fireplace crackles. They huddle inside heavy overcoats. They are comfortable. Too cold and too comfortable.

"A grandson," Yong finally says.

"And god-grandparents." Ping rubs his hands together, shivers.

"The kung fu champ is full of surprises."

"Not surprising at all," Ping says. "His son's been married for two years. It would be a surprise if news never came."

"But no news can never surprise." Yong stokes the kindling. For a moment the fire is large. Smoke roars up through the chimney.

"I'll go to his apartment tomorrow," Ping says. "Tell him that he's made us happy."

"He doesn't care—not really."

"Of course he cares. He's our friend." Ping takes her hand, tries to warm it, but his own are as cold as iron. Over the last few years, he has observed that wrinkles are not good at holding heat. "Anyway, you don't have to come. I'll go myself."

"No," Yong says, turning to him. "We should go together. It will look better. We can stop by some markets afterward. The Spring Festival is coming. We should buy presents for the kids at the orphanage."

Ping pats his forehead with his palm. "Ah, I almost forgot it's that time of year again."

They have been going to the orphanage for five years now, ever since their last—perhaps final—trip to the Lolo mountains. The previous winter, a caretaker brought up the subject of adoption. She said, "You two come every February handing out treats. You have the means. Why not take one home?" *This new generation,* they thought, *they think lost blood can be so easily replaced.* A random child is nothing more than a distraction. Sure, it might alleviate a broken heart for a moment. Sure, there are times when such distractions are necessary, like the holidays, when they have plenty of free time. But an orphan wouldn't change the fact that Little Turnip was still missing, and, in the eyes of their ancestors, caring for another child would appear as if they had abandoned hope of finding their own. Even if Little Turnip was up in the sky sipping on heavenly tea, Yong reasons, he would never forgive her for treating another boy as if he were her own.

"I hope the sellers have squid jerky, spiced beef flakes, dates in brown sugar, or some other succulent treat," Ping says. "Last year they didn't, and the children gave us the most disappointed looks when all we brought them were wooden pistols and dolls."

"That's why we need to go early this year." Yong reaches for a sheet of paper. Her husband has given her ideas for other items to look for.

Together, under a dim gas-powered lamp, they write the list: pickled duck eggs, salted sunflower and watermelon seeds, banana chips, dried turnip in caramelized sugar, chilled pig ears, spicy refried tofu, beef tripe in sweet garlic sauce, and many others. They become excited, laughing in bursts when one remembers a long-forgotten treat from childhood, or another brings up a delicacy they've only heard of and wouldn't mind trying.

They sleep easily that night, the first in a long time, and don't feel cold even after the fireplace has gone out.

69

EARLY NEXT MORNING, JUST AS the loudspeakers are broadcasting the daily news, they decide to visit Haiwu. Nearing the curb to his building, they observe children through tinted windows. A string of firecrackers pops from the tail up to the fingertips of a girl no older than nine or ten. She waves her hand about, yelling, "Hot! Hot! Hot!" Her friends laugh. Most of them have strings in their hands, too, and the girl's momentary misery gives them pause as they decide if they should light their own.

Ping and Yong's driver runs around and opens the car door, and the kids drop their fireworks and swarm the vehicle: a Red Flag CA770, China's first domestic brand. After the civil war, Ping had become one of the company's founding members. He steps out and smiles at the kids.

The children cup their hands, peeking through the window. Their breaths fog up the glass; their fingers skim across the polished black hood. They lean on the fender with their arms crossed. A boy, taking advantage of his distracted friends, lingers behind, picking up a dropped string and lighting it. The noise startles Ping, who turns around and finds the boy crying.

"Be careful with those things!" he yells. "Gunpowder is not a toy!"

He walks to the boy, checks his hands, and brushes away black ash.

"Where are your parents?" Yong asks. "Don't they know children shouldn't set off fireworks without supervision?"

All the kids line up in front of them and look at their feet. Ping sees fear in their faces. They are afraid of the green army coats, the military cap, and the shiny medals. Perhaps a few even remember, not too long ago, their parents being pulled from their homes by men wearing similar uniforms.

"Who are your parents?" Yong waits. "Someone, answer me!"

Ping pulls her back a few steps. He kneels and smiles again.

"None of you are in trouble, and neither are your parents." He looks from face to face, trying to recognize if one belongs to Haiwu's extended family. "Can anyone tell me where the grandpa with one leg lives?"

The oldest girl raises her hand. She is the one who set off the first firecracker, and her puffy, cotton-stuffed jacket hides her neck.

"It's been a while since we've been here," Ping says. "Can you take us to him?"

The girl nods.

"Driver Bao," Yong calls, and points to the other children.

The driver blows a whistle. "*Lai lai lai!*" he says. "Who wants to see the inside?" The other kids become ecstatic again, surrounding the laughing driver. "I think I have some candy in the trunk, too. . . ."

Ping and Yong follow the girl up the concrete stairs. By the time they reach the fifth floor, their breakfast has flipped a dozen times inside their bellies, and they are out of breath.

"Haiwu could've chosen any floor," Ping says.

"He was one of the first occupants," Yong adds.

In front of them, the girl starts walking backward. "Master Haiwu makes us run up and down these steps five times a day. It's part of our training."

"Master Haiwu?" Yong tries to laugh, but it comes out as a cough.

"He says, 'A tree without a tough trunk can never grow branches.'"

"Is that so?" Ping smiles. He is filled with a sudden excitement to see his friend again. He regrets not having done this sooner, and more often.

They come to the door with the black-and-white posters of the latest state-produced war movies: His friend has always enjoyed a good story. Ping gives the door a few gentle knocks. When there is no response, the girl pounds on it with her fists.

"Open up, Master Haiwu! You have guests!" She turns to Ping and Yong. "Sometimes the Master is hard of hearing."

The door finally opens, and an old man with a look of impatience hops on one leg.

"Training doesn't start for another hour—" Haiwu begins to say, and, making eye contact with Ping and Yong behind the girl, he is momentarily silenced, recognition turning into embarrassment. The girl runs off, her steps echoing down the stairs.

"Hello, old friend," Ping says.

"Keeping yourself busy, I see," Yong adds.

Haiwu ushers them in, apologizing for the messy apartment. "If I'd known you were on your way, I would've cooked something," he says, "or at least put on my uniform."

"It's all right. You look as healthy as ever," Ping says.

And he means it. Nearing seventy, five years older than they are, Haiwu is still lean and muscular, his face a shade of pink and orange that reminds Ping of a peach. The apartment, heated by a single boiler hiding in the corner, is barely warmer than it is outside, but Haiwu has his sleeves rolled up. He fans himself with the latest edition of the *People's Daily*, and Ping remembers that his friend grew up in northern Manchuria, close to the Soviet border. This weather must feel only like a brisk breeze.

"And where is Mrs. Haiwu?" Yong asks. Her eyes scan the dusty floor, the half-painted wall and ceiling, and the stovetop littered with unwashed pots and pans. She hardly considers herself tidy, but the room before her brings her back to the years when the three of them lived together on Iron Well Mountain.

"Staying with her parents in Shenyang," Haiwu says. "It's the holidays, and I can't stop her from going. Not that I would want to, either. It's nice to be rid of the nagging for a few days. I can think with a clear head for a change."

"You two enjoying the apartment?" Ping asks. "It's one of the newest in the country."

"As luxurious as the Summer Palace."

Yong crosses her arms. The old man before her is no different from the Haiwu of her youth, the one she has almost forgotten. Their times together rush to her memory now like spools of uncoiling ribbon, and she is greeted by a feeling of annoyance that, at this moment, is not altogether unpleasant.

"You probably know why we're here," she says. "And we want to tell you in person how happy we are you thought of us."

"Who else could it have been?" Haiwu scratches the stubble on his chin. "Or did you think I've forgotten about your rejection of my offer to be my son's godparents?"

To be fair, Yong wants to tell him, they never rejected his offer. It was more accurate to say they never acknowledged it in the first place. Twenty years before, after his wife had given birth, Haiwu had sent them a telegram asking if they would attend his son's first birthday. He was living in another province then and the telegram had taken a week to reach Beijing. At the time, they had just received news of the devastation of the Lolo mountains. They heard the reports of the activities of the beggars' guild there, every eyewitness and local leader telling them that if Little Turnip had survived, he'd most likely be a disabled person—someone with a scarred face, a hunched back, missing an ear or arm. Their grief and worry was made more painful when other members of the politburo advised them to postpone their search for their son until the political situation had settled down. The Cultural Revolution was in full swing, and it did not reflect well on the Party if its senior members engaged in any activity that could be construed as selfish or bourgeois. Haiwu's celebratory letter, like salt on a wound, further burned their hearts.

"That was a different time," Ping says.

"Back then, some viewed the tradition of assigning godparents as out of date," Yong adds, "part of the problematic past."

"I've never heard such a claim," Haiwu says. "Not even at the height of the hysteria." His eyebrows drew close, like those of a fox. "But it doesn't matter anymore. We can make up for past neglect with future devotion. Let's start now. Do either of you have a suggestion for a name?"

70

AN HOUR LATER, WALKING DOWN the stairs, they laugh.

"'Past neglect,'" Ping repeats.

"'Luxurious as the Summer Palace,'" Yong mimics.

"I've missed him."

"I haven't."

Midway through the conversation, it crossed their minds that Haiwu hadn't asked them to become god-grandparents only because they were old friends. His appeal was clever, even calculated. It is only a matter of time before he requests favors: finding his daughter-in-law a reputable gynecologist, obtaining food tickets for milk powder, getting his grandson into a good kindergarten. He knows they have the power to provide these things. And they, for that matter, don't mind helping. Over the years, even unassuming Ping has grown accustomed to the words a subordinate might use when requesting a raise, or the shy way a friend smiles before inquiring about extra food rations, or packages of tea and liquor beside his office door, a note taped to the bottle pleading for him to lighten the sentence of a relative who committed some minor crime.

Still laughing, they are inside the car again, enjoying the warmth of the heater and the softness of the leather in a way that would have embarrassed their twenty-year-old selves. Yong tells the driver they have many more stops, and he tips his hat at the rearview mirror.

Luxury foods are in high demand, especially during the holidays. Restricted by ration policies, vendors can sell only three or four items per person, even to someone prominent. Yong and Ping need to go to a couple markets if they are to gather enough succulent treats for the orphanage. There are lines wherever they go, but their car and uniform draw the attention of the clerks, who approach with pencil and notepad and ask them what they want. They always pay double the worth of their purchase, both in cash and in food tickets, and repeat the clerk's name when they leave so he knows they'll remember this small kindness.

Yong is well aware of supply shortages. In winter, even the capital is not immune. Still, pride swells in her heart when she sees that the citizens in line, far from being annoyed, are talking and laughing, pulling their young ones close, checking to see if they are warm. Most have lived through years that were far worse. For some, the memory of a mother buried on an empty stomach is still close enough to make their hands shake. Others are forbidden to speak of dead siblings during mealtime, the very mention of a name causing dinners to go uneaten.

Yong admits it: Things have steadily improved after Mao's death. Following the return of Deng Xiaoping, whose pro-West chairmanship she had initially opposed, the committees have been given greater freedom to act on their own initiative. Schools have reopened; private companies have started springing up. Layers of restrictions prohibiting the enactment of "bourgeois" policies have been rolled away, and the "Four Modernizations"—agriculture, industry, technology, and military—are in the process of being implemented.

It is here, in these marketplaces, that Yong begins to see the effects of these changes. It is here that she feels her decade-long ideas of a new China finally taking shape.

Their last stop of the day—an unofficial (and illegal) marketplace—lies outside the city limits. Away from the main roads, a bumpy path of wagon tracks and hoofprints lead them to a crumbling, half-enclosed vinegar warehouse. Its roof filled with holes, the ancient building has been long abandoned by its aristocratic owner, no doubt deceased or made humble. When they approach the central bazaar, mules part and onlookers drop their baskets and stare at their car. The people here are a mix of rural and city folk: those with and without a Beijing birth certificate. They trade crops grown in secrecy, haggle using currency or food tickets, and purchase foreign goods like wristwatches and sunglasses.

Driver Bao parks near a trough where pack animals are drinking. Ping and Yong open the door. They smell dung and the lye powder that partially covers it. Yong tells Driver Bao to wait for them here.

"We won't be long," Ping says.

Here, no merchants will approach their vehicle. They aren't sure if the officials inside have come to buy things or hand out fines.

The entrance to the warehouse is a pair of rusty iron doors permanently propped open by two mounds of overpoured cement. Ping and Yong step through a line of people waiting to purchase pork fat, the man at the front yelling for the butcher to even out the scale before declaring a price. They pass a tofu vendor who eyes them suspiciously, and then a trader of plastic trinkets—water pistols, rubber snakes, colorful balloons—who seems ready at any moment to close his briefcase and run away. It is not until they have walked sufficiently into the building, when Ping takes out his wallet in front of a candied peanut stall, that the other merchants drop their guard and stop glancing in Ping's direction.

"Two kilograms," Ping says.

After paying the man, Yong points to another booth where cans of lychee are stacked. They scurry over to the other stall like schoolchildren, nearly tripping on a loose brick. The seller, a woman who claims to have traveled all the way from the southern provinces, spoons a sample into each of their palms.

"Very sweet," she says. "Came from my village."

Ping can tell from her Cantonese accent she's telling the truth. "Five cans," he says.

Rolling the sweet fruit around her tongue, Yong nudges her husband with her elbow.

"No," Ping corrects himself. "Make that ten."

By the time they finish shopping, their arms are so full, Driver Bao has to snuff out his cigarette and rush over to pick up the items that have fallen. Opening the trunk, he helps them throw in the spoils: enough delicacies to fill the bellies of a hundred orphans who haven't tasted sweet or oily foods in months.

When Driver Bao closes the trunk, Ping and Yong notice a man sitting next to the pack animals. Illuminated by the midday sun, he has his legs crossed and is washing his long, unkempt hair with water from the trough. He washes with one hand, because he only has one hand. His other sleeve, tied into a knot, dangles from his shoulder. As he washes, the stump hits the trough's metal wall, the thwacks reverberating like jolts of thunder.

They do not know who has spotted the man first, but when they look at each other, they both have the same question.

"How long has he been there?" Ping asks Driver Bao.

"That bum?" Bao says. "He came up to me just after you went inside, sir. Asked for food. You want me to tell him to get lost?"

Ping shakes his head. He has Bao open the trunk again. Yong grabs a pouch full of peanuts and a can of lychee, and together they walk toward the stranger.

The man is an unusual sight. Beggars are not allowed within city limits, and although the unofficial marketplace is technically outside Beijing, men like the one before them still risk being rounded up by the police and thrown in prison. He must have come from out of town—possibly out of the province—and he must have just arrived.

When Ping and Yong get close, they notice the man is whistling a tune. They don't recognize the language. Is he a foreigner? His pitch changes from high to low often, sometimes within a single word. Is he Mongolian? Russian? Perhaps from the conquered regions of Tibet? No, the man does not have the bald head of a monk, nor brown locks, nor the feral features of the Soviets. Where does his music, which is becoming more familiar with every passing note, come from?

"Excuse me," Ping says.

The stranger stops his washing and uses his one hand to spin himself around. He blinks rapidly, water dripping down dense brows. After his eyes focus, he becomes startled, waving his arm about.

"I'm not a beggar!" he declares. "Please don't take me away! I only look haggard because I've been walking for a long time. Never had a moment to wash until now. And I wouldn't be using this trough if the merchants weren't so stingy. They charge me a *fen* per use of their sink, and I only want to wash my face. . . ."

Ping can't place his accent. Like his singing, it is familiar. Ping is hopeful, but his years of searching have made him hesitant, pessimistic, self-doubting. Surely Old Man in the Sky does not play tricks like this. It is too easy, surely, for this stranger to be his son.

"Stand up," Yong says.

"No, please. Don't do this. I beg you." The man begins to sob.

He shifts his body forward, reaches his arm up, and tugs on Yong's pants. His weeping turns to bawling. Tears come fast, flowing from his face like water from a faucet, and in an instant the man is the epitome of pathos, the essence of tragedy distilled down to its elemental particles. The *atoms*—a word Ping learned after the war—of wretchedness.

"We're not here to nab you." Yong shakes the pouch of peanuts and the can of lychee. "Would someone who's nabbing you carry these?"

The man, still not entirely convinced, stands up. He does not dare look them in the eye, and he continues to sniffle. Even this close, they have trouble determining his age. His hair covers a large portion of his forehead and cheeks, and they are not sure which streaks on his face are wrinkles and which are dirt and grime. He smells like he just woke up from sleeping in a bed of fermenting cabbage.

"Where are you from?" Yong asks.

The man doesn't answer. Perhaps he thinks the question is a trick. After all, anything he says might condemn him.

"That song you were whistling—it's not from these parts, is it?" Ping asks.

"It is." The man nods fiercely. "It's from Beijing. Maybe not the city, but I learned it around the neighboring countryside. I swear, I'm allowed to be here."

Ping shakes his head. "Don't be afraid. Pay no attention to our uniforms. I promise you, we're not *after* you."

He asks Yong to open the pouch of peanuts. Then he takes one out and offers it. The man pops it, shell and all, into his mouth. Yong tells him to have some more. With sidelong glances, he stuffs two handfuls of nuts into oversized pockets. The stitching of the pockets are rough and the brown fabric does not match the rest of the coat.

"Take the entire pouch," Ping says.

The man hurriedly wraps up the pouch and jams it into one pocket. Yong holds out the can of lychee and the man crams it into his other pocket, the peanuts underneath crunching from the pressure.

"The song's from Sichuan," he finally admits, "where I grew up. But I'm from a part neither of you have heard of."

"Try us," Yong says.

"It has no name." The man smiles, all trace of tears having vanished. Throwing another peanut into his mouth, he bobbles his head triumphantly. "Or, maybe it has a name, but I don't remember."

Yong turns to Ping, and for what feels like a long time they stare at each other. They are asking: *Did we hear the man correctly? Did he say Sichuan? Can this be our Little Turnip: our young leaf, once green and vibrant, blown down the mountaintop and returned to us a little wilted, a touch brown, but still ours all the same? Is the man before us an apparition, a trick of the light, someone only we can see?*

Should we dare to believe?

They have many more questions, but it is unwise to talk to the homeless man for too long in public. People are interested in anything out of the ordinary, and a long conversation might draw a crowd. Onlookers might wonder why these officers have not arrested the man, and such speculation can cause the situation to become unnecessarily complex.

"Have you ridden in a car before?" Ping asks. "Not in the back of some carriage or atop a mule, but inside a four-wheeled vehicle whose only purpose is bringing its passengers around in warmth and comfort?"

The man shakes his head, staring over Ping's shoulder at the shiny black car.

"You want to?" Ping asks. "No tricks, no traps."

"A Spring Festival present," Yong says.

The man runs to the other side of the trough; for a moment their hearts sink. But he is only reaching for his belongings—a bulging burlap sack tied to a tree branch—and then he is back.

They lead him to the car. Driver Bao opens the door. He cannot contain a scoff when peanut shells spill from the man's pocket and the man's branch scratches the upholstery. Ping sits up front. Annoyed, Driver Bao asks Ping what their next destination is, and Ping tells him that they are going home.

71

THEIR HOUSE HAS FOUR BEDROOMS, only one of which they use. If Mao had not given the mansion to them, it would have become officers' barracks or a hospital. Upstairs, it has a bathtub with hot running water, one of the few in Beijing. They have barely used it themselves—once every month—to conserve gas and water. In the mornings they wash their hands and faces in a porcelain basin, as they have always done, and at night they use the same bowl to scrub their necks and feet, after which they pour the contents into the pots of ferns and tomato plants. They wax the hardwood floor every week, not to keep it shiny so much as to prevent mold damage. The only artwork they display is a life-size portrait of Chairman Mao hanging prominently on the far wall, above the dining table, under which a victorious battle scene reenacts the dispersal of Japanese troops following the Hundred Regiments Offensive.

"This place"—the man, in a state of awe, seems to lack words—"is very good."

"Go ahead," Ping says. "Walk around. Take a look. Make yourself at home."

The man's head seems to be coming loose from his body. Taking in the high ceiling and the view of the second-floor balcony, he extends his neck so much that his veins turn purple. Ping takes his coat, which is actually comprised of many different coats, and hangs them as one on the varnished rack by the door. Underneath all those layers, the man is very thin, which shouldn't have surprised them. His last shirt, a faded blue sweater, still covers his missing arm.

They want him to unroll his sleeve so they can take a better look. Little Turnip had a birthmark right below the shoulder. A dark splotch shaped like a diamond. Or was it on the other arm? They can't remember exactly. At one point Ping was certain it was on his right shoulder and Yong the left, but they managed to convince each other the opposite was true, and now Ping is certain the mark is on the left and Yong the right.

"We forgot our manners," Ping says. "We never asked what your name was."

"They call me Cactus. Sturdy Cactus. 'Cause my life force is tough. I survive."

"Who calls you that?" Yong asks.

"My friends, travel mates, the other—" He stops himself.

"The other beggars?" Yong says.

He freezes, glances at his knapsack on the tea table and his coats on the rack, trying, it seems, to calculate the likelihood of a successful escape.

"Don't worry." Ping pats him on the shoulder. "Like we said, we don't care. We're not the police. We're army veterans. We don't trouble ourselves with rounding up the homeless." He looks to Yong for support.

"We don't want anyone to go hungry during the Spring Festival. Back at the market, we were buying food for an orphanage."

The man—Sturdy Cactus—gives them a wide, squinting smile, one with a lot of cheekbone. "I can't believe my fortune. The capital's a paradise, they say, and that's why I came north this year, but I never expected to meet anyone so kind. You sure know how to make a chunk of coal feel warm."

"Come," Ping says, directing him to the stairs. "You said you wanted to wash yourself. How about you do so with warm water? Have you ever taken a bath?"

On the second floor, Yong goes to their bedroom and brings out one of Ping's clean shirts and a pair of pants. She sets them on the bathroom sink.

"Put these on after you're done," she says. "A new year calls for new clothes."

Ping shows Sturdy Cactus how to control the water, spinning the knob for cold, then the one for warm. He plugs the drain. Sturdy Cactus watches in amazement as the water gathers, grows higher and higher, steam rising on the surface. He dips his hand beneath the surface, recoils, and then slowly dips it again. Ping reaches for three silver plates—soap, scrubber, and shampoo—and sets them under the knobs. The man lifts up the bar of soap, sniffs it, takes a nibble, and then spits it out.

"For your body," Yong says, "to wash. And this"—she points to the shampoo powder—"is for your hair."

The man nods slowly, as if hearing something profound. He begins to undress, taking off his socks and then his pants, but he keeps his shirt on, in order not to reveal his amputation. He doesn't wait for them to leave before stepping into the water, and for a moment they consider staying, but Ping touches Yong's arm and gently pulls her to the door.

"Take your time," he calls. "Wash every part. When you come down, you'll have a hot dinner waiting."

Outside the door, they linger, pressing their ears to the wood. They hear splashes, and laughter, and cries of exhilaration. They tell themselves: *It's worth it, having him here, even if he turns out to not be their son. Making someone this happy this close to the New Year is an award unto itself.*

72

FOR THE NEXT HOUR, THEY busy themselves with chopping vegetables—carrots, ginger, cilantro, and scallion—and dicing lamb into pieces as small as rice grains. When they run short on meat, Yong returns to the cellar by the back door and reaches for the remaining lamb, which is kept cold under hardened bags of salt, cumin, and other spices. Ping has kneaded flour into dough and is waiting for it to rise enough so that he can slice them into wrappers. They are making dumplings, a dish with a lot of steps.

Luckily, Sturdy Cactus takes his time washing himself. They hear the bathtub being drained, and then refilled. He is using the opportunity to wash his clothes, they guess. Realizing this, Ping stops cooking, unhooks Sturdy Cactus's coats, brings them upstairs, and sets them by the bathroom door.

"Your belongings are by the entrance," he says.

Back in the kitchen again, he hears the door open and close and then the water being turned on for a third time. Satisfied, he resumes kneading the risen dough, cutting thumb-sized cylinders, and then rolling them out into dumpling wrappers.

"What are you thinking, husband?" Yong sets the first folded dumpling onto a sheet of wax paper.

"I'm trying to calculate," Ping says. "He has to be in his fifties."

"Forties, I would say. You need to take into account what he's been through. The homeless always look older than they appear."

"Late forties, maybe. I was twenty-two when the army reached Sichuan."

"I was nineteen," she says.

"I don't think the man can pass for forty-five." Rolling out more wrappers, Ping shakes his head. "I want to believe it, but I'm not sure I can."

Yong goes over to the stove, fills a pot with cold water, and sets it to boil. "I wouldn't be surprised if he was younger," she says. "Late thirties, even."

"We'll find out soon enough."

An hour later the dumplings are ready, but Sturdy Cactus still has not come down. Yong covers the steaming plates with fruit bowls. Ping paces back and forth, trying to decide if he should go up. The sun has already set, and he turns on the electric overhead lights: The occasion is special enough to warrant additional illumination.

Finally, they hear steps on the stairs. Sturdy Cactus walks down slowly, trying, it would seem, to prevent the floorboards from making too much sound. He stops at the end of the stairwell, his face hidden behind a bookshelf. He steps into view with one foot, hesitating, and then pokes his head out. When he notices both Yong and Ping sitting at the dining table, staring in his direction, he walks out. He approaches in small, mincing steps. His back hunched, he appears uncomfortable.

He says, "I'm embarrassed, old-timer, to be wearing your clothes."

What Ping and Yong sees startles them. With the man's hair wet and tied back, his face and forehead are revealed. Wearing Ping's blue button-down shirt and loose gray pants, the man before them—this Sturdy Cactus—looks remarkably similar to the way Ping had looked back in the days when he'd spend hours casting bullets by a portable furnace. The dirt and grime cleared away, the man appears young. Maybe even too young, by their estimates, to be their son. The stump of his amputated limb protrudes from the thin, short-sleeved shirt like a tortoise's head, revealing a black splotch (a birthmark?) right above the meandering, river-like scars where his lower arm was once attached.

They resist the urge to stand up and hug him. *It has been a long time since I've seen the reflection of my young face in a river*, Ping contemplates. *It's as if Old Man in the Sky had molded two clumps of clay that was my husband,* Yong thinks, *and baked them twenty years apart.* Still, they remain cautious. They remind themselves that the mind is most deceptive when it wants something bad enough. One's eyes are its enemy, one's feelings its foe.

"Sit," Ping utters, reaching for a pair of chopsticks.

"Do you want any vinegar?" Yong asks.

Sturdy Cactus pulls out a chair and eases himself down, letting his bottom settle into the cushiony seat. Chopsticks in hand, he waits with shaking fingers as Yong pulls away the fruit bowls. The floury scent of dumplings wafts up to his nose, but he doesn't reach his chopsticks in just yet. He looks at Ping and then at Yong, and then he smiles widely, revealing yellow teeth.

"Go ahead." Ping is the first to poke his chopsticks through a dumpling.

"Then I won't stand on ceremony," Sturdy Cactus says, stabbing his own through three dumplings and bringing them to his bowl.

For a few minutes the three of them don't speak. They eat. They dip a skewered dumpling into vinegar and sesame oil; they roll it around in their mouths before chewing, waiting for it to cool. Soon, Ping and Yong place their chopsticks atop their bowls and watch Sturdy Cactus. They search for any sign that reminds them of Little Turnip. Of course, the only time Yong had ever seen him eat was when he suckled from her breasts. *Are these ravenous lips my son's?* she wonders. Little Turnip was never a desperate eater, as far as she remembers, but then again, he hadn't yet known the rapacious hunger the man before her had surely endured.

The first plates are empty. As Sturdy Cactus waits for the second batch of dumplings to finish boiling, Ping scoots his chair closer to him.

"That place in Sichuan you are from," he asks, "it is in the mountains?"

"Sure, sure. High up in the mountains, where a special kind of cactus grow."

"Why did you leave?" Yong asks from the stove.

"There was no food," Sturdy Cactus says, "and I like to eat."

Ping adds more vinegar into the man's bowl. "What were your parents like?"

"I don't know. I don't remember them."

Stirring the dumplings, Yong lets the ladle fall to the side of the pot. "How can you not remember your parents?"

"I just don't." He shrugs. "It's like how I'm not sure if my mountain has a name. I've been hit here a lot." He taps on the back of his head with his knuckles. "Some travel mates are not so nice. Some push me down, shove me on rocks, steal my things." He turns his head, showing Ping stitches above his ear. "They shake me, but they can't break my roots. I'm a cactus, and I always have my revenge."

"So you don't remember their names," Ping says, "but you know you have parents."

"Well, of course I have parents." Sturdy Cactus laughs. "I'm no bastard."

Yong brings over two new plates of freshly boiled dumplings, and Sturdy Cactus's face is lost in the steam once more.

They decide not to ask him too many questions for the rest of the night. He needs rest. Perhaps he has not slept well in days. A glass of rice liquor, a comfortable pillow, and his head will be clearer in the morning.

They take him to the room next to their own. Once a part of the master bedroom, the guest room was separated to accommodate additional injured soldiers during the Korean War. The walls are thin and do not extend to the ceiling. Lying awake in bed, Ping and Yong hear snores and the shuffling of sheets.

"What are you thinking?" Ping asks Yong.

"I think it's him," Yong says. "I think he's our boy."

Ping nods. "Many things do point in that direction," he says, "but maybe we shouldn't decide so fast. We need to be sure."

Tomorrow they will enlist the help of the only other person who is as familiar with Little Turnip as they are. They plan out their day in whispers, talking under the blanket. Whatever sounds coming from their room can be heard just as clearly on the other side—an unexpected disadvantage of their room selection—and they don't want to fill Sturdy Cactus's heads with any thoughts that aren't his own.

73

FOR A LONG TIME HAIWU sits in the chair opposite Sturdy Cactus, staring like a cat on a ledge, not uttering a word. The four of them are in the living room, listening to the radio—a past broadcast of *Steel Meets Fire*, the one where a Communist platoon saves a village from the bloodthirsty Japanese by digging a tunnel through a copper mine. *Under the cover of darkness, in near-freezing waters, they swim across the tributary. Lugging heavy spades, with a wire cutter between their teeth, the men of the Eighth Route Army drag their mud-soaked bodies onto the shore. The first two Japanese sentries are dispatched of quickly—a slice to the throat—but the next two are close to the barracks, where a thousand white-eared devils sleep. Beyond them, in cages made for pigs, the poor villagers, worked all day without food or water, wait desperately for their rescuers. . . .*

Sturdy Cactus giggles whenever a Japanese soldier is killed and claps when the platoon reaches the cages undetected. His face drops into a deep sadness when a young recruit, hampered by a leg injury, begs his lieutenant to leave him behind lest the enemy passes by and he dooms them all. When the broadcast ends, Sturdy Cactus dabs his eyes with the sleeve of Ping's shirt. Then he sinks his teeth into a chunk of spicy beef jerky.

"I never knew men could be so brave," he says.

Ping glances at Haiwu, whose gaze still has not left Sturdy Cactus. "They're only stories. In real life, it's not quite the same."

"Many good people did sacrifice their lives," Yong says, "many people who aren't mentioned in these programs."

Sturdy Cactus adjusts the knobs on the radio, trying to improve the signal. He wants to hear the preview for next week's tale. "Did you fight the Japanese?"

Yong nods. "We all did. They were everywhere."

"I fought the Japanese, too," Sturdy Cactus says, "but I wasn't a soldier, and I wasn't brave."

"Tell us," Haiwu says, the first words he utters all morning.

"The gang I was in hated them." Sturdy Cactus speaks with his mouth full. "We played tricks on them every chance we got. Sure, we took their money, carrying their bags or polishing their boots, but we'd loosen the seams or cut a tiny hole in the sole, and we'd laugh the next day, seeing things fall out of their bags or their shoes filling with rainwater. They'd chase us around in the streets, but we scattered like rats, into every nook and corner of our city." He is eating peanuts now, balancing the dish of nuts on the sleeve that hides his amputation like an expert waiter. "As I said, we weren't soldiers, but we hated them, too. We weren't going to let them roam around our territory so easily."

"Were they the ones who took your arm?" Yong asks.

Sturdy Cactus opens his eyes wide, like a dragonfly's; a peanut falls out of his hand and rolls under the sofa.

"It's all right," Ping says. "You don't need to tell us if you don't want to."

"No, you need to tell us." Yong turns to her husband accusingly. "It's not good to let such things linger in one's memory. You'll feel better, I promise."

Sturdy Cactus still seems to hesitate. He turns to Haiwu. Perhaps he wants the kung fu champ to share the story of how he lost his leg first. Perhaps he only feels comfortable telling someone who has lost something similar.

Haiwu closes his eyes, nods. "Tell us, kid. There's nothing to be ashamed of."

Sturdy Cactus takes a deep breath. "The Japanese didn't do this. They wouldn't take the time to chop off a limb. They either ignored you or put a bullet between your eyes." His voice quiets to a whisper. "No, my gang leader did this to me. Gave me some opium one night. The next morning I found my arm gone and my shoulder wrapped up. I ran around the yard like a plucked rooster, waking up all the whores. He pulled me by the neck and slapped me. He was doing me a favor, he told me. He said, 'Heaven is forever indebted to those who experience misfortune in their youth.' Really he just wanted me to look more pathetic so I could make him more money." Sturdy Cactus scoffs, his expression turning as stiff as marble. "I tell you, for five years all I thought about was killing him. I thought about mixing his tea with a slow-acting poison, or tying him to a tree and chopping his limbs off one by one. It's a pity the white-eared devils got to him before I did."

"What happened to him?" Haiwu asks.

Sturdy Cactus takes a gulp of pear juice. "He gave the Japanese information, then kept pestering them about his payment. They didn't want to pay and shoved a bayonet through his chest."

Haiwu pulls his leg up to the sofa and crosses it over his prosthetic. Ping and Yong glance at each other and then look to the kung fu champ. Earlier that morning, while in the car, they told Haiwu that one of the things they wanted him to judge was whether the man's story made sense. "We want too much for him to be our son," they said. "We don't have a clear head. We're too invested."

Now Haiwu sits like a Daoist sage, nodding as Sturdy Cactus tells his story. The kid is going on and on about how easy his gang leader died, how he was still on opium and couldn't feel the blade passing through him, and how unfair it was that his own comrades perished in much more painful ways.

When the radio starts to play the next program, a comedy show featuring two air force pilots, Sturdy Cactus abruptly stops talking. He takes the radio and puts it next to his ear.

Haiwu stands and nods in the direction of the kitchen.

"Keep enjoying the program," Ping says. "We'll be in the next room if you need us."

Sturdy Cactus seems oblivious. Ping and Yong follow Haiwu into the kitchen. Yong slides the curtain separating the two rooms.

"Well," Ping whispers, "what do you think?"

Haiwu scratches his head; his face is scrunched up, as if in pain. "First, I'll say there are lots of homeless in our country. Both of you know this. There are lots of people with a missing arm, leg, hand, or feet. You know this as well. The historian Sima Qian once said, 'War is the amputation, limb by limb, of the Middle Country. What is together will separate. What is separate will unite—' "

"We don't need a history lesson," Yong interrupts. "Just tell us if you think he's our Little Turnip."

Haiwu holds out his palm. "With that being said, and with the knowledge that he is from Sichuan and grew up in the mountains, and given that he is roughly the appropriate age and looks somewhat similar to Ping, I find myself wanting to believe, just as you do, that he is our Little Turnip. But—"

They hear a burst of high-pitched laughter coming from the living room. They peek through the curtain, which is now warm from the afternoon sun, and see Sturdy Cactus bent over, his sleeve covering his mouth, trying to contain his laughter.

"But what?" Ping asks.

"But in the end I'm more inclined to believe that it's all just coincidence." Haiwu hops back a step from the entryway and leans against the stove. "Think about it. It makes sense that he's from Sichuan. The province contains some of the hardest-hit areas following the Revolution. It's not unusual for him to be from there. As for him being an orphan—well, that's not so unusual, either, now, is it? Both of you were orphans. We were all orphans. In fact, I think it's safe for me to say the whole country was an orphan. . . ."

Yong frowns. "He still looks like Ping."

"He does," Ping says.

"There is a resemblance," Haiwu concedes, "but people meet others who look like them all the time. Even if by some miracle he is your son, it would do both of you good not to think of him that way. Forty years is a long time. Almost half a century. He's not the baby we held in our arms. Everything has changed. Even his name has changed. You still call him Little Turnip, as if he were still young, but he calls himself Sturdy Cactus, and he's proud of the person he's become, in spite of the misfortunes he's suffered. Don't let that fawning, fumbling exterior fool you. It's practiced. He's had years of experience getting it just right. Take it from a cripple like me: There's nothing that makes us feel better than beating the world that has for so long beaten us."

"We don't care what he's like," Ping says, "as long as he's ours."

"And he *is* ours." Yong peeks through the curtain again. "I see it in his gestures, in his laugh, in how he holds his chopsticks."

"Be careful," Haiwu says. "If what you want to believe turns out to be true, then you should feel happy. But what I'm saying is you shouldn't have any expectations of the man. How can you, having been separated for half a century? You don't have any right to have expectations."

Ping takes Yong's hand into his. He holds it like a sheet of origami paper. What Haiwu says makes sense, and Ping forces out a nod.

To Yong, the kung fu champ's words are fading into an unintelligible language. He might as well have been reciting ancient poetry or declaring himself the emperor of Persia. They go in one ear and come out like tangled string. The only thing sharp in her mind is the person in the other room: a middle-aged man, a homeless traveler, a naïve soul who's known nothing but suffering; someone easily distracted, giggling, now, like a little boy.

74

HAIWU CAN'T STAY FOR DINNER, despite their insistence that he observe Sturdy Cactus for a while longer. "The kids in my building are counting on me," he tells them. "I promised to teach them the Crane stance today." They have Driver Bao take him home. Rolling down the window, Haiwu calls out, "Give me a name soon! I need a name! Do your duty as god-grandparents!" They wave and watch the car pull away, the smell of exhaust fading.

Inside, Sturdy Cactus is taking a nap on the couch, snoring like an outstretched puppy. They tiptoe to the kitchen to make dinner. Ping pulls out the leftover lamb and carrots from a cold corner drawer, the one next to a window, but Yong puts them back.

"We can't make dumplings again," she says.

"Why not? Dumplings during the Spring Festival is a tradition. With the amount he ate yesterday, we know he likes them."

"I'm not feeding my son the same thing twice in a row. He'll get bored with us like we are with those over-broadcasted radio shows."

"Careful." Hearing Yong use the word "son" scares Ping, who is trying to heed Haiwu's warning. "Don't call him that just yet."

Yong ignores him. She reaches to the topmost cupboard and takes down a tin of black bean sauce.

"Noodles," she says, smiling. "We'll make our son noodles."

They drop ground pork into a pan of black bean sauce and the mixture sizzles on the stove. A half hour later it is almost ready. A heavy aroma of garlic fills the kitchen.

Sturdy Cactus walks in sheepishly.

"Can I help?" he asks, looking over Ping's shoulder at the boiling pot.

"No," Ping says. "We didn't want to wake you until it was all ready."

Yong reaches into the pot and pulls out a chopstick-ful of noodles. "I hope you like *mian*," she says.

"Two meals with white flour in two days. I'd never thought it was possible."

Sturdy Cactus sits down at the kitchen table. He grows quiet, looking out the window at some rowdy children throwing sticks at each other. The sticks, part of a ball-balancing game, bounce on the ground a few times before settling down, producing a ringing sound.

"What's wrong?" Ping asks.

Sturdy Cactus shakes his head. "It's nothing. Noodles bring back some bad memories is all."

"I told you we should've made dumplings," Ping says.

"Bad memories?" Yong hands Sturdy Cactus a large bowl drenched in black bean sauce. "You should tell us."

Sturdy Cactus waits until Ping and Yong have sat down with their own bowls. Then he bites into a clove of garlic methodically, as if gathering strength for what he will say next.

"I can count on one hand the number of times I ate flour as pure as this," he says. "One of those times was my marriage day."

He looks from Ping to Yong, who nod, trying their best to not seem surprised. If they appear astonished, maybe he will be too embarrassed to say anything more.

"You can imagine how hard it is for someone like me to find a wife," Sturdy Cactus says. "Each time I bring it up, I can't quite believe it myself. A homeless cripple like me once having a wife. Who would think?"

"You have a handsome face," Yong says. "It's not surprising."

Sturdy Cactus slaps the seat next to him with delight. "Remembering her always makes me sad, but your words have cheered me up."

"Go on," Ping says.

Sturdy Cactus stares at the long, pearly strands slipping from his chopsticks. "She wasn't a pretty girl, though you wouldn't believe me if I told you she was. No, my little rabbit was a skinny bumpkin with a split lip." They met around the time the Japanese were defeated, he continued, following the "Nine-Nine" armistice. The country was in a jubilant mood, and many wealthy families became temporarily generous. During those weeks, Sturdy Cactus followed the parades of homeless, hopping from one ravaged city to the next, taking advantage of the celebrations. His wife was fifteen at the time, and he caught her trying to pick his pocket. "I looked well-off that morning because I had a swim in the river and was wearing a freshly donated tweed jacket. Most people might not have felt her slender fingers, but our gang leader always said you can never out-weasel a weasel—he said this to make sure we thought twice about betraying him. I felt her hand as soon as my coins moved, and I grabbed her wrists and tackled her to the grass."

Sturdy Cactus jerks his hand to his chest, then slams it to the table.

"The charity of those weeks must have been contagious," he continues, "because instead of taking her stuff, as was my right, I bought her dinner. It was from a noodle stand, the flour half sorghum and half wheat." Eating in the light rain, he learned that her deformity had prevented her from becoming a prostitute, so she had spent most of her childhood with other beggars. "She didn't need to lose a limb; she was already pathetic enough. For the next two years she didn't stop following me and calling me 'husband.' At some point I started calling her 'wife' and then 'Little Rabbit.' There were days when I wanted to be rid of her, and I'm ashamed to say that I punched her a few times." Sturdy Cactus picks at the calluses on his hand with his thumb. "Looking back on those days now, I can say they were the best in my life. I miss her so much."

Yong slides him a handkerchief. Maybe it's the way he is telling the story, which reminds her of her father when he was sober, but she sees herself in the girl he's describing. She wants nothing more than to have been Little Rabbit during those days, following Sturdy Cactus around and making sure he was safe.

"What happened to her?" Ping asks.

Hearing this question, Sturdy Cactus's lips quiver and soon he begins to sob. He keeps his mouth closed and his eyes open, like a statue, and his tears come out differently from the other times he's cried.

Ping pats his shoulder. "It was a long time ago."

Yong picks up the handkerchief and wipes the areas below his eyes.

"Both of you are so kind," Sturdy Cactus says, "and all I can talk about on this festive day is sorrow."

"You say whatever you want. Auntie and I don't have much to talk about when we're by ourselves."

Sturdy Cactus tries to smile. He looks at the new calendar hanging on the wall: a fiery red serpent, this year's zodiac.

"Spring Festival is about being with family, right?" he asks.

They nod.

"My family could've been so different if I'd been smarter, braver, or wholer." He presses his face into his empty sleeve, letting snot dribble down to the hem. Then he wipes his nose with the handkerchief.

"There, there," Ping says, glancing at Yong. "If you want, you can think of Auntie and me as family."

"They took them!" Sturdy Cactus suddenly yells. "They pulled them from my side and I couldn't pull them back!" As suddenly as he became excited, he quiets again. "Maybe they didn't want to come back and that was part of it. Maybe they were happy enough to have been tugged away."

"Who pulled who away?" Yong asks.

"They took Little Rabbit and my son, who I drew into the world with my own hand. He was only three."

Yong and Ping sit down. The thought comes to them in a rush: They were once real grandparents. Yong covers her mouth, suddenly unable to breathe. Ping feels his legs growing soft and boneless.

"You had a son?" he asks.

"I *have* a son," Sturdy Cactus says. "I like to think he's still alive."

"Who were the ones who took him? The other homeless? A new gang leader?"

Sturdy Cactus shakes his head. He begins to slurp his noodles again, stirring his bowl forcefully. His expression has grown angry. "The men who took them were soldiers from a retreating Nationalist army. The celebrations were over and war had returned. The soldiers were on their way to Chengdu and then Taiwan. Their general lost his family in the last battle, and for whatever reason he wanted mine. He saw us begging on the street, waving our bowls at the army lines, and he ordered his soldiers to pull Little Rabbit and Cricket into his staff car. I ran after them but couldn't keep up. The bastard even had the nerve to yell back, 'I'll take good care of them.'"

Learning about the details of the child, Ping and Yong feel as if their hearts are also breaking. They begin to sob themselves. They stare at each other, and each knows what is on the other's mind: Is this the right time to tell him who he is? Would he accept them or run away in fear? Would he be consoled to know that although he lost his wife and son long ago, he has gained a mother and father this day? And then there is the situation of the boy, who he says is in Taiwan. Perhaps with the recent changes in the country's policies it will be possible for them to find him.

Yong, moving to the seat next to Sturdy Cactus, asks, "Are you sure the general was leaving the Mainland? Some militias were repatriated later on. He could have surrendered to the Red Army. Do you know his name?"

"I tried asking for it, but the other soldiers just laughed at me." Sturdy Cactus sniffles. "The bastards told me if I wanted to see my family again, I better build a boat."

For a moment the kitchen is silent. Twilight has crept up the walls, and Ping notices in surprise that he can no longer distinguish the features of the two people on the other side of the table. His noodles, which he has barely touched, have become cold and sticky. He feels a kick on his shin, and then Yong has moved next to him again.

"We should show him the one picture we have," she says.

Ping inclines his head toward her, blinking rapidly.

"Remember the one at Yan'an, right after the Long March?"

Of course! Ping understands now. In 1935, after the First Front Army reached the north, the politburo allowed a Western journalist to come to the camps and report on the cause. The man took pictures of all the survivors of the March, including the soldiers from the Third Legion.

Ping remembers his skinny tanned self that day. Following the end of their journey, he barely had enough energy to sit, but he stood in the sun for hours and waited for the Westerner to finish photographing the other divisions. He remembers his black-and-white face being small in the picture and partially covered by a tree's shadow.

Yong is right in suggesting that they show Sturdy Cactus the picture. Having served in the propaganda division for years, she understands better than most the authoritativeness of an image. Why tell their son about his roots directly when a picture could reveal the same truth? Would he see his own reflection in a thirty-year-old photo?

75

THEY TAKE THEIR GUEST TO a room in the back of the house. Next to a coal closet, the door is narrow and covered in black dust. Flipping through his key ring, Ping tries three keys before finding the right one. When the door opens, he coughs. Yong blows away the motes and cobwebs and places the kerosene lantern on a glass cabinet, revealing in it porcelain plates, silverware, and pewter figurines of cats, fish, and camels. A rainbow of light surrounds the edges of the cabinet. The room smells of burnt paper, the flame in the lamp igniting flecks in the air every time it flickers.

"Most things here were not ours," Ping explains. "They belonged to the previous owner of the house."

"A distant relative of Chiang Kai-shek," Yong adds. "He's probably hiding somewhere in Taiwan, like a mole."

Sturdy Cactus takes a thumb-sized horse from the cabinet and studies it by the light of the lantern. Then he puts it back in the same spot next to the carousel.

"We use this room for storage," Ping says. "When we moved into the house, we threw inside everything that wasn't essential. We haven't been back since. I think that was—how long was it again, Yong?—eight or nine years ago."

He points to a collapsed army tent in another corner of the room. Yong picks up the lamp and the three walk over. The tent before them is tarnished to the extent that none of its original color remains, and an opening large enough to poke a head through sits prominently near the collapsed metal pole in the middle. Ping lifts the dome and throws it aside. Like rolling over a boulder in a forest, they discover stacks of letters, rusty knives, bayonets, pins with Chairman Mao's face on them, two empty bandoliers, a dozen red books the size of a wallet, a block of lead, and a tarnished cauldron. Ping kneels and begins rummaging through the loose piles.

"This was the same tent we used on the Long March," Yong says. "Why we kept it all these years, I can't tell you."

This last part isn't true; she realizes it right after saying it. For some reason she doesn't want to admit to her son that the years of retreating with the army had impressed upon her a belief that she should be ready to leave anywhere at a moment's notice. To this day she has recurring nightmares in which she wakes up to retreat bugles and rushes down to this room. In nearly all these dreams she finds Ping already down here. He is young again, standing over the tent, trying to pull the cauldron over his shoulders, yelling, "Too much stuff! Too much stuff!"

"We should've framed the picture," Ping says.

He's gathered the looked-through stacks in a pile with the larger items, and he's raising every fold of the tent and taking out things hiding underneath: bullet casings, cigarettes, hairclips, nails, insect shells, and buttons. He is amazed that he once used some of these items to make weapons. As one of the country's leading industrial administrators, he long ago stopped making things with his hands. After the civil war ended, he confessed to Yong the details of how he caused his friend Luo's death, to which she gave him three hard slaps and told him to never mention his name to her or anyone else ever again. Hearing this, he allowed himself to slowly forget his guilt, along with the craft of weapon making, entirely.

"What's this picture that you want to show me?" Sturdy Cactus asks, squatting over Ping. "Maybe I can help. I don't want Uncle hurting his back."

"You've told us so many of your stories that it's unfair if we don't share some of ours," Yong says. "Believe it or not, your uncle and I had many experiences similar to yours. We stayed at Sichuan during the

Red Road Army's most desperate hour, and we lost a child, too, long ago." She wonders again if now is the time, but Sturdy Cactus, staring at the objects next to Ping, seems more interested in the trinkets than her words. "Of course, during those days many comrades lost loved ones, children included. Even the Chairman had to leave a daughter behind."

"Why?" he asks.

"Well, so that we were not overburdened when we met the enemy, so that we could carry items important for the war, like these."

Sturdy Cactus reaches for a bandolier, stands up, and slings it around his neck. Smiling, he asks, "Do I look like one of you, a revolutionary?"

Yong straightens the bandolier so that it's perfectly diagonal from shoulder to waist. "A spitting image." It's difficult, she finds, to resist the impulse to cry.

"Ah, I've found it!" Ping says.

He pushes himself up, handing her a leather album the size of a shirt pocket.

With Sturdy Cactus and Ping on either side of her, she starts flipping through the album page by page. The pictures are smaller than she remembers, and there aren't many, the album thin enough to pass under a door. The first picture, of course, is a side portrait of Mao. The next few are stock images of other prominent members of the politburo: Zhou Enlai, Deng Xiaoping, Hua Guofeng. Ping and Yong do not remember where they placed the journalist's picture, and each time she flips to the next page, they hold their breath in anticipation.

"So many soldiers," Sturdy Cactus says. "So many heroes."

Finally, Yong reaches the photo of their platoon. It's not exactly how she remembers it: Broadax survived the long trek? She was sure he was killed near Tibet and eaten as a meal. Haiwu kneeling at the front next to the newly recruited Little Red Devils? She always thought he was standing next to Ping, grabbing his arm for support. Still, despite these imperfect memories, she sees her young face, thin as a squid, angry and rude, and her husband's next to it, half in shadows but the other half clearly recognizable. They are standing together, although they aren't holding hands or giving off any indication that they're married. In the picture Ping looks awkward, his arms pressed stiffly to his sides, as if he's standing at attention. He is forcing a smile, much like the one on Sturdy Cactus right now.

"Do you see anyone you recognize?" she asks him.

Sturdy Cactus takes the album and studies it while she hovers the lantern above him. Ping leans closer to the picture, trying to get in Sturdy Cactus's field of vision.

"I see you, Auntie," Sturdy Cactus says. He looks up, squints at Yong, and then turns his head and looks at Ping. "And is that you, Uncle, right next to her?"

"Yes, that's me." Ping believes in his son. Sturdy Cactus will notice the resemblance, Ping is sure of it. Any second now his son will embrace them and call them mother and father.

"Do you see anything else in there?" Yong says, pointing to the image of Ping. "Anything familiar?"

Sturdy Cactus brings the picture closer to his face. It is right above his nose now, Ping's young image visible in his pupils.

"Yes, that's it!" they say together. "What do you see?"

He tilts his head, trying to take in the picture from another angle. Yong moves the lantern so close to his face that it's touching the album.

"Is it this?" he asks, patting himself on the chest. "Is Uncle wearing the same shirt back then that I am right now?"

76

IT IS DARK AGAIN, A moonless night. The wind howls through the cracks of their bedroom window, rocking the frame. When the street-lights shut off, the room appears the same whether their eyes are open or closed, lost in the darkness.

"Give him time," Ping says.

"You're right. We shouldn't force it."

For a few minutes they don't speak. They hear the pipes fill with hot water, and the room gradually warms.

" 'Cricket' is a good name," Ping says.

"Not humble enough to escape the notice of Old Man in the Sky," Yong replies, although she is cheered again by the possibility of being a grandmother.

"What should we call Haiwu's grandson?" Ping asks.

"I don't know." Yong sighs. "I regret agreeing to help him. His son should be the one to choose it. He should be the one to bear the responsibility for the boy's destiny."

"Haiwu pulled one over on us."

They both laugh. Ping is still perplexed by Sturdy Cactus's failure to recognize his own likeness in the picture. The similarity was so obvious. How could he not see it? They gave him the album before leaving the storage room, hoping he'll notice himself when he looks at the photo again. And then there is the other thing: Ping cannot take his mind off Luo's death. Searching through that tent was like reliving the Long

March. He felt the same fatigue in his legs, the same weight on his back, and the same guilt against his temples. He wants to talk to Yong about it, have her forgive him—or punish him—a second time, but he knows it would be a mistake.

"We should take Sturdy Cactus to the orphanage," Yong suddenly says. "Make a formal announcement that he's our son."

"What?" Ping turns and sees Yong's shadowy face staring straight up at the ceiling.

"Think about it," she says. "What better place is there? A captivated, sympathetic, and well-fed audience. The holidays—a time of reunion. We'll make the announcement at the orphanage and then explain the details to him, give him all the irrefutable evidence we've been gathering over these last two days. Afterward we'll bring him to the bureau and do the paperwork. The Party will be shocked, but they won't refuse our request."

"What about Sturdy Cactus? What makes you so certain he'll say yes?"

"Well, for one thing, he'll have a permanent home. Two, he won't go hungry. Three, he'll have parents." Yong wraps the lamb's-wool blanket tighter around her shoulders. "And if none of these things do the trick, we'll remind him that we'll help him find his son—our grandson. Surely he cannot deny who he is after that."

Ping claps. "That's it, then. That's the plan."

"Not so loud," Yong whispers. "He's still in the other room."

"What difference does it make if he hears now?"

"No difference. I just want him to have a good night's sleep."

The bed creaks in the other room, and then there's a bellowing sneeze.

"I can picture the surprised faces of the staff at the bureau when we ask for the paperwork," Yong continues.

"There will be many skeptics," Ping says.

"Who cares? What can they do? It's better to plan out how we'll celebrate than wasting our energy explaining things to subordinates."

"We should listen to Haiwu, though, and remember that he's not *just* our son."

"We'll take him to Sichuan," Yong continues, "and try to find the mountain where he's from. Then we'll retrace the path he took from childhood to adult. We'll make sure the headquarters of the local beggars' guild are no longer functioning and the general who stole his wife, if he did in fact surrender to the Red Army, is doubly punished." Yong goes on to mention that they'll help Sturdy Cactus's friends, the other "travel mates," find jobs despite their disabilities and open up additional facilities across the country to provide for the remaining homeless. "Sturdy Cactus, if he wants, can help govern this new branch," Yong says. "Or, if he's too tired to work, we can just take care of him." Growing warm under the blanket from all the planning, she sits up and slides the sheets toward Ping. "While we're doing all of this," she says, "we'll also be finding our grandson."

Ping pulls the blanket smooth again and replaces it over Yong's knees. He was nodding when she mentioned making the announcement at the orphanage, but the rest of her plan seems overly ambitious. He does not tell her this, of course. It's too early to argue about designs made months in advance, and he decides to try and add to her enthusiasm.

"Don't forget, we may have a daughter-in-law, too," he says. "From the sound of it, they never had a proper marriage ceremony. We can give them one. We'll need to rent a donkey, hire good cooks for the feast, invite all the Party leaders, and have them meet our son."

"Yes, of course," Yong says. "We need to make sure he's taken care of after we're gone. It's a shame, really, how late in life we found him."

This last proposal eases the excitement somewhat, and Yong lies back down. Under the sheets again, she steadies her breathing, trying to fall asleep. Her eyes move rapidly behind closed lids, and she sees again the pristine mountains of the Lolos. Sturdy Cactus is entering the hut with the strings of chili peppers hanging by the door. It's all how she remembers it. Knowing that this hut no longer exists does not diminish the clarity of it in her mind. She follows her son through the beaded curtain. Near the stove sits a young woman with a split lip. She is wearing a red wedding gown, she is smiling, and there is a cradle beside her, one made from the trunk of a thick tree. It is rocking back and forth. Sturdy Cactus reaches inside and scoops up a baby boy. Yong moves closer to get a better look at her son and grandson. When she is within arm's length, she notices, to her amazement, that Sturdy Cactus is holding the baby with two hands now, one supporting the body and the other cupping the head. Sturdy Cactus is wearing the blue button-down shirt of a scholar, and his hair has the sheen of seabird feathers. He lowers his right arm, allowing her to get a better view, and between his hands is an infant so luminescent that he blinds her and makes everything around him fade away. Taking him into her arms, she is filled with a happiness she never thought was possible in this world.

77

THE NEXT MORNING, A CRUST of snow has gathered on the windowsill. Large chunks twirl, cotton-like, in the air. On the other side of the street, the children who threw sticks at each other yesterday have made a snowman, its eyes two coals and its head covered by a green Mao cap. A strip of red slogan tape with the first few characters of *Smash the Four Olds* serves as a scarf, and a ribbon of scrapped tire rubber, bending uncooperatively, is the belt.

Ping and Yong wake up an hour later than usual. They are old, they tell themselves, and there was too much excitement the previous night. Still, they get out of bed with a continued sense of purpose. They do not say anything to each other. They go straight to the guest room.

Ping knocks on it gently a few times, his knuckles rolling on the wood. When there is no reply, he makes a fist and knocks a little harder.

"Do you want some breakfast?" he calls.

Yong cracks the door to a slit, peeks inside, and when she sees that no one is there, she opens it fully.

The bed is not made—not that it was yesterday, either—but the heavy wool blanket rests in a thrown position, half on the mattress and a corner touching the floor. The dresser drawers are open; some are slanted while others have been removed completely and placed on the pillow. The only item she notices missing is a pair of leather work boots Ping wore once, two years ago, while inspecting a newly opened steel mill.

She tries to come up with another explanation for the mess, but deep down she knows Sturdy Cactus is no longer in the house.

"He didn't need to do this," Ping says. "We could have sent him off with whatever he wanted."

Downstairs in the kitchen, the cupboards are parted. Besides treats like jerked meat, preserved fruits, hawthorn flakes, and nuts—all the snacks put away for the orphans—they notice that a kilogram of brown sugar, packaged in newspapers, is also missing. When they check the cellar, the grain is gone, along with the last of their fresh meats: pig ears, chicken hearts, and a few slices of pork belly. In the living room, the fruit bowl with all the foreign candy has disappeared. The cabinet where they keep the radio and loose currency is ajar, empty of the few food tickets and coins that were there the day before. The radio itself is also missing.

At the storage room, the key is still inserted in the lock. The glass cabinet, of course, is thrown open and the miniatures inside taken, but the tent remains in the same position as it was yesterday—to the best of their memory, anyway. Behind the door, they notice there are things that don't belong. There is an old green jacket, one of the layers, they guess, from Sturdy Cactus's coat. And there is the missing brown sugar, spilling out of the newspaper and sprinkling the concrete floor. Finally, they see the photo album, the one they gave Sturdy Cactus yesterday, turned to a random picture of a member of the politburo. Here, Sturdy Cactus must have had too much to carry and was looking for items to unburden himself of.

Ping picks up the album and begins to cry. Yong helps him to his feet again.

When they go back into the house through the front door, they see that all of their heavy winter coats are still on the rack. Sturdy Cactus must have left wearing his old clothes.

"He is so stupid, our boy," Ping says, sniffling.

He holds the sleeve of one of the overcoats on the rack, feeling the weight of it.

"These jackets, these heavy new jackets, stuffed with down and good goose feathers—why did he not take a few of these? He should have been less concerned with money and more with his health."

"And his legs," Yong says. "He'll catch cold without cotton-stuffed pants."

She goes upstairs and takes out two of the thickest trousers. Then she raises them over the rack on the coats. On the off chance her son returns to take more things, he won't forget to grab proper pants.

Suddenly the front door bursts open. They turn expectantly, but it's only the wind: The door was never properly shut. Flurries blow inside and land on their shoes.

They walk to the door anyway. They stick their heads out and peer to the left and then the right. On the sidewalk there is a trail of footprints. Do they belong to their son? The marks are being slowly filled by the falling snow. In a few hours, they will no longer be distinguishable.

The loudspeaker on the nearest power line turns on, playing the first few notes of the "Internationale" and then the daily news:

Good morning, comrades. It is February seventh of the year 1978. A Tuesday. Production of corn and wheat has grown 50 percent this year. Vegetable prices are at an all-time low. Our Mongolian brothers have traded us many kilotons of excess milk, yogurt, and lamb. Nobody will go hungry this holiday! On this festive occasion, the state is happy to report that the mining of uranium has begun on the lands near Kazakhstan. This will no doubt help our plans for the Four Modernizations.

Fear not, comrades. Our tomorrow is bright; our families are secure. Stay tuned for the next program, which commences after the national anthem.

ACKNOWLEDGEMENTS

A BOOK IS NEVER JUST one person, and it's difficult to account for everyone involved in making it a reality. *Lost in the Long March* began as notes about the history of my birth country. I was twenty-seven at the time and knew little about China's past outside of the stories my parents and grandparents had told me. Their references to the Cultural Revolution, the Kuomingtang, and the Japanese occupation accumulated over the years, and I was determined to be ignorant of them no longer.

For several years I immersed myself in the period. Early texts I consulted included *The Great Chinese Revolution, 1800-1985* by John Fairbank, *Red at Heart: How Chinese Communists Fell in Love with the Russian Revolution* by Elizabeth McGuire, *Fanshen: A Documentary of Revolution in a Chinese Village* by William Hinton, *Origins of the Chinese Revolution* by Lucien Bianco, *The Tragedy of Liberation: A History of the Chinese Revolution 1945 – 1957* by Frank Dikotter, *Autumn in the Heavenly Kingdom* by Stephen R. Platt, *Mao: The Unknown Story* by Jung Chang, *On Practice and Contradiction* by Mao Zedong, *Mao Tse-Tung and the Operational Art During the Chinese Civil War, Inside Red China* by Helen Snow, *Confessions: An Innocent Life in Communist China* by Kang Zhengguo, and *Shifu, Soul of Chinese Anarchism* by Edward S. Krebs. Two books that were instrumental in their firsthand accounts of the way communist soldiers lived during this time were Edgar Snow's *Red Star Over China* and *The "Miracles" of Chairman Mao*, collected by G. R. Urban. I also drew inspiration from fictional accounts of the period—Ha Jin's *War Trash*, Andrew Malraux's *Man's Fate*, and Hao Ran's *Lie Huo Jing Gang*, which served as the basis for the "Steel Meets Fire" radio show in Part V—and from my visit to Jingganshan (Iron Well Mountain) Revolution Museum in Jiangxi Province.

At Florida State University, I wrote an early draft of the novel as a section of my dissertation, and I give thanks to my mentors there, Elizabeth Stuckey-French, Ned Stuckey-French, and Mark Winegardner. Before that, I couldn't have written anything without the encouragement and advice from teachers like Anna Keesey, Porter Shreve, Beth Nguyen, Brian Bouldrey, and Patricia Henley, from the creative writing program at Northwestern University and the M.F.A. at Purdue. I am ever thankful to the people at Autumn House Press—Christine Stroud, Shelby Newsom, and Mike Good—for publishing my first book, *Further News of Defeat*, and for giving me the courage to continue revising this one.

Beyond this foundation, I want to profusely thank my agent, Mark Gottlieb, who guided me through the submission and deal process with grace, whose energy and enthusiasm is boundless. At The Overlook Press, I couldn't have asked for a better editor than Tracy Carns, whose uplifting passion for the project made the book so much better. I'm also grateful to the attentive eye of my copyeditor, David Chesanow, and managing editor Mike Richards, to Eli Mock for the strong jacket design, and to everyone else at Abrams, including my publicist Andrew Gibeley and marketing director Christian Westermann, for helping bring this part of my life to readers.

An excerpt of the novel first appeared in *No Contact Magazine*, and I'm grateful to the team there, including Benjamin Pfeiffer, Gauraa Shekhar, and Elliot Alpern, for selecting it for inclusion in their 2021 "Contactless Reading" anthology. A heartfelt thank-you also goes out to my writing friends, James Xiao, Chris Arnold, Jake Wolff, Lori Ostlund, Andrew Bourelle, Tom Noyes, Kristina Gorcheva-Newberry, and the countless others who have helped my writing over the years and given me a sense of community, and to those of the Centrum Writers Workshop, for providing me with the opportunity to write on the shores of beautiful Port

Townsend. To my students, who had endured a semester of reading mostly Chinese subversive literature and who constantly challenge me to do better. Finally, to my family, for their support and stories and for the hardships they had to endure coming to the United States, and to my wife, who guided me through the journey of this book with humor, patience, and wisdom. Thank you all. Thanks a million.